TEXAS
WEDDINGS

TEXAS WEDDINGS

*Three Women Seek Love
That Will Endure Hardship*

JANICE A. THOMPSON

BARBOUR
PUBLISHING

Published by Barbour Publishing, Inc., P.O. Box 719, Uhrichsville, Ohio 44683.

Our mission is to publish and distribute inspirational products offering exceptional value and biblical encouragement to the masses.

ecpa Member of the
Evangelical Christian
Publishers Association

Printed in the United States of America.

Dear Reader,

Welcome to a collection of faith-based love stories set in the place I know best—south Texas! I was born and raised in this great state and have driven nearly every road mentioned in these three romantic tales. And what fun, to have a book titled Texas Weddings. After all, I have four daughters in their twenties, and we've been in wedding-planning mode for the past several years.

A Class of Her Own was my first romance novel, written in 2001. I could relate to Laura Chapman (the heroine) in so many ways. Her desire to go back to college in her mid-to-late forties was a passion I shared. Best of all, I got to plan Laura's "mid-life" wedding. What a blast!

A Chorus of One holds a very special place in my heart. My two oldest daughters got engaged within weeks of each other in 2003, and their weddings were only five months apart in 2004! We were in over our heads as I crafted this story about Jessica Chapman, who longed for a Mediterranean-themed wedding extravaganza. All of my daughters are very musical (and all have been involved in musical theater and/or opera), so placing Jessica's wedding "on the stage" came naturally.

Banking on Love is an "after the wedding" love story. Why did I choose to write a love story about married people? Because I'm always telling my girls, "You're not just planning for a *day*; you're planning for a *life*." In this tale about a young married couple facing the challenges of post-wedding life, I was able to do delve into issues that many contemporary newlyweds deal with and give a few tips about how to keep romance alive along the way!

Happy reading!
Janice Thompson

A Class of

Her Own

Dedication

This book is dedicated to my mother, Shirley Moseley,
an amazing woman of God who, like the heroine in this story,
has endured many hardships and come through them all a victor in Christ.
In my eyes she will always be in "A Class of Her Own." I love you, Mom.

Chapter 1

Laura Chapman stood at the kitchen table, wringing her hands. Something needed to be said, but could she say it? She fought to summon the courage. "I, uh, I'm—"

"What is it, Mom?" nineteen-year-old Jessica asked. "What's wrong?" She continued to clear the dinner dishes from the table, clearly oblivious to her mother's struggle.

"Oh, nothing." Laura attempted to compose herself. This shouldn't be so difficult. She had been through much tougher things than this, especially lately. "See, it's like this, Jessica." She drew a deep breath. "I'm going back to school." *There. No turning back.*

"What did you say?" Jessica looked shocked. The butter knife slipped out of her hand and clattered onto the oak table.

"I said, I'm going back to school." Laura Chapman spoke the words in her most determined voice, though she couldn't seem to hide the tremor. She had wanted to talk to her kids about this for days. Time wouldn't allow her to wait any longer. If she didn't register by tomorrow, there would be no chance—at least not this semester.

"But, Mom," Jess argued, "school?"

"Mom's too cool for school." Fifteen-year-old Kent entered the room with music blasting from the tiny earphones of his MP3 player.

"It's definitely not that." Jessica ignored his obvious attempt at sarcasm. "It's just that you're so, so—"

"So what?" Their eyes met for a showdown of wills.

"Well, you're so—" her daughter stammered, suddenly falling silent.

"Old?" Kent offered, turning up his music to deafen his mother's response.

"Thanks a lot." Laura felt an odd mixture of emotions rise within her as both kids shrugged their response. *I should have expected this.* She tossed her wavy brown hair in defiance, something she might have done at her daughter's age. "You think I'm too old?"

"It's not just that," Jessica argued. "You haven't been to school in, what's it been—nineteen years?"

"Twenty, but I'm sure I can do it." Laura needed a vote of confidence, a confirmation. In the nearly three years since her husband lost his fight with colon cancer, Laura Chapman had lingered on the verge of depression. They were cold,

9

hard years, laced with self-pity and fear. But she refused to give in. She forced herself to get out of bed every morning, dragging herself back and forth to the bookstore where she worked, though it proved to be the toughest thing she had ever done.

When Greg passed away, something in her had died, too. For what seemed like ages, she found herself unable to feel much of anything, unable to dream, to hope. Only in recent days had she begun to come alive again, started to view "tomorrow" as something more than an empty hole to be filled. Surely her children would understand and offer moral support when she most needed it.

"Mom, you just don't understand."

Help me understand. Laura looked into the deep green eyes of her eldest child, her beautiful Jessica—her jewel, her prize. The spitting image of her father, Jessica stood tall and slender, with sleek auburn hair and a light spray of freckles that danced across her cheeks. Her passionate interest in the arts seemed to grow daily, just as Greg's had. She had inherited both his ear for fine music and an eye for the artistic. A fine pianist, Jess always seemed to excel at everything she put her hand to. The grand piano in the living room reminded Laura daily of Greg. He had given it to their precious daughter nearly seven years ago as down payment on her future in the field of music. Now it stood as a reminder that things didn't always work out as planned.

Thankfully, Jessica reconciled herself to studying music at Wainesworth Junior College, a far cry from the university education the anxious teen had craved. She endured it all with little argument—just one in a long list of necessary sacrifices.

Greg would have made sure she received all she needed and more. Laura sighed as she reflected on her husband's great love for their family. A smile instinctively crossed her lips. Just thinking about him could transport her back to better times. Romantic and funny, he had been the perfect mate. There had been a sensitive side to him as well, one that many men did not possess. What amazing memories Laura held of their years together. Their God-given love had run deep. Greg had truly loved her as Christ loved the church, and being his wife had been an honor.

Lord, I miss him so much. No other man could come close to Greg. He'd given of himself day after day, working hard to provide for their family. He'd made himself available to the children and had been genuinely interested in their wants and needs. He'd planned so much for them, so much more than she could give them.

Her daughter's dancing green eyes proved to be a reminder of his spunk, his tenacity, and his undying love. Jessica was, in every way, Greg's child. And yet, Laura had to admit, her eldest also bore a determination that trickled down from Laura herself—a stubbornness that could only be traced back to her own side of the family.

"What don't I understand?" Laura asked, coming back to life again. Surely her daughter could come up with nothing that she hadn't already considered herself. She had argued the negatives and positives of this decision with herself for several nights as she twisted and turned in the sheets.

"Things aren't like they were when you were in school, Mom. They'll eat you alive in college." Jessica gave her a confident, knowing look, one that could not be ignored.

Kent added his two cents' worth. "Yeah, no kidding."

"Thanks for the vote of confidence." Laura's oversensitive heart felt the betrayal, but she bore it with a stiff upper lip.

"Anything I can do to help, Mom." Kent shuffled from the room, earphones still in place and music blaring as loudly as ever.

Jess shook her head, obviously unwilling to give up the fight. "Mom, you don't get it. The students are really crude, the professors are even worse, and the workload is a killer. I barely made it last semester myself. You see how it is. I had homework every night last year—hours of it. How would you make it with your job?"

"I can work part-time at the store in the afternoons and evenings, and take morning classes. Besides, if God is for me, and I'm convinced He is. . .who can be against me?"

"I'm not trying to discourage you," her daughter said with a shrug. "I just want you to be practical, that's all. One of us has to be."

"I am very practical," Laura argued. *I've got a solid plan, a good plan. It will work. You'll see.* "Lots of people do this."

"Young people," Jessica argued, lips tight. "Some of them don't make it when they're working and going to school. Remember Bridget Kester? She dropped out of college last spring because she didn't pass any of her classes. She tried to work at the health club and go to school at the same time. College is tough. And she's young. Bridget's my age."

"I know how old she is, Jessica." *Lord, help me keep my temper in check.* "But you're not giving me much credit. It's not like I haven't been to school before." Laura felt her zeal begin to wane.

"Twenty years ago."

"What difference does it make, really? Besides, we're only talking junior college here—not graduate school. I want to get my associate's degree. That's all. I've wanted it for years. I gave up college when you came along, so I never had the chance to—"

"I know, Mom. You've told me a hundred times." Jessica's face twisted slightly, an indication she already carried the guilt of this situation.

Oh, but it was worth every moment just to be with you. Don't you realize that? Haven't I told you enough? Laura carefully reworded her story. "Jessica, I went to college for one year before I married your father. The second—well, the second year was tough. When you're a new bride, setting up house and caring for your husband feels like the most important thing. Marriage can be a little distracting when you're in school." She smiled, remembering those early days—how torn she had been between schoolwork and decorating their first little apartment. Greg had been so proud of her as she chose fabrics and stitched curtains herself. He lovingly helped her hang them, commenting on their beauty. They'd ended up in each other's arms, curtains hanging lopsided from the rod above.

No, there hadn't been much time left for schoolwork. Not then, anyway.

Laura composed herself, continuing on. "At the beginning of the next semester, I found out you were coming. I just couldn't make myself go back. I never could."

But there were no regrets anymore, not about school anyway. Ever since the catalog had come in the mail three weeks ago, Laura had been making her plans, calculating, counting the cost. She would go back to college, and nothing would stop her.

"It's your decision, Mom," Jessica said. "Though I can't help but think it's the wrong one."

Laura shook her head in disbelief. "I love you, Jess. And I want the best for all of us." She turned toward the bedroom, hoping a few minutes alone would put an end to her frustration. She headed to the vanity, where she sat gazing long and hard at her reflection. "I look as tired as I feel." Her weariness would surely increase as she took on the added responsibility of school on top of a job and child rearing. *I need Your strength, Lord.*

Though she fought to remain strong, her faith had weakened over the last three years, truth be told. Still determined to remain close to Him, Laura found herself calling on the Lord more as the months crawled by. Her moments with Him brought genuine comfort. *"I will never leave you nor forsake you."* The familiar scripture ran through her mind. Laura contemplated the words. *Lord, why can't I feel Your presence like I used to?*

Everything felt different now that Greg was gone. He had been such a good spiritual leader—making sure everyone went to church on Sunday, teaching Sunday school, praying with the kids before bed. Lately, she couldn't even seem to get out of bed on Sunday mornings. Her church attendance had wavered over the last few months. It seemed she found an excuse to stay home nearly every week now. *It's just so much easier.* Facing those happy, carefree people proved far too difficult.

Laura ran a brush through her wavy hair, trying to style it in several different ways. No matter how long she messed with it, the stubborn stuff would only do the same old thing it always had. Her waves cooperated in one direction and only one. She tossed the brush down onto the vanity, ready to admit defeat.

Laura sighed and gazed at the mirror. *Who are you?* she asked the face staring back at her. *I don't really know you anymore. Can you be more than a wife and mother? Can you be a student, too?* An uncomfortable silence lingered in the air.

Reaching over to the bedside table, she picked up the catalog one last time before turning in for the night. In order to obtain the associate's degree she craved, a serious workload lay before her. But, after all she had been through in the last year, it should be a piece of cake. She ran her fingers over the cover, her index finger tracing the letters "WAINESWORTH JUNIOR COLLEGE."

Laura caught a glimpse of her own smile in the mirror. *Nothing to be ashamed of. I have a perfect right to smile. After all, this marks the beginning of a brand-new adventure for me.*

Professor Andrew Dougherty sat at his computer and scrolled through an American Revolution Web site with renewed zeal. The red, white, and blue background held his interest for a while, though his computer seemed to be dragging tonight. "Too many graphics," he observed.

A history buff, Andrew had much to glean from the Web. With only a few days before school began, he certainly didn't have much time to put together a comprehensive list of applicable sites for his students. He leaned back and rubbed at his eyes. The monitor had really done a number on his vision. The flag's colors were all melting into one rather lackluster shade of gray.

Andrew glanced at the clock on the computer—2:45 a.m. "No way." Had he really been online that long? Where had the time gone? Too many nights he seemed to sit alone in this chair, wasting the hours. They always managed to slip by like minutes.

Too much time on the Web, old man. Not that he was old, and not that he had much else to do with his time. Still a bachelor at forty-seven, Andrew found himself completely disinterested in things that had appealed to him in his younger years. The Internet had become a friend and companion, filling his evenings with unspoken words and genuine satisfaction. With so many sites to see, chat rooms to visit, and e-mails to send out, he could easily waste a full evening. Most nights were spent online, when he wasn't up to his ears with papers to grade.

Andrew sighed as he thought about his upcoming classes at the college. He leaned back so far in the chair that it almost toppled over. "Careful now!" He nervously typed in the address to a familiar site. He had heard about it through a chat room he frequented—a computerized dating service. "Only $49.95," the header read. "Money-back guarantee." Andrew had, for some time, toyed with the idea of actually filling out the form and entering a credit card number. It was a game he played with himself quite often these days.

But how would he put it? His mind wandered. "Charming middle-aged man—" No. That wouldn't work. Middle-aged would be a definite turnoff. "Charming, academic forty-something." Nah. But what could he say? How could he possibly begin to describe himself? How did people do that?

His fingers began to trip nimbly across the keys—his heart suddenly releasing him to be free with his thoughts. "Ready for love."

Had he really typed that? After fifteen years of dealing with a broken heart, the time for a change was rapidly approaching. His last relationship had left him wounded in a way that he never wanted to repeat.

Smiling, he continued on. "Romeo is ready to meet his Juliet. Tall. . ." Hmm. A bit of a stretch, perhaps, since he stood at five-ten. "Tanned." He'd be sure to visit a tanning booth as soon as possible. "Blond, wavy hair." "Sandy" would have been a better word, but who cared? And "unruly curls" might have been a more accurate description, but did it really matter? It wasn't like he was actually going to send this thing off, anyway.

Andrew stared at the screen and faced the next question with some scrutiny. Hobbies. They wanted to know what he did for fun. In all honesty, he sat at the computer and browsed the World Wide Web for fun. But that didn't really sound right. "Romantic walks on the beach," he typed with a smile. South Texas beaches were tolerable enough, he supposed—as long as people weren't crammed onto every square inch of them. Besides, that's what ads like these were supposed to say. "Books." That much was true. "And movies." That one wasn't far off either.

There. All done. Andrew's heart pounded in his ears. His palms grew sweatier with each keystroke. The undeniable had occurred. He had actually completed the form. A first. All he needed to do was pull out that credit card and—

"Wait a minute!" he said, startled. "Just what do you think you're doing?" He quickly closed out the site and turned off the computer with a vengeance. This time he had come too close for comfort.

No need to worry about that. The peace and quiet would end soon enough. Within days, his hours would be filled with the usual hustle and bustle of college students entering and exiting his classroom. He felt his pulse slowing as his mind shifted to the thing he loved most. *American history. A subject I can handle. No great risks there.*

There seemed to be a certain comfort to teaching history at Wainesworth Junior College. So what if his classroom had a revolving door? Students enrolled, came, then left quickly. *Lazy. So many of them just don't know what it means to earn their grades.* So he might be a little tough. There were far worse things a teacher could be accused of. No shame in admitting he made his students work hard. Most lived easy lives—too easy, to his way of thinking. His college professors had been plenty tough on him, preparing him for life. These students needed to be just as prepared. He would give them all a fresh dose of reality.

Laura tossed and turned in bed, trying to sleep. Her excitement wouldn't allow it—at least, not yet. She made out the glowing yellow numbers on the clock: 2:34 a.m. Even if she managed to doze off, she would only get in five hours. *I don't want to run the risk of getting off to a bad start. Not on such an important day.*

Laura propped herself up on three pillows, thinking through her class schedule once again.

Her thoughts held her captive, as they so often did these days. Laura had far too much on her mind to sleep. What would she say to Greg, if she had the chance to talk to him? How would she explain her decision about going back to school? She could see his smiling face in front of her, nodding as she explained herself away. His auburn hair shimmered in the afternoon sunlight as he listened intently, and his cheeks held the color of a healthy man.

But she would never talk to Greg again. She would never know how he might have felt about this. As difficult as it might be, she had to begin making her own decisions and sticking with them.

Laura listed the courses in her head again, just to be sure she hadn't forgotten anything. Tomorrow would be a critical day, and she didn't want to risk anything going wrong.

Chapter 2

Excuse me. I wonder if you could direct me to the admissions office." Laura's voice trembled with a mixture of nerves and excitement.

The woman in front of her looked too young for college. *"You think you're getting old when high school students start looking like kids, but you know you're getting old when college students look like kids."* They were Greg's words. She remembered them as clearly as if he had just spoken them.

The girl turned and looked at her curiously. "Up those stairs," she said in a cheery, youthful voice. "Take a left at the first hallway, then follow it all the way to the end. Turn right and go about twenty feet, and then take another right. About three hallways up on the left you turn again. You should see Admissions directly in front of you. There's a bright blue sign just above the door."

Laura couldn't be sure she had absorbed the directions, but she didn't ask the young girl to repeat herself. *This is all so embarrassing, and I feel so out of place.* "Oh, uh, thank you." She found herself distracted by the girl's eyeliner. It was a little too thick on the right eye and smeared a little on the left, a sure sign of puberty. Her skirt was short—a little too short, to Laura's way of thinking.

"Are you registering a son or a daughter?" the girl asked.

How embarrassing. How totally, completely embarrassing. Of course, Laura couldn't blame her for making the assumption. If she had a lick of sense, she would turn around and walk out the door. Instead, Laura shook her head. "I, uh, I'm signing up. I mean I'm going to start classes here." She spoke the words half ashamed, half proud.

"Really?" A sudden look of interest filled the girl's dark brown eyes. "Well, I'm happy to hear it. We need more people your age. I'm Kaycie Conner, head of the English Department."

"What?" Laura tried to decipher this new information, to work it into the equation, but it just didn't seem to compute. *No way.*

"I, uh, I'm Laura Chapman. I'm hoping to get my associate's degree." Her ability to speak coherently seemed to be slipping away more with each passing moment.

The woman nodded and smiled. "Well, good luck to you. Let me know if there's anything I can do to help."

Laura focused on the young woman as she walked away, unable to speak a word. She began to walk in the direction Ms. Conner had pointed, hoping she'd heard correctly. Her heels clicked against the white tile floor, creating a melancholy echo. The sound seemed to scream out, "Look at me," when she really wanted to disappear into the woodwork. At the end of the hallway, Laura turned and headed up the stairs. Which was it again? Right, left, left, right—or left, right, right, left?

Gratefully, at the top of the stairs, a sign reading ADMISSIONS pointed to the left. She followed a trail of clues until she reached the proper office. Finally. The big blue sign. She breathed a sigh of relief, happy to be at her destination. Not that it made much difference. The line went on forever.

Laura took her place at the end of the line, feeling like a wallflower at a junior high school dance. She half-listened, half-ignored a host of young students as they rambled on and on about this professor and that, griping and cursing. Their language proved to be almost as unforgivable as their attitudes. Jessica had been right about one thing: Teenagers were different these days. Crudeness seemed to be the rule of the day. This amazed yet frightened her.

Off in the corner, a couple stood with their lips locked. *Best to ignore them.* Laura pulled out her catalog for one last excited look at her possibilities. There would be no room for mistakes. She had to get this right. She thumbed through the book, closing it willfully. Her mind drifted ahead, into the vast unknown. *Perhaps someday I'll own my own bookstore. It might be a dream but not an unrealistic one.* She would have not only the courage to achieve it but the wherewithal to accomplish it. She would be bold, confident, daring. . .

"Next."

Laura looked up, shocked to find herself at the front of the line. She gazed into the eyes of a young man, about twenty-one or so. He looked tired and irritable.

"Can I help you, ma'am?" His curt words startled her. "We're about to close."

"Uh, yes. I—"

"Are you here to sign up for classes?" he snapped, glancing down at his watch.

"Yes, I am. Am I too late?"

"That depends. Have you seen a counselor?"

"Yes," Laura spoke quickly. "He gave me this." She pushed a card across the counter and smiled in his direction.

His face softened a little as he read it. "Ah. Working on your degree, huh?"

"Yes." Laura smiled, energized at his sudden interest.

"Don't sweat it, sister," he said. "I'm in the same boat. Most of these kids are."

"Really?" *Not that I'm your sister. And not that I'm a kid.*

"Toughest thing is American History, at least for me. Looks like you're gonna end up with Dougherty. He's the only one still taking students." At that, he let out a whistle.

"What? What's wrong with Dougherty?"

"Harsh guy. He makes his students work twice as hard as the others. But you'll make it. You look pretty tough."

Tough? She suddenly didn't feel very tough.

~

Andrew entered the empty room with a large cardboard box in hand. He always loved this part of the year—setting up his classroom. He looked forward to it with an unashamed vengeance. American history would soon come alive for a new group of students. He would see to it. On the other hand, if it didn't come alive to them, he would see to a few other things—like extra assignments, for example.

With great excitement, he began pulling maps from the box. One by one, he secured them to the wall. Lovingly, he ran his fingers across the brightly colored map of North America, tracing the path he had taken from Florida, the place of his birth, to Texas, where he found himself planted. It certainly hadn't proven to be the location of his dreams, but at least he could work in the one field that made him happy. Not everyone could say that.

Andrew backed away from the wall, looking at it carefully, curiously. There seemed to be something missing, but he couldn't quite put his finger on it. *Ah yes.* He groped through the box in search of his prized copy of the Declaration of Independence that lay inside.

"There you are," he said with a proud smile. "Thought you could hide from me, eh?"

He unrolled it with great care, reading as he went along. The edges were frayed and the printing worn, but the words still captivated him, kept him locked in their grip—even after all these years. The founding fathers had worked diligently on the vital document so that he could have freedom, so that he could one day live out the American dream. Just the idea brought a rush of patriotic pride.

"Better get a hold of yourself." Andrew shook his head. "People might start to think you've got a screw loose."

Ah, let them talk. Folks already thought he was an oddball, anyway—forty-seven and still single. They had their probing speculations, to be sure, though he did his best to ignore them. Why bore them with the details, anyway? His heartbreak fifteen years ago wasn't any of their business. They didn't need to know the one woman he had ever given his heart to had jilted him.

No, no one at Wainesworth Junior College would ever have to know.

~

Laura left the crowded college bookstore with five minutes to spare, her arms loaded with textbooks in varying shapes, sizes, and colors. They had to be carried out to the car—which was parked a good half mile away in the farthest parking lot. The weighty stack of books blocked her vision, and her arms ached already.

Laura turned the corner and ran headlong into a tall man with sandy-colored hair. Her books tumbled to the tile floor with a crash, scattering about in every conceivable direction. Her purse flew from her arm and hit him squarely in the belly. He doubled over and let out a groan.

"I'm—I'm so sorry!" Laura dropped to her knees. *I won't look into his eyes. I can't. This is so embarrassing.* "Really, I just wasn't looking where I was going." Her heart beat loudly in her ears. She found herself eyeball-to-eyeball with a man, a nice-looking man, and it scared the living daylights out of her.

"No problem." He reached down to help her pick the books up. "But that purse of yours packs a pretty heavy punch."

Laura groaned loudly. "I'm sorry. I really am."

"You might want to invest in a backpack before classes start next week," he said with a grin. "That's what most of the students carry. You are a student, aren't you?"

Laura looked up at him, grateful for the acknowledgment. "Yes, I am." Frankly, she was so relieved to see someone her own age, she hardly knew what to say. *Hopefully, he's a student, too.* His curly hair was a little unkempt, but not unforgivably so. Their eyes met in an embarrassed glance. The gentleman placed her American History book on top of the pile, looking at her intently.

"Are you taking American History?"

Why is he staring at me? Laura wondered, fighting to balance the stack of books.

"Yes, I just signed up, but I'm not looking forward to it." She shuddered as she remembered what the young man at the registration desk had said.

"Why is that?" The stranger reached to catch the history book as it slid from her grip again.

"Oh," she said, clutching it tighter, "it's not the class. It's the professor."

"Really?" He looked at her curiously. "Who do you have?"

"Dougherty. I hear he's tough. Really tough."

"Tough, huh?"

"Yeah," she said with a sigh. "Hope I'm up for it. What about you?"

"Me?" he said with a look of chagrin. "Me? I'm late for a meeting. Have a nice day." He turned abruptly and walked in the opposite direction.

Chapter 3

Laura buzzed around the kitchen in happy anticipation. Once the registration process drew to its logical conclusion, she finally enjoyed a good night's sleep. The world suddenly seemed a much brighter place. *I'm going to make it.* Laura took a sip from her cup of coffee, glancing out the kitchen window. The yard needed mowing, but even that didn't deter her this morning.

Kent, walked in, yawning. "Morning, Mom." He looked groggy. "What's for breakfast?"

"I signed up for classes yesterday," Laura said excitedly. It wasn't exactly "Bacon and eggs," or "Good morning," but it seemed to be the only thing that would come out of her mouth. She didn't even try to disguise her zeal.

"Yeah, Jessica told me," he replied with a shrug. "She's pretty bummed."

Immediately, Laura felt her expression change. Jessica must really be upset if she took the time to talk to her brother about it. She rarely talked to Kent about anything.

"It's cool, Mom," Kent continued, pulling open a loaf of bread. "You do what you have to do. Don't let her get to you. I know I never do."

"I won't." Laura said the words but didn't really know if she meant them—at least not yet. Truth was, Jessica did get to her. She always got to her.

"When do your classes start?" Kent reached to stick two pieces of bread in the toaster.

"Next Monday." Laura took another sip of her hot coffee, deep in thought.

"Doesn't seem fair," he said, frustrated. "We've already been in school a week."

"I know. But I'm sure you'll have an easier time than I will."

"That's putting it mildly," Jessica said as she entered the room. "What classes did you sign up for, anyway?" She sat at the table and reached for the nearly empty box of cereal.

Ah. So you're speaking to me, eh? Maybe this wouldn't be so bad. "I'm taking Algebra, English, and a fitness class," Laura said. "Oh, and I managed to sign up for American History. That's the one I'm worried about."

"American History?" Jess looked concerned.

"What's wrong, honey?" Her heart began to pound, dreading a confrontation.

"Nothing. At least not yet." There was an undeniable edge to her voice. "Who's your professor?"

"Dougherty."

Jess turned white. "Not the one-fifteen class."

"Well, yes," Laura said. "Why?"

"I already told you, Mother." Her daughter's voice was laced with anger. "I told you I had an American History class at one-fifteen."

"But you said your professor's name was Miller—or something like that. It's not like I planned this. In fact, I was very careful to avoid this situation."

"When I went to sign up, Miller's class was full," Jess explained. "And I got stuck with Dougherty. Trust me, he's the last one on the planet I ever wanted."

"What's wrong with him?" Laura asked, more than a little curious. "Surely he can't be as bad as everyone makes him out to be."

"He works his students to death, and I've already got too many other classes to worry about. But I had made up my mind to get through it somehow. If I had known. . ."

"Neither of us could have known," Laura argued. "I guess it just couldn't be helped. He was the only professor still taking students at that time."

"I know, I know. But can't you take history at another hour?"

"No, I really can't." Laura couldn't possibly adjust her schedule. Everything had been carefully arranged. She needed to be at work by three in the afternoon.

"Mother, you don't understand. I *have* to take an American History class. It's required."

"And you don't seem to understand." Laura countered. "I *have* to take it just like you do. I'm working on my degree, too."

With the shake of her head, Jessica turned and left the room.

⁓

Andrew sat at the small, round breakfast table, swallowing a fried egg and two pieces of bacon. His morning routine hadn't changed in decades. He carefully wiped the edges of his mouth, feeling the draw of the computer. *I've probably got just enough time to check my e-mail before heading up to the college.* Andrew hoped to find something special today—a letter from a colleague with important news.

He placed his plate in the dishwasher, realizing it would be several more meals before he had enough dishes in there to actually warrant turning the dumb thing on. Sooner or later, the plate would get washed. Living alone had its benefits. Anything beat a sink full of dirty dishes and toys lining the stairs. That would be awful. Probably.

Using an antibacterial spray, Andrew wiped down the counter meticulously—not just once but twice. He couldn't be too careful. With school starting in a few days, there would be enough germs to battle in the classroom.

He made his way into the small cubbyhole he called an office and turned on his computer. Barely three months old, it flew on with great speed. Andrew enjoyed investing in the latest technology. He had to keep up with the times, especially today.

What else did he have to spend his money on, anyway? *It's not like I have a wife and kids to support.*

"Snap out of it," he said aloud, shaking his head. He didn't need a reminder about marriage, at least not yet. He sat in silence as the computer booted up, then raced to sign online. *Today's the day.*

The familiar "You've got mail" rang out, creating a little stir. He scrolled through the pieces of e-mail, mostly junk. No letter. He sat back in the chair, feeling the rejection intensely. Hadn't Joe said he would write back today with news of. . .

Aw, what difference did it make anyway? No woman on the planet would be interested in him, blind date or otherwise. Andrew snapped the computer off, not even bothering to shut it down in the usual fashion. He stared at the black monitor, deep in thought.

Karen. He thought about her every day. She was the first thing to cross his mind in the morning, and the last thing he reflected on at night. His Karen.

Just out of graduate school, Andrew had met Professor Karen Norris at a dinner for incoming staff. Of course, that had been light-years ago, in a completely different state. But he had noticed her the minute she walked in the room—dark hair, slim figure, deep brown eyes. Perfect in every way. Karen.

Well, almost every way. They had connected on more than an intellectual level. He fell head over heels for her, and she had for him—at least, that's the way it looked and felt at the time. Their years together escalated into plans for matrimony, a state he had grown to desire. They planned, plotted, and strategized. The future looked like a field of endless possibilities.

And then. . .

Andrew pushed himself up from the chair. *I won't play this game today. Thousands of times I've thought about her, and where has it gotten me?*

No. Today the whole world lay at his feet.

⁓

Laura threw a load of clothes into the washer and tossed in a cupful of detergent. She missed the mark only slightly—about half of the detergent landed on the washer and the other half in it. "What are you doing?" Scolding herself, she swept her hand across the gritty stuff, brushing it into the machine. She slammed the lid shut, turned the button on, and leaned back against the washer to think.

Lord, this isn't working out like I need it to. Show me what to do, Father. Her mind couldn't seem to release the earlier conversation with Jessica. Going back to school might be impossible. Doing so would humiliate her daughter. That much had been made painfully clear.

The hum of the washer coursed her thoughts along. She had already invested so much money into the venture. She couldn't possibly stop payment on the checks she had written. That would be impractical, and she would end up feeling foolish about the whole thing.

Laura turned to look at the kitchen table, piled high with textbooks. She sighed deeply and then made her way over to them. She had really looked forward to the fitness class, and the English class, too. Algebra would be a challenge, but her determination could see her through that, even if it meant spending extra hours in the math lab. But American History—that presented a completely different problem, one she couldn't seem to find an answer to. Laura ran her fingers over the cover of the American History textbook. A picture of the Liberty Bell adorned the front of the book, pealing out the message of freedom, liberty, and failure.

Was this really all that divided her from Jessica—a crazy American History book? Irritated, Laura tossed it on the floor.

Chapter 4

Laura picked up the telephone to call her mother for a heart-to-heart chat. Somehow, with all she had been through in the last few years, she craved her mother's companionship most. Perhaps the fact that her mom had already walked this road ahead of her drew them together.

Laura's own father passed away in his forties, the victim of a massive heart attack. Her mother limped through the grieving process and somehow managed to come through it a stronger woman. She transitioned from victim to victor. Her great faith pulled her through. She'd never let go of the Lord's hand. Her marriage to Buck a few years later led to many happy, comfortable years. Buck was wonderful for her mother. His personality proved to be as refreshing and down-to-earth as his name.

"Mom?"

"Laura? I was hoping you'd call today. I've just got a few minutes. My quilting club meets in half an hour at the church." Somehow just hearing her mother's voice sent a wave of happiness through her. Her mom reflected such joy—and peace. She always seemed to ride a wave of tranquility. Laura needed that.

"I know, Mom. I just needed someone to talk to for a couple of minutes."

"What's up, Laura?"

She felt the familiar knot in her throat. "I went to the college yesterday." She tried to keep her voice steady.

"Good for you." Her mother's voice rose in pitch. "Just what I wanted to hear. Well, how did it go?"

"Not bad, really." Laura dabbed at her eyes with a tissue. "But I've upset Jessica."

"Jessica?" Her mother's voice changed slightly. "What's wrong with our girl?"

"She doesn't want me to go to school with her, and I'm not so sure it's the right thing anymore."

The silence on the other end startled her. When her mother finally spoke, the voice seemed exceptionally stern. "You mean to tell me you're going to let your nineteen-year-old daughter control your chances for happiness?"

Wow. Quite a comment from a woman who prides herself on her soft, gentle nature.

"I wouldn't go that far, Mom." Laura chose her words with care. "She's had such a hard time since Greg died—in some ways, even harder than Kent. And she's enjoying college so far. I don't want to ruin that experience for her."

"Listen to me, Laura Marie," her mother said, suddenly sounding quite motherly. "Once upon a time I almost let you do the same thing to me, remember?"

Laura did remember, and the memory still carried the guilty sting of a teen who had treated her mother badly. *I was so young then and so selfish. If I had it all to do over again, I would. . .*

"There was a time many years ago when I almost stopped my relationship with your stepfather before it started."

Laura remembered all too well. She had behaved very badly. But Buck hadn't seemed right for her mother—at least not at first. Of course, time proved differently, and the guilt she carried over her childish behavior still plagued her from time to time. *We make mistakes when we're young, but time has a way of teaching us the lessons we need to learn.*

"I had just met Buck," her mother continued, "and he invited me out to dinner. You told me, quite bluntly, if I recall, that if I went out to dinner with him, you would never speak to me again."

The knot in Laura's throat began to grow. "But I didn't mean that, Mom. It was just the grief of losing Daddy speaking." Twinges of guilt gnawed at her again.

"Same with Jessica," her mother said firmly. "Just listen to me. I went on and defied you, taking the risk you wouldn't speak to me. Oh, I knew you would eventually, but I really worried my decision might cause a rift in our relationship. I forged ahead and did what my heart told me to do."

"And it's all worked out for the best, hasn't it, Mom?" Laura knew she spoke the truth. No doubt about that. Buck had turned out to be the best thing that could have ever happened to her mother.

"All for the best," the older woman said confidently. "But not without a lot of prayer on my part. Maybe that's what's missing here, Laura. Have you really prayed about your decision to go back to college?"

"Yes, Mom, I've prayed about it for weeks." *I've asked for direction from the very beginning.*

"How do you feel when you've prayed?"

Laura thought about that a moment before answering. Except for the small jittery moments, she had been comforted by an incredible amount of serenity about the decision. "I've had peace," she said, "until now."

"So what you're telling me is you're going to let Jessica disrupt the one decision that has brought you peace?"

"Well, when you put it that way—" Laura felt a resurgence of energy. She'd been excited by the idea of going back to school from the very beginning. It seemed so right.

It *was* so right. Suddenly everything became very clear. "Mom, you're a miracle worker."

"All mothers are. Just keep your wits about you when Jessica gets her skirts all twisted up in a knot. Don't let her control you. Stop it before it starts. You do what's best for you."

"I love you, Mom." The words were heartfelt, genuine. Laura only hoped someday she might be half as amazing as her own mother.

Andrew yawned and folded the evening paper. Politics—the usual rhetoric. That's all he encountered as he glanced through the pages. "Not much worth reading about." But what else could he do? He could squander a few minutes going over notes for his first lecture on the Vikings' exploration of America, but he'd given that lecture dozens of times before. Nothing new there. What would be new was the much-awaited e-mail from his colleague Joe Morris about the promised blind date. He leaned back against the couch cushions and tried to imagine what she might look like.

Funny, the only the face that flashed before him was that of the woman in the hallway at school—the one with the American History book. Andrew suddenly found himself irritated. *I felt sure she would be a great student, a hard worker. But it looks like she's going to turn out to be just like so many of the others. Lazy.*

"Jess, you're home!" Laura looked into her daughter's eyes. They were red and swollen, along with the tip of her nose—a sure sign something was amiss. "What's wrong?"

"Nothing." Jessica headed toward her room with her focus shifted down toward the floor.

Something was wrong, all right. "Jess, tell me."

"It's nothing, Mom."

"Well, I need to tell you something." Laura heard the quiver in her voice as she spoke. She didn't want to hurt her daughter but had to speak these words.

"What, Mom?"

"I've decided I'm going to go—"

Jessica's bloodshot eyes looked directly into hers.

"I'm going back to school, Jess—even if you don't understand. I have to. It's the hardest thing I've ever done, but it's the right thing for me—for all of us."

Andrew tossed and turned in bed, a Technicolor dream enveloping him. He stood near the door of his car, just about to step inside when a beauty with dark brown hair walked up to him.

"Have you got the time?" she asked, eyes glowing. Her soft, pretty face captivated him. Her hair, tied back with a yellow ribbon, flowed down to her waist.

"I've got nothing but time," he answered, swinging the door open. His voice remained rock-solid, his hands steady.

She looked at him with a smile, and his heart began to beat wildly. She clearly seemed interested in him. He would do his best to impress her. "What've you got in mind?" He tried to look casual.

"I was just thinking...," she said demurely.

"Yes?"

"I was just thinking," she said with a smile, "that if you've got the time—you might want to get that tire checked." She pointed to his left rear tire. Flat. The sound of her laughter echoed through him to the very core of his being. She disappeared into the mist.

Andrew groaned in his sleep, twisting among the covers until they caught him in their embrace.

Laura bowed her head to pray, feeling the weight of the day's decisions slowly lifting. Her heart spoke the words that needed to be voiced. The prayer was deliberate and sweet, not so much a prayer of frustration as one of praise. Funny how much better things suddenly seemed. She hadn't been avoiding the Lord— not really. More like holding Him at arm's length.

I should go back to church on a regular basis. Greg had served as Sunday school teacher for nearly twenty years at their local congregation, and she loved the people, but just the thought of attending sent a shot of pain through her heart. The memories were too fresh, too deep. How could she go from being a wife, seated next to her husband in the pew, to a widow, seated alone?

Everything was different. There would be no more couples' parties, no more camping trips with friends. Somehow, when Greg passed away, Laura lost far more than just her relationship with him. She lost everything.

Chapter 5

With her nerves on edge, Laura entered Room 314. Her first three classes had gone far better than expected, but she genuinely dreaded this one. American History. If it proved to be even half as bad as everyone predicted, she needed to be on the ball before the ball even got rolling.

Laura intentionally arrived early, choosing a desk near the front. She hoped this move might win her a little favor with the slave-driving professor she'd heard so much about. She glanced about the room, surprised at its appeal. *He sure takes a serious interest in the subject matter.* She focused on the Declaration of Independence, which hung on the wall.

A familiar gentleman stood near the door. Laura smiled as she gazed at the fellow with sandy curls who had helped her with her books. For some inexplicable reason, her heart skipped a beat as she saw him. "Hey, it's you!" she said with a smile. "Have you recovered?"

"I've recovered," he said with a polite nod. His answer was cool—a little too cool. Laura waited for him to take a seat nearby, but he did not. He milled about the room, looking at the walls. Other students entered the class, most sitting as close to the back as possible. Laura watched and waited.

Just as the bell rang, Jess entered the classroom. Laura glanced at her wistfully, hoping, at the very least, for a nod or a whispered hello. It never came. She turned her attention to the door once again.

Where is this professor I've heard so much about? What does he look like? Will he really turn out to be as tough as everyone says? Her heart raced with anticipation. Biting her lip, she pulled out a notebook and began to write: American History, August 26.

The sandy-haired gentleman hadn't yet found a seat. Laura wondered at his boldness, his apparent lack of fear. *Isn't he as worried about Dougherty as the rest of us?* His eyes met hers for a brief moment before he moved toward the blackboard at the front of the room.

"What in the world...?" she whispered.

He began to write in large, concise letters...M-R. D-O-U-G-H-E-R-T-Y. Everything after that became a blur.

Andrew turned to face his class, letting his gaze fall on the middle-aged woman who sat squarely in front. Her skin had drained of its color; her gaze remained fixed to the board. *Good. Let her suffer a little. If her words last week were any indication, she's just as apathetic as the young ones. She probably never had to work a day in her life—just sits at home, watching the soaps and doing her nails. Well, I'll light a fire under her. She's about to find out what real work is all about.*

"My name is Andrew Dougherty." He pointed to the board. "You can call me *Mr.* Dougherty." The woman's glance shifted to the desk, a clear sign of defeat. *Good. I've got her under my spell.* "I would like to welcome you all to American History—one of the most exciting and difficult classes you'll ever take."

A groan went up from the crowd. This he had grown accustomed to, but it remained part of the drama—and no one could accuse him of not acting his part.

"Oh, I know what you're thinking." He sat on the edge of his desk. "You're thinking, 'I'll transfer out of here and sign up for another class.'"

Another stirring from the troops.

"What sad news I have to convey," he spoke with great drama. "All of the other classes are full. But I promise you this—if you work hard, and if you take great notes, you just might get out of here alive."

Laura managed to keep her emotions in check in the classroom, but once released to the freedom of the hallway, she felt like collapsing. "That class is going to kill me," she said, leaning against the wall.

"I tried to tell you that," Jessica said with a shrug. "But you had your mind made up. Remember?"

All Laura could seem to remember was her run-in with Professor Dougherty in the hall last week. What was it he had said as he reached down to pick up her books? *"Are you taking American History?"*

"Yes, but I'm not looking forward to it." Had she really put it quite like that?

"Why?" It had been a logical question on his part.

"It's not the course," she remembered saying, *"it's the professor."* Laura shook her head, the memory lingering. If only she could take those words back. She had not only judged him—she had accused him right to his face. *I'm going to reap the consequences of that. I can just feel it.*

Jessica's voice interrupted her thoughts. "Mom?"

"Yes?"

"You didn't answer me."

"Oh, I'm sorry," Laura turned to look at her daughter. "What did you say?"

"I said, Nathan's going to be picking me up after math and driving me home. Is that all right?"

"Oh, sure, sure—"

"I just don't understand you, Mom." Jessica shook her head. "There are other people in this world who have problems, too. I have my piano auditions tomorrow and I'm scared to death. Did you remember that?"

Laura shook her head in shame. As hard as this was, it was just as hard on Jessica.

Father, help me to concentrate. I need to stay focused!

"I'll talk to you later."

Laura watched as she headed off to another class. Her gaze remained on Jessica, but her mind drifted elsewhere. Frustrated, she turned toward the car. She had only taken a step when she ran directly into someone, her books taking another tumble onto the floor.

"Oh, I'm so sorry," she said, looking up apologetically at the gentleman. "I. . ."

Could things possibly get any worse than this?

Andrew chuckled all the way to the cafeteria. He had won round one in the great contest he had started with this woman. He could hardly wait for round two. If she survived that, perhaps he would reward her with a pop quiz over chapter one next week. He entered the crowded lunchroom and looked around for a place to sit. Nothing. He made his way up to the counter to order, fighting to get through the mob of teenagers.

"What'll it be, Professor Dougherty?" A plump, dark-haired woman with a friendly face and welcoming voice called out to him from across the counter.

"Well, if it isn't Regina Torres, the best cook in all of Houston," he responded with a playful smile.

"It's Regina Leal now," she said, showing him her wedding ring. "Remember?"

He remembered. "I'm just giving you a hard time. So, how was the wedding?"

"Amazing. But you weren't there! Why didn't you come? I sent you an invitation."

Andrew didn't answer. He had no excuse. It wasn't that he didn't like Regina. Few people at the college treated him with such generosity and kindness. She always made the lunchroom a brighter place with her broad smile and cheery greetings. Her good humor warmed him on days when the cold shoulder from his students left him chilled. No, it had nothing to do with Regina. It was just that the idea of going to a wedding conjured up too many memories of days gone by. It would have been too difficult, far too difficult.

Better to change the subject. "You're back at Wainesworth. I didn't think you'd be working this year."

"Who, me? Leave this place? I could never leave."

"I thought you said that new husband of yours was going to take you off on a cruise or a six-month vacation or something like that."

She shrugged. "Aw, come on, Mr. Dougherty. You know better than that. He works for the cable company. We won't be seeing any European vacations for a long, long time."

Her broad smile cheered him, as always. "Why aren't all women as wonderful as you are?" For whatever reason, his mind shifted to Laura Chapman.

"I guess when the good Lord made me, He broke the mold," she said. "What sort of woman trouble are you having, Professor?"

"Trouble?" he stammered. "No trouble. It's just that most of the women I meet are so...so...." He wasn't sure what they were.

"It's the women, eh?" Regina said. "Couldn't be the problem's on the other end?"

"I'll have a root beer and a bag of pretzels," he said curtly, reaching for his wallet.

"Great combination. What did you do—skip lunch again today?"

He shrugged. "Yeah. I didn't have time between classes—not today, anyway. Talk about swamped."

"You better take care of yourself," she said. "Stay in good shape for that wife we're gonna snag for you this year."

"I beg your pardon?" He looked at her curiously.

"I'm just saying—with the two of us working together..."

"Regina, my love life is none of your business."

"What love life?" she asked as she tossed the bag of pretzels at him. "When was the last time you were on a date?"

"For your information, I'm about to go out on a date."

"Today?"

"No," he said, shaking his head. "But soon."

"With who?"

"A girl named Judy. My friend Joe is fixing me up with her." His heart raced, just thinking about her. *She's the one. I just know it.* After all of these years, it would be so amazing to walk headlong into a romantic relationship. *If anyone deserves it, I do.*

"What's wrong with her?" Regina asked, lips pursed.

"What do you mean?"

"I mean, if she has to be fixed up on a blind date..." Regina's eyes reflected her thoughts on the matter.

"There's nothing wrong with her, just like there's nothing wrong with me. Not everyone is blissfully in love like you are. So just let me have my date, and I'll report back to you when it's over. Who knows? She just might be Ms. Right."

"Well, hallelujah to that!" Regina said triumphantly. "Maybe I won't have to play matchmaker after all."

"Matchmaker?"

"I had my mind made up I would find you the perfect wife this year. It was sort of a challenge—almost made coming back worthwhile."

"Very funny."

Her face suddenly took on a serious expression. "Don't you worry, Mr.

31

Dougherty. I've got my eyes wide open. I'll let you know when I meet the girl of your dreams."

"Gee, thanks, Regina." He popped open the root beer. "Keep me posted. I'm on pins and needles."

He turned to leave, feeling a little better about his life. As usual, she had managed to put a smile on his face. There were a few nice women in the world, after all.

Laura opened the car door, deep in thought. How could her day have ended this way? Just when she had to face a full afternoon of work, she had *him* on her mind. Professor Andrew Dougherty. He had proven to be every bit as tough as people said he would be.

No—worse. He had given the class two chapters to read for homework, along with a work sheet and a biography on Christopher Columbus. *How am I going to get all of this done and still have time to work at the store? Lord, I'm going to need more help than I thought.*

Laura climbed into the car and pulled out of the familiar parking lot. Try as she might, she could not stop thinking about what had happened in the hallway. She did her best to forget it, but how could she?

Lost in her thoughts, she drove to the Bookstop, hoping to make it in time for her shift. How could she possibly handle all of this—classes in the morning, working the afternoon? "I must be crazy." She drove on in absolute silence, her thoughts overwhelming her. By the time she arrived at the store, exhaustion had completely consumed her.

Laura fretted and fumed as the hours rolled by at the bookstore. She found herself pacing around, frustration growing. She couldn't focus on her work because of Professor Dougherty. She could see him now with his cocky expression, walking toward the board, spelling out his name: D-O-U-G-H-E-R-T-Y...very slowly, for effect. His cool eyes had stared into hers as he turned back toward the class. His motives were unmistakable. *Well, I won't let him interfere with my work here. I can't. I need this job too badly.*

"Excuse me?" An elderly woman spoke, interrupting her thoughts. She looked a little lost.

"Yes?" Laura yanked herself out of the daydream to respond.

"Could you please tell me where I can find the biographies? I just love to read about people's lives."

Biographies. *Reminds me—I need to look through some books for information on Columbus.* "Sure," Laura said. "We have a great biography department. Just follow me." She wound her way through fiction and around the children's area to the nonfiction books. *Dougherty would really love it here in this section.* There were biographies galore from his precious American history. She could just see the excitement on his face.

"Oh, thank you, sweetie," the older lady said with a smile. "Just what the doctor ordered. You know, you can learn a lot about a person from one of these books. It always fascinates me to know what makes folks tick—what makes them happy, sad, angry. . ." She rambled on and on, but Laura stopped listening at some point. *There's no way he can expect us to get through two chapters, complete a work sheet, and write a biography in two days. That's ridiculous.* She realized exactly what must be done.

He gave us his number in class, said to call if we had any problems. Well, this is a problem. I'm going to call Mr. Dougherty and see if there's some way to ease the workload.

⏤

Andrew buzzed around his apartment in happy anticipation. The long-awaited phone call from Joe had just come in. His blind date, Judy, would be waiting at The Happy Oyster on Highway 290 and Mangum Road. He had just enough time to get there if nothing went wrong. He slipped on a navy shirt, accidentally tearing a button off as his anxious fingers fumbled with it.

"Oh, man!" He pulled the shirt off and reached for another—a gray-and-white stripe. It wouldn't look great with his dark blue sweater vest, but what did it matter, really? *If she's really interested in me, clothing won't be an issue, anyway.* Andrew pulled on the vest, followed by the jacket. *There. Nearly ready.*

He glanced in the mirror for one last look at his hair. *Curly. Too curly.* He rubbed a little hair gel between his palms and spread it all around. No change, but nothing could be done about that. Andrew sprayed on some cologne with a smile. *I'm going all out for this one.* She would be worth it. He could just feel it.

He grabbed his car keys and raced toward the door, double-checking to make sure he hadn't forgotten anything. Just as his hand hit the doorknob, the telephone rang.

"Forget it." He glanced back. "Let the machine get it." But something in him wouldn't allow that. Could be Joe with a change of plans. Or maybe, just maybe, it was Judy, herself. Andrew dropped his jacket on the bench in the front hall and reached over to grab the receiver.

"Hello?"

Nothing could have prepared him for the voice on the other end of the phone.

"Mr. Dougherty?" The woman stressed his name the way he had so carefully spelled it on the board.

"This is he. With whom am I speaking?"

"Laura Chapman," she said. "C-H-A-P-M-A-N."

"Very funny." He couldn't help but chuckle. "What can I do for you, Ms. Chapman?"

"I'm just calling to make sure I got the homework assignment right. Did you really say chapters one and two, along with the work sheet you handed out?"

"That's right. And don't forget—"

"The biography." They spoke in unison.

"That just seems like a lot of work for two days," she argued. "It's just. . ."

"Just what, Ms. Chapman?"

"Well, I thought maybe I had misunderstood. It just seemed like a lot, that's all."

"Look, Ms. Chapman. . ." Exasperation kicked in. "I know your type. You come into a class like this expecting to breeze through, then reality slaps you in the face. Am I right?"

"Well, actually—"

"Why don't you do us both a favor and drop my class while you can still get a refund? It's obvious this is going to be too much for you." Where the words came from, he had no idea.

"Too much for me?" A renewed zeal seemed to take hold of her. "Who said that?"

"You've done everything but say it. I'm a firm believer in excellence, Ms. Chapman."

"So am I," she echoed. "In fact, you just wait and see, Mr. Dougherty. I'm going to be the best student you ever had."

He laughed out loud.

"I'm not kidding!" she hollered, then abruptly hung up.

Andrew doubled over with laughter. *How delicious!* He dropped down onto the couch, trying to calm himself. He began to picture in his mind the infamous Ms. Chapman—what she must have looked like as she spoke with such energy. What a scene she must have created. A smile crossed his lips as he remembered their first encounter. This woman seemed destined to make him a little crazy.

But wait. Another woman waited for him now. Andrew glanced down at his watch and groaned. He would be late, even if he drove like a maniac. Once again, Ms. Chapman had run him down, though she didn't even know it.

~

Laura shook violently as she placed the phone back on the hook, but she felt some sense of satisfaction. "I guess I told him!" She forced back a laugh. "Let's just wait and see who he thinks he's messing with." Returning to her work, she found herself energized by an undeniable surge of excitement and hope.

Of course, she had made a rather hefty promise. *"I'm going to be the best student you ever had."* She would keep that promise if it took her all day and all night to do so. What did losing a little sleep mean, anyway—as long as she accomplished her goal?

Chapter 6

"Put your books away, and take out a piece of notebook paper and a pen." Andrew spoke the words with a sense of sheer delight. The gaze of every history student locked firmly on him. "We're going to have a pop quiz."

A groan rose from among them. One student in particular held his gaze. Her eyes were unmistakably laced with frustration, but they refused to concede.

"Ms. Chapman," he said, feeling a bit heady, "I noticed from your records that your maiden name is Eriksson." She nodded as he continued. "Our quiz today will cover the journeys of the Viking, Leif Eriksson. No doubt a relative of yours—a great-grandfather, perhaps?" He couldn't resist the temptation, though he regretted the words almost as soon as he spoke them.

The roar of laughter that went up from the class convinced him he had accomplished his goal—humiliating her in front of the group. Doing so suddenly didn't feel very kind, but what could he do now?

With the coolness of a cucumber, she replied, "An uncle."

Her response startled him a little. The class erupted, their laughter suddenly focused on him. His ears began to burn, as they always did when turning red.

"This quiz will be worth ten percent of your overall grade," he announced. "You can leave as soon as you've completed it." The students began to murmur, and rightfully so. *So I'm a little irrational. So what?* Laura Chapman had judged him, slam-dunked him, and all but ruined his date the other night. She wasn't going to humiliate him in front of his students. He wouldn't allow it.

Laura struggled through the pop quiz, amazed at the unfairness of the questions. *"What were the names of Eriksson's children?"* Were they even mentioned in the book?

"Larry, Mo, and Curly," she wrote, lifting her pen with a dramatic flair. If she couldn't beat the professor at his own game, she could surely join him in the lunacy of it all.

The pen slipped from her hand, rolling halfway down the aisle before it stopped. She felt Mr. Dougherty's gaze on her as she crept down the aisle to pick it up.

"Having a problem, Ms. Chapman?"

She glared her response and sat back in her seat, her hands still shaking with anger. She looked down at the pen, noticing ink all over her fingers. "Great." She made her way up the aisle to his desk.

"Can I help you?" he asked, his eyes peering directly into hers.

"My pen broke. Do you have one I could borrow?"

"Certainly." He reached into his top drawer for a black ink pen. "Don't forget to give it back after class."

Laura gripped the pen as she turned and headed back to her seat. She would overcome this—all of this—if it was the last thing she ever did. She sat with a defiant thud and did her best to focus on the paper once again. Question number two seemed worse than the first one. Number three didn't look much better. She took a deep breath, beginning to write. She would give this an honest effort, regardless.

One by one, the class began to empty. Out of the corner of her eye, she could see students marching back and forth to Dougherty's desk to place their papers in the appropriate basket. Each one left with a sigh. As she passed by, Jessica cast her mother an accusing glare.

Laura sat scribbling, marking through, scribbling, marking through. She had read the chapters. Several times, in fact. It was just that these questions were so poorly worded.

She looked up to discover the professor's eyes clearly focused on hers, an undeniable look of satisfaction on his face. *You're insufferable. Nothing like Greg.*

Wait a minute. Where did that come from? Snap out of it. The pen slipped from her fingers once again, hitting the desk and bouncing off to the floor below. It rolled all the way down the aisle, landing just in front of Dougherty's feet. Laura's head dropped to the desk instinctively. *This is partly my fault, Father! I've let my anger overwhelm me. Help me. . . .*

There were still two unanswered questions on the quiz. She couldn't possibly complete them without getting up for the pen. She stood, making her way up the aisle one final time.

"Time's up," Professor Dougherty said sharply.

⌒

Andrew spoke the words with satisfaction. Laura Chapman had already distracted him enough. Thanks to her, his date last night had been a complete fiasco. He arrived at the restaurant fifteen minutes late, much to his own chagrin. Judy, it turned out, wasn't a very patient sort. She wasn't a very intelligent sort, either. She had the looks, no questioning that—a redhead with the appearance of a model but few brains to match. A trip to the dentist would surely have been more pleasant. She spent most of the night whining about everything from his tardiness to the nail fungus under her phony red fingernails. It nauseated him.

Andrew looked again at Laura Chapman as she made her way to the front of the class. She didn't have Judy's figure, and her haircut couldn't compete, but it always seemed to catch his eye. Still. . .

Wait a minute, man. What are you doing?

He forced his attentions back to the where they should be, pushing thoughts of women behind him. They simply weren't worth the trouble.

His eyes met Laura's as she dropped the paper onto his desk. He had clearly upset her, but that had been his intention, after all.

Right?

She left the class in a huff, pulling the door shut behind her. He observed the color in her cheeks as she gave him one last frustrated look.

Andrew glanced through the papers quickly, looking for her quiz. With great satisfaction, he skimmed the page. "That's wrong." He struck a red line through her first answer. "And that's wrong." He added more red to the page.

A sea of crimson ink covered the page before he had finished. Andrew leaned back in his chair and smiled, content. Justified, even. She'd gotten exactly what she deserved.

"Well, Ms. Chapman," he spoke aloud to an empty room. "Looks like you didn't do very well on your first American History quiz. But don't worry—you'll have plenty of others in the weeks ahead. I'll make sure of that."

He gathered up the stack of papers from his desk and prepared to leave. He had one last stop to make—the lunchroom. He hadn't eaten all day. Again.

Andrew made his way across the crowded campus to the familiar hub at the center. Teenagers and twenty-somethings surrounded him on every side. He felt his age more acutely than ever in this place. He worked through the maze of kids to the lunchroom inside, where a familiar face greeted him.

"So," Regina said as he approached the counter, "how was your—uh, your 'date'?"

"My date?" He tried to act innocent.

"Yeah," she reminded him. "Remember? You said something about a girl named Judy. How did that work out?"

"Oh, well, you know," he mumbled, looking past Regina at the food choices. "I'll have some cheese curls and a bag of those oatmeal cookies—and a chocolate milk."

"Are you sure about that?" she asked, looking at his midsection. "We're never gonna get you a wife if you keep eating like this."

"Regina," he said with tightened lips, "I told you, I don't need any help. I'm perfectly capable of—"

"Sure you are, sure you are." She collected his food and placed it on the counter. A silence fell between them, lingering in the air for a moment before Regina finally broke it. "By the way, I heard about that pop quiz you gave today." She let out a long whistle.

"What? What did you hear?"

"A killer. That's what I heard."

"Who said that?" he asked, growing angry.

"Who didn't?" came her swift reply. "It's all over campus. You're a legend, Mr. Dougherty. You know that. But they're saying this one really took the cake."

He shrugged. "It wasn't so bad."

"Well, all I'm saying," she leaned toward him, whispering, "is it sounds like you're mighty frustrated with something and taking it out on these poor kids. Why don't you give them a break and let me help you find a wife?"

"The last thing on earth I need," Andrew said forcefully, "is a wife. I'm perfectly happy with me, myself, and I."

"Laura, it's not that I'm complaining," her boss, Madeline, spoke with what appeared to be some hesitancy. "It's just that a couple of our customers have asked about you—wondering if you were okay."

"What do you mean?" Laura looked into the worried gray eyes of her boss. Madeline wasn't the type to mince words. All business, she prided herself on running the bookstore like a well-oiled machine. This showed in the way she dressed, the way she spoke, even in the way she wore her hair. Never married, Madeline couldn't begin to understand the issues of balancing a home and career.

"Well, they seem to think you're a little...distracted."

The understatement of the century, Laura had to admit. She had been here only in body. Her mind and her emotions had been divided between her children and her classes. Factor American History into the equation and, well—there just wasn't a lot left to bring into the workplace.

"I'm sorry, Madeline." She felt the weight of her words as she spoke. "I've been distracted. I know it. But it's only because I'm trying to get used to my schedule, and I've had a little bit of trouble at school. I can handle this. I really can." She sounded like a kid, trying to convince herself.

"What sort of trouble?"

Laura shrugged, not wanting to get into it. "It's really nothing. Nothing I can't handle, anyway. Everything is going to be fine. Just give me awhile, okay?"

"Oh, speaking of trouble," Madeline interjected, "I hate to be the bearer of bad news, but you had a call from Kent's school just before you got here."

"Kent's school?" Laura asked nervously. "What did they want?" *Lord, keep him safe!*

"He's fine. Something about an incident on the bus."

Laura felt the usual twisting in her chest. Her son had spent much of last year in trouble at the junior high. He really seemed to be slipping since Greg's death. But they had talked about it—at great length—just weeks ago. He had promised this year would be different. They had both hoped for a fresh start. Surely he wouldn't blow it this quickly.

"What sort of incident?"

Madeline shrugged. "I told them you'd call as soon as you got in, but you're already late. Make it a quick call."

"I'm sorry." Laura walked behind the counter and picked up the phone, thumbing through her pocketbook for the tiny phone book she always carried. She located the number for the high school and began to dial.

"Carter High School," a cheery voice rang out on the other end.

"I need to find out about my son. I understand he was involved in some sort of an incident on the bus this morning."

"Ah. You must be Mrs. Chapman." Laura's heart sank instantly. "We've been trying to reach you for hours. Can you come up to the school?"

"I just got to work," she said, "and I can't leave."

"It won't take long, Mrs. Chapman, and we really need to talk to you."

"Where is Kent?" She asked the question carefully, dreading the woman's answer.

"He's here in the office, sitting across from me as we speak."

"You mean he's been there all day?"

"Yes."

"I'll be right there." Laura spoke the words, hoping that Madeline would understand. She hung up the phone, heart racing.

"Please let her understand," she whispered the prayer on near-silent lips, then turned, facing her boss.

"They need me to come to the school."

"Now?"

"It's some sort of emergency; at least that's what they said."

"How long will you be?"

"I don't know," Laura whispered beyond the growing lump in her throat. "But I'll come back just as quickly as I can. I promise."

Madeline sighed. "Do the best you can." She shifted her attention to a waiting customer.

Laura turned at once and headed for the door.

Chapter 7

Laura sat in the courtyard of the college, battling with her emotions. *September 28. Our anniversary. Today would have made twenty-two years.* She wiped away a tear and reached for her American History book. Distracting herself was the best thing. She could get through this. She thumbed through the text frantically, looking for the right chapter. *I've got Dougherty completely figured out. At least I think I do. I can predict there will, without any question or doubt, be another pop quiz today.* His demeanor in the last class left no uncertainty in her mind.

Staying focused seemed difficult these days. Problems at home escalated daily, causing Laura to be even more distracted than before. She suffered from lack of sleep. Night after sleepless night, she promised herself things would be different, but nothing appeared to be changing. She managed to stay awake reading, studying, writing, or worrying.

Things with the kids weren't much better. Jessica remained in a foul mood much of the time, and Kent had been suspended from school for three days because of his fighting incident on the bus. *When Greg was here, things were so different, so much better—in so many ways.* Kent had always been close to his dad, but now. . .

Now everything felt different. Her son grew angrier with each passing day, and it showed in a variety of ways. Looked like they were in for a rough year.

She needed to remain focused on school things. Despite all of her gloating, Laura's grades were slipping dramatically in American History. A sixty-two on the first quiz set the ball in motion. She hadn't done much better on last week's paper. Her best hope lay in the essay she would turn in today on the Declaration of Independence. She'd spent a great deal of time on it. Of course, Dougherty would find plenty wrong with it. He always did.

Why this particular professor had singled her out remained a mystery to Laura. Surely he couldn't still be holding a grudge after all of this time. There must be something more. But what? Did he hate women in particular, or just her?

Sighing deeply, Laura closed the book. Studying seemed to be pointless. His pop quizzes defied logic, anyway. She made her way toward the class, wondering about Jessica. How would her daughter treat her today? Would it be the cold shoulder, or a friendly hello?

Will things be like this forever, Lord?

Somehow, in the midst of the battle, it seemed they would.

Andrew watched Laura Chapman carefully as she entered the room. His disappointment in her had diminished greatly over the past month, replaced with a growing amazement at her tenacity. He hadn't shown that, of course. Andrew looked forward to this class on Tuesdays and Thursdays above all others. All of these changing emotions perplexed him, but not overwhelmingly so. On the surface, she seemed just like any other woman.

Or did she? He looked at her with curiosity. Today she wore a pair of jeans and a soft blue sweater—quite a sight for his sore eyes. Her hair had a shimmer that held him captivated. *She's really very pretty. And maybe she's not as apathetic as I made her out to be. She seems to be trying.*

He quickly changed gears, hoping not to attract her attention. "Class, please turn in your essays on the Declaration of Independence." He watched as she rose, stepping into the aisle with paper in hand. His gaze never left her. She carried herself with grace. Andrew hadn't yet figured out her story. Was she divorced, widowed? No wedding ring adorned her left hand, and yet she had a daughter, Jessica.

Ms. Chapman placed her paper on the desk—typed, double-spaced—just as he had requested. She certainly seemed to be doing everything in her power to conform. Perhaps the time had come to declare a peace treaty. Enough damage had been done. Clearly she struggled, not just in this class, but with deeper issues. Her eyes were often weary, and her shoulders down. He would change that. He would be a better man. He would step up to the plate.

"Ladies and gentlemen," he said to the class, "today we're going to have an open discussion on the Declaration of Independence. Whom did the authors intend to include? Whom did they exclude? How do you feel about the men who signed, etc.?"

The class erupted into a lively debate—touching on everything from the lives of the men who had framed the document to those excluded from the rights of the Declaration because of the issue of slavery. He kept a careful eye on Ms. Chapman, who never stirred once during the entire discussion. She seemed frozen in place. Finally, when he dismissed the class and the other students left, he approached her. "You were unusually quiet today, Ms. Chapman."

She shrugged her response, but he noticed the frustration in her eyes.

"Nothing to add to the conversation?"

"I just think one subject was overlooked today." She offered up a shrug. "Maybe I should've mentioned it."

"What's that?"

"Well, what about a woman's right to independence—and, in particular, her right to vote? No one even touched on that subject."

"Could you elaborate?"

"I mean, for all the good it did, the Declaration of Independence still didn't provide for the women of those original thirteen states. It excluded them, didn't it?"

"Well, to some extent, perhaps," he said frankly. "But women were viewed differently in those days." *Things are about to get touchy. I can feel it.*

"How so?"

"Well," he said hesitantly, "they were viewed much more as..." How could he put this? "They were viewed more as possessions than as thinking people. When a man took a wife, she became his property."

Laura had taken to staring, her jaw hanging open in surprise. "Well, thank God that has changed."

"Yes. Thank God." He paused and then added, "I think that women are completely entitled to their right to vote, as are all American citizens of voting age." He did. No question about that.

"But..." Laura looked at him intently.

He chose his words quite carefully. "Well, it's just that some of the women I know aren't exactly nuclear physicists, if you get my drift." Visions of his blind date danced in front of his eyes. Judy's nail fungus had been far more important to her than political matters, that was for sure. Of course, she wasn't like many of the woman he had known, so he couldn't judge them all by the way she'd acted.

"You mean, 'men are smarter than women,'" Laura argued.

Andrew noticed how pale her face had become. It intrigued him but worried him as well. He certainly didn't want to create an even larger rift between the two of them. "Well, no," he stammered, trying to make the best of this. "We're not all smarter..."

"All?" Her eyes began to sparkle with anger. Had he said something wrong? No. Every word he had spoken could be backed up with intelligent and accurate statistics.

"Men, as a rule, have a higher intelligence quotient than women," he argued, "but that's because we've been privy to a history of learning, whereas women have only been allowed full access to all of the academic opportunities this country has to offer for a short time. We've got several hundred years of university education under our belts." *There. That should satisfy her.*

Apparently not. She stared at him in silence—deafening silence.

"What I mean to say," he stammered, "is that you—I mean, *women*, haven't had the same access to a college education. You've missed out on many years of possibility." Could he get any plainer than that?

"Are you really saying what I think you're saying? You honestly believe men are smarter than women?"

Her words were heated, and they stirred something in him. She didn't seem to understand where he was coming from. Her stubbornness wouldn't allow it.

"That's not what I. . ." he tried to interject another explanation. He found himself completely frustrated with the direction of the conversation. *How can I turn this around?*

"All you have to do is look around you, Ms. Chapman. You'll find a good many women here at Wainesworth your age but not many men. I'm sure Jessica's father, if he didn't have his degree yet, would head to a major university to obtain his bachelor's or master's. That's true of most men. But you're going to a junior college. See what I mean?" He smiled in her direction.

"I think it's time for me to go," she said, turning to leave the room. Her eyes widened with his last comment, a sure sign she had misunderstood his words. Laura disappeared down the hallway, never looking back. Andrew sprinted after her. He needed to say something to her—obviously something more carefully thought-out than his last statement.

"Ms. Chapman," he called out her name, but she kept walking. "Ms. Chapman." Nothing. "Laura!"

At this, she turned and looked at him, ashen-faced. "There is one thing you should know, Mr. Dougherty, one very important thing."

"What?"

"My husband died nearly three years ago after a terrible battle with cancer. Does that answer your question about why I'm struggling? He never cared if I had a degree or not. He didn't put a lot of stock in things like that. He loved me for who I was. He respected me. He would have been proud of me for going back to school—even if it was only a junior college."

Andrew swallowed hard, and his heart pounded in his chest until he felt like it would explode. "I'm so sorry. I. . ."

"Except for my kids, I'm alone. Up until now, I've been doing the best I could to get by, no thanks to you. I may not be the smartest woman in the world, but until today, I've given this my best shot. Apparently my best wasn't good enough for you."

Andrew's heart sank to his toes. How could he begin to redeem this? "I'm a tough teacher. Maybe a little too tough; I don't know. But I'm really sorry if I've said anything to hurt you. We can work this out."

"I don't want to work it out. I'm tired of trying. So I'm dropping your class, Mr. Dougherty. Isn't that what you wanted? You've won." Defeat covered her like a shroud.

I haven't won. Neither of us has won. I've caused this—caused her to fail. But how can I stop her? "Laura, please don't."

"That news should make you happy. I'm not going to be around to make fun of anymore."

He never had a chance to respond. She turned to walk in the opposite direction.

Laura made her way to the car, jaw clenched. She just wanted to leave and never come back. She couldn't blame it on the school. Her other classes were going well. Even the younger students all treated her with respect and dignity. It was only *him*—only that professor. *Why do I let him get to me? What is it about him that bothers me so much? He's not worth it. The class isn't worth it.*

Laura climbed in the car and rested her head on the steering wheel in defeat. "Now what?" she asked herself. She knew the consequences of dropping the class. It meant she couldn't possibly get the degree within the two-year period. It messed up everything. *He* messed up everything. Her thoughts deepened from melancholy to hopelessness. Without a degree, she would never make it out of her dead-end job. *Unless they fire me, of course.*

September 28. Looks like I might not make it through the day, after all. The tears began to flow. Frustrations were mounting. And now, thanks to Mr. Dougherty, the sky was falling.

Chapter 8

Come on, Matt—just tell me," Andrew coaxed the young man in the admissions office. "I just need Laura Chapman's work number so I can call her about something that happened today after class."

"Why are you so hard on everyone?" Matt asked. "Why don't you just give this one a break?"

"Is that what everyone thinks—that I'm too hard on people?"

Matt smiled. "Well, yeah."

Andrew shook his head, miserable. "I really need to apologize, but I can't if you won't give me the information."

"You're gonna humble yourself and do the right thing, eh?" Matt said. "Think you'll regret it?"

"Probably not." He couldn't possibly regret anything more than he did the mess he'd gotten himself into already.

Matt typed a few words into the computer. "Here you go," he said finally. "She works at the Bookstop on Tully. The number's right here."

"She works in a bookstore?" Interesting.

"Yeah. Do you want the number or not?"

"Sure. Sure." Andrew quickly scribbled down the number, but he'd already decided on a better plan. A bookstore. What a logical place for a college professor to turn up. Nothing contrived. He would simply be one in a number of shoppers, especially in a store the size of the Bookstop. Maybe, just maybe, he would find her there.

~

Laura drove up to the store, anxious to get inside and start working. The harder she worked, she reasoned, the quicker she could put this afternoon's incident out of her mind. And that's exactly what she had to do in order to maintain her sanity.

"Laura, everything all right?" Madeline asked.

"Yeah. Rough day." She opted not to elaborate. "But I'm fine. Really. I want you to know things are going to be better, Madeline. With me, I mean."

"What do you mean?"

"I mean," she said, with a look of determination, "I'm going to drop a class or two, and that should relieve my schedule a little." *Madeline will appreciate this news. She, of all people, knows how stressed I am.*

"But your plans. . ."

"Never mind my plans," Laura asserted, putting on her best face. "I'm going to be fine; just wait and see. Now, what needs to be done?" There would be no time to dwell on the day's events if she had her mind on her work.

"Well, I've been thinking of revamping the inspirational section," her boss said. "That area's not getting a lot of business, and I think maybe it's because of the way we've got it set up."

Laura nodded. "Sounds great." Just the titles alone in the inspirational section would cheer her up. She moved forward, into a newer, brighter day. She would put Mr. Dougherty and this whole fiasco out of her mind.

Andrew pulled up to the Bookstop and anxiously looked toward the door. He glanced at his reflection in the rearview mirror before getting out, wet his fingers, and ran them through the lopsided curl in the center of his forehead that never seemed to lie down. *Useless.*

He made the short walk to the entrance of the large store. A poster in the window advertised Grisham's latest book. Looked like they were also having a sale on art books. None of that interested him at this moment. Only one thing captivated his mind: He had to find Laura Chapman.

Laura pulled books off the dusty top shelf with a little more force than usual, placing them onto the cart in front of her. She looked around her, trying to imagine what this section would look like in a few hours. With her help, it could be a showcase. This area could be improved in so many ways. What they needed were posters and promos, drawing people to this corner of the store. Perhaps a center table with inspirational best-sellers available at a glance.

Laura thumbed through a few of the books on the cart. Some of them looked a little dull, but others really caught her eye. One in particular stood out—*Put Your Troubles in the Blender and Give Them a Spin.* She didn't recognize the author's name, but she could certainly relate to the title. Who would have thought inspirational books could be humorous? She gave it a once-over. The text was clever, funny—yet packed a real punch in the emotional department. *Lord, are You trying to tell me something?*

Andrew wound his way through the bookshelves, nervously looking for Laura. He rehearsed the words over and over again in his mind—what he would say when he saw her. He would start with a practical apology. He owed her that. He would then shift into an explanation of why he had said what he had. He would do his best not to further damage his case. Rather, he'd try to make himself look like the reasonable man that he was. Being a reasonable woman, she would respond in kind.

At least he hoped she would. He rounded a corner, practically running into a cart full of books. *Looks like I've found her. Now who's running into whom?* He smiled warmly, attempting to regain his composure.

Laura glanced his direction, her face falling. "What are you doing here?"

"Me?" He tried to look calm. "I come here a lot, actually. Interesting you should work here."

"Very."

"Laura—"

"Ms. Chapman." She stressed the words.

"C-H-A-P-M-A-N." His meager attempt at humor didn't seem to go over very well. She didn't smile. "Look, Ms. Chapman, I really felt like we needed to talk. Do you have a few minutes?" His heart pounded in his ears, making it difficult to hear her response. He watched her lips as she spoke.

"I think we've covered all the basics, don't you?"

She has a point, but won't she even give me a chance? "I just wanted to say how sorry I am."

A baffled look crossed her face as he forged ahead. His gaze shifted to the ground. "I'm so sorry. I don't want you to quit the class. I really don't." He meant it. He hated to see any student give up, truth be told, but there was something special about this one. She needed to get through this—for psychological reasons as well as any other.

"I have to work and I really don't have time to deal with this. I'm going through enough at home and here at the store."

"What do you mean?" Nosiness kicked in. There seemed to be so much he didn't know about her, about Jessica.

"Never mind," she said, moving toward the door.

Just be direct. Get to the point. "So, will you come back?"

"Why should I?"

"I just hoped—" No, he wouldn't go that far. He didn't want to let her know that he had grown accustomed to seeing her, looked forward to every class with her.

"Can you give me one logical reason why I should come back to your class, Mr. Dougherty?" Laura asked, her face set.

Should he tell her that he enjoyed seeing her there, that she brought a smile to his face with her wit and her persistence? Should he let her know how impressed he was by the effort she took to raise her kids, work, and go to school? "I, uh. . ." He started, then hesitated slightly as fear caught hold of his tongue.

She shook her head in disbelief. "I thought so."

———

Laura watched as Dougherty sauntered out of the door, making his way to an old sedan with worn black paint. The car suited him—outdated and not terribly pretty. He deserved a car like that. She watched as he pulled out of the parking lot and sped down Tully with tires squealing.

Laura immediately set her mind back on her work. So much needed to be done, and she had lost time—thanks to him. He had quite a way of spoiling things. She quickly moved back toward the inspirational section, ready to dive in headfirst. She picked up a Bible to place it on the cart with the others. Her fingers lingered across the cover. It had been weeks since she picked up her own Bible to read. Somehow, just holding one now made her feel better.

She turned it open to the New Testament, her fingers racing along the words. They were as familiar as an old friend, and yet stirred an emotion in her she was unprepared for. Her index finger rested on a verse in 2 Corinthians that startled her. She couldn't remember ever reading it before.

"If anyone has caused grief, he has not so much grieved me as he has grieved all of you, to some extent—not to put it too severely. The punishment inflicted on him by the majority is sufficient for him. Now instead, you ought to forgive and comfort him, so that he will not be overwhelmed by excessive sorrow."

"Forgive and comfort him?" She spoke the words softly, struck by their simplicity. But it couldn't be that easy! Laura closed the Bible quickly, placing it on the cart. Surely she wasn't supposed to comfort a man like Professor Dougherty. He was beyond help.

But, then again, why had he come here? Her mind began to drift to their conversation. Did he really feel bad about what he had said, or were there darker forces at work?

Madeline walked up.

"I guess you pretty much figured out who that was," Laura said.

"The infamous professor. Yeah, I've got it—and I hope you don't mind my saying this, but he doesn't seem like the ogre you made him out to be. He's a cutie."

Laura groaned—loudly, for effect.

Madeline grinned. "What did he want, anyway?"

"Actually, he wanted to apologize and asked me to come back to the class."

"Are you going to?" A smile made its way to her boss's lips. "I mean, I'm just saying if I had a professor who looked like that, I'd go back."

Laura thought carefully about her words before answering. "If I do, it won't have anything to do with him. I'd be going back for myself."

"Good girl. I'm proud of you."

"You are? I thought you didn't like the idea. Balancing work and school is a real pain."

"Like the idea? I'm so proud of you, I could burst! You make me want to go back myself."

"I do?"

"You do."

"Well," Laura said with a sigh, "it's a lot tougher than they make it out to be.

I'm not sure how I'm ever going to get through this American History class if I do go back."

Madeline's eyes began to sparkle immediately. "Oh, Laura!" She grabbed her cell phone and lifted it triumphantly. "I have the most amazing idea!"

Chapter 9

Laura sat in the college cafeteria, clutching her colorful American History book. She slowly worked her way through a chapter on indentured servants, fascinated by the material. She glanced up occasionally, slightly distracted. She looked back and forth—from her book, to her watch, to all of the people. The noisy room provided some degree of comfort—trays clattering, soda cans popping open, students chattering incessantly—these were all things she had grown to love. Even so, Laura found it very difficult to focus. The whole thing was nerve-wracking, especially under the circumstances.

"Come on, come on."

He should be here soon. She took a bite of her sandwich and chased it down with a mouthful of soda, then glanced at her watch nervously. *Not much time left. He'd better come quickly, or there really won't be much point to all of this.* She tried to keep her attention on the chapter but found it extremely difficult. She stared at her watch as the minutes ticked by. *He should definitely be here.*

"Are you Laura Chapman?" A deep voice rang out.

Laura looked up into the twinkling eyes of a gentleman with peppered hair and a well-trimmed gray beard. "I am," she answered. "And you must be Richard."

"Dick DeHart," he responded, extending his hand for a firm handshake. "Madeline says you need some help in history."

"Help is an understatement," she confessed. *How much should I confide in him?* Then again, it might be better to let him know what he was up against. She spoke hesitantly. "If I don't pass this course, I might as well drop out of school."

"Well, we can't have that, can we?" He sat next to her then pulled his chair a bit closer. "You've come to the right place."

She couldn't help but notice his dimples, not hidden in the slightest by his beard. He was a nice-looking man, just as Madeline had said—probably fifty-two or fifty-three, somewhere in that neighborhood. Not that it mattered. It was just that Laura had looked for a tutor in her own age group, not from among the students at Wainesworth. Things were rough enough this way.

"I don't know what my sister told you about me," Richard explained, "but I used to teach here at the college until about three years ago. That's when my wife passed away."

"I'm so sorry," Laura said. "I'm a widow, myself. In fact, my husband has been gone three years, too."

"Really?" He looked more than a little interested.

Laura immediately grew nervous.

"I think I've seen you at the store a couple of times. I've been doing a lot of research."

"What sort of research?"

"History, naturally," he said excitedly. "I've taken to writing college textbooks since I left the teaching profession."

"That's fascinating." Madeline had simply described him as a history buff.

"In fact," Richard said, pointing to her American History text, "I had a hand in writing that book."

"You wrote this textbook?" she asked, turning to the cover for a quick glance. Sure enough, *Richard DeHart & Jonathan Frisk* jumped off of the cover at her. "For heaven's sake."

"I had a particularly tough time with that chapter you were reading when I walked up." He reached for the book. "May I?"

"Of course!"

"You're just starting the unit on slavery, right?"

"That's right." She looked at the open book with new admiration and respect. "Why did you have a tough time?"

"There's a shortage of documents concerning slave groups brought over from the Caribbean." He frowned. "I wanted to include a well-researched section on their story, but I couldn't track down everything I needed. What you're reading there is just a shell of what I had hoped to include."

"Looks pretty thorough to me," Laura observed.

"Still, we may have to do a second edition. There's just so much material to cover."

"If you don't mind my saying so, there's plenty of material in this book as it is. Getting through it in one semester is going to be rough. And Dougherty—well, he's not making my life any easier."

"Professor Andrew Dougherty?"

Laura nodded.

Richard let out a whistle and shook his head.

"You know him?"

"Know him? We used to be archenemies—seemed to be an ongoing battle over who could be the better teacher. Also, there was that *dean* issue."

"Dean issue?" She grew more curious by the moment.

"Well, yeah," he said, "but I hate to talk about it. I was named dean of the History Department here at Wainesworth about five years back. Apparently Dougherty felt I had one-upped him. I don't know that he ever quite forgave me."

"Sounds like he carries a lot of grudges," Laura said. "Actually, that's part of my problem. . . ."

"Got on his bad side right away, did you?" Richard laughed.

She nodded, embarrassed. "Yeah, but it really wasn't my fault."

"It rarely is. Dougherty's got a real chip on his shoulder. But you're barely two months into the school year. There's plenty of time left in the semester to make things even worse."

"Very funny. But I'm serious. He hates me."

"Hate is a pretty strong word," Richard said, suddenly looking serious. "Besides, I think he's just covering for something."

"Covering for something?" He must know quite a few things about Andrew Dougherty that she didn't. Not that she cared.

"I think he must have had his heart broken somewhere along the way," Richard said with a sly grin. "At least that's what I've gathered."

Really. Interesting tidbit of information. For the life of her, Laura couldn't imagine any woman entering a relationship with a man like that.

"Well, let's forget about our dear Professor Dougherty, shall we?" Dick pulled his chair even closer. "Looks like we've got our work cut out for us."

"Yes, we do." She tried to sound confident, but the smell of his cologne distracted her. Greg had worn the same brand in their earlier years together. Somehow, just the aroma made her feel a little out of sorts.

"I think we should go over this unit before you head into class today." He pointed to the book.

"You're right." She turned her attention to the chapter on slavery. It looked, for once, like she had a logical, workable plan.

⌒

Andrew entered the cafeteria, hoping for a quick bite to eat before teaching his last class of the day. *What a madhouse.* The sights, sounds, and smells were dizzying, making him claustrophobic and completely uncomfortable. He needed order, control. What had made him think grabbing a baked potato and soda would be easy? Nothing proved to be easy here.

He forced his way through the mob, heading to the counter. "Oh, excuse me," he said, as he bumped into the back of a chair. He looked down instinctively. Only then did he realize Laura Chapman's eyes gazed directly into his. "Laura..."

She didn't respond immediately. Instead, her gaze shifted to the man sitting next to her.

Richard DeHart. What's he doing here? Andrew hesitantly extended his hand. "DeHart."

"Professor Dougherty." Dick shook it with a firm grip.

"What are you doing here?" It was a fair question. After all, the man didn't teach at the school anymore.

"Ms. Chapman has asked me to tutor her."

"In history?" Talk about throwing a kink into his plans to offer to help Laura.

This guy had no business...

"Naturally," Richard said. "What did you think?"

Andrew looked back and forth between Laura and Richard. Something about the combination almost made him feel sick. He sought out Laura's eyes. "How did you two meet? If you don't mind my asking."

She looked up at him with a confident smile. "Richard's sister is my boss, Madeline."

"That's right," Dick said. "She told me about Laura's plight, and I rushed right over."

Laura's plight? What is that supposed to mean? Andrew's heart quickened a beat, looking at the two of them together. Not that Dick DeHart was a bad guy. He was great. Maybe a little too great.

⌒

Laura observed the look of confusion on Professor Dougherty's face. "Richard tells me he wrote our text." She closed the book and held it up under Andrew's watchful eye.

"Yeah. Knew that."

Great show of support for his colleague. "We were just discussing this week's chapter. I'm finding it very enlightening." *That might be stretching it just a bit.*

"Are you?" He didn't sound very convinced.

"We were just about to enter a lively discussion on indentured servants," Richard added. "Would you like to join us, Dougherty?"

"No, thank you." He looked at Laura but spoke more to Richard. "I, uh—I've got a ton of other things to take care of. And then I have to teach a class. I still do that, you know."

They stared at each other until Laura grew uncomfortable. She turned her glance to the textbook in question, trying to change the direction of the conversation. "This is so well written," she commented, pointing to a particular passage. "How did you ever think to phrase it that way?"

Richard's eyes beamed. He spoke in earnest. "I just felt passionate about the subject matter and wanted to express it in the most ardent way I could so that the reader would be drawn into the discussion. That's all."

"Good grief." Andrew turned on his heels to leave.

"Sure you won't join us, Dougherty?" Richard called out, a smile crossing his lips.

"No, thank you." He turned to walk in the direction of the counter, leaving her to face Richard DeHart alone.

⌒

"That's the one," Regina said, looking Andrew in the eye.

"I beg your pardon?" He followed her finger until his gaze fell on Laura Chapman.

"That's the one I've got picked out for you."

"Oh no, not that one. Anyone else but her!"

"Why not?" Regina asked, insulted. "Not good enough for you?"

"It's not that. She's just—well, she and I don't exactly get along."

"I'm sure it's your fault. She seems like a nice enough lady."

"Thanks a lot."

She smiled. "Even though your heart is in the right place, your people skills are a little lacking."

"Meaning I'm not really the tyrant everyone thinks I am?"

"Of course not. But you've changed the subject. I want to talk about finding you a wife. Thank goodness you have me; otherwise I don't know what you'd do."

"I don't need a wife," he said defiantly.

"You don't need all that butter and sour cream, either," Regina said, pointing to his baked potato, "but I notice you're still eating it."

Laura looked up from her conversation with Dick DeHart, her gaze resting on Andrew Dougherty. He remained deep in conversation with a woman across the counter. She had dark hair and complexion and looked to be in her early forties. *A real beauty.* Not that it made a difference.

Laura noticed they had been talking for quite awhile. An odd mixture of emotions shot through her. More than anything, she found herself extremely intrigued by the woman. How could any female on the planet look that comfortable with Andrew Dougherty?

Chapter 10

Andrew passed out the exams, pausing as he placed one on Laura Chapman's desk. Nearly three weeks had passed since that awful day when she threatened to quit his class. Each day he breathed another sigh of relief when she walked in the door. However, he had mixed emotions when it came to her sudden and obvious association with Richard DeHart. *I can't stand that guy. What a lady's man.* Laura Chapman certainly didn't need that in her life. *Wait a minute. I've got no right analyzing what Laura Chapman does and doesn't need. It's none of my business.*

Still. . .

He glanced down at her wavy hair, his hand accidentally brushing against it as he handed a paper to the girl on her left.

"Sorry," he said quietly. Truthfully, he wasn't sorry. One touch had been enough to send sparks through him. Just the thought of it scared him to death.

Laura reached up instinctively, her fingers pushing through the spot where the professor's hand brushed against her hair. It had been an accident, surely, but his lingering gaze left her more than a little curious. Irritated, she turned away from him. She was about to prove a point—a very strong point.

"You may begin." Professor Dougherty gave the go-ahead.

Lord, help me. She turned the paper over and began to read through the questions—first, with fear; then with overwhelming relief. She knew this stuff. A couple of questions might present a challenge, but they were essay questions. Surely she could come up with something for those. As for the multiple-choice questions, they would be a piece of cake.

Laura looked up at Andrew's desk, where he sat silently grading papers. He seemed lost in his work. She turned back to the questions, breathing a huge sigh of relief. At one point, she glanced across the room to where Jessica sat, stone-faced, staring at her exam paper. Try as she might, Laura had not been able to get her daughter to study with her.

She focused on the test, answering questions rapidly and accurately. A short time later, she walked to Professor Dougherty's desk and dropped the exam into the appropriate basket with a smile. She had a lot to smile about. For once, she'd actually accomplished her goal. She'd proven, at least to herself, that she could excel. Soon enough, he would know it, too.

The professor looked confused. For a moment Laura felt a twinge of guilt, though she couldn't quite figure out why. She had nothing to feel guilty about. *I've done all of the right things, so why do I feel so bad?*

Dick DeHart had turned out to be a regular Romeo. Picking up on the fact that he seemed interested in far more than her mind, she carefully chose when and where they would meet to study. *I could never be interested in a man like him.*

Her gaze fell on Andrew Dougherty once again. His rumpled hair stuck up on his head. He wore a mismatched shirt and tie, and his pants had gone out of style years ago.

Still. . .he did have a certain charm about him. He looked up at her with a smile and she almost returned it. Almost.

⌣

Andrew waited until the classroom cleared before shuffling through the stack of exams to find the one he was looking for. "Miller, Johnson, Tanner, Breckenridge. . . Chapman." Ah yes. Laura Chapman's exam. He scanned it quickly and made it to the bottom of the first page. No errors so far. He turned to page two. Flawless. A little glitch in an essay question on page three—worth about two or three points at most, but page four appeared to be perfect. She'd aced the exam. Aced it.

Amazed, he checked it once again. Only one conclusion could be drawn: Her study sessions with DeHart had been effective. Very effective. That confirmed something he'd worried about for days. She and Dick DeHart must have spent a lot of time together.

A twinge of jealousy shot through him, stirring up an odd mixture of emotions. *I'm so proud of her. She's turned out to be a much harder worker than I gave her credit for.* But on the other hand, how could she give so much of her time and attention to someone as unscrupulous as DeHart? He struggled with the thought. *Maybe she hasn't figured him out yet. Maybe someone needs to warn her.* Andrew tossed ideas about, clearly confused over the whole thing. If her academic performance improved with Dick's help, how could he possibly go about approaching her now?

⌣

Laura heard the ringing of the phone as she turned the key in the front door. "Come on, come on. . ." She struggled to get the door open. By the fourth ring, she made it into the living room. "Hello?" She dropped the armload of books, still panting.

"Ms. Chapman?"

A man's voice—probably one of those annoying telemarketers. They called a lot. She glanced at the Caller ID. "Unavailable."

Oh, why did I even pick it up? "Yes?"

"I was hoping to catch you." Why did the man's voice sound so familiar? "I've been meaning to talk to you about your work in my class."

Bingo. Andrew Dougherty. What in the world did he want with her? Her hands began to tremble. She forced her voice to remain calm as she clutched the receiver. "What about my work?"

"I'm really pleased with it. In fact, I just graded your exam."

"So soon?" Something must have happened to prompt this.

"Uh, yes. You got a ninety-seven."

Ninety-seven? That's awesome! And yet, she wouldn't let her jubilation show. She couldn't. "Well, thank you for letting me know." She tried to keep her voice on an even keel. "Though I'm not sure why you took the time to call. You could have just told me in class."

"I'm pleased with your grade," he continued, "but. . ."

"But what?"

"Well, to be honest, I was hoping to talk with you about Dick DeHart."

"Oh?"

"I just think you need to know that DeHart has a. . .well, a past." He seemed to be choosing his words very carefully.

"A past? What does that have to do with anything?" Laura grew angrier by the moment. "This is really none of your business."

"I just thought you might like to know."

"I'm not interested in gossip, Professor. In fact, I'm stunned that you are. To be perfectly frank, if I had anything to say about Mr. DeHart to you, it would all be good." Granted, Dick DeHart acted a little too close over the last couple of weeks, but she certainly wasn't ready to admit that to Andrew Dougherty. "He's gracious and kind," she continued, "and seems to see something of value in me. It's clear he has my best wishes at heart."

"Among other things."

"I beg your pardon?"

"His reputation precedes him, Laura."

"Ms. Chapman."

"Ms. Chapman," he said slowly, deliberately, "I've got your best interest at heart. Really, I do."

"Well, thank you just the same, but—"

"If I were you—"

"Well, you're not," she said emphatically. She had just about reached wit's end with this guy dabbling in her personal life. She wouldn't allow it. "Besides, this is really none of your business, Professor."

"Fine."

"Fine," she echoed. "Was that all you were calling about?"

"That's all."

"Well, if it's all the same to you, I really need to hang up. I've still got to work today. Good-bye, Mr. Dougherty."

"Ms. Chapman."

With a click, he disappeared. Laura still clutched the phone in her sweaty hand. She slammed it back down, shifting her gaze to the books she'd carelessly tossed on the coffee table. The American History book sat at the top of the stack, a grim reminder that this battle had just begun.

Irritated, she shoved the book to the bottom of the stack.

Andrew stared at the receiver, dumbfounded. *There's no winning with this woman.*

Yet he couldn't get those amazing eyes and wavy brown hair out of his mind.

Chapter 11

"Y"ou want to what?" Laura turned to face Dick DeHart, who had come into the store for a visit.

"I want to take you out to a movie this Saturday night." He slipped his arm across her shoulder.

"But I . . ." Uncomfortable, she pulled away from his embrace. Laura couldn't seem to get the professor's words out of her mind—something about Richard DeHart's past. She had no idea what he meant, but she wasn't taking any chances.

"There's a great new movie out on the Civil War," Dick said, giving her what looked to be a rehearsed pout. "We could look at it as an educational date."

"I'm not sure I'm up to any kind of a 'date,'" Laura said. "I'm just not ready for that yet."

"Well, we don't have to call it a date, then," he argued. "We could go to dinner afterwards and have a, uh—a study session."

Laura had seen just about enough of his study sessions already. She spoke very candidly. "I don't think so, but thanks for the offer."

"Aw, come on, Laurie," he wooed.

"It's Laura."

"You know you want to spend time with me. I'm irresistible."

"Is that what you think?" she asked incredulously. "You think I'm that easily swayed?" *He's got to be kidding.*

"You're a woman." He shrugged. "That about says it all, doesn't it?"

Laura's blood began to boil. She couldn't stand men with an attitude like this. She hadn't tolerated it in the professor, and she wouldn't in this man either.

"I may be a woman"—Laura tried to keep her voice steady—"but that doesn't mean I don't know how to use sound judgment and reason. I'm perfectly capable of doing that."

His expression never changed. "Aw, come on," he coaxed. "I didn't mean anything by that comment. Let's go out Saturday night and have a good time. We'll paint the town red. I promise to have you back home before you lose your glass slipper."

"I don't think so." Laura turned back to her work. "In fact, I don't think I'll be needing any more tutoring sessions either. I'm doing pretty well on my own."

"Sure you are. Just like you were before I came along."

Laura stared at him in disbelief. *This guy is too much.*

"You'll change your mind." He turned to leave. "And when you do—call me."

She wouldn't call him. She would never call him.

⌣

Andrew signed onto the Internet and scrolled through his e-mail—junk mail, a letter from a colleague, and a quick note from his friend, Joe, asking if he'd be interested in going to a high school football game Saturday night to watch his son play.

A high school football game? Andrew barely tolerated sports, and the idea of sitting out in the cold to watch a bunch of kids toss a ball around sounded anything but inviting. Still, Joe was his friend, and he owed him for the blind date thing. Might as well balance the scales by going. "Why not?" Andrew said aloud. He had little else to do, anyway.

⌣

"Mom, the homecoming game is Saturday night." Kent sounded nervous.

"Do you have a date?" She gazed into her son's eyes as she posed the question. He looked too young to even consider dating, and yet the inevitable seemed to be upon her.

"Yeah, I'm going with Mandy. The dance is after the game. That's what I wanted to talk to you about."

"She needs a mum, right?" It wouldn't be the first red-and-white mum she'd made over the years.

"Yeah." He looked like a nervous wreck. "I need it by Friday morning."

Laura smiled, realizing this would be Kent's first school dance. Her heart began to ache, realizing that Greg wouldn't be here, snapping pictures as he had so often in the past as Jessica headed out the door.

"You'll have it by Friday morning," she promised.

"Great. But that's not all."

"What else?"

"The band is playing at the game. Are you coming?"

A football game? *Lord, you know I can't stand football. Surely You wouldn't ask me to do that.* "I don't know, Kent. . ."

"Aw, come on, Mom," he argued. "You go to all of Jessica's piano recitals."

He had a point there.

"I guess so, but I might leave after halftime. I have a lot of homework this weekend."

"That's cool." Kent smiled. "Just as long as you watch me play the trumpet, you can go whenever you want."

He bounded from the room with his usual zest, and she was left alone with her books and her thoughts. Not that she minded. It had been a long day, and the silence felt just right.

Andrew slipped into bed for the night, television still running. A sappy love story played itself out on the screen. Whether he meant for it to happen or not, he found his attention glued to the set.

"Aw, don't do it, man," he said to the character on the screen. "Don't give your heart away to her. She's not worth it."

He stared in disbelief as the man in the movie told the young woman that he loved her. She responded by slapping him in the face.

"I tried to tell you." Andrew shook his head. "But you wouldn't listen."

What's wrong with women these days? That's all Andrew really wanted to know. What did they want? And how in the world could any man ever succeed in being everything they expected him to be? He quickly snapped off the TV, determined to put females out of his mind. Unfortunately, when he closed his eyes, all he could see was Laura Chapman's face. She had an amazing smile—when she bothered to smile—and the cutest dimples he'd seen in ages. How could he possibly go about winning a woman like her? He didn't stand a chance in the world.

Andrew wrestled with the sheets, trying to get comfortable. Would there ever be someone—anyone—to call his own? Perhaps some people just weren't meant to have love in their lives. Maybe that was part of some sort of master plan. Who knew?

His mind reeled back to Karen instinctively. She had been so ideal, so perfect. And yet she hurt him. Terribly.

"We all make mistakes," he whispered to himself as he remembered some of the words he'd spoken to Laura in those first few days of school. He had been deliberately cruel. Even Karen, in breaking his heart, hadn't acted maliciously. She'd simply followed her heart.

Suddenly, lying in the stillness of his room, Andrew Dougherty managed to forgive the woman who had broken his heart fifteen years ago. For the first time, he felt completely free to love again.

Chapter 12

Laura put the finishing touches on the red-and-white mum, then handed it to Kent.

"Looks great, Mom." He held it gingerly, as if afraid it might break.

"It ought to," she responded. "I had to mortgage the house to buy all that stuff." *A slight exaggeration—but only slight.* "What time is the game tomorrow night? I'm hoping Jess and Nathan will want to come with me."

"Seven-thirty." He bit into a muffin then spoke with full mouth. "You gonna leave after halftime?"

"It depends on how the team is playing," she said with a chuckle. "Nah. If I leave, it will only be because I've got a lot of—"

"I know," he interrupted. "You've got a lot of homework. Trust me, I understand."

"Just promise me this." Laura looked at her son with as firm an expression as she could manage. "Promise me you'll do your best not to get into any trouble."

"It's cool, Mom. I'm fine."

"I sure hope so." She gave him a peck on the cheek. "Get on out of here. Go to school." He headed out the door, whistling as he went.

Thank You, Lord. He's doing so much better! As he left with the mum in hand, she couldn't help but think of the one she'd worn her senior year in high school, so many years ago. It had been blue and white, a gift from Greg. His mother had worked diligently on it. To this day, it hung in her closet, though the cloth flower had faded over the years.

"Mom?" Jessica's voice sounded surprisingly sweet.

She turned to face her. "Good morning, Jess."

"Mom, I was wondering if you'd like to go to breakfast with me."

"Breakfast?"

"Yeah," Jess said with a smile. "I need to talk to you and thought I might do it over breakfast. Sound good?"

Laura smiled, in spite of herself. Jessica wanted to spend time with her. A first—in quite awhile, anyway. How could she turn that down?

"I'd be delighted. Where do you want to go?"

"Your choice, but this is my treat. I've still got a little birthday money left from Grandma."

"Okay then," Laura said, standing. "Pancake House on the freeway. Their waffles are incredible. Blueberry pancakes—"

"With blueberry syrup," Jess added with a smile. "I know. I remember."

"Why the celebration?"

"You'll see, you'll see. Go get dressed and let me get you out of here for a little while." Jessica looked anxious. Something must be up. Suddenly Laura knew the answer. It had something to do with the piano scholarship. Jessica had gotten the news she'd been waiting on and wanted to share it with her.

"Are you sure?" Laura could hardly contain her excitement.

"Yep. I'm sure."

Laura bounded off to her bedroom, erupting five minutes later in a sweater and slacks.

"Better?"

"Much better," her daughter said, smiling.

Fifteen minutes later, they sat in a corner booth of the Pancake House, sipping cups of hot coffee. *What a wonderful treat!* Laura hadn't felt this spoiled in ages.

"Mom, I need to tell you something." Jessica looked serious for a change.

Laura's heart began to pound instantly. *Why do I always assume the worst?*

"Don't look so scared."

"What is it?" *Whatever it is, I can take it.*

"Well, you know that I planned to audition for the piano scholarship, right?"

"Planned to?"

"Well, I . . ."

"What, honey?" Laura asked. "You can say it."

"I couldn't do it, Mom. I was too scared to go in and play."

"You what?" Laura felt stunned. "But you've waited for that audition for weeks. You didn't even go in?"

Her daughter's beautiful face fell immediately. Laura knew she should try to be more understanding, but once the words started, she just couldn't seem to help herself.

⌣

"She can't stand me," Andrew said as he sat across from Regina in the nearly empty lunchroom. With no classes scheduled today, only faculty and staff drifted in and out. Regina took advantage of the break, plopping down onto the chair across from him at the lunch table.

"Oh, pooh!" Regina said. "She just doesn't know you yet."

"No, she knows me. And she really can't stand me." Andrew sighed deeply. "I tried to call her."

"You called her?" Regina asked excitedly. "To ask her out?"

"No, of course not. I just wanted to talk to her about her grades."

"Oh." Regina's face fell. "Well, that was a romantic touch."

"You don't understand." He felt his shoulders sag in defeat. "It's not that easy for me. I don't know how to talk to a woman."

"You're talking to me."

"That's different." Surely she could see that.

She gave him a look. "What's that supposed to mean?"

"I mean, you're like a sister to me—not like a woman."

"Well, thanks a lot."

"I can't say anything right."

"I sure hope you do a better job than that when you're talking to her, or the game will be over before it even starts."

"It's already over," he said, standing. "And we're not even in the second quarter yet."

Laura struggled through the afternoon at work, her thoughts in a jumbled mess. *Jessica didn't get the scholarship.* The words went round and round in her head, disappointment filling her.

"I, uh. . ." Laura shook her head, not wanting to talk. The knot in her throat wouldn't allow it anyway.

"That's all right," Madeline said. "I'm just worried about you, that's all. This doesn't have anything to do with my brother, does it?"

Laura laughed, in spite of herself. "No," she said, grateful for the relief the laughter brought. "Nothing to do with your brother."

"That's good," her boss said. "Because I thought for a minute there, I was going to have to hurt him. You just let me know."

Let her know? Should she let her know her brother had one thing, and only one thing, on his mind—and it wasn't American history?

"Would you mind taking over the register?" Madeline asked. "I need to check a new shipment that just came in."

"No problem." Laura headed to the cash register, her mind still reeling.

Jessica didn't get the scholarship. The words still tossed themselves around in her head. She shouldn't be this disappointed, but money didn't grow on trees, and with two of them in college, things might get tight by the spring.

"Uh, umm. . ." A man in front of her cleared his throat, trying to get her attention. "Are you going to wait on me or not?"

"Oh, I'm sorry. My mind is on other things."

"That's obvious."

"Will this be all?" She glanced down at the book he'd placed on the counter: *One Hundred Ways to Become a Better Person.* Intriguing title. She would have to remember to look at it later.

"Yeah, that's all." He pushed the book toward her. "My wife says I have to read this."

"Really." She didn't mean it in an accusing way, but he glared at her, just the same. "Well, I hope you enjoy it. That will be $22.95 plus tax—a total of $24.78."

"That's a lot of money just to become a better person," he grumbled, reaching for a credit card.

"I'm sure you're worth it, sir."

He smiled warmly—for the first time. "Yeah, I guess I am. Who knows? Maybe this book will help."

"If it does," she said, "come back in and let me know so I can buy a copy for myself."

The gentleman headed toward the door, his expression totally changed from when they had begun.

"Looks like you had a nice effect on him," Madeline said, returning with a tracking slip in hand. "He's one of my worst customers. Comes in here every few months to buy another self-help book his wife has recommended."

"I've never seen him before. But he wasn't so bad, really. Sometimes people just..." She glanced at the floor. "Have a rough day." She smiled lamely at her boss, hoping for a positive response.

"Laura," Madeline said, looking at her intently, "it seems like nearly every day has been a rough one for you lately, but you're going to get through all of this. I know you are. You're a lot stronger than you think."

"Then why don't I feel it?"

"It doesn't matter what you feel. You just have to begin to act on it." Laura smiled warmly at her boss, thankful for the encouragement. *I sure hope you're right.*

Chapter 13

Kent bit into an apple, then spoke with his mouth full. "You didn't forget about the game tonight, did you, Mom?"

"No." She glanced through the refrigerator for something that might resemble lunch. There wasn't much to choose from—a stale package of bologna and a half-eaten can of sliced peaches. Neither sounded appetizing.

"You're gonna freeze to death if you stand there all day." He reached around her to grab a half-gallon of milk.

"Yeah, I know." She closed the door, opting to skip the food idea. *It's not like things aren't already cold enough in this house already.* Ever since her breakfast with Jessica yesterday morning, little more than a word or two had been spoken between them. *I need to apologize.* But every outward sign convinced her Jessica wasn't ready to hear it yet.

Kent poured a tall glass of milk then left the carton standing open on the counter. "Is Jess coming with you?"

"I don't think so."

"Bummer." It was only one word, but it genuinely reflected her feelings.

Andrew pulled his jacket out of the closet and slipped it on. For late October, today proved to be particularly chilly. *I don't know why I'm going, anyway. I've got no interest in football. What an illogical game.* Then again, Joe had been a good sport about the whole "Judy" thing, and his eldest, Jonathan, was like a son to Andrew. For that reason alone, Andrew would go. He would endure the crowd and the noise. He would put up with their lousy band and their childish bantering back and forth.

Andrew made the drive to the stadium with the radio playing softly in the background. A love song streamed from the radio. For some reason, a picture of Laura Chapman came to mind immediately—the way her hair framed her face, the richness of her smile every time she received a good grade. She seemed to be receiving a lot of those lately. Just thinking about her made him smile.

Laura made her way through the crowd, shivering. Already, she regretted her decision to wear a lightweight sweater instead of her heavy coat. She gazed out onto the field where cheerleaders warmed up. They leaped about like gazelles and shouted their chants, clearly ready for the game to begin.

It feels so awkward, coming here by myself. Almost as bad as sitting in a pew alone. She hadn't managed to do that for quite some time either. Her mind began to wander back to another game, just two years ago, when Jessica had been nominated for homecoming queen. *Greg would have been so proud.* Though their daughter hadn't won the coveted crown, she had certainly excelled above the other girls in Laura's eyes. *In every conceivable way, she was a queen that night.*

Just the thought of her daughter caused Laura's brow to wrinkle. The strain between them grew more with each day. The gap seemed wider than the football field below, and there didn't appear to be a way to narrow it.

"Andrew, over here!" Behind her, a man's voice rang out, almost deafening her. Laura looked up to find Professor Andrew Dougherty waving from a distance. Their eyes met. She immediate dropped her gaze to the ground. *Great.*

Andrew's heart skipped a beat the minute he saw Laura. She looked beautiful in her soft peach sweater. With her hair pulled back like that, she almost looked like a teenager. In fact, she looked remarkably like Jessica tonight. Should he tell her so? Would that be inappropriate? He made his way up the steps to her row, pausing momentarily to nod in her direction. She nodded back with less enthusiasm.

Joe acted a little more interested. "Glad you could make it," he said as he reached out to shake Andrew's hand. "I was starting to think you'd changed your mind."

Thank goodness I didn't. "Oh," he said finally, "I, uh. . .I got caught up in traffic." He sat quickly, gaze fixed on the back of Laura's head.

Truth was, he had pulled his car off the road to listen to the love song on the radio. It sparked something in him that he hadn't felt for some time. And now, the very one he'd been thinking about sat directly in front of him, completely alone. *This has to be more than coincidence. I'm not that lucky.*

Joe slapped him on the back. "You look like you're a million miles away tonight. Rough day?"

"No, not at all."

"Well, I hope you're ready for a great game. I hear they're playing a tough team tonight."

"Really? That's nice."

Joe laughed, slapping him on the back once again. "You're a laugh a minute. No wonder Judy never asks about you anymore." He erupted into laughter, and Andrew did everything in his power to change the subject, hopeful Laura hadn't heard.

"Who did you say they were playing again?" he asked as he looked toward the field.

"Westfield High. They're a tough team."

"Oh yeah. I've heard that." Not that he cared. Football was a sport he deliberately avoided.

"We'll whip 'em." The proud papa beamed.

"Speaking of 'we,' where's Jolene?" Andrew asked, looking around. He still chuckled, thinking of their names. Joe and Jolene. The all-American couple.

"Oh, she's at the junior high tonight," Joe answered with a shrug. "Brenna's in a play of some sort. You know how it is when you've got a houseful of kids. You have to divide your time."

No, I don't know. Andrew often wondered if he ever would. He turned his attention back to Laura's hair. A soft breeze played with her tiny ponytail, causing the peach ribbon to dance around in the wind. He stared at it, fixated.

The field below came alive as the game got under way, yet Andrew just couldn't seem to concentrate on it. Laura's perfume pulled at him in a way that boggled his mind. *What is that smell—some sort of flower or something else?* He couldn't quite put his finger on it, but talk about alluring. *And that hair of hers— that amazing, wavy brown hair—it's making me a crazy man.* He wanted to run his fingers through it, to nuzzle close and smell it. *What's come over me? Is Laura Chapman some sort of unattainable dream? Do I really need a woman in my life?*

"Snap out of it!" he whispered to himself, shaking his head. *What am I doing, thinking about her that way? She's certainly not making any moves to communicate with me.*

Perhaps she had plans to meet someone. A fear gripped him as he considered the idea. Maybe Dick DeHart would take the place on the bench in front of him. Maybe he was already here. Maybe. . .

"Andrew, are you listening to me?" Joe's voice shocked him back to reality.

"I, uh. . ."

"Are you okay, man?" His friend looked concerned. "You're not acting like yourself."

"Yeah, yeah. . ."

"You're sure acting strange," Joe said. "I know what you need. You need food. I'm gonna go get a hot dog and a soft drink. You want the same?"

"Oh, sure," Andrew said as he fished for his wallet. "Whatever you say."

"What I say is, you're in need of some serious help, my friend." Joe flashed him a grin as he left. Andrew sat in silence, trying to decide what to do next. *Should I talk to her?*

Laura watched in silence as the professor's friend left the stands, realizing he sat alone behind her.

Please don't let him talk to me. The words flashed through her mind like an alarm going off. She couldn't bear another confrontation tonight. She'd been through enough over the last few days.

68

His voice interrupted her thoughts. "Laura, how are you?" *The moment of truth.*

"Fine." She glanced at him briefly. She deliberately looked back down at the field, hoping he would take the hint. He didn't.

"I didn't realize you still had children in high school," he commented. Then he moved to sit next to her. *That took some nerve. What does he think he's doing?* Laura knew she should say something to him—make him go back to where he came from. She turned, prepared to do battle—but no words came out. Something about the way he wore his hair tonight seemed a little different, but she couldn't quite put her finger on it.

"Uh, yes," she said finally. "Well, just one. My son Kent is in the band." She pointed to the section below where red and white reigned alongside silver and gold instruments. Suddenly the cold air gripped her. She began to shake, and goose bumps made their way up each arm.

"You're cold!" Andrew pulled off his jacket. "Please, put this on."

"Oh no, I couldn't," she argued. He draped the coat over her shoulders and she instinctively pulled it tight, grateful for its warmth.

"Kent, did you say?" the professor asked with interest. "Which one is he?"

"He plays the trumpet. He's the one with the brown hair on the end of the fourth row."

"Ah. He looks like you," the professor said with a nod. "Same hair."

She shrugged, still shivering. "I guess so."

"No, it is," he said firmly. "Your hair is brunette, just like his."

Brunette? It was brown—plain dull, boring brown. She'd never thought of it as anything else. Somehow "brunette" made it sound more intriguing.

"His hair looks a lot more like yours than Jessica's does," Andrew observed. "Her auburn hair isn't anything like yours."

Had he actually spent time thinking about this? The notion blew her away. "She takes after her father. Greg was a redhead." She inwardly scolded herself for talking about her husband to a man she barely knew.

"Ah, that would explain the temper, too," he said with a laugh.

"You think Jessica has a temper?" Her own quickly rose to the surface.

"And you don't?"

He has a point. Jess had even used that temper in his class a time or two to gain attention from him.

"I'll bet you're really proud of her."

"Sure. I'm proud of both of them." He had struck a nerve—flattering her kids. Was he serious or just trying to smooth things over with her?

"No, I mean the news. . ."

"What news?"

"I just found out yesterday afternoon myself," he continued. "Of course, it's all over campus."

"What are you talking about?"

"The scholarship," he said, looking at her incredulously. "The music scholarship."

Laura's heart began to race. Something must be wrong here—very wrong. Just yesterday morning, Jessica sat across from her at breakfast, telling her that she *didn't* get the scholarship.

"That's not right," she said, shaking her head. "Jess didn't get the music scholarship. She didn't even audition. I know all about it."

He looked at her in disbelief. "Sure, she did. Her vocal coach, Barbara Nelson, is a friend of mine. We talk about Jess all the time. She's doing really well in her voice lessons."

"Voice lessons?" Laura struggled to maintain her composure. There must be some mistake here.

"Sure. They say she's a natural. Haskins was anxious to hear her the other day. From what I heard, she really knocked his socks off. He said there was something about hearing that hymn sung with such depth that almost brought tears to his eyes."

Haskins? Hymn? Laura's head began to spin. She started to tremble uncontrollably but not from the cold. Her emotions were in a whirlwind. This made no sense at all. *Jessica is a pianist. She went to audition for a piano scholarship. When did she start taking voice lessons?* To be honest, Laura had been so busy, she wasn't sure what classes her daughter had signed up for.

"Haskins?" she stammered.

"Sure. The choral director. He was very impressed—said she sounded like she'd been singing for years."

"Singing for years. . ." Laura's voice trailed off. *This is awful.*

"That Haskins really knows his stuff, so she must be good. He told Barbara that he might be willing to commend Jess for the Houston Grand Opera's Youth program if she continues to work hard. He feels she'd be an asset to their program."

"An asset to their program. . . ," Laura stammered.

"I'll bet you're really proud," Andrew said with a smile.

"Really proud. . . ," she echoed softly. Laura nodded numbly, not knowing what to say next. *Jess won a scholarship. That's what she was trying to tell me yesterday morning.* Laura had been so impatient, she hadn't even waited to hear the news. Shame suddenly flooded her heart. *I'm a terrible mother. The absolute worst.*

Andrew watched as Laura's eyes filled with tears. *What did I say?* Something had gone terribly wrong, but what? "Laura, is there a problem?"

She nodded, biting her lip. "I, uh. . .I have to go." She stood abruptly, trying to step across him, the jacket dropping down onto the bench below.

"But your son. . . He hasn't even played yet."

"I know, but I have to go."

She looks almost frantic. What did I say?

She made her way down the steps, disappearing into the crowd below. Andrew wasn't sure what he'd done, but somehow he had done it again.

⌒

Laura pulled the car up the driveway, relieved to see Nathan's car parked there. *Father, for once let me get this right. Help me to lay down my crazy, foolish pride and show my daughter the kind of love she needs and deserves. Help me to use the right words.* She bounded up the walk to the front door, knocking instead of reaching for her keys. Jessica answered. Nathan stood just behind her.

"We just got here, Mom, I promise," Jess said defensively. Apparently she had prepared herself for an argument.

"I trust you, Jessica, but I really need to talk to you. Do you mind, Nathan?"

"Of course not," he said, reaching for his jacket. "Should I go?"

"No, please stay," she said. "I want you to hear this, too." She stood silently for a moment, trying to decide what to say and how to say it.

"What is it, Mom? Are you gonna stand there all night?" Jess's voice had a sarcastic edge.

"Jess, I'm so sorry." Laura's mind shot back to one of Greg's favorite Sunday school expressions—the twelve words to heal any relationship: *"I am sorry. I was wrong. Please forgive me. I love you."* She would say them all before this conversation ended, no matter how difficult.

Jess looked at her dubiously. "Sorry about what?"

"About getting angry. About the scholarship. It was really wrong of me. Why didn't you tell me?"

"Tell you?"

"About the vocal scholarship."

Jessica's expression changed immediately. "You know?"

"Yes," Laura explained. "I just found out."

"Who told you?"

"Professor Dougherty."

"What? When did you see him?" Jessica looked stunned.

"He was at the game tonight."

"You're kidding. What's he doing—following you?"

"Of course not. It was just a coincidence, but I'm glad he was there. He told me what a great job you did and how proud your vocal instructor is. He told me that you got the scholarship."

"That's what I've been trying to tell you for days, Mom."

"I know that now." Laura reached out to embrace her. "Jessica, I'm so proud of you."

"Right." Her daughter pulled away.

"I am, honey. I really am."

"Well, anyway," Jess said, "it's five hundred dollars. That part should make you happy. I'm going to be less of a burden in the spring than I am now, I guess."

"Jess, please don't talk like that."

"Isn't that what you're thinking?"

"No, it's not what I'm thinking at all." Laura felt a knot in her throat. "What I'm thinking is how very proud I am of you—and how much I would love to have your forgiveness."

Jess shrugged.

"And something else, too," Laura continued. "I love you. I hope you know that."

Her daughter moved toward the door, shaking her head. "Sorry, Mom. Nathan and I were just about to leave. We're going to a nine o'clock movie. Maybe later."

Nathan glanced in Laura's direction, then looked at Jessica. "We don't have to go. This is important. You guys need to talk this out."

"We don't need to talk." Jessica glared at him. Laura couldn't help but see her own reflection in her daughter's countenance.

Nathan shrugged. "Whatever," he said. "But I really don't feel like seeing a movie anymore. I think I'd better go home."

"But—" Jessica never had time to finish her sentence.

Nathan gave her a quick kiss on the cheek and headed to the door. "See you tomorrow," he called out. The door shut behind him.

Jessica's eyes sparkled with anger. "Do you see what you've done? Do you see?"

"What I've done? I just wanted to ask you to forgive me and to tell you that I love you. I've been so wrong about so many things. I'm so sorry."

"Don't you get it, Mom?" Jessica said angrily. "You ruin everything for me. Everything!" With that, Jessica stormed into her room and slammed the bedroom door behind her.

Unwilling to let it go at that, Laura followed closely behind her, speaking through the door that separated them. "You can shut me out of your room, but you can't shut me out of your life."

Silence.

"I'm going to make mistakes, Jess. Lots of them."

"No kidding." Her daughter's voice sounded muffled.

"I'm human. But I don't ruin everything for you, and I won't stand by and let you say such a thing. You have no idea what it's like to be in my position. Someday, when you have kids. . ."

"That's what all mothers say." Jess opened the door abruptly. "I can't wait until then to understand what makes parents tick. I know that you're so stressed out about everything that you don't even have the time to spend with Kent and me like you used to. You're no fun anymore, Mom."

Laura looked down at the floor, unable to respond past the growing lump in her throat. "All I can say is I'm sorry, honey. I'm doing my best." A lone tear rolled down her cheek. She brushed it away, embarrassed.

Jessica's face softened slightly. "Mom, I didn't mean to make you cry. I do love you, but I miss things being the way they were. I want life to go back to normal."

"Me, too, honey." Laura reached to give her a hug. "Me, too." They held each other for a few moments before Jess backed away and disappeared into her room.

Laura headed off to the privacy of her own bedroom, her thoughts rolling. She pulled on her flannel pajamas, then reached over to slam the closet door. Greg's suits still hung in the closet, just where he had left them. The time had come to give them away, to put them and the pain of losing her husband behind her. But she couldn't seem to do it. They had remained in the closet this long. They could stay a little longer.

Just looking at Greg's suits reminded Laura of Andrew, of the jacket he so carefully placed across her shoulders earlier this evening. Was it an attempt to reach out to her? To be nice? If so, did she feel ready for that?

Laura tossed herself across the big queen-sized bed for a good, long cry. Her heart hurt so desperately, she hardly knew how to begin mending it. Perhaps it couldn't be mended. The hole left by Greg's death had grown to immense proportions. No one, nothing, could ever fill it. Not now. Not ever.

"Surely I am with you always. . . ." The words from the scripture came to her mind. What brought them there, she could not tell. *"Surely I am with you always. . . ."*

"Who?" she cried out to the stillness of the room. "Who is with me always?" Greg certainly wasn't here. She couldn't wrap herself up in his arms and ask him to make everything all better. She had no one to fill the emptiness she felt. There would never be another human being loving enough to fill that hole, no matter whom she turned to.

What she needed to fill the gaping hole in her life, no human could fill, no mortal man could conjure up. She needed God's assurance. She needed His peace, His strength. She needed Him to move in and take over the loneliness and become the lover of her soul, to be more than just Someone she called out to in her moments of extreme need.

Problem was, she couldn't seem to let go of the pain long enough to allow Him to do that. Maybe she never could.

———

Andrew drove home in silence, contemplating what had happened at the game. He wanted to call Laura right away, as soon as he arrived home, but he didn't have the courage. What would he say, anyway? Clearly, she hadn't wanted to share her thoughts with him. Maybe she never would.

Chapter 14

I did it again," Andrew said with a sigh.

"Did what?" Regina's eyes were more curious than accusing.

"I blew it." He looked at her for some show of support, hopeful her response wouldn't be negative. He needed a pat on the back, needed someone to tell him he wasn't a total and complete failure.

"Tell me what happened," she said soulfully, as she took a seat. "I don't have to be back behind the counter for fifteen minutes. Will that give you enough time?"

He nodded lamely. "I think so."

"What happened—and be specific."

"I was at the ball game the other night with Laura—"

"You were?" Regina let out a squeal, which caused a lunchroom full of students to turn and look at them. "You asked her out? Well, it's about time. I knew you would. I just knew it."

"No. No, I didn't," he said, trying to quiet her. "I didn't ask her out."

"But you said—"

"I said I was at the ball game with her," he tried to explain. "I didn't say I asked her out."

Regina looked confused, but he plowed ahead. "Anyway, we were sitting there and I don't know what I said, but she just jumped up and ran off."

Regina let out a whistle.

"What?" he asked, avoiding her eyes.

"Must have been pretty awful. What'd you say?"

"That's just it. I didn't say much of anything. I was congratulating her on the music scholarship her daughter just received, and before I knew it, she jumped and ran."

"Maybe her pumpkin was waiting." Regina smiled. "She didn't by any chance drop a shoe when she ran off, did she—'cause, you know. . ."

"I'm trying to be serious here," he interrupted, getting irritated. "You're supposed to be cheering me up. That's what you do. I come in here and whine, and you cheer me up. That's your job."

"And it's what I'm trying to do, but this time, I think I'm really on your side. Doesn't sound like you did anything wrong. Did that ever occur to you?"

He shrugged.

"Maybe she had something on her mind. Could have just been a bad day.

That happens to other people, too, you know. You don't need to take everything so personally."

"I know." He had already considered that possibility. But why had Laura run off at that very moment—just when he brought up Jessica?

"Professor," Regina said, looking at him seriously, "I'm going to give you some sage advice."

He looked into her eyes. If anyone could give advice worth taking, Regina could. She had a depth that seemed undeniable.

"I think it's time to back off and just let nature take its course."

"Let nature take its course? In that case, I might as well forget the whole thing."

"I said, 'back off,' not drop out of the race. There is something you could be doing in the meantime."

"What's that?"

"I'm just wondering. Are you a praying man?" She spoke the words quietly, but with an assurance that seemed to come from deep within.

"A what?" How in the world could he go about answering a question like that?

"A praying man. . ." She said it again, this time looking him right in the eye.

His gaze shifted immediately. It wasn't that he never prayed; it was just that he hadn't for a while—a long while—say five, ten years. "I suppose."

"Well then, why don't you stop all your whining and just get down on those knees of yours," Regina said, "and get busy praying? She'll come around if it's God's plan."

God's plan? "Are you saying I'm supposed to pray for a wife? Is that how desperate I've become?"

"No, of course not." She stood. "You've always been that desperate. You just never knew what to do about it."

"Regina, I never know how to take you. You're kidding, right?"

"No, I'm not. That's how I found my Daniel. I prayed for a godly husband, and before I knew it, Daniel Leal just waltzed into my life. And now that we've already got this woman picked out for you. . ."

"Picked out? Regina, you are too much."

— · —

"What are you talking about?" Laura asked the man at the front door. "I paid the electric bill last week."

"Better check again, lady," he said, placing a slip of paper in her hand. "According to the office, they never received a payment."

She shook her head in disbelief. "I thought I paid it." *Of course, with every-thing going on in my life, I could have forgotten.* "Could you wait just a moment while I check?"

"Won't make any difference. I can't take a payment at the door. I'm just here to shut you off."

"But. . ." *This is crazy. I know I paid that bill.*

"You could make a payment online, but they usually take a couple of days to post."

Is he kidding? This house is all electric. We'll freeze to death in here.

"If you want your power turned back on by tomorrow, you could go to one of our payment centers. There's one about five miles from here, on Robinson."

"You look like a very understanding man." She forced a nervous smile. "Would you really do this to us three weeks before Thanksgiving?"

He shrugged, a look of compassion crossing his face. "I just do what they tell me, Ms. Chapman. You understand."

Within minutes the house sat in cold, stony silence. The rattle of the dishwasher no longer hung in the air. The gentle flow of warm air no longer emanated from the vents. The refrigerator ceased to hum. Laura would have missed them all, if she had let herself. But the anger was far too hot in her heart for that. *I know I paid that bill. I remember writing the check.* She thumbed through her checkbook until she came to the one made out to the electric company. *I forgot to mail it. I can't believe it. I've never done anything like that before.*

A surge of emotion raced through her. "It's not fair!" she shouted, though no one was close enough to hear. She leaned against the wall as her knees gave way. Everything seemed to be crumbling around her, and she couldn't do a thing about any of it. Nothing had prepared her for this. Nothing.

She gave herself over to the tears without a moment's guilt. They were long overdue. She had played the role of valiant widow long enough. She couldn't keep the game going any longer. Her heart ached with a fierceness she hadn't known in all of the time since Greg's passing. The full gamut of emotions tore through her. Anger. Pain. Fear. Loneliness.

This can't go on, Lord! I'm asking for Your help, Father—but more than that, I'm asking You to forgive me for not trusting in You. Increase my faith. Give me courage. I love You, Lord!

Chapter 15

Laura shuffled back and forth between the bookstore and home, working until her body passed the point of exhaustion. For over a week, she'd covered both Madeline's hours and her own. It couldn't be avoided. Madeline's bout with the flu required someone to fill her shoes. Laura was the logical candidate. Unfortunately, she'd missed several classes as a result.

The lights might be back on at home, but everything else remained in the dark. Jessica hadn't spoken to her in days. Laura managed to get a few words out of Nathan—something about Jess moving out—but there had been no sign anything like that was actually going to happen.

I'll show her the same patience You've shown me, Lord.

On top of everything, the car broke down. One evening, it just wouldn't start. A dead battery would have been bad enough, but the source of the problem turned out to be an alternator. As usual, when it rained, it poured—at least in her life. But something felt different. Somehow, in the middle of her turmoil, Laura found peace. In the very middle of her storm, she felt anchored.

Her only real regret was being away from school. She had missed two days this week—Tuesday and Thursday. Any more, and she might never get caught up. Her English teacher had been amiable, even offering to e-mail her assignments. Her math homework would have to wait. And American History—well, there just didn't seem to be much hope that she would ever catch up in that class, so why bother trying?

Andrew sat at the dinner table, listening to his fellow professors drone on about unimportant things. He was up to his ears as they rambled on about economics and politics. To be honest, he didn't give a rip about the latest stock market analysis. He had far more important things on his mind.

Laura Chapman. He couldn't release himself from the image of her wavy hair and silly smirk. . .her soft, smooth skin that carried the bold pink hue of a hot temper when she got riled up. . .her voice, trembling with anger as she spoke. Her "I told you so" smile when she proved him wrong. He missed those things, and so much more. Laura had been absent for the last two classes. With only two weeks before Thanksgiving, he started to worry that she might not come back at all. Truthfully, he missed her. There didn't seem to be any other way to put it. He missed the look of anger in her sparkling eyes. He missed her furrowed brow as she leaned over those unreasonably hard pop quizzes he gave.

For nearly two weeks, he had thought of little but her. When she ran off from the football game that night, she left behind far more than the scent of her perfume. The undeniable lingered in the air. Regina had been right all along. Andrew didn't hate Laura. He liked her—maybe a little too much. What he had grown to feel couldn't be explained without some amount of stammering on his part.

Did he really have room in his heart for someone like Laura Chapman? He hoped so. Perhaps, once the semester ended, he would feel comfortable entering into a relationship. Perhaps.

"Andrew, are you with us?" Sociology professor Mack Brewer, asked.

"Yeah, yeah. . ."

"We were just asking about your position on yesterday's big story out of Washington. Where do you stand?"

"Oh," he said, trying to focus. "I think it's awful, but I've got faith in our leadership. I'm sure they'll bring us through it all in fine style—if we don't mind hanging in limbo until then."

"What are you talking about?" Mack laughed. "I was asking your opinion on the renovations taking place at the National Art Gallery. What were you talking about?"

"Oh, I, uh. . . ," Andrew stammered. "I'm sorry. I guess I wasn't paying attention."

"Well, that's obvious. But at least we're all aware of your political views!"

Those at the table had a good laugh at Andrew's expense. He turned his attentions back to Laura.

⌒

Laura tossed and turned in bed, unable to sleep. She reached across the sheets. In that moment, Laura felt a sudden breeze blow through the room. She gazed at the window. *Surely no one would have opened it in the middle of November.* No, thank goodness, it was closed. But the breeze. . . Where had it come from? She lay, transfixed, watching, wondering. She began to sense an undeniable warmth, a somber satisfaction.

"Surely I am with you always." There was that scripture again. God was taking the time to call out to her, to let her know He was still here. He hadn't gone anywhere. Greg's spot in the bed might be vacant, but she didn't have to be empty.

"Lord, I'm here. Please don't leave me."

"I will never leave you nor forsake you." Another of her favorite scriptures came to mind almost immediately, doing its work to fill the void within. She was not forsaken! God hadn't left her at all. He hadn't been far off. In fact, He was so close, she could almost reach out and touch Him. Laura's heart began to dance within her. She was almost giddy as the words tripped across her tongue, "Thank You, Lord! Thank You!"

Suddenly everything became clear. She had been walking through the valley of the shadow, where the darkness had all but overwhelmed her. But this was a new day. *I'm going to be just fine.* God, the very lover of her soul, was there to remind her of that—and what a sweet reminder!

Emotion gave way to exhaustion and a peace like she hadn't felt in quite some time. Laura fell into a deep, well-deserved sleep.

Chapter 16

"Ms. Chapman?"

Laura looked up from the bookshelf into the eyes of Professor Andrew Dougherty. Her heartbeat immediately quickened. *What's he doing here?*

"Professor. . ." She said the word slowly, hesitantly.

He took a step in her direction. "Can you call me Andrew?"

"Mr. Dougherty." She looked the other way. "Is there something I can help you with?"

"I was going to ask you the same thing."

"What do you mean?"

"Well, we've missed you in class this past week, and I thought maybe you'd like your assignments."

Is he actually here on a goodwill mission? "I'm. . .I'm sorry. I've been working a lot of extra hours."

"That's all right. I understand completely. I just wanted to make sure you weren't staying away because of me."

Interesting remark. Laura looked into his anxious eyes. "No." Had he really been worried about her? Was that possible? "It doesn't have anything to do with you." She straightened the books as she spoke.

"That's good." He sounded relieved. "When you left the game last Saturday night, I felt sure I'd said something wrong. You may recall that I'm pretty good at putting my foot in my mouth."

"I do." She smiled, in spite of herself. "But you didn't do anything wrong this time. To be honest, I didn't know about Jess auditioning for the vocal scholarship. I guess I felt a little left out. I don't know."

"Oh, I'm sorry."

I can't blame him. It's certainly not his fault. "You were just happy for her—which I should have been—but wasn't because we had spent the whole weekend not speaking to each other." Suddenly Laura felt a release to talk, to really talk. For the first time in a long time, it felt great to have someone to share with, even if it was Professor Andrew Dougherty.

———

Andrew stood, mesmerized, listening to Laura speak. He learned much about her family during those precious minutes—far more than he had counted on. *She's a beautiful woman, inside and out. I can't believe she's taking the time to share all of this with me.*

His heart beat in his ears as he tried to work up the courage to ask her the question on his mind. "Do you get a break anytime soon?"

"I have been here all day, but I haven't gone to lunch yet. Why?"

Why? Because I have plans, if I can just work up the courage to implement them! "There's a deli a couple of doors down," he said nervously. "Have you ever been there?"

"Sure."

"Well, I was hoping you might have time for lunch." *I can't believe the words are coming out of my mouth. Then again, it's not as difficult as I thought it would be.*

She hesitated for what seemed like an eternity. "I, um. . . I'll have to check with Madeline."

He followed her to the front of the store, where her boss's broad smile let him know instantly that she could go. *I can't believe it. I'm actually going out to lunch with Laura Chapman.* Try as he might, he couldn't wipe the silly grin off his face.

"Are you ready?" Laura looked directly into his eyes and his heart flip-flopped.

Am I ever! "I'm ready." He pulled the door open for her. They stepped out onto the sidewalk, then turned in the direction of the deli.

"Laura, is that you?" Andrew heard the voice, somewhat familiar, and turned. Richard DeHart stood just behind them.

"Dick?" *Talk about lousy timing.*

"I was just coming in to ask you to lunch." DeHart frowned. "Am I too late?"

Andrew jumped in quickly. "We're just headed out—the two of us."

"I'm so sorry." Laura looked from Dick to Andrew and back.

"No problem." Dick reached out to take her arm and a shiver ran down Andrew's spine. "You're both hungry. So am I. What do you say we all go together?"

Andrew's eyes searched out Laura's. He hoped she would say something.

"I don't think—" Laura began.

"You're right," Dick said. "I don't think it's such a bad idea either."

Andrew's pulse quickened. *Dick DeHart is the last man on the planet I'd want to go to lunch with.* He watched out of the corner of his eye as Dick patted Laura's arm. *This guy infuriates me. I should do something about this.* He looked at Laura intently, hoping for some sign of her feelings. Her face looked slightly flushed, but she didn't seem to show the same level of anxiety he felt. Either that, or she was better at hiding it. Worse still, maybe she wanted to go to lunch with Dick DeHart.

"We're just headed down to the deli," Laura said. "I really don't have long, anyway."

"Well then," Dick said, "I'm awfully glad I got here when I did. Talk about great timing."

Yeah. Talk about great timing.

Laura sat at the table between the two men, completely confused and frustrated. Andrew's ears grew redder by the moment. Dick—well, Dick was content to barrel away, pounding Andrew into the ground with his expertise on early American presidents. She could slip away, and they would probably just go right on bickering. She tried, at several points, to enter into their conversation, but they seemed to be talking around her, not to her.

"So," she said finally, "I guess you'll both have to agree to disagree." They'd argued about the difference between the administrations of John Adams and John Quincy Adams for the last ten minutes.

"Are we boring you?" Andrew looked her in the eye.

Boring? Are you kidding me? She was half-asleep already. She shrugged, unwilling to speak her mind. She felt bored, yes, but more irritated than anything—like a third wheel, stuck directly between two flat tires. "I have to get back to work." She stood, relieved to be leaving.

"So soon?" Dick looked at his watch. "We're just getting started."

"Well, I'm sure the two of you will have a lot to talk about once I'm gone." She turned quickly and noticed Jessica, who stood just outside the window.

Oh, dear. Just when I thought things couldn't possibly get any worse.

Andrew stood and pulled out Laura's chair. *She looks frustrated. I don't blame her. This isn't how things were supposed to work out at all.* He had planned a long, lingering lunch over an exhilarating conversation—just between the two of them. *Leave it to Dick DeHart to mess things up.* "Are you sure you have to go?" He gave her his most imploring look.

She turned away from him as she spoke. "I'm already late."

"Would you mind if I stopped by the store in a few minutes?"

"Whatever."

Is she disinterested or just plain mad? Laura quickly moved toward the door, taking his hopes with her.

"Looks like it's just the two of us," Dick said with a sly grin.

"Great." Andrew reached to take another drink of his soda. "Just what the doctor ordered."

"Jess, what are you doing down here? Is something wrong? Is Kent in trouble again?"

"Mom, calm down. Kent's fine. Everything's fine. I just wanted to talk to you."

"Talk to me?"

"Yeah, is that so surprising? But it looks like you already have enough people to talk to. You certainly don't need me." She turned abruptly.

"Jessica," Laura said sternly. "This is not what it looks like. Professor Dougherty came by to. . .well, to talk to me about school stuff. He offered to take me to lunch. On the way out the door, we ran into Dick DeHart, and then things got complicated. I just couldn't seem to get rid of him."

"Whatever."

"Jess, stop it. Besides, it's not like I was having a good time." She waved her arms toward the deli to indicate her frustration. "They're both so egotistical and self-serving, they never even saw me."

A faint smile crossed Jessica's lips, the first sign of compromise. She gazed into the window of the deli. Both men seemed to be engrossed in conversation.

"Despite what you might think, I don't like either of them. I really don't. I wouldn't go out with Dick DeHart under any circumstances, and the professor. . ."

"Yes?" Jessica asked. "What about the professor?"

"Well, he's a nice guy, but. . ."

"Not your type?"

Laura hesitated slightly. "To be honest, I'm not sure what my type is anymore." She gazed through the deli window at Andrew, who looked miserable sitting next to Dick DeHart. *I almost feel sorry for him.*

"Look at them," Jessica said with a smirk. "They're two peas in a pod."

"Aren't they? Let's get out of here and leave them alone." That thought seemed very appealing to Laura.

She and Jessica walked toward the bookstore, laughing and talking about the professor, the tutor, and her daughter's apparent misunderstanding. Laura didn't mind being misunderstood, as long as things were made right again. Within moments, they chatted like youngsters. For the first time in a long time, Laura felt comfortable around her daughter.

They stopped just outside the door of the Bookstop. Jessica's expression changed abruptly. "Mom, there's something I need to talk to you about. That's why I came down here in the first place."

Laura nodded, waiting for her daughter to continue. No one ever wanted to "just talk" anymore, especially not Jess. "What is it, honey?"

"It sounds stupid now, after just blowing up at you. In fact, I've been doing that a lot lately. I can't seem to control my emotions. But that's why I'm here. I, uh. . .I just wanted to apologize."

"For what, honey?"

"Mom," Jessica said tearfully, "I'm just so sorry about everything that's happened this whole semester. I feel like I've ruined everything for you. I should have been more supportive when you told me you wanted to go back to school. You've been through so much these last couple of years, and I couldn't even give you any support at all. I'm selfish. There's no other way to put it." At that, Jessica burst into tears and buried her face in her hands.

"Jess. . ." Laura reached to put her arms around her precious daughter as she spoke. "We've all been through a lot. Ever since your father passed away. . ." The tears filled her eyes as well. "Ever since your father passed away, I've had to become mother and father. Nothing in life prepared me for that. It's hard enough just being Mom. I don't have any idea how to be Dad, too."

"You don't have to be." Jessica lifted her head. "Don't even try. We'll be fine with just you."

The words were freeing. Laura began to weep uncontrollably. Customers passed by. Many gazed at her oddly, but she didn't care.

"I just don't want to get in the way," Jess continued.

"You're not in the way. You never were, and you never will be."

"But I'm such a pain in the neck."

"Yeah," Laura said with a smile. "But aren't we all, sometimes? I mean—I'm a pain, too. Don't you think?"

"Do you really want me to answer that?"

Laura shook her head. "Not really, but we're all grieving, Jessica. And the way you've felt—about the music, about my going back to school, about Nathan, even. . ."

"What about Nathan?"

"I know things have been tense between the two of you," Laura said. "It's pretty clear."

"I don't know what to do about that either. I don't know what to do about anything."

"I think it's time for a fresh start," Laura said firmly. "For all of us. Time to start everything over again."

"How? How do we do that?"

Laura suddenly came to life. "Well, for one thing, I think we need to go back to church on a regular basis. None of this in-and-out stuff."

"I know I could use it," Jess agreed. "My spiritual life has been, well, almost nonexistent."

"I'm sure we could all do with a little spiritual help. Besides, I miss being in Sunday school and singing in the choir. Most of all, I long for the closeness I used to feel when we were there together as a family."

"Yeah," Jess responded. "To be honest, I've really missed being in the youth group and all that. Heaven knows, Kent could use it."

"True."

"But, Mom," Jessica said suddenly, "there's something else I want to do. It's actually the reason I came down here."

"What's that?"

"I want to come to work for you."

"What do you mean?"

Determination etched Jessica's face. "I mean, I want to work some of your hours

84

here at the shop so you can get back into your classes and finish the semester."

"But—"

"I've got it all worked out, Mom. I can give at least two or three hours a day and still keep my schedule at the school. I've even talked to Madeline about it. She's totally cool with the idea. I'll have to miss a couple of history classes, but I'm okay with that. I haven't missed any until recently."

"Madeline wants you to take some of my hours?"

"That's right," her boss said, appearing behind her. "I think it's a great idea, don't you?"

To be honest, Laura didn't know what to think.

Chapter 17

H ey, you!"
Regina's voice rang out, waking Andrew from his lethargy. He had been grading papers—one after another—and welcomed the interruption. Regina stood in the doorway of his classroom, looking as nervous as a cat.

"What's up?"

"Just wanted to come by and let you know something." She walked into the empty room. "I've got news."

"Me, too," he said excitedly. "But you go first. What's up?"

"Nope. You first. Is it something to do with the infamous Ms. Chapman?"

"Maybe."

"Well, come on. Spill the beans. I don't have all day."

"You'd be proud of me," he said with a smile. "We had lunch together."

"You did! You actually did it?"

His gaze shifted to the ground as he spoke. "Sort of."

"Sort of? Tell me."

"I went to the store where she works to talk to her, and there was this deli next door—"

"Good boy, good boy."

"So I asked her if she wanted to go and talk for a while."

"And she said yes?" Regina's voice reflected her glee.

"Uh-huh."

"Andrew, that's great! Then what happened?"

He felt his face fall. "Then DeHart walked up on us."

"Oh no. That weasel."

"Yeah."

"I hope you got rid of him."

Andrew shrugged.

"Don't tell me. . ." Regina stared him down.

"He came to lunch with us."

Regina slapped herself in the head. "I'm about to give up on you, Professor Dougherty. In fact, that's what I came to tell you. You're on your own after today."

"What do you mean?"

She hesitated slightly. "I, uh. . ."

"Spit it out." *She's obviously got something on her mind.*

"Today was my last day in the lunchroom."

"You quit? Why?"

"Had to," she said. "I'm just too tired."

Don't tell me she's sick. Bad things don't happen to great people like Regina. If anyone deserves a break, she does. "Tell me about it," he said finally. "I mean, if you want to." *I don't want to get too personal.* She stepped toward his desk, half-sitting on the edge. He waited for her explanation.

"It's like this. I—I'm going to have a baby."

He shot out of his seat instantly. "A baby? Are you serious?"

"I'm serious. But my doctor says he wants me off my feet. I'm no spring chicken, you know. Turned forty last month."

"You don't look a day over twenty-nine."

She gave him a thankful smile. "Well, anyway, I just wanted to come over and say good-bye, wanted to make sure you could handle this romance business without me. You're really not very good at it, you know."

"I'm not so sure about that, but I'll do the best I can." He reached over and gave her a playful hug. "Congratulations, Regina." He felt a lump in his throat. "I'm very happy for you. Please tell Daniel for me."

"I will." She returned the hug. "In fact, he's waiting for me in the car. We're both tickled pink." She paused. "Better make that blue. He's holding out for a boy."

———

Laura entered the American History classroom, struggling with her emotions. She wanted desperately to be here and yet felt terrified at the same time. As she came through the door, she saw Andrew with his arms wrapped around the lady from the lunchroom in a warm embrace. Laura stood, transfixed. She couldn't seem to move forward. She didn't want to go backward.

"I'll see you later, Andrew," the woman said, passing by her at the doorway. Laura noticed the woman stared at her. A twinge of jealousy shot through her, though she wasn't sure why.

"Ms. Chapman." She looked up into the eyes of Andrew Dougherty, amazed at the twinkle she found there. "You're back?"

"I'm back," she said, trying not to let her emotions show. "I've got to get through these last few weeks somehow."

He smiled a warm, inviting smile. "It's going to be just fine, and I'm going to help you."

———

Andrew's heart pounded so hard, he could scarcely breathe. Laura had returned. His trip to the store must have made the difference. He looked at her inquisitively. Was she here because she really wanted to be? Did it have anything to do with him at all?

"My daughter is going to miss class today," Laura explained. "She's taken some of my hours at the bookstore."

Ah. So, Jessica made all of this possible. Well, thank goodness for Jessica! "I'll be glad to send her work home with you."

"Thank you—for everything." She offered up a smile, one that warmed him to his toes.

Andrew fought to keep his composure. He wanted to know what made her tick, what gave her such tenacity. He wanted to take back everything he had ever thought about her being lazy. Laura Chapman had turned out to be one of the hardest workers he'd ever come across in his years as a teacher. Should he tell her, give her some sort of confirmation she would make it?

Andrew watched as she sat at her desk and pulled open the textbook. He turned his gaze to the board, where he wrote questions from today's lesson, then turned slightly to see if she had watched him. No, her head remained buried in the book. She seemed to be lost in her own world.

She probably thinks I'm going to give another pop quiz. Well, not today. No, he would take it easy on his students for a change. For some reason, he felt like a new man, invigorated, alive. As the rest of the students entered and took their seats, he made a silent pact with himself to give them a break.

"Welcome, everyone." He turned to face the class. "I trust you all managed to get through the work sheet I gave you when we met last."

A slight rumble went up from the students, who reached for their papers.

"Well, let's forget all about that and take a look at something else." They looked up at him, obviously startled.

"You mean we don't have to turn them in?" one of the boys asked.

"Not this time."

A look of relief flooded several faces. Still others looked puzzled. "Are you feeling all right, Professor Dougherty?" one of the girls asked.

"Never better." He turned his attention to an enlightening discussion on the Industrial Revolution, trying to remain focused. The students chimed in, creating a lively discussion. From the front of the room he kept a watchful eye on Laura. What was she thinking? Had he said anything to offend her?

No, she appeared to be smiling, enjoying the conversation as much as the others. All through the class, Andrew couldn't seem to take his eyes off of Laura. She seemed different, somehow—more peaceful than before. The angry edge was gone, replaced with the closest thing to happiness he had observed in quite awhile.

His heart continued to race as he concluded the class. Andrew hoped for a way to keep Laura after class, to ask her. . .

What he really wanted to do was ask her out, but he couldn't even say the words to himself. A date. He wanted a real date with her. But would she? Maybe after the semester ended? She certainly hadn't shown interest in him at the deli the other day. Then again, that was Dick DeHart's fault. He had ruined the afternoon entirely.

Andrew dismissed the class, waiting to see if she would linger behind the group. Their eyes met for a brief moment. He turned his gaze to the papers on the desk, embarrassed that she had caught him looking at her. He looked back up again, disappointed to find she had slipped out of her seat and was headed toward the door.

"Ms. Chapman?"

"Yes?" She turned, looking at him.

"I wonder. . . I wonder if you could stay after class for a few moments," he said, feeling his hands begin to shake.

"Why?"

"Well, I, uh. . ." The other students disappeared down the hallway, leaving them alone.

"I want to tell you how happy I am to see you. I'm glad you're back."

She looked startled. "You are?"

"Certainly. Haven't you figured that out yet?" He fought to continue. "I enjoy your company, Ms. Chapman." Andrew searched her eyes for a response.

Her face flushed as she whispered hoarsely, "Call me Laura."

"Laura." His hands shook uncontrollably now. "That's why I wanted to take you to lunch the other day. I'm so sorry about the way everything turned out."

"Me, too."

"I wanted to spend some time alone with you, to get to know you. I wanted to make up for the time I've spent poking fun at you or making assumptions."

"It's all in the past. I hope you can forgive me for the day we met."

He smiled, remembering. "Done." He paused slightly. "Do you still think I'm so tough?"

"In a good way. Most of these kids need a little push. I know you've made me a better student."

"I have?"

"If nothing else, you motivated me, made me want to be the best I could be. That's what every good teacher strives to do, right?"

"Right." Andrew stared at her in disbelief. *She's so giving.* "Look," he said, feeling strength well up in him, "I've been trying to work up the courage to ask you something."

She looked up, their gazes locking. "What is that?"

"This probably isn't the right time or place. . . ." He looked toward the door. Any moment now, students from his next class would be arriving. It was now or never. "I've been wanting to ask you out on a date. A real date. Just the two of us."

"Are you serious?"

"Never more serious."

She bit her lip before responding. "I'm not sure if I'm ready for that yet."

His heart twisted inside him as he took her hand. "Will you let me know when you are? I don't want to rush you, but I'd love to spend some time getting to know you better."

She nodded silently. "I'll do that."

His heart swelled. "That would be great." Just then, two students barreled through the door, laughing at one another. Laura quickly pulled her hand from his and moved away. "I really need to get to work. Jess has been so good to cover for me, but I'm sure she's ready for a break." She smiled, then left the room in a hurry.

Andrew turned toward the board, erasing the notes from the last class. His heart soared as he contemplated her words. "Andrew Dougherty," he whispered, "I do believe you're making progress."

Chapter 18

Kent? Jessica? Are you guys ready?" Laura called out in an attempt to rush them. "We're going to be late to church." Something about the words reminded her of when they were children. Many a Sunday morning had been spent looking for missing shoes or socks or arguing over appropriate church attire. She and Greg had always managed to get them out the door and to church in time for Sunday school.

Kent appeared at the top of the stairs, still in his pajama pants and T-shirt. He stretched, letting out a loud, rehearsed moan. "Mornin'."

"What are you doing, Kent? I told you to get ready nearly an hour ago."

"I fell back asleep," he said with a yawn. "Just go on without me."

"Go to church without you? But—"

"Aw, give me a break, Mom. I've had a tough week at school. I'm beat."

Laura felt the disappointment deeply. *I wanted this to be a family affair. Well, at least Jessica will go with me.*

"Jess?" She called up the stairs. Her daughter appeared, dressed in a trendy blouse and skirt.

"You look great."

"Thanks." Jessica smiled. "So do you."

"Did you say Nathan wanted to sit with us this morning?"

"He's meeting us there. He always rides with his parents, anyway." She pulled the door shut behind them, and they headed out to the car. The air outside felt crisp and cold. Laura shivered, pulling her jacket tightly around herself. Doing so reminded her of the night at the football game when Andrew pulled his jacket over her shoulders to keep her warm. *Andrew.* Thinking of him brought an unexpected smile. *Is it possible I'm beginning to have feelings for this man?*

"It's almost Thanksgiving." Jessica interrupted her thoughts as they climbed into the car. "Can you believe it? It seems like the semester just started."

"Seems more like an eternity to me, but I'm happy the holidays are coming. It means I'm one step closer to being done with my first leg of the journey."

"You've done a great job, Mom. I'm really proud of you."

Laura felt her heart swell. "I never thought I'd hear those words—not from you, anyway."

"Well, just like you've been saying—today's a new day."

They drove to the church, chatting about everything from Christmas gifts to Thanksgiving dinner. It was a truly wonderful trip.

⁓

Andrew changed the channels on the TV, frustrated. *Church services*. He certainly wasn't interested in any of those. . .or was he? One, in particular, caught his eye. It was a room full of people, singing, worshiping. They seemed to be happy, in an odd sort of way.

"What phonies. Like anyone could be that happy in church."

And yet, he couldn't seem to change the channel. Something about those people held him captivated—something in their expression intrigued him. They didn't look like they were faking anything. In fact, they looked perfectly natural, genuinely comfortable.

"Comfortable in church. Now that's something I've never felt." It wasn't like Andrew had never been to church. He had been raised in one. His strict mother had pulled him out of the arms of his agnostic father every Sunday until Andrew turned about twelve or thirteen. That's when he rebelled—started staying home with his dad for one-on-one conversations about the things that really interested him—explorers, navigators, maps, and so much more. That's where the fun had been. He certainly never experienced any joy sitting in a pew.

Joy. There seemed to be so little of it in his life. His passion for teaching brought him joy, but not the kind that really lasted. Those people on the television looked like they had something that superceded what he felt in front of the class-room. Their joy seemed to come from something inside, something he couldn't quite understand. "I don't get it," he whispered, "but I'd sure like to figure it out."

He watched as the pastor brought the congregation to laughter with a joke about children. "No, I never went to a church like that." He spoke to the empty room. "But maybe someday I will."

⁓

"Turn with me to Colossians, chapter three," the pastor said. "Verses twelve through fourteen."

Laura turned through her worn Bible until she found the passage. She had always loved this one, but somehow, in the middle of things, she had simply for-gotten about it.

The pastor's voice rang out against the silence. " 'Therefore, as God's chosen people, holy and dearly loved, clothe yourselves with compassion, kindness, hu-mility, gentleness and patience.' "

Kindness? Patience? Laura had shown little of these traits over the last several months, in spite of her good intentions.

" 'Bear with each other,' " the pastor continued, " 'and forgive whatever griev-ances you may have against one another. Forgive as the Lord forgave you.' "

She had forgiven everyone, hadn't she? After all, she excused Jessica for giving her the cold shoulder. She pardoned Kent for complicating their already complicated lives with his shenanigans. She had forgiven Greg... Wait a minute! Greg hadn't done anything wrong. Why should she have to forgive him? Could she possibly be holding him in unforgiveness—after all this time?

The pastor continued on, oblivious to her inner turmoil: " 'And over all these virtues put on love, which binds them all together in perfect unity.'"

Love. She and Greg had been in love—the kind that surpassed romance. The kind that could have lasted forever—at least that's what she always thought. Gentle tears began to course down Laura's cheeks. She reached for a tissue but found none. Jessica quickly handed her one, then reached out to touch her arm.

"It's all right, Mom," she whispered, eyes glistening. "I know how you feel."

The pastor went on to talk about the steps to mend broken relationships. Laura took notes, scribbling down as many words as she could on the back of an offering envelope. Jess handed her the church bulletin, pointing to a blank spot on the back. "There you go, Mom," she whispered.

Laura reached to pat her hand, a gesture of thanks. *Lord, thank You so much for sending Jessica with me. I love spending time with her.* She paused from her note-taking, content to sit with her hand wrapped around her daughter's. She could go on sitting like this forever.

The service ended some time later, but Laura couldn't seem to pull herself from the sanctuary. Even after most of the others left, she remained. She slowly made her way up to the front, a place she had often visited as a child. Funny how the altar still cried out to her. Jess had disappeared to the foyer with Nathan, so Laura took advantage of the situation by kneeling for a few moments alone.

"Lord, I'm here," she whispered. "I made it. And I'm back to stay this time. I'm not going anywhere." She felt the presence of God overwhelm her. "How did I stay away so long?" She spent a few more minutes opening up her heart to her Father. How wonderful it felt to be back in this place, the very place Greg had loved so much.

"Greg." No sooner did she speak his name than she realized what she must do. "I have to forgive him, Lord. Help me."

Her daughter appeared behind her. "Mom, is there anything I can do?"

"No, Jess." She looked up with a smile, dabbing at her eyes.

"I'm worried about you."

"No need to worry. This is a good thing."

"Are you sure?"

Laura nodded. "Yes, but I'm not sure I can explain what I'm feeling right now."

"Could you try?" Jessica knelt down beside her.

Laura took her hand and clutched it tightly. "When your father died..." That was all she got out before the tears came again.

"Tell me, Mom."

Laura took a deep breath. "When your father died, I blamed God. I didn't realize it until months later. I was so angry with Him that I never wanted to come back into a church again. In fact, I even told Him that."

"You did?"

"Yes, but it was wrong of me. I knew that, after awhile. That day—when you came up to the store—I realized then that I was also angry at you kids."

"At us? Why? What did we do?"

"It wasn't anything you did, exactly. The situation I found myself in had reached a crisis point. Don't you see? I've been completely responsible for the two of you with no one to help me. Since I had locked God out, I sure couldn't look to Him for help. That left me on my own. But that day you came up to the store, God began to show me this."

"Really?"

"Yes. He showed me that unforgiveness is like a prison. It holds us in its grip until we can't breathe. Eventually we become so bitter, we're no fun to be around. I don't want to be like that!" At that, Laura began to cry unashamed. "Can you ever forgive me, Jess? I'm so sorry about everything!"

"Mom, of course I do, and I know Kent will, too. But you have to forgive us, too. We haven't exactly made things easier." They embraced for what seemed like an eternity.

"There's something else," Laura said finally. "And this is the worst part. I didn't realize it until just this morning. I really didn't."

"What, Mom?"

"I've been angry with your father." She spoke through the tears. "I've been so angry with him, I couldn't think straight. He left me. He abandoned me."

Jessica held her tightly. "I do understand, Mom. More than you know. I've been mad at Daddy, too. I've been so mad, sometimes I fight with him in my dreams."

"You what?"

"I dream about him," Jessica explained, "and we always end up fighting. I argue and argue but never seem to win. He always wins. But then I wake up and realize what's happened—that it's just a dream—and try to put it out of my mind. But the dreams don't go away."

"Jess, I never knew."

"I know," she said sadly. "I never told you. I just wake up in a bad mood and take it out on you and Kent. I have a feeling things are going to be better after today, don't you?"

"It felt really good to go back to church." Laura smiled through the tears. "I mean, it was hard—seeing all of those women sitting there with their husbands beside them, but it still felt wonderful."

"I thought so, too. I missed having Daddy next to me, trying to sing bass."

"He had a terrible voice," Laura said with a smile. "Do you remember?"

Jess laughed. "How could I forget?"

He hadn't been the best singer in the world, but he had certainly made up for it by being the best husband.

"Jess, would you pray with me before we leave?"

"Here?" Her daughter looked around. "Out loud?"

Laura nodded. "If you don't mind."

Jessica began to pray aloud, hesitantly at first, then gaining strength as she went. Her prayer was passionate, heartfelt. As she continued on, Laura's heart swelled with joy inside her. She had truly come home.

Andrew paced back and forth across his tiny living room, the words from the television still on his mind. Something the TV pastor had said intrigued him. He couldn't seem to shake it: " 'Be transformed by the renewing of your mind. . . ,' " or something like that.

"Transforming your mind." He repeated the words. Andrew understood the concept of strengthening his mind by gaining knowledge, of bettering himself. That's why he had spent so many years in college, and why he felt driven to teach.

But this idea of transforming his mind. . . Now that was certainly something new, something to think about.

"Does he mean I should gain more knowledge?" he asked, pacing across the room. "Or is there something more?"

He headed to the computer, rapidly signing online. "Surely there's got to be some sort of Bible online I can read," he spoke aloud. "I'll get this figured out."

Before he knew it, three hours had passed. Bleary-eyed, Andrew reached to shut down the computer, his mind reeling. If the scriptures he'd read were true, bettering his mind didn't have anything to do with education.

It had everything to do with inspiration.

"I'm sorry. . .what did you say?" Laura felt sure she had heard the voice on the other end of the phone correctly, but she didn't want to believe it.

"This is Officer Meyer with the Harris County Sheriff's Office. Your son was in an accident on Interstate 45 about half an hour ago and has been taken to Northwest Hospital."

Please, God, no! "I'm on my way." Laura suddenly felt faint. She hung the phone up, trembling as she called, "Jess!"

Her daughter appeared quickly, a look of fear crossing her face when she saw her mother. "What is it?"

"It's Kent."

"What about him?"

"He's been in an accident."

"What? What happened?"

"I don't know. They didn't say."

"Where is he?"

"Northwest. Can you drive?"

Jessica nodded, taking the keys from her hand. "Of course. You just get whatever you think you'll need. Do you have his insurance card?"

Laura nodded lamely, letting her daughter take charge. If nothing else, it felt good to have someone else in control—at least for the moment.

Laura felt numb as they made their way outside.

"When we get there, I'm going to let you off at the door," Jess explained as they got into the car. "Then I'm going to park. Getting a parking space at Northwest isn't easy. Did they say where to go? Is he in the Emergency Room, or have they moved him?"

"I—I don't know." Laura tried to speak over the lump in her throat. "I forgot to ask."

"Well, we'll start there. Don't worry, Mom. I know he's going to be all right."

Laura nodded numbly, trying to collect her thoughts. She hadn't asked for any information at all. *I don't know who was driving, how many other people were injured, or if Kent was badly hurt. I only know that he needs me—and quickly.* The ride to the hospital seemed to take forever. *Are they ever going to finish these interstates? This construction is ludicrous.* "Take the back way."

Jessica followed her instructions, and they quickly reached the hospital. "Just stay calm, Mom. Don't let Kent see you upset. You need to be strong."

Laura didn't feel strong. She felt completely unprepared to face whatever lay on the other side of that door, but she had to put her best foot forward—for Kent's sake.

"I'm Mrs. Chapman," she said to the first official-looking person she came in contact with.

The elderly woman nodded compassionately. "They've taken your son into surgery."

"Surgery?"

"Yes, ma'am. The doctor will tell you all about it when they're done. In the meantime, a police officer is here, waiting to speak with you." She pointed to her right.

Laura made her way to the officer, who sat filling out papers. "I'm Laura Chapman. Could you tell me what happened to my son?"

"Officer Meyer." He stuck his hand out to grasp hers. "Nice to meet you. I'm sorry it has to be under these circumstances."

"Please tell me something."

"Your son was in a major collision on I-45," the officer explained. "Apparently, a friend of his was driving under the influence."

Driving under the influence? "Who? What friend?"

"We're still trying to determine that, ma'am. He came in without any ID, and your son was in a state of shock—unable to identify him. The doctor will give you details when he comes out of the operating room, but I can tell you, Kent's in pretty bad shape. A paramedic mentioned the possibility of internal bleeding. We had to Life Flight him here."

Laura spoke over the knot in her throat. "How did you know to call me?"

"Kent had his permit in his wallet," the deputy explained. "Wish the other boy had."

"But you're sure Kent wasn't driving?"

"We're sure. The other boy is pretty cut up—took some damage from the steering wheel and the air bag. He didn't have a seat belt on."

"Oh no. . ."

"Would you please come and have a look at him for us? We're really hoping you can help identify him."

Laura followed him to the room where the boy lay unconscious, hooked up to various machines. He was almost unrecognizable—the cuts on his face and head were bandaged, covering much of his face.

"I know him," she whispered. "His mother is a good friend. His name is Josh. Josh Peterson. He's just a kid. . . ."

"An intoxicated kid who lost control of his car and hit the railing on the interstate. He managed to hit two other cars."

"Did he hurt anyone else?"

The officer shook his head. "No, not this time. But we need some information on Josh. Do you have a phone number? We'll need to contact his parents."

"Is he going to be alright?" She quickly scribbled the number on a piece of paper and handed it to him.

"He looks bad, but the doctors say his wounds are superficial. If I were you, I'd focus on Kent. In fact, I'll ask an aide to walk you down to the surgical waiting area so you're there when they finish with him."

Laura followed the aide down the long hallway, a prayer on her lips the entire way. *Father, I'm asking You to guard the surgeon's hands as he operates on Kent. He needs Your healing, Lord. Help him. Help Josh. Help us all.*

Laura collapsed numbly into a chair in the waiting area. Jessica arrived, breathless, a few minutes later.

"That parking garage is a madhouse," she said, panting. "What did they say? Is he here?"

"They've taken him to surgery," Laura said, giving way to the tears.

"Surgery? Why? What's wrong with him?"

"I don't really know. The doctor will tell us when he comes out. I guess we'll just have to wait and see."

"Wait and see?"

"There is something you can do, Jess," Laura said, gathering her strength. "I need you to call Grandma, and I need you to give the Petersons a call, just to make sure they got the message."

"What message? What do the Petersons have to do with this?"

"Josh was driving the car. He was. . .the policeman said he was driving under the influence."

"No!"

"That's what he said. But please, just make the calls. Don't tell them that part—at least not yet. Just make sure they come. I've got to go in and see Josh again, make sure he's okay. I feel like someone needs to be in there with him." She reached out to embrace her daughter, squeezing her tightly.

"I know everything will be okay. We'll get through this. If God is for us—"

"Who can be against us," Laura finished the scripture with her daughter's hand tightly clutched in her own.

Chapter 19

Andrew stood in his classroom, silent after a long day's teaching. He'd just received the news that Laura's son had been in an accident, and Andrew found himself torn. *Surely I should do something, but what? Send flowers? Drop off a card?*

Did he dare go up to the hospital? Would that be too forward? Andrew paced nervously to the board, erasing all that had been written there during the last class.

I should go. I should. It didn't take much more to convince himself.

———

"Mom? Are you all right?"

Laura awoke suddenly, fearfully, looking toward the hospital bed. An immediate fear gripped her. "Kent?"

"No, Mom. It's me, Jess. I didn't realize you were sleeping. I didn't mean to wake you."

Laura's nerves calmed immediately. She turned to face her daughter, who stood in the doorway. Just the tone of Jessica's voice soothed her. "Oh, that's okay. I shouldn't have been dozing."

"Why not? If anyone deserves to rest, you do. You've been shut up in this hospital room for three days now."

That was true, though Laura wouldn't have had it any other way. How could she possibly leave Kent's side? He was still not out of danger. Though the surgery to remove his lacerated spleen went well, there was still the broken arm to contend with. The orthopedist insisted Kent needed to stabilize before he could surgically repair the fracture. That surgery had taken place just this morning. It didn't matter how long any of this took. Laura would stay regardless of how much it taxed her.

"He's been sleeping for hours." She yawned loudly.

"You need a break," Jess said. "I thought I'd stay awhile."

"I could stand some food." Laura felt a surge of strength rise within her. "Maybe I could go down to the cafeteria. Have you eaten?"

"Yep. Stopped off at the cafeteria after class."

Laura's heart twisted within her as she thought about the classes she had missed. "How was school? Were you able to make it to all of your classes?"

"Yep. Everything at school is fine." Her daughter reached into her backpack to pull out some papers. "These are from Dougherty. He said he hopes to see you soon—whatever that means."

"Did you tell him?" Laura didn't know why it seemed important that he know. . .but it did, somehow.

"Yeah." He looked pretty shook up but said not to worry about class, that everything would be fine. He knows you're a good student."

"Humph. Don't know about that."

"Well, anyway. I told him you were shut up here with little to do, so he sent some work over. Hope that's all right."

"Sure. Whatever. I need something to pass the time." While she had been intent on staying by Kent's side, there had been little to do but watch TV, chat with the doctor about his condition, and pray. Laura had done a lot of praying over the last few days.

"Anything else?"

"I talked to Madeline. She also said not to worry—you've still got a few sick days coming to you."

"Yeah, but the day after Thanksgiving is the busiest day of the year," Laura said nervously. "I know she'll need me then."

"Let's just take this one day at a time, Mom."

Laura nodded. She was right. Besides, Laura couldn't do anything about it, anyway. "Anything else going on that I need to know about?"

"Nope."

"Well, in that case, I'd love to get some coffee and something to nibble on." Laura looked around the room, still feeling a little unsure about leaving.

"Go on. . . ," Jess urged.

"I'll be in the cafeteria if anyone needs me. And I may stop by the chapel for a few minutes." *I've meant to do that for days.*

Jessica gave a nod. "Go on, Mom. Get out of here for a while. I'll hold down the fort."

Laura turned to leave the room. As much as she hated to go, she felt she had to get out for at least a few minutes. She made her way down to the cafeteria, finding a spot at a table where she could be alone to drink her coffee and nibble on a banana. She then headed back toward the room, walking slowly through the now-familiar halls of the first floor of Northwest Hospital.

Laura paused at the chapel door. *I should go inside.* To be honest, she had avoided it for days, though she couldn't put her finger on a legitimate reason. A hospital chapel shouldn't frighten her. She tiptoed into the empty room, making her way to the altar where a Bible lay open.

Quietly she sank to her knees, though doing so felt a little awkward. Once there, the tears began to flow. She hadn't planned them. They just seemed to erupt from a deep place within her—a place that needed comforting. Where the words came from, she wasn't quite sure, but they began to flow, too.

"Father, do You ever get tired of hearing how much I need You? If it's a lack of faith on my part, then give me more. I need You more than ever. I don't know how to make it through this alone. I can't do it on my own. Take care of Kent, Father. Heal him. Mend his broken heart so he can let go of the anger he's been holding onto. Lord, I pray that Your work would be complete, not just in Kent, but in me. Take away the things in my life that aren't pleasing to You. Make me the woman you want me to be. Help me to know how to show Your love to the people You've placed in my life."

Laura poured her heart out to the Lord, begging Him to spare her son, and asking Him to forgive her for every conceivable thing she could think of. Somehow, at the end of it all, she felt the burden lift.

Andrew Dougherty stood outside the chapel of Northwest Hospital, listening. Jessica had said he might find Laura here, though he was completely unprepared for the way he found her. She was praying, actually praying out loud, and on her knees.

As a child, he had spent many hours on his own knees—punishment from a stern mother who used prayer as a means to an end: to bring him to repentance for his thoroughly wicked deeds. He had spent more time daydreaming than praying back then, but if he had known prayer could be this simple, he might have tried it.

Andrew had never heard anyone pray like this before. Laura's words were genuine, heartfelt. They spoke volumes. He felt like a traitor as he strained to hear each and every word. They weren't his to hear, and yet somehow they sounded as comfortable and comforting as anything he had heard in a long, long time.

"Be transformed by the renewing of your mind. . . ." The scripture ran through his head once again. For the first time in his life, he began to understand just how possible that could be. *Lord, is it really that easy? Do I just talk to You like she's doing? Can it be that simple?*

Relief flooded his soul. Perhaps this wasn't something he would have to earn. Maybe it wouldn't require a huge amount of study on his part. Perhaps all he had to do was just believe.

The sound of a man's cough at the chapel door roused Laura from the altar. She wiped at her eyes and tried to get control of her emotions. She didn't want anyone to see her like this, even a stranger. Laura reached for a tissue but couldn't seem to find one.

"Are you looking for this?" A man pressed a tissue into her hand.

She didn't dare look up. "Thank you."

"I hoped I'd find you here," he said softly.

Laura suddenly recognized the voice. She turned, finding herself face-to-face with Andrew Dougherty. Instinctively, she reached out to take the hand he offered, letting him pull her to a standing position. His arm slipped around her shoulder in a warm, sincere hug. There was nothing uncomfortable or awkward about it.

Wrapped in his embrace, she felt completely free to let the tears flow. Her face found its way to his shoulder, where she buried it, sobbing uncontrollably. He wrapped both arms around her, whispering gentle words of reassurance. "It's going to be okay." His fingers brushed against her hair and Laura found comfort in his touch. He had come at just the right moment. She needed someone to be there just then. She'd longed for it for quite some time, though she hadn't realized just how much.

But Andrew Dougherty?

Funny. His touch was tender, loving, nothing like she would have expected. He caressed her hair with his fingertips, pausing to brush it from her eyes. None of this made sense, and yet she couldn't deny the feeling of peace and satisfaction she felt wrapped up in his arms. The whole thing felt perfectly natural. It felt good.

Too good.

After a few moments she pulled away and forced her gaze in another direction. Embarrassment filled her. "I'm so sorry. I don't know what came over me."

"Please, don't be sorry." Andrew felt his heart swell. "I wanted to be here for you. It's the least I can do."

Laura Chapman had felt good in his arms. So very good. The scent of her shampoo lingered, dizzying him. It had been years since he had been close enough to a woman to smell that. His fingers had run through her hair with a mind of their own. That lustrous hair of hers had always been a temptation for him. Andrew's arms ached to reach for her again, to wrap her up into them and whisper comforting words to her. It felt so right.

Andrew could no longer deny his feelings for Laura Chapman. He desired to know her as a friend and as much more.

He spoke softly. "That prayer of yours. . ."

"You heard me pray?"

"Yes. That prayer was beautiful. I haven't heard anything so incredible since I was a kid in Sunday school."

"You're making fun of me."

"No, I'm not." He meant every word of it.

"You were a Sunday school kid? That's hard to believe."

"I know, but it's true," Andrew said with a sigh. "Somewhere along the way, I turned my back on God. When I got to my teens, I guess. I remember accepting

Christ at an altar when I was nine. It seems like a lifetime ago. But I never learned to pray like that. Never."

"I'm just remembering how to do it, myself. Turns out it's pretty simple. You talk, He listens. He talks, you listen."

Andrew shook his head in disbelief. "In the academic world, everything has to be earned—every grade, every promotion. Everything. Nothing comes easy."

"Prayer should."

"I can see that. Now. I'm not sure what I've believed about God since my days in college. It's like I put Him away on a shelf and forgot about Him."

"What about now? What do you believe?"

"I believe. . ." Here Andrew hesitated. He wasn't completely sure how to go about saying what was in his heart. "For years, I have been frustrated. So many things have happened to make me give up on God and on people—mostly women."

"Women? Why?"

How could he begin to explain why? "I was engaged once, but something happened on the way to the church."

"She broke your heart?"

Andrew nodded lamely. "Yeah."

"I figured as much."

"What do you mean?"

"It wasn't so hard to figure out that someone must have hurt you at some point along the way. Is that why you're so angry with God?"

"What do you mean? Who said anything about that?"

"Isn't that what this is all about?" Laura asked. "I know I've had to struggle with that. Ever since Greg died, I've been so mad at God, I hardly knew how to function. But admitting it is half of the battle. It gets easier after that."

Andrew laughed and shook his head in disbelief. "You are something else. Just about the time I think I've got you figured out, I find out that there's so much more."

"I'm not such a bad person," Laura said with a smile. She looked down at her watch and gasped. "I have to get back up to the room. Jessica is up there alone with Kent, and I need to be with her."

"Would you mind if I came along?" He almost dreaded her answer.

To his relief, she shrugged. "No, come if you like. I'm sure Jess would be glad to see you."

He walked beside her, chatting all the way. What he wanted to do—what he longed to do—was to pull her close to him and tell her everything would be all right. Would she think him awful if he reached for her now? No, that wouldn't be the appropriate thing to do. What had happened in the chapel had been perfectly natural, perfectly comfortable, but anything more would spoil an otherwise perfect moment.

Andrew continued to ramble on about everything from the weather to his latest history quiz. Truth be told, he was so nervous, much of what he said didn't make a lot of sense. Not that she seemed to notice. Laura's mind appeared to be a million miles away.

Chapter 20

"Hello there."

Laura looked up as Andrew peeked in the door of the hospital room. Her heart skipped a beat as their eyes met. His visit yesterday had been unexpected, but today she had secretly hoped he would come. He stood in the doorway, clearly hesitant.

Laura laid down the magazine she had been reading. "Well, hello."

"How's our patient today?" He turned his gaze toward the bed, where Kent lay sleeping.

"Better. But they are keeping him pretty sedated. He's been sleeping most of the day."

"What about you?" Andrew took a couple of steps into the room. "Have you had any sleep?"

She shrugged. "A little." An embarrassing yawn worked its way to her lips.

He pulled a small bouquet of flowers from behind his back. "I thought these might cheer you up."

Yellow roses. I love yellow roses. "Are they for me or Kent?" She suddenly felt like a shy schoolgirl.

"They're for you." He handed them to her. She clutched them tightly, suddenly unable to breathe correctly.

"I actually have something else for him, when he wakes up, that is." Andrew reached inside his coat and pulled a small package from the pocket.

"What is that?"

"It's a CD. Dizzy Gillespie. He's a trumpet player."

"Dizzy Gillespie? How in the world did you know—"

He laid it on the bedside table. "The football game, remember? After you left, I stayed to watch Kent play. I don't know much about trumpets or trumpet players, but he looked like he knew his stuff."

Laura nodded, stunned. She couldn't seem to get past the fact that Andrew had handed her three yellow roses, which she still held tightly. They smelled incredible. She ran her finger over one of the blossoms. "And I'm sure he'll love it. It was very thoughtful of you." *Very thoughtful.*

"No problem. I enjoyed shopping for it. I'm not much of a contemporary music person, but I love to browse through the old stuff." Kent stirred slightly in the bed. "Sorry, I guess I'm too loud," Andrew whispered.

"No, trust me. Nothing could wake him." Laura stood and carried the roses toward the bathroom. "I need to get these in some water." As she crossed in front of Andrew, their eyes met. He held her captive for a moment with his smile, and her heartbeat accelerated slightly. Laura glanced at the ground nervously, then chose to keep walking.

"I'll just be a minute," she said, then entered the bathroom. She quickly turned on the tap water with one hand, unwrapping the roses with the other. She glanced around for something to put them in. The only thing she could find was a small glass. "This will have to do." She broke the stems off at the bottom, then placed them in the glass, which she filled with water. They leaned a little too far to the right.

"I think I'll put them on the windowsill." She walked past him once again, feeling his eyes on her hair. *Why am I so nervous? It's not like I've never been alone in a room with him.*

"I was hoping you might be able to take a little break."

"A break?"

"Yeah. I thought we might grab something to eat in the cafeteria."

"I don't know." Laura looked nervously at Kent, who lay in a sound sleep. "He might need me." She yawned again. "I am hungry. And I haven't been out of this room all day. Maybe I could just stop by the nurses' station and tell them where I'll be."

"Sounds good."

She went to Kent's bedside, stopping to brush a kiss across his forehead. Her heart twisted as she gazed at him. *I won't do it. I won't get down about this. The doctors say he's going to be fine. I can be strong. I will be strong.*

She turned to face Andrew, immediately relieved by his presence. "I think I'm ready now."

He smiled and led the way out of the door.

~

Andrew sat across the table from Laura in the hospital cafeteria, mesmerized by her conversation. "And then what happened?"

"Then I told the kids that they were never allowed to eat peanut butter and jelly again—at least, not in the living room!" She chuckled then sighed deeply. "It feels good to laugh. It really does."

"You've got a great laugh."

"What do you mean?"

"Oh, come on. You know. Some women have those really high-pitched, annoying laughs. They hurt your ears. And some have that terrible snorting laugh. That's the worst."

"And I'm neither of those?"

"No, you have the perfect laugh."

"You can't imagine how long it's been since I've felt like laughing. Lately it seems like my life is just this never-ending cycle of. . ."

"Stuff?"

"Yeah."

"I can relate to that," he said, feeling it was safe to open up. "I keep pretty busy with all of my students."

"What about your family?"

"My mother passed away three years ago," he explained.

"Oh, I'm sorry."

"I am, too. She was a difficult woman, but I still miss her keenly. I spent a lot of time trying to figure her out. She was always so bitter, so frustrated. I never really knew why."

"Some people get like that as they age. Life doesn't go the way they expected it to, and they can't seem to gauge their reactions."

"She always took everything to heart. Wore her emotions on her sleeve. Guess that's why it bothers me to see women like that."

"What about your father?" Laura took a bite of her sandwich.

"My dad died when I was in my late teens." Andrew's heart ached with the memory. "He was such an amazing man. He knew everything there was to know about history, about everything."

"Everything?"

Not everything, Andrew had to admit. His father had been very well schooled, had learned much about the world he lived in. But he had never really cared to learn about the things that seemed important to his mother—church, faith, the Bible. . .

Maybe that's why she was so bitter.

"Andrew?" Laura gave him an odd look.

"Oh, I'm sorry. I lost my train of thought. I was just remembering how my dad treated my mom. He didn't care for her religion."

"She was a religious woman?"

"Oh, very."

"What do you mean by religious?"

Andrew shrugged. "She went to church a lot. Took me along for the ride. Like I said, I was a Sunday school kid. She preached at my dad a lot, always tried to get him to go with her. But he wasn't interested. After a few years, I wasn't either. It just seemed like my dad was more exciting. He was so smart, one of the brightest men I ever knew."

"If you don't mind my asking, how did your father. . . I mean, how did he. . ."

"How did he die?" Andrew began to tremble slightly, remembering. He took a deep breath before continuing. "It was a couple of days before my seventeenth birthday. My dad was late coming home from work. My mom got supper ready, as usual, but he just never came. Finally, after a couple of hours, she started making calls. In the middle of all of that, there was a knock at the door—a police officer."

"He'd been in an accident?"

"His car was struck by an eighteen-wheeler," Andrew said, shaking his head. The memory still carried the pain of a seventeen-year-old boy's broken heart. "When my dad died, something in me just sort of gave up, too."

"I can understand that," Laura said softly. "When my husband passed away, I felt like I couldn't go on. He was so much a part of me. Or vice versa. I don't really know how that works, but it hurts so terribly when they're gone."

Andrew looked at her tenderly. "I'm so sorry."

"So your mom was a widow at a young age."

"Yeah, I guess you could say that. She was in her forties when he passed away." Andrew suddenly realized what he was saying and how closely it paralleled Laura's story. "Oh, Laura."

"I think I can understand where some of your mother's bitterness came from. I've struggled with it since Greg died. But last Sunday. . ."

"What about last Sunday?" His curiosity grew.

"Last Sunday, something happened at church. I'm not sure if I can explain it exactly, but God did something in me. He. . . He. . ."

Andrew's heart raced. *Last Sunday. Something was stirring in me, too.*

"I spent some time at the altar Sunday morning after everyone else left the service. I think, for the first time, I was really able to deal with my unforgiveness."

"Unforgiveness?"

"Remember I told you the other day in the chapel that I had been angry? Angry at Greg?"

He nodded.

"I needed to deal with that. It's one thing to carry around anger and frustration. It's another thing to get rid of it, to give it to God."

She makes it sound so easy.

She glanced at her watch, suddenly coming to life. "Oh no. We've been gone nearly thirty minutes. I really need to get back to Kent. He might be waking up, and I want to be there for him." She rose abruptly, wiping crumbs from her blouse.

Andrew stood to join her. "I should probably go, anyway." They stared at each other in silence for a moment before either spoke.

"Thanks for the roses."

His heart leaped as she reached to squeeze his hand. "You're more than welcome," he said, not wanting to let go.

Chapter 21

On Thanksgiving morning, Andrew visited the hospital once again.

By now, Laura had grown accustomed to seeing him. He had become as familiar as the flowers from friends at church, which lined the windowsill. However, she hadn't expected him today. *Not on Thanksgiving.*

She stood as he entered the room. "Why are you here?"

"I just had to see for myself. Jess told me he was up walking around this morning."

"Jess? You've talked to Jessica?"

Kent groaned loudly, interrupting them.

"Looks like he's awake, all right."

"I can use all the sympathy I can get." Kent struggled to roll over in the bed. "My arm is killing me." He let out a dramatic moan.

"I'll bet," Andrew said with a laugh. "But this too shall pass. I'm Andrew Dougherty," he said, nodding in Kent's direction.

Laura watched for her son's response. "Kent Chapman." There was an extended pause as he looked Andrew over. "So you're the infamous professor. We meet at last. Thanks for the CD, by the way."

"You're welcome. But I see my fame precedes me."

"Oh yeah." Kent nodded. "I'll say."

"I'm not sure how to take that," Andrew said with a laugh. "So I'll just take it as a compliment."

Kent looked up his mother. "He's not half as bad as you said, Mom. He actually looks like a pretty nice guy."

Laura groaned loudly. "Kent. . ."

"So," Andrew said, looking her in the eye, "what has your mom been saying about me?"

Laura's heart hit the floor. She sent a glaring look Kent's way, but it didn't seem to phase him.

"She says you're tough as nails." Kent looked up at her curiously. "What's that other name you use so much, Mom?"

Laura's gaze shifted to the floor. *Slave driver.* But she couldn't force herself to say it. Why did she suddenly feel like such a heel?

"Hateful?" Andrew guessed, looking at them both.

"Nah. That's not it." Kent shook his head. "It was something else. . . ."

"Prideful?"

Laura looked up on that one. He had been prideful, though she had never said so.

"No," Kent said. "I think it was. . ." He lost himself in his thoughts for a moment before answering. "Slave driver. She said you were a slave driver."

Andrew shook his head, then gave Laura a nod. "Can't argue with that one," he said, almost playfully. "Looks like she hit the nail right on the head."

"Well, anyway," Kent said, "you don't seem like such a bad guy. I don't know what she was talking about."

"Thanks, Kent," Andrew said. "I'm glad someone in here sees me for who I am."

Laura groaned aloud at that one.

"So, what are you doing here, anyway?" Kent's question was blunt, but frankly, Laura had been wondering the same thing. Why did Andrew keep showing up day after day? She looked up at him. Just a few short months ago they had felt so differently about each other and now. . .

Now she didn't know what to think. He had become a regular member of the family.

"I'd do the same for any of my students," Andrew said, his eyes looking straight into Laura's. She felt her face flush.

"Sure you would," Kent said.

"Anyway, Jess said to tell you 'hello.'" Andrew reached over to straighten up the flowers in a nearby vase.

"You've seen Jessica today?" Laura asked incredulously. How could that be? Her daughter hadn't been up to the hospital since early morning, and it certainly wasn't a school day.

"Yeah. Well, I took a turkey over to your place before coming here." He spoke the words with a slight tremor in his voice. His focus shifted up to her face.

"You did what?" She couldn't believe it. He had actually been to her house. "How do you know where I live?"

"Oh, well, I. . ."

Ah. Of course. His friend in the registrar's office. *I'll have to remember to report him later.*

"Jess says she wants you to come home and have Thanksgiving dinner with her," Andrew explained. "She misses you."

"I have to stay here. Kent needs me." As much as she would love to go home for a few hours, she simply couldn't. Her conscience wouldn't allow it. How could she leave Kent alone?

"Aw, Mom, I don't need you. I'd feel better if you went home and had Thanksgiving with Grandma and Buck."

"My mother and stepfather are coming over later this afternoon," Laura explained. "In fact, my mom plans to bring a turkey, too, I think."

"Well, there should be plenty for all, then," Andrew said with a laugh. "So why don't you go on home, and I'll stay here with Kent?"

"You would do that? Why?" Why would he make such an offer?

"Sure. Why not?"

She stood for a moment, contemplating his offer. Maybe she could go home for a few hours. Kent didn't seem to mind, and she would love to take a shower and get cleaned up before coming back to the hospital for the night. A Thanksgiving dinner certainly wouldn't hurt either.

"Are. . .are you sure you wouldn't mind?" Laura asked as she looked back and forth between Kent and Andrew.

"I don't mind if he doesn't mind," Andrew said.

"Get out of here, Mom. You deserve a break."

"I won't be gone long. Maybe a couple of hours."

Andrew dropped into a chair. "Take your time. We can play cards, or watch TV, or something."

Laura looked intently at him, hardly recognizing her own voice as she spoke: "Well, maybe you could. . .maybe you could join us for Thanksgiving dinner in about an hour and a half. That is, if Kent doesn't mind staying here alone for a while."

"I told you, Mom, I don't need a sitter. Go home and eat until you're sick. Just bring me some turkey when you're done. And some sweet potatoes."

"You've got a deal." She headed for the door but then turned back, looking at Andrew once again. "An hour and a half?"

"Great," he said, then directed his attention to Kent.

She left the room, headed out into the hallway. It was only when she was about halfway to the car that she realized what she had done. "The professor's coming to my house for dinner."

She thought about him as she made the drive home. She'd grown attached to him over the past few days and had come to rely on his visits. Beyond that, she had learned to enjoy his company, really enjoy it. He was a good man, a kind man.

Is that wrong, Lord? Are my feelings wrong?

She prayed as she drove, trying to come to grips with her changing emotions. By the time she reached the house, she could no longer deny the obvious. "I think I'm falling for this guy." How or why it had happened, she couldn't be sure, but she was sure of one thing. She liked him. A lot.

Laura approached the house with a smile on her face, anxious to see her family. She opened the door and called out, "Is anyone home?"

"We're here, Mom." Jessica exited the kitchen wearing a flour-covered apron.

"What in the world?"

"I'm helping Grandma. We just finished rolling out the homemade biscuits.

I mixed them myself." Jessica threw her arms around her, planting a floury kiss on her cheek.

Laura acquired a noseful of the white, powdery stuff and sneezed. "Uh-huh. I can see that. How long till dinner's ready?"

"A little over an hour," Laura's mother said, popping her head out of the kitchen door. "And don't be late."

"That gives me plenty of time for a shower." She headed for her bedroom. "I feel grungy."

"Well, we certainly can't have that at the dinner table. Go take your shower, Mom. We can smell you from here."

Moments later, Laura relaxed under the steady stream of warm water. It felt like heaven. Every time she closed her eyes, she saw herself, head tightly pressed against Andrew's shoulder in the chapel of the hospital. He certainly hadn't seemed to mind. She hadn't either. In fact, she had enjoyed the moment, more than she would have admitted just a few short days ago.

"This is so crazy," she said, leaning against the shower wall. Laura's mind drifted to the smell of his jacket, a brand of cologne she hadn't recognized. Nice. Not too strong, not too light. It suited him.

"Is my heart ready for this, Lord?" she whispered.

The peace that followed suddenly motivated her. Laura reached for the shampoo bottle, pouring a large dollop of the golden liquid into her palm. "The professor's coming to my house, and I'm standing here as nervous as a schoolkid."

Energized, she flew into action.

⌒

Andrew nervously knocked at the door. Jessica answered with a shocked look on her face.

"I'm here." He offered up a brave smile.

"You're here," she echoed. "Uh, come on in." She hesitantly opened the door. Awkwardness kicked in. "Didn't your mom tell you I was coming?"

"She must have forgotten that, but she's been a little preoccupied lately."

"That's understandable."

"Please come on in. I'm sure she'll be out of the shower soon. We're having dinner in about thirty minutes. Are you hungry?"

"Starved."

"Well, have a seat." She gestured to the couch.

He sat reluctantly.

"You the fellow who brought the turkey?" An elderly man entered the room. Andrew rose, extending his hand.

Jessica made the introductions. "This is my grandfather, Buck Timmons. I'm sure he'll keep you occupied till dinner's done."

"Guess she thinks I've got a big mouth," Buck said, "but that ain't true. I like to talk with the best of 'em, sure, but I know when to quit. What is it you do for a living again, Mr. . . ?"

"Andrew. Andrew Dougherty. I teach at the college. In fact, Jessica and Laura are both in one of my classes."

"Well, I don't know anything about your teaching skills," Buck said as he joined him on the couch, "but you sure know how to pick your turkeys. I just carved your bird, myself."

"I'm glad to finally have an excuse to cook it," Andrew felt the weight lift off of his shoulders. "To be honest, someone gave it to me awhile back, and it's just been taking up room in my freezer. I don't have any family in the area, so I started to think it would stay in there forever."

"No family, eh?" Buck gave him a wink.

"Uh, no, sir."

The elderly man dove headlong into a discussion about the merits of family. Andrew sat quietly, listening as he rambled on and on about every conceivable thing. Their conversation transitioned from families to the battles Buck fought in the Korean War. "You fight in 'Nam, boy?"

"No," Andrew said. "I was just a kid."

"Probably for the best. I tell ya, fighting for your country can be a blessing and a curse all at the same time. Wait. Didn't I hear someone say you taught history?"

"Yes, I teach American History," Andrew said, smiling.

"Well then, if anyone knows your battles, you do."

The older man transitioned into another story about his journey across the Pacific on a battleship as Andrew politely listened. He found himself slightly distracted by the photos of Laura and her husband on the wall across the room. Another smaller snapshot of the whole family sat on the end table next to him. Without thinking, he reached to pick it up and ran his finger over Laura's brown hair.

"That Laura. . . ," Buck exclaimed. "She's a pretty filly, ain't she? I always said she was the spittin' image of her mother. They both just get prettier every day."

Andrew nodded, not sure how to answer. He found himself captivated by the face next to Laura's. This had to be her husband. He had been a handsome man—fair-skinned, with auburn hair and an inviting smile. His eyes glowed with a warmth that spoke of friendship.

"Greg was a great man. Did you ever meet him?"

Andrew shook his head, suddenly apprehensive.

"A great man," Buck repeated with a sigh. "Just about the best father a kid could ever have. And so good to Laura. They were still very much in love, just like young kids. It like to broke her heart when he passed, it really did."

Andrew set the picture back down, not wanting to hear anymore. Suddenly he felt like a stranger in this place, a man who didn't belong. He could never fill the shoes of the man in this picture. Why would he even try to? He stood suddenly, knowing he must leave. He had to back out of this thing before it was too late, before. . .

Laura stuck her head out of the bedroom door, shouting, "Jessica, could you get my jeans out of the dryer?" She had tossed on an old terry-cloth robe and wore a towel around her head but didn't figure her mother or Buck would mind. "Jess?" No answer. Laura stepped out into the living room, hollering a little louder. "Jess!"

"Laura?" She looked up at the sound of Buck's voice to find herself face-to-face with Andrew Dougherty.

"Oh, my goodness!" She clutched at her robe. "I'm—I'm so sorry. I didn't know you were here. You're early." For a moment, Laura felt a familiar frustration rise up within her. Then, just as suddenly, it was replaced with an odd sense of satisfaction that he had come. *I can't let him see me like this.* She backed toward the bedroom.

"Kent fell asleep," Andrew explained, "and the nurse said she didn't see any point in my staying. His medication should keep him out like a light for a couple of hours—at least, that's what she said. I just came on over. I'm sorry. I should probably go."

But I don't want you to. She gave him an imploring look. "No, please don't go. If you'll excuse me, I'll just be a minute." She backed into the bedroom, overcome with embarrassment. "Jess!" she called once more, peeking her head out of the door. She watched as Jessica raced across the living room, a pair of jeans in her hand.

"I'm coming, Mom. I'm coming." She practically knocked the professor down as she passed by him. She entered the bedroom, closing the door behind her.

Laura trembled as she pulled the towel off of her hair. "Help me, Jess," she whispered as she flipped on the blow-dryer and ran a brush through her hair.

"What's wrong with you, Mom? What's got you so shook up?" Jess teased.

"Nothing. Just help me." Laura fought with her brush until her hair was nearly dry. She grabbed her jeans, struggling to slide into them. Her hands shook so hard, she could barely get them up.

"Mom. . ."

"I don't have time, Jess."

"Mom, you're putting your jeans on backwards."

"Oh." She turned them around and tried again.

"Much better," Jessica said. "What'll you wear with them?"

"Get my peach sweater out of the closet." Laura put on a pair of earrings.

"You mean your 'special occasion' peach sweater?"

"It's Thanksgiving, Jessica. That's a special occasion, isn't it?" Her hands still trembled as she fought to put her earrings in.

"What's wrong with you, Mom? You're acting like a giddy schoolgirl with a crush."

"That's crazy." Laura tried to avoid looking her daughter in the eye. Why was it so hard to admit she actually liked this man? *I do like him, very much. More than I could admit to Jess or anyone else.*

She quickly applied some lipstick and blush, then ran the brush through her hair one last time. "Do I look okay?" she asked, turning for Jess's approval.

"You look great, Mom. Now get out there and knock him dead." Jessica clapped her hand over her mouth, realizing what she had said. "I'm so sorry. I didn't mean. . ."

Laura grinned a silly grin. "It's okay. It's about time we got back to joking around here. You just be yourself, and everything will be fine."

⁓

Andrew tried to compose himself as Laura entered the room. Keeping his emotions in check proved to be very difficult. Her hair was still slightly damp, but it carried the familiar aroma of flowers. She wore the same sweater she had worn at the game—the one he remembered so well. She completely took his breath away.

"I hope you didn't mind waiting." Laura looked as nervous as he felt. "I just had to change before going back up to the hospital. You understand."

Of course he understood. He would have understood if she had decided to paper and paint the living room before going back.

"Everything smells great, Mom." Laura gave her mother a hug. "Professor Dougherty, have you met my mother, Violet Timmons?"

"Just call me Vi," the older woman responded.

He shook Violet's hand firmly and smiled, knowing from her easygoing smile she would be easy to like.

"Well, why don't we all go on into the dining room," Vi said, leading the way, "before everything gets cold."

⁓

Laura watched Andrew carefully as he made his way into the dining room. Buck pulled out the seat that had always been Greg's and gestured for Andrew to sit down. Immediately, Laura's heart began to twist inside her. *Greg's chair. No one else should sit there. No one. Not yet, anyway.* She reluctantly sat across from Andrew, unable to focus.

"Let's pray, shall we?" Buck said with a smile as he looked around the table.

Laura glanced in Andrew's direction, trying to read his reaction. How would he feel about this? Would he be offended, or. . . She was relieved to see that he bowed his head reverently and closed his eyes. She did the same. Buck began to pray a deep, genuine prayer, thanking God for Kent's recovery and for the food provided. He added a special prayer of thanks for Andrew's gift of the turkey, but

Laura barely heard it. Her eyes were once again fixed on Greg's chair.

Heads lifted, and the food began to make its way around the table. Everyone chatted and laughed as if nothing in the world could be wrong. But something felt wrong, very wrong.

"Laura, honey, would you pass the potatoes?" She numbly passed them to her mother, trying to focus.

"I'll have the dressing, Laura," Buck said, reaching out for it. She nodded but never touched it, her focus drifting once again to the chair.

"Mom, are you okay?" Jessica asked, looking at her curiously.

"Oh. Yeah, sure." *I'm not.* A war had suddenly and inexplicably risen up inside of her. There was no logical reason why she should feel this sudden anger, but she couldn't seem to stop it.

"I'll take a roll," Andrew said, looking directly at her with a smile. She picked up the basket, clutching it tightly. She couldn't seem to release it.

"Mom?" Jessica gazed at her with a worried expression.

"Oh, I—" She passed the rolls without further explanation, turning her attention to her own plate. She could do this. She wouldn't humiliate herself or anyone else. Not today, not when everything was so perfect. She looked up again, and a very clear picture of Greg seated in the chair greeted her. Suddenly, Laura could take it no more. "I—I have to get out of here," she said, standing.

"What do you mean?" her mother asked.

"I—I have to get back to the hospital. I'm sure you all understand. Kent needs me."

Andrew stood immediately. "Maybe I should leave. It's getting late, anyway."

"No, please don't go, Mr. Dougherty," Buck said. "You're our guest. You just sit right down and eat."

"Really," Laura said, trying not to look at him. "Just because I'm leaving doesn't mean you have to." She practically ran to the front door, throwing it open. "If anyone needs me, I'll be at the hospital."

She stepped outside into the cool autumn air and leaned back against the house, where her tears flowed freely.

⌒

Andrew stood up from the table, excusing himself. He needed to catch up with Laura before she left. He had so much to say to her. She couldn't just slip away— not this time. He had lost her this way before, and he wasn't about to let it happen again.

He opened the front door, expecting to find her in her car, but she was propped up against the side of the house, sobbing.

"Laura?"

She looked at him fearfully. "I'm—I'm sorry. I have to go."

He reached out to take her arm, but she eluded him. "Laura, please wait.

I need to talk to you."

"I can't talk to you right now, Andrew." She moved away from him.

"I just want to tell you something. Please." He felt like his heart would burst if he didn't say it.

"Can't it wait?" she asked impatiently.

"No, it can't. I can't." His ears were ringing now. *Just get through this.*

"What's so important?" She took a few steps toward her car, obviously trying to avoid him. He followed her closely.

"You remember that conversation we had in the hospital cafeteria yesterday?" he asked breathlessly. "Something really, I don't know. . .amazing happened to me when I got home last night. For the first time in years, I found myself able to pray."

She looked up at him with tears in her eyes. "Really?"

"Yes. I asked God to forgive me for being so angry with Him. That happened because of you, Laura." He reached to take her hand. She let him hold it for a moment, then pulled away. "Don't you see? I would never have had the courage to face the truth if it hadn't been for you."

"The truth. . . ," she stammered. "It's the truth that's killing me right now. The truth of how I felt about Greg. The truth about how scared I am when I see someone else sitting in his chair."

"So that's what it is."

"Yes." Tears filled her beautiful eyes again.

Andrew reached out to brush them away, but she pushed his hand away. "Can't we at least talk about this?" he implored. "Please?"

"Maybe someday," she said as she pulled the car door open.

"When?"

"I don't know," she spoke through the emotion. "I just can't right now. I can't." She jumped into her car and sped away, leaving his heart in a state of chaos. With his head hanging, Andrew climbed into his car and drove away.

Chapter 22

Mom, it's been two weeks, and you haven't even spoken a word to him. That's not fair."

Laura did her best to ignore her daughter. Frustration overwhelmed her these days. She seemed to always be in a bad mood at home. She had thrown herself into her work with a vengeance. "I don't expect you to understand, Jessica," she said finally. "I'm just confused, that's all. I need time. Space."

"Confused about him?"

"Him who?"

"You know who, Mom. The professor. The one you've been avoiding for the last two weeks."

"I haven't been avoiding him," Laura argued. "I've been going to class, haven't I?"

"Yes, but you haven't said a word to him," Jessica commented. "Everyone's noticed. The whole class is talking about it."

"The whole class?"

"Yes."

"What are they saying?"

"They're just wondering what's up. The kids loved the bickering that went on between the two of you, and now it's just nothing but silence. It's boring. You're boring."

"Thanks a lot."

"No, I mean it, Mom. You've got to snap out of this. Whatever he's done, you need to forgive him. Remember, we talked about that. Forgiveness is everything."

"It's nothing he's done, Jessica. That's the problem."

"What do you mean?"

"I mean. . . ," Laura hesitated. "I mean, he's not your father. He never will be. There will never be another man like your dad." Surely Jessica would understand.

Her daughter looked her squarely in the eye. "You're right, Mom. He's not Daddy. But did you ever consider the fact that God might be bringing you something—someone—completely different?"

"He's different, all right." Laura smiled.

"Maybe you shouldn't be looking for someone like Daddy at all. Maybe you should just be open to any man God might bring into your life, no matter how different he is."

"What?" Laura was stunned at her daughter's tenacity.

"No one can ever take Daddy's place—that's true. But you don't have to worry that we'll forget him, Mom. He's always here, in my heart." Jessica's voice trembled with emotion as she continued. "But you've got things all confused where the professor's concerned. Maybe all he needs to do is just be himself."

"You're right, Jess. I know you are," Laura said softly.

But what could she do? There were too many bridges crossed, too many things left undone.

Three weeks and counting. Andrew paced around his classroom, tormented by the struggle that ensued in his heart and his head. His head convinced him he should give up—not pursue any type of relationship with Laura Chapman, friendship or otherwise. His heart cried out for more, much more. As the semester came to a close, he faced an inevitable deadline. Grades for American History had just been averaged. Laura's good, solid A had been earned without any assistance from him. She had aced his class. Not many people could boast of that.

Of course, it might not have happened if Dick DeHart hadn't gotten involved. Andrew's skin began to crawl. The idea of any other man looking at Laura—his Laura—made him so angry, he could hardly see straight. *But she's not my Laura. She doesn't want to be with me. She made that abundantly clear on Thanksgiving.* It had started. . .when had it started, again? *Ah yes. When I sat in that chair.* A light tap on the door distracted him. He looked up, shocked to see Jessica standing there with a concerned look on her face.

"Professor Dougherty," she said hesitantly. "Can I come in?"

"Sure, Jess. What's up?"

She looked a little nervous. "I just wanted to talk to you. Of course, my mom would kill me if she knew I came."

"What do you mean?"

"I mean," she said, "I think you need to know that she's, she's just. . ."

"Just what?" He waited anxiously to hear the rest of the sentence.

"Scared," Jessica said finally. "She's scared to death."

He dropped into a chair, his forehead breaking out in a sweat.

"You don't look like you're in much better shape than she is," Jessica said with a laugh. "This is really pathetic."

"I'm not very good at this."

"I'll say. That's why I'm here to help you."

"Help me?" *She's just a kid. How can she help me?*

"Yep. My mom's at the Bookstop, and I want you to go there to see her."

"She's back at work?"

"Has been for a week and a half. Kent's back in school and doing great," she explained.

"That's good."

"Yeah. Well, anyway, she's back at work; but her mind isn't on her work, I'll tell you that much."

"It's not?"

"No, it's not."

"If you don't mind my asking—" he stammered.

"She can't stop thinking about you," Jessica explained. "I know because she talks about you all of the time. She's scared of how she feels, that's all."

"I can relate to that." Andrew looked at the ground. "I'm pretty, well, I mean—I'm a little scared, too."

"You two are like a couple of kids," Jessica said finally. "But don't you worry. Just leave everything up to me."

Andrew's heart beat so fast, he could barely breathe. "Are you sure about this?"

"More than sure," Jessica said.

He suddenly knew what he had to do. He would go to her. Somehow, someway he would communicate his love for her in a way that wouldn't threaten the memory of her husband. He could do that. With the Lord's help, he could do that.

"Can I ask you a personal question?" Jessica looked him in the eye.

"Sure. Why not?" Everything he had ever kept hidden had already come out over the past few days.

"Do you pray, Professor Dougherty?"

He paused before answering. "If you had asked me that question a few weeks ago, I would have answered so differently. But I do pray, Jessica. Believe it or not, I've been spending a lot of time in prayer over the past few weeks." He had felt years of coldness toward the Lord melt away in the process.

"Well then, if you want to see those prayers answered, get on over there to the bookstore and tell my mom how you feel. If she's half the woman I know she is, she won't break your heart. At least, I don't think she will."

The words "at least" nearly drove a stake through Andrew's fragile heart, and yet they propelled him to his feet. "I'll do it," he said, suddenly energized. "It may seem crazy, but I'll do the impossible."

"Professor," Jessica called out to him as he bolted through the door. He turned and looked at her one last time.

"Yes?"

" 'With God all things are possible.' "

" 'With God all things are possible.' " He repeated the words, feeling the smile return to his face. "Thanks, Jessica. Thanks for everything."

"Hey," she hollered, as he sprinted down the hallway toward the parking lot. "Does this mean I get an A in your class?"

Andrew didn't answer. After all, he didn't want to spoil what had suddenly become a perfect moment.

Laura passed through the inspirational section of the bookstore, taking another look at the book that had long captivated her attentions: *Put Your Troubles in the Blender and Give Them a Spin*. She stood in silence, thumbing through the book. Funny in some places, it struck a serious nerve in others. Many of the situations in the book were not unlike her own. Somehow this author, also a woman, had triumphed over her tragedies and turned them into victories using humor.

"It should be so simple," Laura mumbled as she placed the book on the shelf. "So, what do you think, Madeline?" She turned to look at her friend. "Do you think I should or I shouldn't?"

"Should or shouldn't what?" the woman asked.

"Should I or shouldn't I..." Laura's heart beat so hard, it took her breath away. It had been many, many years since talking about a man had made her this nervous. "Take a chance," Laura stammered finally. "With the professor." She looked nervously at Madeline. What she found there was warmth and understanding.

"I've been hoping for quite some time that you would find someone."

"Really?"

"Yep."

"I wasn't even praying for this," Laura said with a sigh.

"Don't you see?" Madeline interjected. "That's exactly what makes it so special. God knew what you needed and wanted even before you did. Besides, it's about time you had a fella in your life. To be honest, I had hoped my brother would be the one, but..."

"I'm so sorry, Madeline, but Dick just wasn't my type." She said the words firmly. Perhaps a little too firmly.

"I know. He's a Romeo, that's for sure," Madeline responded. "It may make you feel better to know he's already dating someone from the university."

"Good grief." Somehow knowing that did make her feel a little better.

"So do you think I should go up to the school and see Andrew?" Laura asked. "He's probably still there. I think so, anyway."

"I wouldn't waste another minute. You get in that car of yours and make haste all the way down to the college. Go. Don't worry about the shop. I'm here."

"Are you sure?" Laura's heart raced, making it difficult to breathe.

"Completely sure," Madeline said. "Get out of here."

Laura sprinted to the door. "See you later, Madeline." She raced toward the car, turning the key in the ignition. *I can't believe I'm doing this! I'm actually going to tell him how I feel.*

Andrew drove like a maniac along the interstate, fighting traffic all the way. "Come on...," he grumbled at the cars in front of him. They crawled along, ignoring his pleas. "Just a couple of miles. It's not that far." He had already decided what he would say. He would tell her exactly what he felt, what his intentions were. If she rejected him this time, he would give up. Plain and simple. Andrew reached the exit for Tully, pulling off onto the feeder road. In just a couple of minutes he would see her.

He would tell her.

Chapter 23

Is Laura here?" Andrew asked, his eyes bearing down on Madeline's.

"Oh, dear. Oh, dear," she said, looking as nervous as a cat. "I'm so sorry."

"She's not here? Where did she go?"

"Well, actually, she went to the college to try to find you," Madeline explained.

"To find me? Why?" *This is too confusing.*

"She wanted to...," Madeline stammered. "She was going to... It's like this..."

"Could you please just say it?" Andrew hollered, feeling his face go hot.

Madeline stood frozen, saying nothing.

"Fine," he said, turning toward the door. "You say she's at the school? I'm going back to the school." Andrew groaned loudly as he headed back to his car.

~

Laura paced back and forth in the empty classroom, her heart feeling as if it would break.

"Where is he?" The door stood wide open. He never left it open unless he happened to be nearby, but he didn't appear to be anywhere.

She plopped down onto the edge of his desk, deep in thought. Her eyes traveled the familiar room, drinking in the things that Andrew loved. American history. She had somehow managed to make it through his course with flying colors, with or without assistance from Dick DeHart. If nothing else, she could be very proud of that.

But something else captivated her mind, something that wouldn't rest. She had to talk to Andrew, had to tell him how she felt. She did have feelings for him, she had to admit—strong feelings. Her conversation with Jessica had convinced her of that. God had arranged all of this. But she had treated Andrew so badly on Thanksgiving. Would he forgive her?

Laura's thoughts shifted, wandering back to the day when she had walked in on him in this very room—a day when a dark-haired woman sat in the very spot she found herself. Was it possible? Was Andrew involved with her, the girl from the cafeteria? They had been seen together on more than one occasion, deep in conversation.

And yet Andrew had swept her into his arms with such tenderness that day in the chapel. The look in his eyes spoke of more than friendship.

Laura stood and walked across the room toward the door. She gave the walls one last glance as she left, running her finger across the Declaration of

123

Independence. She pulled the door shut behind her, realizing it could very well be the last time she would ever step inside this room.

Andrew raced back out to his car, immediately climbing inside. "Please be there," he whispered as he turned the key in the ignition. So many unanswered questions lingered in his mind. *Why did she go back to the school? Is it possible. . . ?*

Moments later, he entered the interstate, accelerating much faster than usual up the entrance ramp. He raced along, honking his horn at any driver who had the nerve to drive the speed limit. Finally he arrived at the school. Anxiously, he turned into the parking lot.

He raced from the car to the history classroom. *Please be here.* He made his way up the hallway, quickly opening the door to his classroom. *Empty.* Andrew made his way to his desk, dropping into the chair. He buried his head in his hands. "This is too much. I can't do this anymore."

"Well, what happened?" Jessica appeared at the door.

"She wasn't there. Madeline said she was on her way here. Have you seen her?"

"Nope. I've been waiting in the cafeteria with my nose buried in a book. I had a feeling you'd come back here afterward."

He sighed deeply. "This is such a mess."

Jessica plopped down in a chair, staring up at him. "I'm really sorry about all of this."

"It's okay. I should probably just go home and sleep it off. Maybe I can try again tomorrow."

"Well," Jessica said, "I have this one little problem."

"What?"

"I need a ride home. You don't really mind, do you?"

Mind? Of course he didn't mind. He lived for days like this. "Come on," he said, reaching for his keys once again. "Let's get out of here."

Laura climbed into the shower, talking to herself. "What's wrong with me?" she mumbled. She allowed the water to run over her hair to cool her down. "Andrew Dougherty probably thinks I'm the biggest flake on the planet."

She pulled out her favorite shampoo, working it into lather. Scrubbing her head vigorously, she continued the conversation with herself. "I'm crazy to think I need a guy in my life. I don't need anyone. I don't."

She leaned against the shower wall, tears cascading down her face. Her heart began to beat so hard, she could barely breathe.

"I may not need him," she whispered to herself. "But I love him."

She stepped out of the shower, agitated. "Of course he wasn't at the school," she grumbled. "Why should he be at the school just because he teaches there?" She wrapped herself in her bathrobe, still upset. "Where else would he be? He probably doesn't want to talk to me, anyway."

Frustrated, she pulled a towel up around her wet hair and looked in the mirror. "It's not like I'm pretty," she said, staring at her reflection. "I'm not even close to pretty." What Greg had seen in her, she had never understood. A solemn reflection met her gaze—an ever-present reminder of the fact that she was average, ordinary.

Laura reached up into the medicine chest and pulled out a container. "Not that this will do much good." She smeared the gooey mask all over her face. When she finished, the only things left visible were her mouth and eyes. "Anyway, it's not like he's such a great catch," she reasoned with herself. "He doesn't even know how to dress. His clothes are wrinkled, and his ties are older than my children. He's as hopeless as I am."

Laura made her way across the bedroom, still talking to herself. Somehow, it made her feel better. "And his hair," she continued. "It wouldn't hurt the man to use some hair gel. It wouldn't wound his ego that much, would it?"

Frustrated, she pulled the bedroom door open, feeling the mask begin to harden. A cup of hot chocolate would make everything better. It always did.

"Men," she exclaimed, stepping out into the living room. "They don't know what they're missing, anyway."

"Mom?"

"Yeah?" She didn't even look up, still lost in her private conversation.

"Uh, Mom?"

"What, Jessica?" she asked, exasperated.

"I just thought you might want to know we have company."

Laura turned abruptly, finding herself face-to-face with Professor Andrew Dougherty. Her heart leaped into her throat. Suddenly she wasn't sure whether to throw her arms around him or to turn and run.

⁓

Andrew took one look at Laura and started laughing. He couldn't seem to control himself. Whether the laughter came from the sheer relief of finding her at last, or the fact that her face was covered in the thick green mask, he couldn't be sure. How comical, yet how endearing. He had never seen anything like it on any woman, let alone the one he now found himself helplessly, hopelessly in love with. "Laura?" It was more question than statement.

She instinctively put her hands up over her face, clearly embarrassed. "Oh, no... Not now. Not like this!"

"Please don't hide your face," he said, reaching for her hands. "It's beautiful." His hands trembled uncontrollably as they clutched hers.

"You're making fun of me," she pouted, backing toward the bedroom.

Andrew's heart pounded loudly in his ears, which were heating up more with each passing moment. He could hardly breathe, let alone think or speak like

125

a rational man. "Laura, the last thing on earth I want to do is make fun of you. I think you're beautiful—green face and all."

"You do?"

"I do." He spoke the words almost prophetically. There would be no more broken hearts in his world. He had waited for Laura Chapman all of his life, and she was well worth the wait.

She continued to take tiny, nervous steps backward until she ran smack-dab into the living room wall. Jessica stood off to one side of the room, giggling helplessly.

Kent stuck his head in from the kitchen, his jaw dropping. "Mom?" He looked more than a little surprised.

"Kent," Andrew said, turning toward him, "your mother and I are having a little conversation. You don't mind, do you?"

"Not a bit," Kent said, heading back into the kitchen.

"Jessica," Andrew said firmly, turning to look at her. "I think your brother needs your help in the kitchen." He gave her a look that could not be misunderstood.

"Whatever you say," Jessica agreed. "You're the teacher."

Laura looked up into the sparkling eyes of this man who had captivated her. How clear everything suddenly seemed.

"I feel like I've known you forever, not just a few months," he said as he reached to touch her crusty cheek.

Months? It seemed she had always known Andrew, always felt drawn to him as she did now. It was true that he could never take Greg's place. But, then again, maybe he wasn't supposed to. Maybe, like Jessica said, he only needed to be himself.

But how could she begin to break through the layers of unspoken words that had traveled between them over the last several weeks? Laura had rehearsed the prepared speech in her head so many times. She would tell him how she felt, what her heart had been longing to say. And yet, no words seemed to come at all. She found herself completely and utterly speechless. Part of that, she had to admit, came from the fact that the mud mask had completely hardened, leaving her with little or no facial movement.

"Ms. Chapman," Andrew said, moving closer to her. She looked up into his eyes. They were kind eyes, loving eyes. They seemed to reach into the very depths of her soul and touch a spot that had not been touched for a long, long time. For the first time, she saw herself in their reflection. It was wonderful, amazing.

"Yes, Professor Dougherty?" She fought to form words through tightened lips. The "professor" part was just for emphasis, but it seemed to work like a charm. A grin spread across his face. *I love this man. I love him!* She struggled to catch her breath with the reality of the thought.

"Your very wise daughter asked me today if I was a praying man."

"What did you tell her?" Laura spoke slowly, forcing the words.

"I told her that I was," he answered. "I've taken to praying quite a bit these past three weeks."

"You have?" She tried to smile, but her cheeks refused to cooperate.

"I have, and I can say I'm a firm believer in the power of prayer." A look of determination filled his eyes—a fiery look.

"Really? Is that what you came to tell me?" she asked, half-teasing.

"I came to tell you that you aced my class." He moved closer still.

"I did?" She asked breathlessly, cradling her head in his hand. "I got an A?"

"You got an A," he said, coming so close that her heart began to race. "But that's not the only reason I came."

"It isn't?" Her knees suddenly grew weak, and she felt a little wobbly. The only thing that kept her standing was the wall itself, which she had firmly pressed herself up against.

"Nope," he said, slipping both arms around her neck and pulling her to himself. How right it felt to be in his arms, how totally and perfectly right. "I came to tell you, Ms. Chapman, that, no matter how many students I have, you're absolutely in a class of your own." His breath lingered warm against her lips.

She looked up at him, wanting like crazy to smile, but unable to with her face frozen in position by the mask. "Does that make me the teacher's pet?" she whispered, feeling her heart about to break wide open with the joy that consumed it.

Andrew never took the time to answer. His lips spoke more than words could ever say.

Chapter 24

Laura glanced in the full-length mirror, then turned to look at Madeline. "What do you think?" she asked, as she fussed with her hair.

"What do I think? What do I think?" Madeline's face lit into a broad smile. "I think you're the prettiest bride I've ever seen."

"Exaggeration doesn't suit you," Laura said with a sigh, "but I appreciate the effort."

"I wasn't exaggerating, thank you very much," Madeline said with a smirk. "I meant every word."

After another glance in the mirror, Laura attempted to tame a loose hair, but her trembling hands wouldn't allow it.

"Need help with that?" Madeline gave her a sympathetic look.

"Y–yes." Laura chuckled nervously, then looked in the direction of the door as she heard a knock.

"Mom, are you almost ready?" Jessica's voice rang out.

"Yes, come on in." Laura looked up as her daughter entered the tiny room the church secretary had designated the "Bride's Chambers."

Jessica took one look at her and her eyes filled with tears. "Mom, I always pictured this the other way around. You would be helping *me* dress for *my* wedding. *I'd* be the one in the wedding dress."

"It's not exactly a wedding dress." Laura twirled around to show off the ivory lace dress she had selected for this special day.

"It's a wedding dress all right," Jessica said. "And Andrew's eyes are going to pop when he sees you in it."

"You think?" Laura felt her cheeks flush.

"I think."

Another knock on the door interrupted their conversation. Laura's mother popped her head in the door and began to cry as soon as she saw her daughter. She stepped inside the tiny room and reached inside her purse for a tissue. After just a few seconds, she managed a few words. "I don't think I cried this much at your first wedding." Immediately she clamped a hand over her mouth, as if she'd said something wrong.

Laura took a couple of steps in her direction and offered up a reassuring nod. "It's okay, Mom. I don't mind. And you're right. . .you didn't cry this much at my first wedding."

"I'm just so happy for you, is all," her mother said as she wiped her eyes. "We all are."

Jessica and Madeline nodded their agreement, and all of the women entered into a group hug. For a minute, Laura couldn't speak. She thought about all of the pain she'd felt for so long, the fear. How loneliness had gripped her. And now... why, now she could practically soar, she felt so happy. *You've resurrected me, Lord. You've done the impossible.*

Just then, another knock sounded at the door. "Is it okay to come in?" Kent's voice sounded muffled from the other side.

"Come in," Laura called.

When Kent entered the room in his tuxedo, everyone gasped.

"You're a...a...a man!" His grandmother swept him into her arms.

"A man who reminds me a lot of his father." Laura couldn't help but make the observation. Standing there in his tuxedo, Kent looked for all the world like Greg. A very young Greg, of course, but what a likeness!

"Hey, this day is supposed to be about you." Kent took his mother's hand and gave it a squeeze. "And I happen to know that Andrew is having a fit waiting for you."

"He is?" Laura's cheeks warmed at the thought of it.

"He is." Kent extended his arm. "So let's get this show on the road. The guests are all seated."

Laura drew in a deep breath.

"You can do this, Mom," Jessica whispered. "You'll be just fine."

They left the tiny dressing room together and headed out into the foyer of the church, where they were met by Buck, who gave a little whistle. Even from here, Laura could hear music playing from inside the sanctuary.

Madeline switched into wedding planning gear and started giving instructions. "Okay, mother of the bride, you're first."

Laura watched with a smile as Buck took her mother by the arm and ushered her through the doors into the sanctuary.

The music changed, signaling time for the bridesmaids to enter. Madeline led the way, followed by Jessica.

"Looks like it's just you and me, Mom." Kent gave her a wink, and her heart flip-flopped.

"R–right." She attempted to swallow the lump in her throat, but found it difficult.

As the music for the bridal march filled the auditorium, Kent took her by the arm and they began the long walk down the aisle. Even from here, she could see the tears in Andrew's eyes and noticed the tremor in his hands. *Thank goodness! He's as nervous as I am!*

Maybe nervous wasn't the right word. Overwhelmed? Overjoyed? Yes, that was surely it. She felt overjoyed. So much joy spilled over, there seemed to be no place to contain it.

After what felt like the longest walk in history, Laura reached her husband-to-be. The pastor cleared his throat, then posed the familiar question: "Who gives this woman to be wed to this man?"

Kent's voice shook as he responded, "My sister and I do."

At this point, Kent moved to the front to join Andrew as his best man.

Everything after that was a blur. A joyous, nerve-wracking, blissful blur. Vows. A beautiful solo, sung by Jessica. Exchanging of rings. The kiss. . .

Ah, the kiss! In that moment, as heaven and earth seemed to touch, Laura Chapman. . .no, Laura *Dougherty*. . .found herself wrapped in the arms of the man who would walk with her—arm in arm—through the next season of her life.

Funny. Knowing that almost made all of those ridiculous pop quizzes worthwhile.

Epilogue

Laura sat alongside her fellow students, anxiously waiting her turn. Any moment now, she would hear her name. She glanced across the large auditorium to where her family sat in the stands. Kent waved frantically, his new girlfriend, Bridget, joining in. They had only been dating a few weeks, but Laura loved her like a daughter. She was a strong Christian and had made quite an impact in Kent's life. In fact, just this morning Laura had heard the two of them discussing plans to work in the youth ministry at church. *God is so good.*

Her eyes traveled to her mom and Jessica, who sat at their right. As usual, Buck was nearby, a broad grin on his face. They smiled and waved, and Laura's heart began to race in anticipation of what was about to take place.

She glanced to and fro, looking for Andrew. *Ah. There he is, seated just behind them, with a fistful of yellow roses. I'm so glad he's here. He's my biggest fan.* She grinned at them all, waving madly. He blew her a kiss in response. She pretended to catch it, nearly knocking the cap off of the boy sitting next to her.

"So sorry."

"No problem."

Laura turned her attention back to the speaker at the podium, trying to concentrate. He spoke of hope, of potential, of possibilities. They were words she fully understood. In fact, she appreciated them now more than ever.

Laura's two years at Wainesworth Junior College had paid off and then some. With her associate's degree in hand, she had transferred to the university a couple of years back. She would cross the stage to accept her bachelor's degree in Business Management any moment now.

The whole thing had been her husband's idea, really. Laura looked up at Andrew once again, a smile instinctively spreading across her face. His sport jacket and tie were terribly mismatched, and his rumpled hair desperately needed combing. Not much had changed over the years.

She hoped it never would.

A Chorus
of One

Dedication

This melodic tale is dedicated to my very "vocal" daughters—
Randi, Courtney Rae, Megan, and Courtney Elizabeth.
(Yes, I really have two daughters named Courtney!)
The Lord has truly gifted each of you for His purpose,
and I'm thrilled to watch you step into the roles to which you have been called.
Recognizing and developing your God-given artistic gifts
has positioned you to discover your "use-ability" within the body of Christ.
Remember—as long as you continue to keep your hand in His,
you will never be "A Chorus of One."

Chapter 1

"That's it! That's the one." Jessica Chapman let out a squeal of triumph as her gaze fell on the most beautiful wedding invitation imaginable.

Her fiancé, Nathan Fisher, looked up from the book of samples, clearly stunned. "The beige one?"

"It's not beige, Nathan. See?" She pointed. "It's cream linen." Jessica spoke with dramatic flair then leaned down for a closer look. "Besides, there's a lot of color in this exquisite lettering. Don't you just love all of the detail?"

"I guess." He shrugged.

"But you know what I love most about it?" She reached down to run her finger across the embossed print. "The European design reminds me of *La Bohème*."

"Let me guess—an opera, right?"

"Not just an opera." Jessica's voice swelled with excitement. "It's an amazing love story about a young woman who dies in the arms of the man she loves. Tragic, really." Tears sprang to her eyes, and she quickly brushed them away so that Nathan wouldn't poke fun at her.

"Uh-oh. Here we go again."

Jessica pulled her hands to her chest and sighed deeply. Could she help it if she loved the theatrical?

"The way things are going, we might as well sing this whole wedding." Nathan looked up with a playful smile. "That's what I'd call tragic."

"Very funny." She jabbed him in the ribs, and he doubled over, pretending to be in pain. Nathan had often accused her of turning this wedding into a production, but that's what the most special day of your life should be, after all. Surely he would grow to understand her sense of style, even appreciate it.

"Problem is," he continued, "I'm tone-deaf, as you well know. So singing our vows is out of the question. Unless you give me a few voice lessons between now and then."

"I'm not sure lessons would do much good, all things considered."

"Oh, you're a laugh a minute."

"But really." She turned back to the book. "What do you think of this invitation? I just love the fancy print." She ran her finger across the raised letters with their curly edges. "It looks so elegant. And see how reasonably priced they are? They're definitely within our budget."

"If that's what you want, I'm fine with it." He turned another page. "But before we make a final decision, what about this one? I really like it." He pointed to a stark white invitation with crisp, gold lettering.

Nathan clearly didn't relate to her overall plan for a muted Mediterranean theme. Otherwise, he would never have given this one a glance. "It's okay. Not really what I had in mind, but if you like it. . ."

"We both need to like it." He sighed. "I just wonder if we're ever going to agree on anything."

He gazed into her eyes with a woeful expression, and Jessica's heart melted immediately. "We both agree that we're in love." She reached up to plant tiny kisses on his cheek. "And we agree that it's the happily-ever-after kind. True?"

He slipped his arm around her shoulder and gave her a tight squeeze. "True. But if we can't even pick out a simple wedding invitation, I hate to think of the trouble we'll have naming our children someday."

"Oh, that won't be a problem." She chuckled. "If we ever have a son, we'll call him Jim-Bo or Billy-Bob."

"Naturally."

"And if we're blessed with a daughter, we'll name her—"

"Carmen Aida Don Giovanni," he said with a wicked grin. "That's a musical name, right?"

"Bravo!" Jess stuck out her hand for a high five. "See? We agreed on something. And you obviously know more about opera than you've been letting on."

He shrugged. "Another thing I think we would agree on is that our daughter had better have your looks and not mine."

"Don't be silly. If she looks like you, she'll be—"

"Tall? Skinny?" He lifted his hands in mock despair.

Jess stood back and gave him a careful look. Nathan was tall, nearly six feet, and a little on the thin side. Years of study had kept him off the basketball court and in the classroom, but she felt no need to complain. He might not have an athletic build, but he looked just right to her, and she wouldn't argue a bit if their children shared his looks. His sandy, lopsided curls always kept her entertained, especially when he attempted to force them into place. As if that were possible.

Nathan brushed his lips against her cheek. "No, she'd better look like you. Those freckles, that red hair. . ."

"Auburn, thank you." Jess groaned. If anything, she felt plain, ordinary—and the hair color didn't help anything. She had always longed for rich, dark hair or even shocking blond, but she'd been stuck with a lackluster shade of red-orange instead.

"Auburn," he echoed, then turned his attention to the book of samples once again. "Now, if we can just get these invitations ordered, we'll be one step closer to the big day."

The big day.

Jess and Nathan's wedding wouldn't take place until mid-May, eight long months from now, but Nathan's classes at the university would begin next Monday. Finishing up his master's degree in financial management would take his undivided attention, and wedding plans would have to take a backseat. That's why getting the details ironed out now seemed critical.

Jess leaned her head against his shoulder, and they continued to look through the samples together. She had adored Nathan Fisher for as long as she could remember. Everyone in high school had known they would someday be married. They were meant for each other. Over the years, her schoolgirl crush had developed into full-blown love. And Nathan had proven his commitment to her over the past few years, walking her through some of the darkest moments of her life.

Jessica paused to think about all she had been through. She still marveled at how the Lord had turned the bad situations in her life around for the better. When her father passed away her junior year of high school, she never dreamed she would experience joy—real joy—again. But so much had come into her life she scarcely knew where to begin thanking God for everything.

Through it all, her mother had proven to be the best example of godliness and strength a daughter could have asked for. Despite her pain, Laura Chapman had done a fine job of caring for Jess and her brother, Kent. This had always made Jess so proud. Her mother was such a woman of God—one who she could only aspire to be like. And the Lord had blessed her mother's dedication, meeting every need above and beyond all expectations.

Jess smiled as she remembered the giddy excitement her mother had experienced two years ago, when the Lord brought a new man, Professor Andrew Dougherty, into her life. He could never replace her wonderful father, of course, but he had been good and kind to everyone in the family and had proven to have an amazing sense of humor. How wonderful to think her mother had found love twice in her lifetime. Was such a thing really possible?

A popular love song drifted out of the store's sound system. Nathan looked up and pointed to the speaker in the ceiling. "Now here's a song I really like. I definitely think we should have it at our wedding. Or at least the reception. What do you think?"

Jess wrinkled her nose.

"Don't you like it?"

"Well, yes, but. . ." How could she explain that the music she had always dreamed of for her wedding would probably be in Italian? Country music would definitely not be an option. "It's nice," she said. *There will be plenty of time to discuss this later. One challenge at a time.*

"I never knew putting together a wedding would be so much work." Nathan rubbed his brow.

"Me, either," Jessica added. "But I don't suppose we have to make a decision about the invitations today. We've got plenty of time."

"True."

"Besides, we really can't order them until we know how many people we'll be inviting, and we're nowhere near finished with the list." Far from it, in fact. To date, her mother had given her over one hundred names, and Nathan's mother. . . well, that was another story altogether.

"I know my mom's not going to be done with her list for a while." He closed the book.

Jessica sighed.

"You okay?" He brushed a lock of loose hair out of her eyes.

"Yeah." She lost herself in her thoughts for a moment. Nathan's mother had great suggestions for the wedding, no doubt. All of her ideas were wonderful, but a little costly. Of course, Jess would never dream of arguing with her, but wondered if the words "wedding on a budget" would ever be fully understood by all involved.

She appreciated all that her own mother had done so far, and Andrew, in his fatherly way, had surprised her by offering to help, as well. But Jessica felt very strongly that she should contribute as much as possible, in part to pay her mother back for all of the years of sacrifice. Unfortunately, Jess's part-time job at the church barely covered her car payment and insurance, let alone a wedding dress and invitations. But she would manage. Somehow.

"Jess?" Nathan said, bringing her back to the present.

"Yeah?"

"Let's go get some dinner, okay?" he said. "I'm famished."

"It can't be dinnertime already. We haven't even been here an hour, right?"

"Try two and a half hours." He yawned.

Jessica's heart lurched. She looked down at her watch in horror. "It's five forty-five? I'm supposed to be at the Wortham for a vocal audition at six fifteen."

"What? Tonight?"

Her gaze remained fixed on the watch: 5:46. "Yes. The Houston Grand Opera is holding auditions for *Rigoletto*."

"Did you forget?"

"No. I brought my music with me. I just lost track of the time." Jessica had waited for this day for weeks. She felt privileged to be recommended by her college professors at the prestigious Moores School of Music at the University of Houston. If all went well in tonight's audition, she might find her place alongside other mezzo-sopranos in the chorus of one of her favorite operas.

If she made it to the audition.

"Can you get me there in a hurry?" She shot a glance at her watch once again.

"In less time than you can sing an aria."

Jess took his hand and gave it a tight squeeze. "Thank you."

"Come on, Madame Butterfly." He clenched her hand in response. "Let's fly this coop."

Together they sprinted toward the car.

Chapter 2

Jess leaped from the car and ran across the large veranda of the Wortham Theater. Nathan gave the car horn a couple of quick beeps, and she turned to wave as he steered the vehicle away from the curb. He would be waiting in the diner across the street when she finished.

She pulled open one of the large front doors of the theater and found herself in the spacious lobby. Grand escalators stood in front of her. Jessica glanced at the note in her hand. *Main stage.* She glanced up nervously.

"Can I help you?" A security guard stopped her in her tracks.

"Um, yes." Her shoulders slumped in defeat. "My name is Jessica Chapman. I'm here—"

"For the auditions," he finished for her. "Your name is right here on the list. I was starting to think you were going to be a no-show."

"Am I late?" She glanced at her watch. No, thankfully. One minute to spare.

"Just on time, if you hurry." His smile gave her hope. "Do you know how to get to the main stage?"

"Yes. I'm just a little flustered."

He patted her on the shoulder. "You'll do fine, I'm sure. Just head up the escalator, straight across the lobby, and into the theater. The man you're looking for is a Mr. Gabriel. He's the one with the silver hair."

"Thanks so much. I owe you." Jess sprinted to the escalator and bounded up the stairs, two at a time, not waiting for the slow-moving ride to the top.

She entered the auditorium at six-fifteen and was met by a stern-looking older woman almost immediately. "Jessica Chapman?"

"Yes. I'm Jessica."

"I'm Catherine Caswell. Let me introduce you to rest of the panel. Then you can give your music to Karyn, our pianist." Jess allowed her gaze to follow the woman's extended finger to the massive stage where a thin young woman sat at a massive grand piano. She drew in a deep breath and tried to steady her nerves. *I can't believe I'm actually going to sing on that stage. Finally.*

Ms. Caswell took off toward the front of the theater, and Jessica followed in her shadow. By the time they reached the front row, she found herself completely out of breath.

"Jessica Chapman. . ." Ms. Caswell nodded in her direction. "Meet your judging panel—Mr. Gabriel of the Houston Grand Opera, Ms. Venton of the New

York Metropolitan Opera, and Mr. Colin Phillips of the Dallas Metropolitan Opera."

"Nice to meet you." She nodded in their direction. Mr. Gabriel never looked up. Ms. Venton briefly glanced up over narrow bifocals, but Mr. Phillips from Dallas extended his hand.

"Just relax, Miss Chapman." He stood and led the way toward the stage as Ms. Caswell disappeared toward the back of the auditorium once again.

Jessica nodded and followed him up the side stairs to the grand stage. From here, she could see the entire theater in all of its beauty. Many times she had seen productions from the opposite viewpoint, but she longed to see the audience from this angle. "I could get used to this," she whispered.

"Excuse me?"

"Oh, I just said I could get used to this." She gave him a girlish grin.

He winked at her. "Then sing your heart out."

She pulled the sheet music for "When I Have Sung My Songs" from her portfolio and handed it to the pianist, who briefly scanned it, then sat at the piano.

Jess instantly realized she had forgotten to give them her résumé. She pressed it into Mr. Phillips's hand. He took it with an encouraging smile.

"Thanks. Go ahead and warm up a little. Oh, and Jessica?" He turned as he headed down the stairs.

"Yes, sir?"

"Break a leg."

She felt his calm reassurance and nodded in appreciation. The pianist played a broken chord, and Jessica quickly began to vocalize. Her voice trembled. *Lord, help me. Please.* As she finished the warm-up, she breathed deeply and felt her nerves calm a little.

"Any time you're ready, Jessica," Mr. Gabriel called out.

She stepped to center stage and took one last sweeping glance across the theater before nodding to Karyn. As the music began, she prepared herself, both physically and emotionally. *I've waited for this moment all my life.*

The first few words seemed to stick in the back of her throat, but by the time she reached the chorus, Jessica seemed to feel a little more secure. She looked down at the panel members, who rarely even glanced her way. Only Mr. Phillips looked up occasionally with a warm smile. As she started the second verse, Jessica found herself lost in the emotion of the familiar lyrics. She had specifically chosen this song because it impacted her on many levels, emotionally and spiritually. Her voice, strangely unfamiliar, seemed to leap and dance across the amazing auditorium. By the time the song ended, Jessica felt confident and bold. Almost daring.

"That was beautiful, Miss Chapman." Ms. Venton looked up over her bifocals as she spoke.

"Thank you for auditioning," Mr. Gabriel added. "Results will be posted next Monday on the backstage door."

She nodded and made her way to the piano to pick up her music. "You sounded great," the pianist whispered. "Best I've heard all afternoon."

"Thanks." Jessica whispered her response as she headed for the stairs. Mr. Phillips met her there. For the first time, she noticed more than just his broad smile. He was young, probably late twenties or early thirties, at most. His eyes were lit with excitement, which he wasn't doing a great job of hiding. He extended his hand to help her down the stairs.

"Great job," he said, as she made her descent. "You have quite a range for a mezzo-soprano."

"Thanks." Her hand trembled in his. "Do I exit out the back?" She gestured toward the rear of the auditorium.

"Yes."

She made her way up the aisle with her knees knocking all the way. The security guard met her in the lobby. "Done so soon?"

She nodded, suddenly feeling as if she might be sick.

"You don't look so great. Should I call a cab, or do you have a ride?"

"My fiancé's in the restaurant across the street," she said. "And I'll be okay. Just nerves, I think."

He walked with her to the front door and pulled it open. "Good night, Miss Chapman. Maybe I'll be seeing more of you after tonight."

"I hope so." She shook his extended hand, then made her way across the veranda to the busy downtown street. It wasn't until she was seated across from Nathan in the restaurant that her stomach relaxed and she finally felt free to breathe a natural, comfortable breath.

"You okay?" He took a swig of coffee and glanced at the television overhead.

She nodded. "That was about the scariest thing I've ever done."

"Did they make you eat a live chicken?" He glanced her way with a smile.

"Very funny. But speaking of chicken. . ." She grabbed a menu and scanned it quickly. "I'm starved. Seen a waitress lately?"

He motioned to get the waitress's attention, and Jessica quickly ordered a chicken club sandwich and fries. Then she leaned back against the seat and poured her heart out to Nathan. He gave her several encouraging hand squeezes and assured her of her ability.

Then, just as her food arrived, Jessica finally let herself think of something other than the audition. "I've been looking at wedding dresses in magazines," she said after swallowing a couple of fries.

"Find anything yet?"

She shook her head. "It's tougher than I thought. If I had a great figure, this would be so much easier."

"You do have a great figure, Jess. Why are you always cutting yourself down?"

She shrugged as she finished a big bite of the sandwich. "I don't know. Just insecure, I guess. Not fishing for compliments or anything, if that's what you're thinking."

"No need." He reached over and squeezed her hand. "You're perfect just the way you are, and I'll always compliment you."

"You're sweet." Jess took another bite then settled back for a relaxing meal. Her thoughts were suddenly interrupted by an oddly familiar voice.

"Miss Chapman?"

Jess looked up to find Colin Phillips standing next to her. She very nearly choked on the sandwich. "Mr. Phillips? What happened? Is something wrong?"

"No, actually. I'm thrilled to find you here. I hope you don't think I was following you. It's just a coincidence, I assure you."

"Okay."

His face lit up. "Actually, I had already planned to phone you at home tomorrow, but this is certainly easier. Do you have a few minutes?"

"Sure."

Colin pulled a chair up to the table, and she quickly introduced Nathan, who then turned his attention to the television for a stock market report.

"Miss Chapman," Colin began.

"Please. Call me Jessica."

"Jessica. This is a little awkward, but I feel like I'm supposed to ask you a question." He pressed his hands together in a tight grip.

Her heart now raced, though she tried to stay calm. "Go for it."

"I'm from Dallas," he explained.

"Right."

"Well, see—we're starting a program in the Dallas area for children. Preteens, mostly, who are interested in the opera. I'm heading up the program. Technically, anyway. But I'm looking for someone who has experience with children to do much of the legwork. This has to be a vocalist, someone who can help train the kids and prepare them for our Christmas production, *Amahl and the Night Visitors.*"

Nathan cleared his throat a little too loudly, and Jessica tried to gauge his thoughts. "There's something I need to tell you, Mr. Phillips," she began.

"Please. Call me Colin." The gentleman's rich brown eyes gazed into hers.

"Colin."

She took a deep breath, but he interrupted her before she had a chance to continue. "I forgot to mention that you would also be offered an internship with the Metropolitan Opera in Dallas, which would mean that you would be assured a place in the chorus of both our fall and spring productions. On top of directing the children, I mean."

Her mouth flew open in surprise. "Really? Which operas?"

"*Madame Butterfly* in the fall," Colin said. "November, to be precise. And in the spring we'll be doing *The Bartered Bride*."

"Wow. Two of my favorites."

Nathan shifted in his seat, but Jessica didn't pause for a moment. Her excited thoughts forged ahead. *A place in the chorus. Assured. And working with children to help them develop their vocal gifts. What more could I ask for?*

"Jess?"

Nathan's voice brought her back to her senses. She gazed into his nervous eyes and knew immediately what her answer would have to be.

"I'm sorry to have to turn you down so quickly, Mr. Phillips," she explained, "but we're in the middle of planning our wedding. Nathan and I are getting married in May."

"Ah. I see." Colin paused. "Well, congratulations are in order then." He extended his hand in Nathan's direction. Jessica couldn't help noticing the look of pride in her fiancé's eyes.

"I couldn't possibly leave right now," she continued. "I'm sure you understand."

Colin turned toward her with a penetrating gaze. "Actually, what I'm suggesting would be a six-month internship. You'd be back in plenty of time for the big day. And you'd only be in Dallas, after all."

Nathan cleared his throat again, then shifted his gaze to the television.

"Your voice is unique, Jessica," the handsome young director continued. "And untapped. I could tell from your résumé that you had some amazing opportunities to perform in college, but what I'm talking about would give you the opportunity to train alongside some of the best voices in the country."

"Well, I. . ." *Lord, this is such a wonderful opportunity, but how could I possibly accept it?*

Colin stood. "All I ask is that you think about it. I know this is all pretty sudden, but I've just got a strong feeling God is in the middle of all of this."

"God?" She looked up at him to make sure she hadn't misunderstood.

"Sorry. Forgot I was supposed to leave my faith out of this." He shrugged. "I forget that a lot, actually." He smiled and handed her a business card with his name, address, and phone number.

"It's okay. I appreciate your honesty. I'm a believer myself." Jessica extended her hand, and he shook it firmly.

"Great."

She pulled her hand from his after another penetrating look from Nathan. "Thanks for the offer, Mr. Phillips," she said. "But right now I think I'd better wait and see what my options are here in Houston. I did just audition for a place in *Rigoletto*, after all."

"I know. And one of the better voices we heard all day, I should add."

Wow. "Thank you."

"I do feel like a bit of a traitor stealing you from them, but something in my gut just tells me. . ." Nathan turned an accusing glance his direction. "Well, I've kept you too long. Thanks so much for your time." He left the restaurant in a rush, and Jessica turned her attention back to her fiancé.

"Can you believe the nerve of that guy?" Nathan grumbled.

She wrinkled her nose as she contemplated his remark. "I thought he was nice."

"You're not actually thinking of going, are you?"

"Of course not." She reached over and gripped his hand. "How could I? It's not just the wedding standing in my way—"

"Standing in your way?" A flash of resentment clouded his eyes.

"You know what I mean," she explained. "I've got my job at the church. The kids are counting on me."

"Right."

"And who knows? I might be offered a part in *Rigoletto*. That would be amazing."

He nodded. "That's my girl. Always hopeful."

She nodded and tried to turn her thoughts to her audition, but they gravitated once again. *Dallas.* Amahl and the Night Visitors. *A place in the chorus of* Madame Butterfly *in November.*

"So," Nathan interrupted her thoughts once again. "Tell me about this wedding dress you're searching for."

She looked up into his smiling face.

Chapter 3

Jessica made her way across the driveway to the mailbox at the curb's edge. She knew she must open it, though she dreaded the news it probably held. Sure enough, the large black box contained the much-anticipated letter from the Houston Grand Opera Society.

She held the sealed envelope in her trembling hand and fumbled with the flap, attempting to loosen it. "Come on. Open up." Then again, why bother? Jessica knew what it would say, even before reading it.

"We are sorry to inform you. . ." The rest would go on to say that while they appreciated her talent and effort, they simply didn't have enough space to give everyone a position in *Rigoletto.* Then they would welcome her to audition again in the future.

These things Jessica knew because she had already seen the list at the Wortham Theater two days ago. Her name had not been on it. She had swallowed both her pride and her disappointment and had given Nathan the news. He had shrugged it off in his usual good-natured way, assuring her of his love, regardless. In fact, he had looked strangely relieved.

But now she must face the letter in her hand. Somehow just reading the news in print would make it seem more real, more awful. Jessica ripped the envelope open and scanned the typed words. Just as she expected. A rejection. She brushed back a tear as she read the words, "You have a lovely voice, and this decision is in no way a reflection of your talent or ability." She shook her head in defeat and wadded up the letter into a tight ball.

"Honey, is everything okay?" Jessica's mother appeared at the curbside. Jess quickly brushed away a tear as she looked up with a numb smile. "I guess." She gripped the paper ball a little tighter.

"Your letter from the Houston Opera?"

"Uh-huh. But at least I knew ahead of time." She sighed deeply. "It's no big surprise."

"I know." Her mother's brow wrinkled in concern. "But I'm really sorry, honey. You've got such a beautiful voice, and I know the Lord is going to use you to minister to others with that gift. I guess this just wasn't the right time."

"Or the right place." Jessica fought to swallow the ever-growing lump in her throat.

"There will be plenty of operas in your future." Her mother placed her arm

146

around Jessica's shoulder. "And in the meantime, you've got a lot of work to do with the children's choir at church, right?"

"Right." But that didn't lessen the pain of rejection she felt in this moment.

Her mother patted her on the back. "The kids need you, honey. And so does Mrs. Witherspoon. She wouldn't know what to do if she lost you."

Jessica didn't know how to respond. The elderly Mrs. Witherspoon, truth be told, had a knack for dealing with the children. In fact, she could take charge of the whole thing in a heartbeat, if need be. But right now Jessica needed to be needed.

Somewhere.

She reached to close the mailbox and looked up into her mother's kind eyes. "Do you think maybe God is trying to tell me something?"

"What do you mean?" Her mother looked concerned.

"Well, I know I'm supposed to be singing classical music," Jessica explained. "That's what I've trained for. But there's not much opportunity at church for that sort of style. So the opera has always been my goal."

"Right."

"I'm just wondering. . . ." She paused.

"About the position in Dallas?" Her mother seemed to read her thoughts.

"Uh-huh." Relief washed over Jessica. "I mean, doesn't it just sound like God had the whole thing set up in advance?"

"It would be a marvelous opportunity." Her mother walked alongside her as they approached the house. "But whether it's in the Lord's plan is another thing. Just because something is easy doesn't always mean it's from the Lord."

"I guess." Jessica heaved a sigh. "But how will I know unless I try it?"

Her mother stopped and looked her in the eye. "You're actually thinking of going to Dallas in the middle of planning a wedding?" She gave her a curious look.

"I don't know, Mom. I'm just thinking out loud."

"Does Nathan know you're considering this?"

"No." She pulled the front door opened and stepped inside. "I'm afraid to talk to him about it at all, to be honest. He's so busy with his new classes and seems a little distracted. But it's such a great thing they're doing up there." She paused then looked at her mother for a bit of encouragement.

"Well, pray about it, honey. God will show you what to do."

Jessica's shoulders slumped as she crossed the house to her bedroom. She tossed the letter in the trash can right away, determined to put the whole thing behind her. Then she reached into her bedside drawer and pulled out another letter—one she had received just yesterday, in fact.

A letter from Mr. Phillips. A "just in case" move on his part, or so it had said. In his carefully crafted note, he had formulated a plan for the internship, offering

Jessica a "creative, interactive, and educational environment in order to promote and develop an appreciation of opera as an art form; to provide educational opportunities for all ages and cultures; and, therefore, to supply the opportunity for lifelong learning." He described the youth apprentice artist program in a way that had intrigued and excited her.

Twenty exceptional artists will be selected by vocal audition from applicants from the Dallas Metroplex. Each young artist selected will be given many of the skills necessary for a professional career. The program director will assist each child by providing personal attention and instruction, and significant performing opportunities. These artists work with a team of highly experienced professionals and will receive coaching in standard operatic repertory. They will also be offered multiple performance opportunities.

Jess stretched out across her bed with the letter in her hand. "It almost sounds too good to be true." But how could she balance this against her wedding plans? Would Nathan think she had lost her mind?

Her thoughts gravitated to her fiancé. He was so sweet—and such a good guy. She had always appreciated and loved his understanding heart. While he clearly didn't share her love for the opera, he had never discouraged her from following her dreams. Perhaps he would begin to see this possibility as a part of God's plan for her life, her future.

"Only one way to know for sure." She picked up the telephone and dialed his cell number. He didn't answer until the fourth ring. When he did, his voice sounded hushed, strained.

"Hello?"

"Nathan, is that you?"

"I'm in the middle of class right now," he whispered. "I forgot to turn off my phone. Everyone's looking at me."

"Oh, I'm so sorry. Call me later." She quickly hung up and shook her head in despair. "Great."

A tap on the door interrupted her thoughts. "Come in."

Her mother entered. "I just wanted to let you know that Andrew and I hoped to take you and Nathan to dinner tonight. We were thinking of that new seafood place up in The Woodlands. Sound good?"

"Very." Her mouth began to water, just thinking about it. "But I'll have to get back to you about Nathan. He's in class right now."

"Okay, honey. We just thought it would be a good time to discuss plans for the wedding—get a few things down on paper."

"Sounds good."

Her mother left the room, and Jessica rolled back over on the bed. Within minutes she fell into a deep sleep. She dreamed of *Amahl and the Night Visitors*—the hauntingly beautiful Christmas story. It seemed strangely twisted into the plot of *Madame Butterfly*, which made for a colorful, yet confusing, dream. She played the role of the beautiful young Japanese woman in love, betrayed by the man who had captured her heart. Just as she stepped to center stage to sing her big solo, Jessica heard the sound of a familiar voice.

"Wake up, sleepyhead."

She propped herself up on her elbow and squinted up at Nathan, who stood in the doorway with a grin on his face.

"What time is it?" she asked with a yawn.

"It's five forty-five. You called me at two o'clock."

"No way." She rolled over to look at the clock.

"Is it okay to come in?"

Jessica nodded, and Nathan stepped into the room. "Your mom called me about an hour ago to ask if I wanted to go out to dinner with you guys," he said. "So I'm here."

"I can't believe I slept all afternoon." She yawned again and sat up. As she did, her letter from Dallas fell to the floor.

"What's this?" Nathan reached down to pick it up. "Your rejection letter?"

"No, I uh. . ."

"Your mom told me it came today." He gripped it tightly. "She figured that's why you needed the sleep, to recover from the bad news."

"Uh, no." She snatched it from his hand. "It's, uh. . ."

A worried look crossed Nathan's face.

"It's just a letter from—"

"That guy from Dallas?" Nathan asked.

"Yeah. But he's not actually back in Dallas yet. He's going to be in Houston for another couple of weeks."

"I see."

"There's nothing to see, Nathan."

"He just won't take no for an answer, will he?"

Jess shrugged. "Actually, I've been thinking—"

"There's nothing to think about." Nathan reached out and took her hand. "He can't have you."

"But—"

"You're a Houston girl, and you're all mine."

She nodded and let her head fall onto his shoulder. As he stroked her hair, he continued. "And speaking of being all mine. . ."

She looked up into his eyes, which twinkled merrily. "What?"

"I have some good news. But let's go out into the living room so I can tell everyone at once."

Jess quickly touched up her lipstick then met them in the living room. There, Nathan gathered the whole family around him to make his announcement.

"I have some news." He paused momentarily, then proudly announced, "My parents have decided to spring for a European honeymoon."

"Europe?" Jess immediately began to weep. She had always longed for a trip to Italy. For years, she had talked of it with such longing. Venice would be the destination of choice. And Florence, of course. There were so many places to visit, so many historical and musical sites to take in.

But why would Nathan's parents go to such trouble? They must have been listening to her childish babblings all along. Suddenly she felt completely overwhelmed at their generosity. "That's the sweetest thing I've ever heard," she whispered.

"I thought you'd like it." He smiled. "My mom has a friend who's a travel agent, and they set the whole thing up today. We'll fly into Frankfurt."

"Germany?" *That's curious.*

"Yes, I've always wanted to take a boat trip down the Rhine. Then we'll go on to Paris and London from there."

"Paris and London?" That all sounded great, but how did Italy fit into the plan?

"A fabulous ten days of sightseeing and exotic foods for my new bride. British tearooms, double-decker buses. . . The best."

Laura and Andrew immediately began to chatter about French foods, and Jessica's brother, Kent, overlapped them with a conversation about German automobiles. Nathan tried to keep her attention by telling her about their flight, their hotels, and their detailed schedule, but Jess felt lost in the muddle of it all.

Somehow, Italy had slipped right through her fingers, and she felt the loss more acutely than a rejection letter from Verdi himself.

Chapter 4

Jessica spent the following Saturday afternoon making a to-do list for her wedding. She tried to push all thoughts of Dallas as far away as possible. With so much planning ahead, she shouldn't have much difficulty pressing misguided images of *Madame Butterfly* out of her mind.

"Photographer. Invitations." She mumbled aloud as she wrote. "Flowers. Candelabra. Roman columns." She paused a moment before erasing the last entry. Nathan would never agree to Roman columns, in spite of her best explanations and pleas. "Fruit, vegetable trays, quiche. . ."

Jessica continued to write, scribbling down only the things she knew the two of them together would come to agreement on. After some time, she laid down the lists and reached for a bridal magazine. She thumbed through it in bored silence as she carefully examined each dress. To be honest, they all looked the same to her. *White with long train. White with short train. Beaded with short sleeves. Beaded with long sleeves.* Did it matter anyway? They were all dreadful. Would she ever find one that appealed to her?

Jessica's eyes grew heavy as she turned the pages. In her mind's eye, she could see her gown. It would be so different from anything in these magazines. So vastly different. She rested back against the sofa and tried to stay alert, but it grew more difficult. For some reason, every time she tried to focus on wedding plans, she grew weary with the process almost immediately.

Jessica allowed herself to contemplate something else for a moment. *Just a minute or two of dreaming won't hurt.* In her mind's eye, she saw herself on a stage, singing her heart out. She wore an exquisite, flowing dress in shades of cream and burgundy. To her left, a beautiful set filled the stage—an antiquated Italian city with houses, fountains, and cobbled streets. From inside the window of one of the houses, a man sang to her in a rich baritone voice, which resonated across the theater.

She responded to his words in Italian. Her soprano voice paralleled his, as they joined together in harmony to complete the song. He disappeared momentarily, only to reappear in the doorway of the house. The tall stranger with dark hair moved toward her, never taking his gaze off of hers. He swept her into his arms and sang lovingly to her, as he danced her across the stage. She found herself captivated by the moment and completely lost in his gaze. They seemed to mirror each other perfectly.

151

As if anything could be that perfect.

"I've got to stop this." Jessica tried to shake off the image. She tossed the bridal magazine onto the coffee table and stood with a yawn. Enough with the dreamy schoolgirl imaginations. Life was staring her in the face, and she had work to do. Lots of work.

And yet she didn't feel like working on the wedding. She wanted to think about—dream about—singing. *Why, Lord? I thought my life was settled. I really thought I could have it all—the husband, the family, and the music. Was I wrong, Father? Show me what to do.*

The telephone rang, startling her. Jessica felt her hands begin to tremble as she picked it up. *Don't read too much into this.* "Hello?"

"Jess? Is that you?"

Her heart lifted as she heard Nathan's voice. "Yep. What's up?"

"Just wondering what you're up to."

"Oh. I—I was just sitting here making plans for the wedding."

"Good girl." He paused. "Listen, my parents were wondering if you wanted to come over for dinner. My mom's fixing lasagna and Caesar salad. I know they're your favorites."

Jessica's mouth watered. "Mmm."

"And I think she's nearly finished with her guest list for the wedding, and she'll want to talk to you about that. She needs to feel wanted, if you know what I mean."

"I do."

"Also, my dad's been on the Internet again," Nathan said. "He's printed up some pictures of the hotels we'll be staying at on our honeymoon. He's anxious to show them to you."

"What time should I be there?"

"Six thirty?"

She glanced at her watch. "Sounds good. Gives me just enough time to take a quick shower and change into clean clothes. I'll see you then."

"Great. Love you, babe."

"Love you, too." She hung up the phone with a click and picked up the bridal magazine for one last glance. *Lord, is this Your answer to my question?* Though she still didn't feel completely settled on the issue, the phone call seemed entirely too coincidental.

As Jessica climbed into the shower, she finally felt some sense of resolution on the matter. She loved Nathan. He loved her. She had a lot of work to do right here in Houston. Everyone needed her. There would be plenty of time to think about her career later. Timing was everything, after all. Her favorite scripture from Ecclesiastes reminded her of the fact. *"There is a time for everything, and a season for every activity under heaven."*

This simply wasn't the time for leaving.

By the time she finished dressing for dinner, Jessica knew what she must do. She reached for Mr. Phillips's letter one last time, scanning it only briefly to find his cell number. Once located, she picked up the phone and dialed it. She would give him her answer.

Her final answer.

Colin sat on the balcony of the downtown Houston hotel, drinking in an unexpected evening breeze. From inside the room, his cell phone rang, rousing him from a near-catatonic state. He sprinted inside. Just as he approached the phone, Colin stubbed his toe on the sharp edge of the dresser. He began to hop up and down, then grappled to pry the flip phone open before he lost the call altogether. "Hello?"

"Mr. Phillips?"

The female voice sounded oddly familiar. Colin placed his aching foot back on the ground and winced in pain. "This is he."

"Oh, hello. This is Jessica. Jessica Chapman. We met last week."

His spirits lifted immediately, and his foot suddenly felt better. "Jessica, it's so good to hear from you. You got my letter then." He had taken a chance by sending it, to be honest. In fact, he had prayed the carefully crafted note wouldn't seem too forward, too pushy. But he knew in his spirit this girl was the one he had been praying for.

For the internship, of course.

"Yes. Well, that's why I'm calling." She hesitated. "I hope I'm not interrupting anything."

"No. As a matter of fact, I'm still here in Houston. I've been in meetings all week, but I'm back at the hotel now."

"Ah. Well, I'm glad I picked the right time to call," she said.

"With good news, I hope." He drew in a deep breath and waited for her response.

"Actually. . ."

Colin's heart suddenly felt heavy. He dropped down onto the sofa to await her reply, rubbing his aching foot as she spoke.

"I've really given this a lot of thought," she said. "And I've prayed about it, too. But—"

He switched the phone to the other ear. "You've decided against it?"

"I'm afraid so."

She sounded as if she would cry, and Colin suddenly realized the struggle she must be facing. "I'm sorry to hear that," he said.

"There's just so much going on right now," she continued, "and leaving in the middle of everything would present too many challenges."

Colin struggled with his disappointment but quickly opted to do the right thing, for her sake. "Jessica, thank you so much for calling," he said. "And thanks for considering the internship. I knew from the get-go that your answer would probably be no, but I was so taken with your voice and your love for children that I couldn't help pursuing it. To be honest, I was only thinking of what you could do for us, how you could benefit our organization—not the other way around. That was selfish of me, and I'm really sorry if I've been too pushy."

"Oh no," she said. And then her voice broke. "I–I'm so flattered you would think of me. It means so much to hear your kind words, and I know the Dallas Metropolitan Opera could have opened great doors for me. Just the opportunity to perform with such amazing professionals in the field—"

"Yes, well."

"I'd honestly love nothing more than to come," she said with a sigh. "In my heart, I'm there already."

"You don't have to say anything else," Colin interrupted. "Just please know this, in case you ever doubt it. You have a unique voice, a God-given talent. And there will be plenty of opportunities for you in the music world. Promise me you won't ever give up on that gift, okay?"

"Okay." She practically whispered the word.

"And if your situation changes in the next few weeks. . ." No, he wouldn't say it. He didn't want to be guilty of manipulating her in any way. Besides, the Lord had the perfect person in mind for the job, and Colin didn't want to interrupt the Almighty's plans.

Even if it meant losing the one person he had felt so strongly about from the very beginning.

Chapter 5

"What do you think of this one, Grandma?" Jessica turned in a prissy circle to display the white Cinderella-style wedding dress she wore. The romantic gown with its long, full skirt and fitted bodice accentuated her waistline, but something about it still didn't feel quite right.

"Hmm." Her grandmother, never one to mince words, crossed her arms and gave Jessica a penetrating look. "Turn around one more time, so I can give it a fair analysis."

Jessica swished the elaborate gown as she pivoted once again.

"I don't know, honey." The silver-haired woman shrugged. "Something about this one just doesn't seem to suit you. I don't want to burst your bubble. If you like it, that's all that really matters."

"I like it." Jess looked in the mirror once again. "But I don't *love* it; you know what I mean? I want my wedding gown to be perfect. This is close, but—"

"Not quite the right fit?"

"Nope." She shook her head and gave a defeated sigh. "None of them seems to suit me and, to be honest, I just don't know how many more of these I can try on. I'm so frustrated. The last one made me look like a ballerina. That tulle skirt was just too much. Felt like a tutu. And the one before that—"

Her grandmother laughed. "I know, I know. Made you feel like a prom queen."

"That shiny fabric made me a little nervous." She swished in front of the trifold mirrors once again, then leaned against the wall in defeat. "What's wrong with me, Grandma? Why can't I find anything that's just right for me? Am I really that difficult?" She slumped down into a nearby chair.

"You're just looking for the perfect fit, and that's not easy to find."

"I suppose," she said. "But nothing's going to be perfect, right? I mean, truly perfect." She sought out her grandmother's expression for an answer.

"You can force something to fit, but that doesn't make it right. Living with something that's uncomfortable or 'not quite right' is never a good thing."

Jessica tried to swallow the lump in her throat before responding. "What are you saying?"

Her grandmother's eyes watered a bit. "I'm just saying—if you could have anything you wanted, absolutely anything, what would it be?"

"Are we talking dresses here, or something else?"

"You tell me." The older woman suddenly took on a determined, maternal look. "Tell me about your dream wedding, Jessica."

"My dream wedding?"

"Yes. If you could have anything you wanted, what would you have?" The silver-haired beauty eased her way into a chair.

Jessica pursed her lips as she thought of her answer. "Well, the wedding of my dreams, the one I've always hoped for, would be very romantic but also a little theatrical, which I know Nathan would absolutely hate. There would be a stringed quartet playing in the background and candles all over the place. I know a church wedding would be nice—traditional—but I really see a more surreal setting, more like a—a. . ." She knew what she wanted to say, but didn't dare.

"A theater?" Her grandmother finished for her.

Jessica shrugged. "Yes, or something like that. Anyway, the music would be the foundation for the whole event, and all of the love songs would definitely be sung in Italian. There would be a backdrop—like a set, with painted scenes from Italy. Maybe some Roman columns—to add a little romance—with swags of sheer fabric draped between them and some twinkling lights reflecting through."

"Sounds beautiful."

"And," Jessica continued, more excited now, "if I had my way, I wouldn't even wear a traditional wedding dress at all. I'd pick something with a long, flowing skirt. Chiffon, maybe. Lots of flow. Loose, romantic sleeves. Something very dramatic."

"More like a costume from one of your operas?"

"Yes, actually." Jessica felt a sense of relief as the words were spoken. "And not necessarily white," she continued, "which I know would probably upset everyone. But I just see this as a nontraditional sort of wedding—a staged event."

"Right, right."

"I'd like to see a little color, even in my gown. Muted, of course. If we're going with a Mediterranean theme."

"*Are* you going with a Mediterranean theme?"

"Well, I've tried to tell Nathan my ideas, but he's got a more traditional approach in mind. Not that he's being stubborn. He's not." Jessica drew in a deep breath. "He's almost too nice about it all, but I can see it in his eyes. He's very 'in the box'—which is fine. That's just who he is, and I appreciate that about him. He's solid, stable."

"Romantic?"

"Well, I can't expect everything from one person," Jessica said slowly. "But I'm fine with that. I really am."

"Humph."

"Besides," Jessica said, trying to turn the conversation in another direction, "I don't want to hurt him by insisting on having my own way. That would be wrong. And I'm more than willing to compromise."

"Your wedding plans, you mean?" Another penetrating gaze.

"Of course. What else would I be compromising?"

Her grandmother's wrinkled brow alarmed her. "You're a wise girl, Jess. And I know you'll make the right decision."

"About the dress or the Mediterranean theme?"

"About everything. Your happiness is my first concern." Her precious grandmother suddenly grew more serious. "I'm sorry I said that, honey. Truth be told, finding God's perfect will in all of this is my first concern. After that, your happiness is right up there. I want you to be so blissfully in love that you can't see straight."

Jessica smiled. "Thanks."

"But," her grandmother continued, "I also want to see you fulfill your dreams in other areas of your life. Your father worked hard so that you could have music lessons as a child. I don't ever want you to forget the musical gift he saw in you from the time you were young. It's still there, you know."

Jessica felt tears begin to well up in her eyes and pushed them away with the back of her fist. "I know that."

"Just don't forget it, that's all I'm saying. It's one thing to be happy in love, another to be happy in life. A healthy bride needs both."

"Aren't they one and the same?" Jessica tried to force the lump down her throat, but it refused to budge.

Her grandmother shrugged. "Sometimes it seems that way, but answering the individual call of God in your life is critical. Before those vows are taken, I mean. So many people try to do it the other way around. They marry without ever discovering who they are, first."

"I . . ." Jessica couldn't seem to finish the sentence.

"When your grandfather passed away, I thought my life had ended," the silver-haired woman continued. "At first I was terrified. But those years alone gave me a chance to rediscover who I was, the things I had hoped and dreamed for as a young girl. By the time I met Buck, I was more sure of myself than I had been for years. When I married him, he knew he was getting a bride with some self-confidence."

"You're a strong woman. I know that. And I am, too."

"Jessica." Her grandmother stood and placed her hands on Jessica's shoulders. "Turn and look close." Together, they turned to face the tri-fold mirror. What Jessica saw staring back at her was a downcast bride-to-be in a wedding dress that didn't quite fit. "There's so much inside of you waiting to be discovered, and I'm not trying to discourage you. I'm really not. Just set out on that journey, and God will show you what's around the bend. In your gifts, in your occupation, and in your relationship with Nathan."

Jessica reached up and embraced her grandmother, not even trying to stop the tears. "I know you're right."

"You're going to be a beautiful bride, honey, and that radiance is going to shine through like a light that can't wait to escape the darkness, because it will spring up from your innermost being. In the meantime, promise me you'll take the time for a little self-discovery."

Jessica nodded, and as she turned toward the dressing room, tears tumbled freely down her cheeks. She carefully slipped out of the wedding dress, contemplating all her grandmother had said. *It's one thing to be happy in love, another to be happy in life.* Had she really heard correctly?

Lord, I don't want to be selfish with these wedding plans. Help me to find my happiness in You, and not in others.

Or my music.

Jessica dejectedly pulled on her jeans and T-shirt. As she exited the dressing room, she turned to look in the mirror once again. A somber face greeted her. She forced a smile. *I'll work harder at being happy,* she assured herself. *Even if it means putting my dreams on hold awhile longer.*

With a renewed vigor in her step, she turned to face the challenges of the day.

Mom, I appreciate your efforts, but—" Colin never had a chance to finish the sentence before his mother cut him off.

"Colin, you're avoiding the subject."

He quickly shifted the cell phone to the opposite shoulder. For thirty minutes she had been sharing her concerns about his lack of a personal life, and the phone had grown warm to the touch. It was actually beginning to bother his ear a little. With both hands on the steering wheel, there was little he could do about that. He guided the car north on Houston's busy Interstate 45 as she spoke.

"You're twenty-eight years old, Colin." She never missed a beat. "It's time you settled down. Found yourself a wife. Had a few kids. I mean, the opera is a good thing, but there's certainly more to life than music. It's one thing to follow your dreams; it's another to give up your personal life."

"I know, Mom." He turned on his signal to change lanes, nearly dropping the phone in the process.

"It's not like you haven't had plenty of opportunity. I don't know how you could resist all of those beautiful young women in the company. There have been dozens I would have picked out for you. Dozens."

Colin groaned inwardly. To be honest, none of the women who currently sang with the Dallas Metropolitan Opera suited him at all. Many were prima donnas, and the few who weren't already happened to be involved in relationships. Besides, the Lord had someone unique in mind for him. Someone who had given her heart to the Lord and shared his passion for the lost. Someone who recognized that any gifts she had were given by God and not something to be flaunted or admired.

In short, the woman he was waiting for might be a long time in coming. But Colin didn't mind the wait. Sure, he had grown a little lonely at times, but the busyness of his schedule helped. And once he returned to Dallas and the children's chorus kicked off, his free time would be zapped with a host of additional activities.

"Are you still with me?"

His mother's words brought him back to his senses, and he quickly responded in his most reassuring voice. "I'm here."

"I don't want you to think I'm lecturing, honey," she continued. "I know this is your own business. It's just that sometimes I wonder if I'll ever have grandchildren."

Colin smiled. Many times, he had thought of what his future would be like. A houseful of kids would be sheer bliss. He couldn't wait. But what choice did he have, really? "You'll have grandchildren, Mom," he assured her. "I'm looking forward to being a father someday."

"You'll be a great one." Her voice lifted. "And they'll be beautiful if they take after you."

"Mom."

"Just hear me out on this, Colin," she urged him. "Your career is very important to you. I know that. And I know you've been given a serious, God-given gift that few can comprehend or appreciate. But that gift, no matter how fully developed, will never be able to replace relationships. You need a healthy balance of both."

"I know." He sighed. "But, Mom—"

"Colin, I hate to do this," she said abruptly, "but there's someone calling on the other line. I've been waiting on a call from the cable company, so I'd better get it."

"I love you, Mom."

"I love you, too." With a click, she hung up.

For the next few moments Colin fought to focus on the road. His mother's words carried a sting. Many times he had wondered if he would ever marry, even wondered if perhaps God might require him to remain single so that he could accomplish more for the sake of the gospel.

But his heart told him otherwise. Truthfully, he longed for someone to love, someone to share his heart, his home, his life. . .his passion for music.

Lord, I know I might not find everything I'm looking for in one woman. If she's out there, Father, then please bring her to me. I don't want to miss Your plans for my life. I want someone to love. I want the joy—the happiness—that a relationship would bring.

In the meantime, Colin surmised, life at the opera would have to do.

159

Chapter 6

Jessica clutched Nathan's hand as they moved through the crowd of people at Houston's annual Grand Opera Benefit Gala. She looked out across the beautiful foyer of the Wortham Theater, her hands tightly clutched to her chest. "I almost sang here."

"What, honey?" Nathan raised his voice to be heard above the din.

"Oh, nothing. I was just thinking out loud." Jessica paused as she looked around the room teeming with people. "I do love this place. Don't you?"

"It's okay." He shrugged.

"Just okay?" She looked around at the beautiful room with its exquisite décor and was reminded immediately of the day she had raced so quickly across this lobby, barely noticing its beauty.

"At least tonight won't be a total waste."

"What do you mean?"

"I'm taking mental notes. Looking at that buffet table is giving me ideas for our wedding reception." He pointed to their right.

"Really? Me, too." A beautiful array of foods was spread out before the opera patrons, beckoning, tempting. Smoked salmon, luscious fruit platters, finger sandwiches shaped into musical notes. It was all too amazing to take in. "So what were you thinking?"

"Basically, that all of this is just too frilly, you know what I mean? We should do more basic foods. None of this buffet line stuff. We need a sit-down dinner with good, solid food. Guy food."

Jessica's heart lurched. She had always envisioned a beautiful reception with a wonderful array of foods. Not expensive, of course. But everything would look and taste expensive. And the guests would be overwhelmed at the artistic beauty of it all. Grapes and strawberries would dangle over the edges of crystal bowls and a luscious fruit dip would sit nearby. Vegetable trays would be adorned with carrots cut to look like flowers, and broccoli sculpted to look like actual trees. She had a plan—an elegant, creative plan.

"All this talk about food is making me hungry." Nathan turned toward the buffet line. "What about you?"

"Nope. Not yet," she said. "Besides, I need to find Professor Wallace and see if he needs me. I'm supposed to be here to help." Tonight's event would benefit the Houston Grand Opera in a number of ways. Despite their recent rejection, Jessica still felt compelled to support the organization in any way she could. Besides, her favorite professor from the University of Houston had called specifically to ask for her assistance. She was to meet him at the school's booth on the northeast side of the room. If only she could find it.

"Go on." Nathan turned toward the food line. "I'll catch up with you later."

Jessica fought her way through the crowd, looking for the Moores School of Music booth. She located it—off in the distance, to her left—though she could barely make out Professor Wallace through the crowd. She quickly made her way in his direction, hardly able to squeeze through the throng of people. "Excuse me." She apologized as she accidentally bumped into a tall gentleman who blocked her way.

"No problem."

Jessica looked up in surprise as she heard the familiar voice. Colin Phillips stood directly in front of her. "Mr. Phillips."

His face lit up immediately. "Jessica." He extended his hand. "I wondered if I would see you here tonight. I take it you're an opera supporter as well as an amazing vocalist."

She felt her cheeks warm with embarrassment. "Yes, my music professor," she said, gesturing across the room, "got me involved during my junior year. I've seen every opera for the past three seasons. That's why I was so excited to finally get the chance to audition." Her voice faltered slightly. "But anyway, I'm really late."

"I'll walk with you, if you don't mind."

"Of course not."

She turned and began to make her way through the crowd with Mr. Phillips on her heels. Why her heart fluttered, she had absolutely no idea.

Colin followed along behind Jessica Chapman as she made her way through the boisterous crowd. In her soft blue evening gown, with her auburn hair swept up like that, she wasn't difficult to keep track of. He envisioned her standing on a stage, singing in that beautiful blue dress.

All the way across the room, he fought the urge to ask her, one last time, to reconsider his offer to come to Dallas. *No. I won't do it.*

When they arrived at the university's booth, Colin had to smile. Jessica's professor, a short, bald gentleman, looked a little frazzled as he crawled up from under the table, where he had obviously been searching for something.

"Jessica!" The older man's face lit immediately. "I'm so glad you're here. I'm at my wit's end. I can't seem to find our brochures. And I need someone to visit with all of the potential students who stop by."

"Of course. I'd be happy to."

"I started a list for people to sign." He gestured toward a clipboard at the far end of the table, then immediately went to his knees again, resuming his search through a large cardboard box.

Colin smiled, in spite of himself. This fellow was quite a character.

Jessica went to retrieve the list, then began to chat with a young woman about music scholarships. Colin marveled at how easily she talked to strangers and how comfortable she seemed to be. *She has such an easy way about her.*

Professor Wallace stood, proudly waving a stack of brochures in his hand. "Found them!" He placed them on the table, then gave Colin a curious look.

Colin suddenly came to his senses. "I should introduce myself. I'm—"

"Jessica's fiancé, of course!" the older man added with a smile. He grabbed Colin's hand. "It's great to finally meet you."

"Actually, sir—"

"I've heard so much about you," the professor continued excitedly. "You've got quite a girl, let me tell you. She's got a voice like an angel, that one."

"Oh, don't I know it." Colin nodded emphatically. "Never heard anything like it, and I hear a lot of great voices."

"It's Nathan, right?" The professor began to spread the brochures out across the table.

"Well, actually, I'm—"

"I hate to brag, but I consider your fiancée to be my prodigy," Professor Wallace interrupted. "When she transferred to the university her sophomore year, I discovered her. She was in my choir at the time. But once I heard her sing solo. . ."

Jessica approached in the middle of his sentence. She gave the professor a look of curiosity.

"I know what you mean," Colin said excitedly. "The first time I heard Jessica sing, I just couldn't believe it. She reminded me of Beverly Sills. At a young age, of course."

"I agree completely!" The professor waved his arms dramatically. "Same quality. Same tone. And talk about a range."

"She's better than most of the professionals I've heard," Colin added. "And I've heard quite a few."

Jessica looked up at him, clearly stunned. "Beverly Sills? Better than most? Those might be slight exaggerations, gentlemen."

"You're one lucky man, Nathan." The older man extended his hand.

Colin caught Jessica's shocked expression. "Actually, sir, I—"

"But with your obvious love for music, I'd have to say that Jessica hasn't fared too poorly herself," the professor interrupted. "You know, it's not always easy to find someone who understands a vocalist's world. In fact, many of the mismatched musical relationships I've witnessed have ended on a sour note, if you know what I mean." He chuckled.

Jessica turned pale. "Professor Wallace, this isn't Nathan. This is—"

"The luckiest man on earth, if you ask me," the older man interrupted. "But, regardless of your name, young man, you'd better be prepared to hang on for dear life if you're marrying this girl. She's going places. And fast. She's already auditioned for the opera; did you know?"

"Yes, sir. Actually, I was there," Colin explained.

"Then you know what a jewel she is. And if I haven't said it already, you're one lucky guy." At that, the professor turned to speak to someone else.

Jessica grabbed Colin's arm. "Did you tell him you were my fiancé?"

"No."

"Where did he get that idea?"

Colin shrugged. "I have no idea."

"This is so embarrassing." She buried her face in her hands.

Colin reached out and gently pulled her hands down so he could see her eyes as he spoke. "It might be embarrassing," he said. "But it's also been enlightening. He was right about your voice, Jessica. He only confirmed what I already knew to be true. You are going places."

Her eyes filled with tears, and he let go of her hands so she could dab at them. "Do you mean that?"

"Of course." Colin gestured toward the professor. "He knows it, and I know it, too. But what about you? Do you know it? Have you made a decision about what you're going to do with this gift you've been given?"

Jessica sighed. "It is a gift," she acknowledged. "But I don't know what I ever did to deserve it."

"When God gives a gift, He doesn't attach any strings," Colin said. "We don't have to qualify for it. And I have it on good authority that the Lord is a lot easier on us than that audition panel you faced."

"No kidding." She chuckled.

"He invented music, you know. And I happen to believe He loves it."

"He does." A smile suddenly lit her face. "And I love it, too. I love the stories in the songs. I love the sound of the instruments warming up. I love the way it feels when the overture begins and the music swells. The whole auditorium just seems to come alive with an electricity that I can't explain." She closed her eyes, as if off in her own world. "And I know I'd love to have the privilege of actually standing up on the stage instead of just sitting in the audience." Her eyes flew open. "I'll get there someday."

"Someday." He dared not say another word.

Jessica's brow wrinkled. "In the meantime, I'm content to go on working to help others reach their dreams." She pointed to a young woman at the end of the table. "I just met that girl down there. Valerie. She's been interning with the junior division of the Houston Grand Opera, and she's considering the University of Houston for her education. I think I helped her make that decision just now."

"That's great, Jessica." *If only you could see how good you'd be at helping lots of young people like her. In Dallas.*

Jessica's fiancé appeared at her side with a plateful of food in his hand. He poked at it with a plastic fork. "How are you supposed to know what any of this stuff is, anyway? None of it looks edible."

"Nathan." She placed her hand on his arm.

"Hmm?" He seemed too preoccupied with his plate to pay much attention.

"Nathan," Jessica continued, "you remember Mr. Phillips."

Nathan looked up immediately, and, as their eyes met, Colin detected a look of animosity.

"Oh yeah. The music guy. From Dallas."

Colin extended his hand. "Please. Call me Colin."

Nathan shifted the plate and briefly shook hands. Very briefly. "So what were you two discussing?" he asked.

"Actually, I was visiting with Jessica's professor," Colin explained. "We were talking music."

"I don't know how anyone could handle all of this opera mumbo jumbo," Nathan said. He pressed a piece of salmon into his mouth and then continued. "But most of these people seem to be cut from the same mold."

"Nathan's not terribly musical," Jessica explained as she slipped her arm around his waist. "But he's learning."

Colin nodded in understanding.

Nathan shrugged. "I'm more at home with numbers. But that's what makes us so perfect for each other." He pulled Jessica close with his free arm, clearly conveying his message. "You know what they say about opposites attracting." He planted a kiss on her cheek.

"Yes, well," Colin said, "if you'll excuse me, I should probably head over to the other side of the room to meet up with the rest of my party. We've got some fund-raising ideas to talk over before I leave for Dallas."

"Are you going back tonight?" Jessica asked.

"In the morning, actually." Colin extended his hand in her direction. "It was nice to run into you once again, Miss Chapman. Maybe I'll have the opportunity to hear you sing again one day."

"Maybe." She gripped his hand longer than he had anticipated, and unspoken words traveled between them. When she withdrew it, her gaze shifted to the floor.

Colin nodded and smiled in her direction, then turned to leave. He couldn't help thinking of all Jessica would be missing, though he did not feel at peace about pursuing the discussion. The Lord clearly had someone else in mind.

The words "You're one lucky man!" rang out across the cacophony of sounds in the room. Colin turned to see the professor waving. He returned the gesture then headed in the opposite direction.

Chapter 7

Jess made her way up the aisle to the front of the church. Though the Sunday morning service had ended nearly half an hour ago, she felt compelled to linger a bit. Explaining this to Nathan had taken some doing, but she just couldn't leave the sanctuary. Not yet. Several issues weighed heavily on her heart, and she must find some answers. As a believer, she knew exactly where those answers would come from.

As she approached the altar area, Jessica felt the urge to drop to her knees. Perhaps the weight of life's decisions drove her down. Whatever the reason, she had to get alone with God—had to get His perspective on the issues at hand. As she knelt in prayer, Jessica poured her heart out. All of the things she had struggled with over the past few weeks now drove her to speak. Finally. God could be trusted with her thoughts, her emotions. He had created them, after all. The words seemed to tumble forth like autumn leaves on a crisp evening breeze.

"Lord, I know You love me. I feel Your love, Father. And I know You have a plan for my life. I don't want to make a mistake or waste time doing the wrong thing. I want to go where You want me to go and do what You want me to do. Anything else would be wrong. I'm tired of walking in my own strength, Lord. I'm tired of trying to make everyone happy and even more tired of pretending to be happy myself. What I need to know is what will make You happy. I want to please You, Father. I really do."

Then the tears started.

After a few moments of weeping in silence, Jessica drew in a deep breath. From out of nowhere, she suddenly felt compelled to sing. A worship song poured forth from her heart and lips. It reverberated across the room and seemed to take her to new heights, freeing her from the turmoil inside. As she sang her self-composed hymn of praise, courage arose inside, which prompted her to stand. She continued to sing as she made her way to the platform area of the church. From here, she could see the entire room. Though empty, she imagined it full of people and sang her heart out.

When the melody ended, she trembled uncontrollably. *What are You doing in me, Lord? Where did that song come from?* Had she composed it herself, or did it come from the very throne of God? On wobbly legs, she made her way down the steps and began to walk to the back of the sanctuary. She knew that something extraordinary had taken place. Something was stirring. Something big.

"Daughter."

Jessica stopped in her tracks and listened intently for the Lord's unspoken words.

"Daughter, I love you. You may not see, but I have awesome plans for you—plans for a hope and a future. Don't be afraid of what you can't see. I can see clearly enough for both of us."

Jessica wept until her chest ached. *Lord, I trust You.* The song of praise came to her lips again, and she sang as if kneeling at the throne of God. All the way out of the building, she sang. In the car, she sang. All the way home, she sang.

By the time she pulled the car into the driveway, Jessica knew what had to be done. She felt an inner peace she had never known before. Surprising words tripped across her tongue, and yet they felt just right. "I'm going to Dallas," she whispered with a smile.

Now came the hard part. She must tell the others. They were inside, probably already seated at the dinner table. She would tell them all at one time. The task would be easier that way. Jessica made her way through the front door and into the dining room, where they all looked up at her with expressions of curiosity.

"You okay?" Nathan asked as she seated herself.

"Great." She smiled warmly.

"We saved you a piece of chicken." Her mother gestured toward the platter on the table. One lone piece sat waiting. Jessica reached for it then loaded her plate with mashed potatoes, gravy, green beans, and a biscuit. Everyone went back to his or her prior conversations. No one seemed to notice her nervous condition except her grandmother and Grandpa Buck, who gazed at her with a knowing look from the opposite end of the table.

After a few bites, Jessica tapped the edge of her water glass with her spoon. When no one noticed, she cleared her throat—loudly. All faces turned her direction. "I have an announcement to make." The words trembled across her lips. All of the courage she had felt in the car seemed to have vanished.

"Don't be afraid, Jessica."

"What is it, honey?" Her mother reached over and patted her hand. "You and Nathan aren't moving up the date, are you?"

Nathan stopped chewing long enough to answer. "Definitely not."

"No, that's not it. I have something else to announce."

"What's up, Jess?" Nathan used his napkin to wipe gravy from his mouth.

She swallowed hard before speaking. "I've decided to accept Mr. Phillips's offer and move to Dallas for the next six months. I'm going to take the internship—if it's not too late."

Chaos immediately erupted as they talked over one another. Jessica couldn't make much sense out of any of it until Nathan's voice rose above the rest. "You're doing what?" he asked.

"I'm going to Dallas."

"Jess, are you sure about this?" Her mother twisted a cloth napkin into knots.

"Yes, I am." She placed her fork down on the table and prepared herself for a lengthy conversation on the matter.

Kent reached across the table and grabbed the potatoes. "Big mistake, sis. Long-distance relationships never work out."

"We can make this work." She sought out Nathan's gaze. He didn't look terribly convinced. "I know that God has big plans for my life."

"Marrying me is that big plan." Nathan's words seemed to rock the table.

"Part of it," she said softly. "But there's more to me than just being someone's bride."

From across the table, Jessica saw her grandmother's nod of assurance and forged ahead. "If I don't take the time to find out who I am—and what God's call on my life is—then I won't be a good wife. I won't be a good mother. I might not even be a good person. It's critical for me to discover God's will for me, personally."

"What are you saying?" Nathan's brow wrinkled.

"I'm not putting a stop to the wedding plans, if that's what you're worried about. I'll be coming back and forth nearly every weekend. At least every other. It's just a four-hour drive, after all. And we have the Internet. We can stay connected online every day with instant messages and e-mail. This doesn't have to be complicated."

"You've just got so much going on already, Jess," her mother said. "I hope you can handle it all. Once you get up there, your workload will be really heavy."

"I know, and I'm looking forward to that. It's not like I haven't thought all of this through. I have. Carefully. I've prayed about it. I've weighed my options. And I know this is right. I just hope you can all trust my judgment to make this decision."

The room grew silent, and Jessica felt like a criminal at an inquisition. *Lord, is this what it feels like to be alone in your principles?*

Her grandmother grinned mischievously then tapped her own water glass. "I have a few comments to make on the matter," she said. Everyone turned their attention in her direction. "I, for one, trust my granddaughter." The older woman spoke slowly, deliberately. "She's proven herself to be reliable over the years, and I have no cause to doubt her judgment now. If Jessica feels the Lord is leading her to Dallas, so be it. Whether right or wrong, she will discover His plan in the process. I think we should let her be the grown-up woman that she is, and that's all I have to say on the matter." She leaned back in her seat and folded her arms.

Once again, the room erupted in lively conversation. Jessica let her weight rest against the back of the chair and turned her head from side to side as comments flowed freely. Only when she looked to the opposite end of the table, into her grandmother's adoring eyes, did she feel the strength of agreement.

"Mr. Phillips? Mr. Phillips!"

Colin brought the church choir to a halt as eighty-two-year-old Walter Malone fought to get his attention. "What's up, Walter?"

"Your cell phone is going off. Even with my bad ears, I can hear it." The older man pointed to his hearing aid and grinned.

Colin heard the ringing then but shrugged. "I can call them back—whoever it is. We're in the middle of practice right now, and with all the weeks I've missed, you guys are out of shape." The thirty-some-odd choir members of His Word Community Church began to grumble. Colin didn't mind. In fact, he had grown used to it. For three years now, he had served as volunteer choir director at this small community church on the north side of Dallas. Its members, most in their golden years, lived to torment him. He loved every minute with them.

"Never know—could be missing the most important call of your life!" Walter shook his head.

"Could be your future missus on the phone," seventy-four-year-old Ida Sullivan added. "But if you don't want to take the call, that's your choice. 'Course, it's about time you found yourself a girlfriend, if you want my opinion on the matter. Not that anybody ever listens to my opinion." She began to grumble under her breath.

Colin chuckled. "Okay, okay. I'll get it." He reached to pick up the phone but noticed he had already missed the call. He glanced curiously at the area code. *Someone from the Houston area. Lord, is it possible. . . ?*

Suddenly his heart began to race. "Why don't we take a break for about five minutes, and then we'll go over that last section again." He bounded from the stage and made his way to the back of the auditorium as he redialed the number. It rang once, twice, three times, then a familiar voice greeted him.

"Hello?"

"Jessica, is that you?" Colin felt his spirits lift immediately.

"It's me." She sounded more cheerful than before. He liked that sound.

"It's good to hear from you." He continued to walk, though Walter now joined him. Ida stood nearby, clearly straining to hear.

"Do you have a minute?" Jessica asked.

"I do." He tried to signal Walter away with his eyes, but the older man simply wasn't taking the hint.

"I have something to tell you," Jessica said. "Something I hope will be good news."

His heart pounded double time. *Lord, are You really this good to me? Have You answered my prayer for a director of the children's chorus?* "I could use some good news," he responded.

"I just wanted to let you know—I mean, if the offer still holds—that I'd like to come."

"Really? You're coming to Dallas?" He let out a whoop that nearly sent poor Walter reeling. "Jessica, that's great. What did your family say? What about your fiancé? Is he okay with this?" Immediately Colin regretted asking. These were personal questions and really none of his business. Besides, at the word *fiancé*, Ida waved her arms in defeat and turned to walk the other way.

"They'll get used to the idea," Jessica said. "But I have to follow the Lord's leading."

"And He's leading you here. Are you sure?" *Lord, I want her to be very, very sure. I don't want to take her away from anything You've planned for her there.*

"I'm sure," she said. "I'll be traveling back and forth on weekends as I'm able. I know I can make this work. And, to be honest, I can't wait to meet the kids and get to work. Which reminds me, when should I come? Also, do you have any ideas about housing? And what sort of vocal materials should I bring with me for warm-ups and practices? I've got some great children's pieces."

"We really need to talk more about this," Colin agreed. "There will be quite a few details to iron out. But the Dallas Met is prepared to offer you a place to stay—all expenses paid, plus a modest salary. And, as I said before, a place in the chorus of our upcoming shows." At that, Walter elbowed him in the ribs. "Uh, could I call you later tonight? I'm, uh. . ." Colin whispered into the receiver. He looked into Walter's imploring eyes. "I'm in the middle of something right now."

"Oh, sure. I'm leaving for our evening service at church in about an hour, but I'll be back around nine. Is that too late?"

"Nope. Should work out just right."

"Well, thank you for calling me back," she said. "I feel a lot better now that the decision is made. You know how that goes."

"Yes, I do. And thank you for taking the time to reconsider," he added. "I'm so anxious to see what the Lord is going to do."

"Me, too. Well, I guess I'll let you get back to work now. Have a great evening."

"You, too, Jessica." He hung the phone up and turned to face thirty pairs of inquisitive eyes.

" 'You, too, Jessica,' " Walter spoke in a lovey-dovey voice.

"Now, Walter. It's not like that."

"I'd say. Especially if she's already got a beau," Ida threw in. " 'Course, I haven't met him yet. Don't rightly know if he's the right man for her, but that's for the Lord to determine, not me. Not that anyone ever listens to my opinions anyhow." She began to mutter again, and Colin turned his attention to getting the choir back in place on the stage.

Somehow, though, he couldn't keep his thoughts or the tempo of the music straight. Everything seemed to have suddenly, ridiculously gone askew.

Chapter 8

Colin spent the last Saturday in September thumbing through a stack of children's résumés. He stifled a yawn as he read over them for the umpteenth time. He tried not to let his exhaustion stop him from the task at hand, though he had slept precious few hours over the past week. Thankfully, auditions for the adult performance of *Madame Butterfly* had gone well. With a full cast firmly established, rehearsals would soon be under way.

However, narrowing the list for the children's production of *Amahl and the Night Visitors* might prove to be a bit more difficult. Fifty talented children would be auditioning tomorrow afternoon. Colin held their résumés in his hand. Out of that group, he could choose only twenty. How would he ever decide who to keep and who to cut? Which hearts would be encouraged, and which ones broken?

Thankfully, he wouldn't have to make those decisions alone. Colin would have Jessica Chapman's help. He glanced at his watch. She should be arriving—actually, she should be pulling into the Dallas area right about now, if everything went according to plan. He'd give her the day to settle in, then call her first thing in the morning, perhaps even invite her to church. Then, armed and ready, they would dive right into the auditions.

Colin leaned back in his chair, and relief washed over him. For years, he had dreamed of starting a children's company in the Dallas area. God had answered his prayers just a few short months ago when the board of the Metropolitan Opera agreed to finance his dream. He had been given free rein to oversee the project, but with so much on his plate already, selecting a vocal director had been critical to his own survival.

His mind drifted to Jessica once again. Colin had thanked the Lord daily for providing just the right person for the job. And what a job it would be. With fifty children slotted for auditions, he could easily predict a couple of sleepless nights ahead. His eyes grew heavy as he glanced through the children's résumés one last time. *Lord, help us make the right decisions. I want to give opportunity to the ones You've chosen. Help us, Father.*

Jessica chatted with her mom by cell phone as they caravanned into the Dallas area. "Are you getting sleepy?" she asked as she caught a glimpse of her mother's car in the rearview mirror.

"Not too bad," her mother said with a yawn. "What about you?"

"I'm wide awake." Jessica fought to balance the cell phone against her ear as she glanced over at Nathan. He sat snoring in the seat next to her. "Nathan's passed out, but that's a good thing. He has an exam Monday morning, and he needs all the rest he can get. I didn't mind driving, anyway," she added. "I need to get used to it." She glanced over at him, nearly dropping the phone in the process. It warmed her heart to see him sleeping so peacefully after his rough week. He had been so good to give up his Saturday to help her move, especially in light of his objections.

"I suppose." Her mother sighed. "How much farther?"

"Mmm." Jessica glanced down at the printed e-mail. "Looks like we're only about twenty minutes from the exit. How are you guys doing back there?" She peered into the rearview mirror once again.

"We're fine, honey. Your brother is preoccupied with his new pocket organizer, and Andrew's reading a history book."

"Figures. What about you? How are you holding out?"

"I'm a little stiff from driving so long. I'll be glad to get there."

"Me, too." Jessica stretched. "But it's good to talk to you. Again. What did we ever do before cell phones?"

"I can't remember. But speaking of phones, I should probably hang up now. I need to save all the minutes I can. With you living in Dallas now..." Her mother's voice seemed to break.

"It's going to be okay, Mom," Jessica said. "You'll hardly have time to miss me before I'm home again. Wait and see."

"Okay, honey. Guess I'll talk to you when we get there."

"I love you."

"I love you, too."

As she ended the call, Jessica leaned back against the seat and yawned. She glanced at the clock. *Only 4:16? It feels more like midnight.* Then again, her day had started pretty early. Loading the car had taken awhile. Though a furnished apartment awaited her in Dallas, Jessica still had to pack her clothes, music, and personal items. As for kitchenware, her mother had pressed enough of that into her trunk to last Jess a lifetime.

Not that she planned to spend a lifetime away from home. The next six months would fly by. She felt sure of it. With September drawing to a close, Jessica had just a few precious weeks of fall left to prepare a team of youngsters to perform in their first Christmas opera—after tomorrow's auditions, anyway. And what fun she would have getting them ready!

Jessica's mind wandered. Her distraction nearly caused her to miss the appropriate exit. Thankfully, she looked up just in time. With a nervous glance in the rearview mirror, she discovered her mother had made the exit, as well.

Within minutes, she pulled her car to the front of Northgate Crossing apartments. As she stopped and shifted into park, she glanced over at Nathan, who still snored loudly. *Let him sleep a few more minutes. He deserves it.* She climbed from the car and stretched before waving to her mother and stepfather. They gave the apartment complex an admiring look.

"Not bad," Andrew said.

"It is nice, isn't it?" Jessica felt a wave of contentment pass over her as she turned toward the office. "But I'd better get in there and pick up my key. I think they close at five. I'm cutting it pretty close."

Minutes later, she turned the shiny silver key to open the door of her very first apartment. Stepping inside, she gave a whistle. "Wow." She looked over the spacious living room, fully decked out with plush furniture and complementary décor.

"Looks like you won't be suffering much, sis." Kent pushed past her with an armload of clothes. "Where do you want these, anyway?"

"In the bedroom." She led the way into the large front bedroom. It, too, took her by surprise. She could certainly learn to adapt to her new surroundings without much trouble.

"Not bad, not bad." Kent dropped the clothes on the bed, then headed out to the car for more. "If this is how opera singers live, I might want to take a few voice lessons myself."

"Very funny."

Nathan entered the room with a suitcase in hand. "Found a closet yet?" he asked.

"I'm guessing it's through that door." She pointed to her left. He stifled a yawn, then tossed the suitcase inside and turned back toward the front door.

Jessica gave the place a thorough looking over, more than pleased with her new home. *Thank You, Lord. You've been too good to me.* She could almost envision sharing this home, this beautiful home, with Nathan after their wedding. Almost. *Stop thinking like that. He would never agree to move to Dallas. This is just for a season, not a lifetime.*

"Knock, knock!" A chipper female voice brought Jessica back to reality. She turned to discover a young woman, blond and extremely tanned, standing in her open doorway. "Just wanted to stop by and say howdy," the petite beauty said with a smile. "I'm Kellie."

"I'm Jessica." She made her way to the door and extended her hand in greeting.

"I know." The girl's eyes twinkled merrily. "My sister has been talking about you for days."

"Your sister?"

"Katie. She sings with the Dallas Metropolitan Opera," Kellie explained. "We live right next door. She helped Colin find the apartment for you. Of course, she'd do anything for that guy. She's head over, if you know what I mean."

"Oh, I see. Well, thank her for me, okay?"

"I'm sure you two will be best buds." The blond sighed. "But me, well. . ." She laughed. "I'm completely tone-deaf. Don't care a thing about opera. Hope that doesn't offend you."

"Doesn't offend me." Nathan approached with another armload of clothes.

"Me, either," Jessica added. "Honestly."

"I can brew a mean cup of coffee, though." Kellie's lips curled up in a cute smile. "And I'm great if you ever want to chat about boyfriends or broken hearts or stuff like that."

"Thanks." Jessica glanced up at Nathan, whose eyes seemed fixed on the blond bombshell. "Um, speaking of boyfriends. This is my fiancé, Nathan."

Nathan nearly dropped the armload of clothes as he extended his hand. Kellie shook it vigorously.

"Nice to meet you," the perky young blond said.

"You, too." Nathan glanced at the ground and withdrew his hand.

"So," she said, "is there anything I can do to help?"

At that moment, Kent passed through the open doorway with a box of pots and pans. He nearly tripped over his own feet as his gaze fell on Kellie. "Uh, Jess?"

"Yeah?"

"Could I, uh, talk to you in the bedroom?"

She trudged along behind him, leaving Nathan alone in the doorway with the blond.

"Who is that?" her brother asked, barely above a squeak.

Jessica shrugged. "She's just a neighbor who stopped by to say hello. Why?"

"Introduce me."

"Get a grip, Kent."

"No, I mean it." He spoke insistently. "Introduce me. But make me look good. Say something great about me."

With a groan, Jessica made her way to the doorway once again, this time taking pains to carefully introduce her brother to Kellie. When the vivacious young woman offered to give the newcomers a tour of the complex, Jessica declined, but Kent followed behind the boisterous blond like an obedient puppy. *Great. Now I've lost him completely.*

Jessica continued to unload the car with some assistance from her mother and Nathan, while Andrew drove off in search of a restaurant for dinner. She could hardly keep her thoughts straight. When they finished, she plopped down onto the sofa, completely exhausted. *If I sit here much longer, I'll fall asleep.*

Her mother joined her, letting out a groan as she sat. "I'm getting too old for this."

"Mom!" Jessica shook her head in disbelief. "You're not old."

"I haven't helped anyone move in years. It's a lot of work."

"No kidding." Nathan dropped into a wingback chair across from the sofa. "And to think we have to move you back in six months. Then move again into our own place. That's a lot of moving in one year's time."

Jessica shrugged. "I'm sorry. I really am."

Andrew appeared in the doorway. "Anyone hungry?"

"Starved," Jessica and her mother said in unison.

"I found a great Mexican restaurant just a couple of blocks away," Andrew said. "Let's grab a bite together before we head back home."

"Good luck finding Kent." Jessica chuckled.

"Where is he?" Andrew glanced at his watch.

Nathan stood and stretched. "Who knows. But don't worry. I'll track him down. The sooner we get on the road, the better. I've got a lot of studying left to do before the weekend is over." He headed outside to look for Kent.

Jessica enjoyed a few moments of quiet conversation with her mother and Andrew until her brother burst through the door.

"I'm in love!" He clutched his heart and acted as if he would faint.

"Honestly, Kent." Jessica rolled her eyes. "Not again."

"This time it's the real thing. I think I'm moving to Dallas."

"Nothing impulsive about this boy." Andrew patted him on the back.

"Well, before you up and marry this girl, would you like to have some dinner?" his mother asked. "Mexican food."

"I guess." Kent sighed loud enough to alert the entire apartment building.

As they gathered up their belongings and headed to the door, Jessica realized Nathan still hadn't returned. "Anyone seen my fiancé?" she asked.

"Oh, he'll be here in a minute," Kent said. "He and Kellie are talking about the stock market. Turns out, she's a broker. Isn't that amazing? I mean, isn't she amazing?"

"Amazing." Jessica smiled at her brother's antics.

Nathan soon appeared at the door, and they headed out to the restaurant. Over a plateful of enchiladas, Jessica decided to share some things that had been weighing heavily on her heart. She chose her words carefully. "I don't want any of you to think I've lost interest in planning the wedding."

Nathan shrugged his response. "I'm not worried, babe."

"No need to be." She gave him a hug.

"We know you better than that, honey."

"I know there's still so much to think about," Jessica continued. "We'll need to settle on some invitations when I come home weekend after next."

"True." He scooped a chip full of salsa into his mouth. "Or," he said after swallowing, "I guess I could just leave that part up to you. I've got a lot on my plate between now and then. No pun intended." He gestured to his half-empty plate and grinned.

174

"You wouldn't mind?" She looked at him curiously.

"Nope. I'm so busy with school. Besides, anything you pick will be great. I trust your judgment."

"Really?" *That's odd.* Jessica tried not to read too much into his lack of enthusiasm.

Her mother reached out and grasped her hand. "I'll give you as much help as you need or want."

"Thanks, Mom."

"And I'm only a phone call away. Promise me you won't be a stranger, Jess." Her mom's eyes grew misty.

"Trust me. I won't. I'm going to miss all of you so much." Tears sprang to her eyes, and she brushed them away. "But I know that God has a plan for me, and I'm so excited about what He's doing. Thank you, all of you, for being so understanding."

Jessica's mother reached over and gave her a warm embrace. Andrew smiled his reassurance from across the table. Kent went on talking about Kellie, the love of his life.

And Nathan. . .

Nathan seemed to have drifted off to sleep, sitting straight up.

Chapter 9

The first two weeks in Dallas flew by. When the auditions for the much-anticipated children's production drew to a close, Jessica finally had a moment to catch her breath. The whole process had placed her squarely in the center of a musical whirlwind. She loved every whimsical moment and immediately grew to love the children selected for the prized roles, as well.

In her heart, Jessica knew she had been born for this very thing—to train and mentor young people in the classical vocal style. In the same way that her father had supported her musical gifts, she would encourage these budding stars. Already, Jessica could see that her input would have tremendous payoff, both vocally and psychologically. Nothing could make her feel better.

The knowledge that she would soon be singing alongside some of the best-trained voices in the country left her speechless. Jessica could hardly wait to join the chorus of *Madame Butterfly*. Her formal audition for the company would come in a couple of weeks, though her position in the chorus had already been secured by Colin, who—she had recently learned—would play one of the major roles in the production.

Her lips curled upward in an unexpected smile as she thought about Colin Phillips. More than a mentor and guide, he had already turned out to be a great friend. And his vocal ability left her speechless. When she heard him sing to the children for the first time, Jessica felt an unexplainable kinship with him. His rich baritone voice had reminded her of someone, something—though she couldn't put her finger on who or what.

Jessica truly came to know herself in Dallas. Somehow life just seemed more exciting here. The city itself seemed to be alive with electrical energy. In spite of a few moments of homesickness for Nathan and her family, Jessica never once regretted her decision to move to this thriving metropolis. Not that she had much time to ponder the matter. In no time at all, it seemed, she was on her way back to Houston for a weekend visit.

As she drove, Jessica spent a great deal of time in thought and in prayer. *Lord, You've been so good to me. I know I don't deserve all of this, but thank You. And thank You for trusting these children to my care. Help me to be a good example to them. I know it's not specifically a Christian environment, but help me to shine Your light in any way I can. And help me to balance my life in Dallas with my life at home. I pray Your perfect will is done in my life, Father. Amen.*

She continued south on Interstate 45, completely lost in her thoughts. On more than one occasion, Jessica challenged herself to think of other things besides the goings-on in Dallas. So much in her life had changed, and yet she must remain focused on the task at hand. Nathan would be waiting at home. Together, they would finalize their guest list, and then she would place an order for invitations. In all truthfulness, she had scarcely spent more than a moment or two thinking about the wedding, what with all of the events of the past few days, but this weekend at home would help.

Home.

Somehow traveling back to Houston put things in perspective. And seeing Nathan again would be great. She could hardly wait, in fact. There were so many stories to share—so much news to relay. He would be thrilled to hear it all.

Then again, he hadn't had much time to call or send e-mails over the past two weeks. Between his work schedule and college classes, he seemed to be almost as swamped as she. *Never mind that. We'll have the whole weekend together. It will be great.*

Jessica arrived home a couple of hours later, breathlessly anticipating all that lay ahead. Her mother greeted her at the door with a kiss on each cheek and excited squeals. "I've missed you so much!"

Jessica felt tears in her eyes as she melted in her mother's arms. "I've missed you, too, Mom." It felt wonderful to be home once again, and she could hardly wait to catch up on all that had happened.

"Well, look who's here." Andrew appeared in the doorway. "The lost sheep returns home at last."

"I wasn't lost," Jessica said with a smile. *In fact,* she pondered, *I feel like I've finally found myself.*

"Well, come on in, stranger." Andrew grabbed her suitcase and ushered her into the living room.

Kent joined them, and everyone promptly began to ask question after question.

"What do you think about...?"

"Have you had a chance to...?"

"I can hardly wait to tell you..."

On and on they went. After a few moments of talking over one another, the conversation finally fell into some semblance of order, and Jessica was able to share her heart. She told them about the children. She told them about the magnificent theater and its intricate design. She shared some funny stories of things her boisterous neighbors, Katie and Kellie, had done to welcome her to the neighborhood. In short, she finally had a chance to put a voice to all of the Lord's goodness in her life over the past two weeks.

Andrew and her mother laughed at each antic and added their own stories of all that had transpired since her absence. They had missed her terribly but had managed to take advantage of the spare bedroom by purchasing a new computer and desk to replace her missing furniture. Kent admitted, with reddened cheeks, that he had e-mailed Kellie on a number of occasions but had yet to hear back from her. He claimed her computer must be broken, though Jessica certainly knew better.

"Tell me about the church," she urged everyone. "How are the kids? How is Mrs. Witherspoon?"

"Oh, you've missed so much already!" Her mother lit up with excitement. "The children are going to be performing a Christmas musical. Something with an angel theme. Believe it or not, Mrs. Witherspoon has already held auditions. Rehearsals start next Sunday afternoon."

"You're kidding."

"No, I'm not."

Her mother laughed. "She's really in her element, but who would have guessed it?"

"No kidding." Jessica couldn't be more surprised. Funny, she also felt a tad bit of jealousy creep up at the news.

"She's always been such a 'behind-the-scenes' sort of gal—letting you take charge of everything," her mother continued. "But you should have heard her talking to Pastor Meeks about the set design and costumes. She's amazing."

"Wow. That's great." Though startled, Jessica breathed a huge sigh of relief, recognizing that this, another piece to the puzzle, had been orchestrated by the Lord.

They tumbled back into lively conversation, and time flew by. Jessica stayed up well past midnight, filling her family's ears with every wonderful detail of the past two weeks. When at last it came time to rest, she could hardly keep her eyes open. She fell asleep on the sofa, too tired to argue with the lumpy pillow or the itchy cushions. She awoke on Saturday morning with a stiff neck. However, her heart seemed to be dancing.

Jessica could hardly wait to see Nathan. After a brief phone call, they arranged to meet at a local pancake house for breakfast. He met her at the door of the restaurant thirty minutes later and swept her into his arms.

"How's my girl?" he asked as soon as their lips parted.

Her animated response seemed to flow like water. "I'm great! But I've missed you so much. How are you? How is school? How's work?"

"Whoa, whoa!" He put his hands up in protest. "Too many questions. Too fast."

"I'm sorry." She wrapped her arm around his waist, and they entered the restaurant together. "I just feel like we have so much to talk about and so little time."

"Yes, well. . ." He drew in a deep breath. "Less time than you know."

"What do you mean?"

"I have an appointment at noon," he explained. "Then I'm supposed to meet my study group at three."

"You're kidding."

"Wish I was. But let's not let that stop us from having a good time while we're together." He took hold of her hand.

"I just miss you." She pouted. *How could he schedule a study session on my weekend at home? Doesn't he know how much I need to be with him? And why did he have to have a meeting today, of all days?*

Nathan gave her a curious look just as the server appeared. "Well, I miss you, too, Jess." His voice dropped to a hoarse whisper. "But I'm not the one who moved away, remember? And I still have things to do, things that can't wait."

She followed in numb silence to a table at the rear of the room. Suddenly, everything she had wanted to say seemed to vanish from her mind. A distance seemed to have opened up between them. *What's happening here?*

Jessica immediately determined to narrow the gap as best she could. Instead of telling Nathan any of her stories, she listened attentively while he shared all that had happened at college over the past two weeks. She held her tongue when he told her of an idea his mother had given him regarding the wedding reception. She nodded in agreement when he talked about the upcoming honeymoon to Germany.

In short, she kept all of her excitement inside, in the hope that this feeling of sadness would disappear. And yet, as his conversation shifted to less appealing things—the stock market, his latest accounting classes, and the advantages of lower interest rates—all Jessica could think about were her own tales. She tried to push them down, but they would not go away.

By the end of the meal, Jessica felt as if she could hardly remain quiet any longer. She quickly shared a few details of the past two weeks, and Nathan listened intently. *He is interested.* He seemed especially curious to hear about her neighbors and their antics, asking on more than one occasion if Kellie had corresponded with Kent. By the end of the meal, Jessica felt safe and secure once again.

They parted with a quick embrace, and Nathan assured her of his love. *He just misses me. But everything will be all right as long as we get some time alone together.* She would make sure that happened. Somehow. In the meantime, she would stay focused. That would certainly help.

The rest of the day seemed to fly by. Jessica thumbed through dozens of invitation samples but couldn't seem to settle on anything she thought they would both like. Sunday morning arrived quicker than she could have imagined, and she attended church with her family. Then, before she even had time to think about it, Jessica found herself on the road once more. All the way back to Dallas, her mind reeled. She tried to concentrate on wedding plans but instead found her thoughts drifting to the opera, and especially to the children awaiting her at home.

Home. Hmm.

So many exciting adventures lay ahead, and she had a lot of plans to make. Thankfully, she wouldn't be alone in any of them.

Jessica smiled as she thought of Colin. What a wonderful, godly man he had turned out to be. His love for the opera was surpassed only by his love for the Lord. *And the children.* He seemed to be completely taken with each one. She fully understood and appreciated his dedication to them, especially the ones who came from underprivileged families in the inner city. Many would never have received an opportunity to be trained at no cost if he hadn't implemented this program.

Thank You, Lord, for giving Colin this idea. How wonderful for these children to get the chance to sing in front of a real audience. And thank You for letting me partici-pate. I'm so excited, Father.

Jessica consumed herself with thoughts of the upcoming week. Though she already missed Nathan terribly, she would see him very soon. In fact, he would be flying up next Saturday afternoon to escort her to a lavish fund-raiser dinner for the new children's program. She could hardly wait. In the meantime, she still had rehearsals with the children and her audition for *Madame Butterfly*.

With so many thoughts tumbling madly, Jessica could barely keep her mind on the road. By the time she arrived back in Dallas late Sunday evening, she felt fully awake and alive with excitement. Tomorrow simply couldn't come soon enough.

~

Colin checked the time on several occasions Sunday afternoon. He knew Jessica would be driving back today and prayed for her safety. As he headed off to church for choir practice, he planned the week ahead. There were so many details to at-tend to. *Thank You, Lord, for giving me someone to share that responsibility.* Some-how, just knowing Jessica would be back on the job tomorrow morning made everything fine again.

As he steered his car into the church parking lot Sunday evening, Colin's cell phone rang. He grabbed it, then glanced at the number. "Oh no. Not again." For weeks, he had been fending off calls from one of the young women in the com-pany. Katie Conway. She had expressed more than a little interest in him. *I don't want to be rude to her, but. . .*

Would it be wrong to simply ignore the call?

On the fourth ring, he answered. *Might be something urgent.* After all, she was a key player in the upcoming opera and needed to be assured, even pacified a lot. He didn't really mind—for the sake of the show. "Hello?" He spoke hesitantly.

"Oh, Colin, I'm so glad you answered." Katie immediately dove into a lengthy discussion about a problem she appeared to be having with a particular vocal number in the opera. "Would you mind, I mean—you don't have to. . . But would you mind coming by my place later this evening?" she asked. "I'm having such a difficult time with this one section of music, and having you here to sing along with me would be so helpful."

Colin glanced at his watch and started to explain that he was running late for choir practice. Just then, he heard a tapping on his car window. He looked up to see Ida Sullivan, standing with her arms crossed.

"You're late." The older woman mouthed the words and pointed to her watch.

Colin shrugged and gestured toward the phone, trying all the while to think of an answer to Katie's suggestion. "I, uh. . . I'm in the middle of something right now," he spoke quietly into the phone. "Actually, I'm at church."

"Oh, I'm sorry." He thought he heard a little sniffle. "I shouldn't have bothered you. I know you're so busy."

"It's no bother," he assured her. Ida continued to tap at his window. "But I'm afraid I've already got plans tonight, so I won't be much help to you."

Katie sighed loudly. "That's okay. Jessica will be back in town in a while. I know she won't mind giving me a hand with the music. She's great on the keyboard, anyway, and she's such a good sport."

She'll be exhausted.

"I guess I'll see you tomorrow then." Katie's voice lifted slightly. "And thanks so much for being such a great friend, Colin."

"Good-bye, Katie." He hung up, feeling like a traitor. *Lord, I don't want to lead her on, but I don't know how to let her know I'm not interested without hurting her feelings.*

Just then, Ida knocked on his window again. Colin opened the car door and stepped outside.

"Talking to your girlfriend?" she asked.

"Nope. Just a business acquaintance." He began to walk toward the church. She trudged along behind him.

"How am I ever going to get you married off if you won't settle on a girl?"

"Ida, really."

"What sort of lady are you looking for anyway? Maybe I can be on the lookout. I was quite a matchmaker in my day."

Is that why you never married? He didn't dare ask the question. "I'm not looking." Truthfully, Colin didn't see the point. When the Lord was ready to bring him a bride, she would simply appear—he prayed.

"That's half your trouble." Ida shook her head. "How can you ever expect to find something if you're not looking for it?"

He shook his head in disbelief. "You sound like my mother."

The older woman broke into a broad smile and slipped her arm into the crook of his as they approached the building. "Why, that's the nicest thing you've ever said to me." She paused and looked up at him intently. "Tell you what," she said with a broad grin, "if neither of us is married in a year, why don't we just bite the bullet and marry each other?"

"Ida," he said, then chuckled. "To be perfectly honest, I don't know if my heart could take it."

Chapter 10

Jessica sprinted, nearly breathless, to the baggage claim area of the Dallas–Fort Worth Airport. She managed to locate Nathan standing in the midst of a crowd of people, his hand tightly clutching the handle of his rolling bag. He looked anything but happy. She waved her hand to get his attention and hollered, "Nathan! Over here."

He shook his head as she approached. "This is the craziest excuse for an airport I've ever seen. I can't believe this mob."

Jessica couldn't argue the point. In fact, she had perused the parking garage for nearly half an hour in search of a place to deposit her car. After finally locating a spot, she had walked a good half mile to get to the baggage claim area.

"I was starting to think you'd forgotten about me." Nathan gave her a forced pout.

"How could I forget about you? I love you." She reached up and gave him a playful peck on the cheek. "I've just been stuck in traffic. And the parking situation is terrible. This airport is a mess."

"No kidding." He looked around at the throng of people and shook his head.

They walked hand in hand to the parking garage. Jessica tried to lift his spirits by telling him some of her ideas for the wedding. By the time they arrived at the car, he seemed to be far more relaxed. His broad smile let her know everything was right with the world once again.

"So, what's the plan for tonight?" he asked.

"It's going to be so wonderful." Jessica came alive with excitement. "All of the children are going to be there, along with nearly three hundred financial supporters of the program. The kids will be sharing one of the songs from the production. But don't get your hopes up too high." She paused as she thought about the anxiety level of the children. "We just started rehearsals a couple of weeks ago, and they're still on a learning curve."

Nathan shrugged. "Wouldn't know the difference."

As they climbed into the car, Jessica continued. "We'll be going back to my apartment first to get changed. Then we'll meet Colin and the others at the theater at six fifteen."

"Colin?" Nathan gave her an awkward glance.

"Sure. He's in charge of tonight's event. Anyway, we'll be meeting him to

183

finalize some plans for the kids, who will arrive at six thirty. Dinner will be served at seven. They tell me it's going to be wonderful."

"No more buffet lines?"

"Nope. This is a sit-down affair. But even if I get busy, you won't be completely alone. My neighbor Kellie will be there."

"Really? Why would she come to something like this? I thought she couldn't stand opera."

"She can't. But her sister, Katie, sings with the company, remember? In fact, she is playing one of the leads in *Madame Butterfly*. I'm sure you'll hear all about it before the night's over. Katie has a tendency to talk your ear off."

"Great."

"When she's not trying to get Colin's attention, that is." Jessica smiled as she thought about Katie's ridiculous antics to win the attentions of the man she called, "Verdi himself!" Colin was either blind or not interested. He didn't seem to pay much attention to the vivacious blond, though she fought with every ounce of strength to be noticed.

Jessica continued to fill Nathan in on the details as she drove. By the time they arrived at her apartment, they had just enough time to quickly change into evening attire and prepare to leave once again. Jessica had selected a new dress for the occasion and could hardly wait to show it off. As she entered the living room in the sage green gown with beaded straps, she awaited Nathan's response.

"What time did you say we have to be there?" He stared at his reflection in the mirror as he straightened his tie.

"Six fifteen."

He turned her direction but seemed to see right through her. "Shouldn't we be going then?"

Jessica glanced at her watch. They should have just enough time if she hurried. She tightened a bobby pin to hold a loose curl in place, then smiled at Nathan. "I'm ready when you are."

Jessica was on pins and needles as she drove to the theater. She tried to envision how the evening would go—how she would comfortably work Nathan into all of her plans. The last thing she wanted was to make him feel left out. She would make sure that didn't happen.

Jessica pulled the car into the parking garage at 6:13. "We need to make a run for it." Hand in hand, they raced toward the beautiful lobby, where carefully decorated tables with elaborate centerpieces had been set up ahead of time. Once inside, Jessica couldn't help noticing Nathan's look of admiration.

"This is quite a place," he said.

"I know." She sighed. "It's beautiful here." She located a place for the two of them to sit and asked Nathan to wait for her while she tried to track down the children. Jessica fought her way through the ever-growing crowd heading in the direction of the rehearsal room at the south end of the lobby. She found herself distracted on more than one occasion by chatty new friends, who all enthusiastically told her how lovely she looked. She thanked them all and tried to keep moving, though she couldn't seem to locate Colin anywhere.

Lord, don't let him be late. I can't do this by myself. As if in direct answer to her prayer, she made him out through the crowd. In his sleek black tuxedo, he almost looked like a character from a movie. His dark curls seemed a little less unruly tonight, and his cheeks were flushed with excitement as he talked to a friend. Though she certainly didn't intend to, Jessica found herself staring. *He's really in his element.*

Just then, her neighbor Katie approached with a curious smile on her face. "That fiancé of yours is quite a catch," she said with an admiring grin.

"Oh, you met him?" Jessica glanced back at Nathan, who still sat alone. He looked bored out of his mind and, for a brief moment, she regretting leaving him.

"Sure did," Katie said. "Interesting first meeting, I don't mind telling you."

"What do you mean?"

Her friend giggled. "He thought I was Kellie. Called me by the wrong name."

"Oh."

"I played along with him," Katie said. "But do you know what he said to me?"

Jessica shook her head.

"He told me he'd rather be watching the news channel. Wanted to know if I felt the same way." Katie laughed.

Jessica's heart sank. "You're kidding."

The blond shook her head. "Nope. Then he made some sort of joke about music. I take it he's not an opera fan?"

"I'm working on him." Jessica bit her lip as she stared at Nathan once again.

"Still, he's a cutie," Katie said admiringly. "With a face like that, who needs to like opera?"

Jessica looked up to see Kellie approaching her fiancé. What appeared to be a look of relief crossed his face. He immediately dove into an animated conversation with Katie's twin sister. *Why can't he light up like that when we're talking?*

"Jess, are you with me?" Katie looked at her curiously.

"Oh, yeah." She turned her attention back to her friend. "I'm just a little preoccupied. But I need to stay focused. I need to connect with Colin quickly so we can get the kids ready."

"I happen to know right where he is." Katie's face lit up. "Let me take you to him. It will give me an excuse to spend some time with him. You don't mind, do you?"

"Of course not." Together they pressed their way through the crowd to Colin's side.

He looked up with a broad smile as they approached. "Wow." He gave an admiring whistle. "Must be my lucky night. You both look exceptionally gorgeous."

"Thank you, kind sir." Katie curtsied, and he bowed in response.

"And, I might say," Colin turned in Jessica's direction, "that shade of green is exquisite with your beautiful auburn hair, Miss Chapman." He gestured for her to turn around, and she did so with embarrassment washing over her.

"You flatter me." She extended her hand, and he kissed it with a theatrical flair. For a moment, Jessica could hardly breathe. *Stop it. He's just playacting.*

Katie cleared her throat and extended her hand, as well. Colin repeated the gesture, though his gaze never seemed to leave Jessica. She felt her cheeks warm and wondered what he might be thinking. "I, uh, thought we should probably meet with the children soon." She glanced at her watch.

"You're right. Let's get a head count then take a few minutes to run through the first part of their piece as a warm-up."

She nodded and attempted to stop the butterflies that suddenly seemed to fill her stomach.

"Are you okay?" Katie nudged her.

"Yes, why?"

"I don't know." Her friend looked at her nervously. "You're a little flushed."

"Oh," Jessica stammered. "It's warm in here—that's all. I'll be better off when we get to the rehearsal room. I'm sure it's cooler in there."

"Do you need my help?" Katie's lips turned down in a rehearsed pout as she looked back and forth between Colin and Jessica.

"I think we'll be fine," he said, "but thanks for the offer." He turned to face Jessica. "Are you ready?"

She smiled her response, and they moved through the crowd together.

⌣

Colin couldn't seem to wipe the silly grin off of his face all evening. He directed the children as they sang one of their selections from *Amahl and the Night Visitors* in front of three hundred excited patrons. Though they struggled a bit in one small section, the youngsters did a fabulous job, in spite of any obstacles. With only a few days' rehearsal under their belts, even the adult company would have found the complicated piece a challenge.

And Jessica. . .

Colin couldn't be prouder of his new coworker. She led the children through their brief rehearsal and cheered them on with a vengeance. When she stood before the crowd to introduce the youth program, she did so with dramatic flair, drawing both the chuckles and sighs of those in attendance. All night long, she remained his fiercest ally. Colin overheard many excited comments about her participation, and he knew beyond a shadow of a doubt that God had certainly brought her to Dallas for such a time as this.

As the evening drew to a close, he caught a glimpse of Jessica from across the room. She stood, arm in arm, with her fiancé. *I need to get to know Nathan better.*

186

I'm sure he's a great guy. He'd have to be, to win her heart.

A giggly female voice interrupted his thoughts. "What are you thinking about?" He turned to face Katie. She was all smiles, as usual.

"Not much," he said thoughtfully. "I'm just so proud of the kids."

"You have a lot to be proud of. They did a great job." She took his arm and looked up into his eyes longingly. "You've done a terrific job with them, Colin."

"I, uh. . .thank you." He gazed into Katie's bright blue eyes and noticed, for the first time, how they sparkled with joy. The two entered into a lively conversation about the children, and Colin felt himself relax a little. *She's a great girl. Why am I trying so hard not to like her?* For some reason, he immediately thought of Ida and wondered what she would think of Katie. Would she approve?

From across the room, a burst of joyful laughter rose above the cacophony of sounds. His breath caught in his throat as Jessica captured his attention. As she played with one of the little girls, her rich auburn hair slipped out of the barrette and bounced across her shoulders. Her green dress shimmered under the room's subtle lights and brought out the rich glow in her face. Bright freckles seemed more pronounced than ever across those flushed cheeks.

For whatever reason, Colin couldn't seem to take his eyes off of her.

Chapter 11

Jessica sat in the spacious Dallas Opera House and lost herself in her own imagination. Like the Wortham Theater in Houston, this room also seemed to call out to her with its carved walls and sweeping stairways. The stage loomed before her, beckoning. She trembled slightly as she glanced over her music one last time.

Jessica's formal audition for the Dallas Metropolitan Opera would take place in a few short minutes. Colin had assured her position with the organization, even going so far as to offer their letter of acceptance in advance. However, this audition would serve to meet the requirements of her contract. Regardless, she still felt oddly unsure of herself today.

Jessica took slow, deep breaths and tried to relax. *Father, I place this into Your hands. Surely You wouldn't bring me this far to turn me back around now.* She tried to relax as she leaned back against the plush velvet stadium seat. She glanced to her right, where Colin stood visiting with the opera director, Eugene Snyder. The balding, middle-aged man had made a brief appearance at the fund-raiser dinner, sweeping in just long enough to hear the children sing. Even then, he seemed to look down his long, thin nose at her, and she felt strangely uncomfortable around him already. However, Colin gave her a reassuring smile, and her nerves began to calm.

Jessica turned her attention to her left. The gilded balconies seemed to rise almost to the sky. *I wonder what the view is like from up there.* She glanced up at the stage where she would soon stand to sing. Its broad wooden floor seemed to stretch forever across the vast expanse of the theater's front side. A retractable orchestra pit loomed before it. Though empty at the time, Jessica could imagine the area filled with violins, cellos, and French horns. The instrumentalists would play something beautiful, something familiar. . . .

The wedding march. They would play the wedding march as she entered from the back of the theater, dressed in an eye-catching chiffon gown she had designed herself. *Did I dream all of this?* She would make her way across a carefully designed bridge to the stage, where her anxious groom would await. With the minister, of course.

A beautiful set would frame the back of the stage. Florence itself would come to life. Cobblestone streets. . . Antiquated homes. . . Fountains and storefronts would provide the perfect backdrop for the most blissful of all wedding ceremonies. She and Nathan would be married between large, draped columns in the center of the stage.

Nathan. Hmm.

Jessica sighed quietly as she roused herself from the daydream. *It was only a dream, anyway. Don't make too much of it.* Her fiancé would never agree to a wedding like the one she envisioned now. *If I even suggested getting married onstage, he would probably—*

"Miss Chapman?"

Jessica looked up into Mr. Snyder's narrow, gray eyes. "Yes, sir?"

"I'm ready to hear you sing now."

She approached the stage with her knees knocking against each other. *Keep me calm, Father.* From a distance, Colin urged her on with a wink and a smile. The whole thing felt slightly reminiscent of her audition in Houston just a short time ago. Entering the stage seemed to boost her courage, and once she faced the auditorium, the butterflies all but disappeared.

As Jessica began to sing, the whole world seemed to close in around her. Once again, she found herself in that private place, that safe haven. Nothing—no one—could disturb her here. When the song ended, she turned her attention to Mr. Snyder, who looked at her with renewed interest.

"Very nice, Miss Chapman. I'll have no trouble placing you in our current production. Welcome to the Met."

"Thank you, sir." She made her way to the edge of the stage and shook his outstretched hand. His eyes shone with excitement.

"In case I haven't said it before," he added, "we at the Dallas Metropolitan Opera would like to thank you for all of your work with the children. Colin here tells me you're doing a magnificent job."

"Did he?" She felt her lips turn up as she looked at her coworker.

"He did." Mr. Snyder looked at his watch then turned on his heels, still talking as he walked away. "And I was fortunate enough to catch a glimpse of the two of you in action the other night with those children. Terrific work, and in such a short time, too."

"Thank you." Jessica could hardly contain her joy.

"I'd love to chat with you again soon, Miss Chapman." He stopped and glanced over his shoulder at her. "I'm sorry, but I'm late for a luncheon now." With little more than a quick "Good-bye," he sprinted from the room.

"Nice to meet you, sir." Her voice echoed across the theater. Jessica turned to face Colin once again. "Thanks for the compliment," she whispered.

He shrugged. "I didn't make it up, you know. You're great with those kids, Jessica. You seem to truly relate to them."

"I *do* relate to them." Jessica felt her excitement growing. "I know how important it is for young musicians to have the moral support of a grown-up. When

I was a little girl. . ." She paused as she debated whether to continue.

Colin gave her a reassuring nod. "Go ahead."

"When I was a little girl," she continued, "my father made sure I had both a piano and private music lessons. It was a sacrifice on his part. I know that now." A lump rose in her throat as she remembered her father's loving voice. *You'll wow them all someday, honey. Just wait and see.* At the time, her fingers had nervously trembled across unfamiliar keys. Now they seemed to sail. "He really poured so much into my life," she said. "And when he died. . ." Her voice broke. Jessica fought to regain her composure. "When he died, I thought I'd lost the music forever. It seemed to disappear with him."

"I'm so sorry." Colin looked at her sympathetically. "I had no idea you'd lost your father."

She nodded and wiped away a loose tear. "It was nearly a year before I touched the piano again. When I did, God used the music to heal my broken heart. And then the words came. I started to sing and couldn't seem to stop."

"You mean you had never trained as a vocalist?" He looked stunned.

"Never. I was well into college when I stumbled into my first voice lesson. To be honest, the whole process nearly scared me out of my wits. I can't believe I stuck with it. But my mom was there to support me. And Andrew. He and my mother haven't been married very long, but he really has been like a father to me."

Colin gazed at her with a new light in his eyes. "That's great, Jess."

"Yeah. He's been great," she said. "They've all been very supportive. But my grandmother. . ." Jessica's words took on a new life as she began to pour out the story of all her grandmother had done in recent days to assure her move to Dallas.

"I'm awfully glad you took her advice," Colin said as she finished the tale.

"Me, too." Jessica gave a relieved giggle. "It took me long enough though."

"Nah. You were right on time."

She gazed into his eyes and, for the first time, Jessica truly noticed what a rich shade of brown they were. Her cell phone rang out, and she quickly fetched it from her purse. "I can't believe I forgot to turn this off," she said. "I'm glad it didn't go off during the audition."

Colin turned away to give her some privacy as she pulled the phone from her purse. Jessica's excitement grew as she looked at the screen. *Nathan. I can't wait to tell him!*

"Jess, is that you?"

Her heart lifted at the sound of his voice. "It's me."

"How did your audition go?"

"Great." She dove into a full explanation. When she reached the part about her conversation with Colin afterward, Nathan grew oddly quiet.

"Are you still there?" she asked.

"Uh-huh."

"Is something wrong?" Her heart fluttered in anticipation of his response.

"It's just that Colin guy," Nathan said. "Something about him bugs me. Are you having trouble figuring out that he likes more than your voice?"

"Nathan, that's crazy." She had never considered the possibility. Colin Phillips was a great guy, to be sure, but he had been a perfect gentleman in every way. He certainly knew about her relationship with Nathan and had never indicated any interest in her other than their musical working relationship. "I think you're reading too much into things," she spoke nervously into the cell phone. "And besides, you've got nothing to worry about. I'm going to be your wife soon, and that's the important thing."

After a long pause, he spoke. "I know." A deep sigh framed his next words. "I guess I'm just feeling the pain of this separation. When are you coming home, Jess?"

"Weekend after next." She glanced at her watch. "But right now, I have to let you go. I'm late for a rehearsal. I'll call you tonight."

"That won't work. I've got a meeting."

"Tomorrow at one?"

"I'll be in class."

She groaned. "Well, I'll connect with you as soon as I can. I've really got to get off of here now. The kids are waiting. I love you, honey."

"I love you, too." The line went dead, and she closed her phone with a click then sprinted toward the rehearsal room.

As Colin made his way across the front of the rehearsal room, he pondered Jessica's story about her father. *No wonder she takes such an interest in the children. There's a lot more to Jessica Chapman than I knew.* He silently thanked the Lord, once again, for bringing someone so miraculous and kind to fill this position.

Just as he turned to face the crowd of children, she made a breathless entrance. "Sorry I'm late."

"No problem."

They carried on with the rehearsal, and everything went well. The talented group managed to perfect the song they had performed at the fund-raiser and start another without much difficulty. Colin continued to marvel at Jessica's ability to get the children to listen and obey with enthusiasm. *How does she do that?*

When the session ended and the children scattered to the winds, he and Jessica were left alone in the large room. Colin turned his attention to a pressing matter. "I wanted to ask your opinion on something." He gazed into her wide, green eyes, still sparkling with excitement from her work with the children.

"Sure." She pulled up a chair and sat down.

"I'm trying to decide which spring production to choose for the kids."

"Ah."

"I've been thinking about *The Magic Flute*."

She wrinkled her nose. "Too overdone."

"*Hansel and Gretel*?"

"Kind of scary for children," she said with a shrug.

"Yeah, I guess you're right."

"It's not one of my favorites," she added. "But it's your call."

"What would you suggest?" He truly wanted to hear her opinion on the matter.

"Hmm." Jessica seemed to lose herself in her thoughts for a moment. "What about *The Left-Behind Beasts*? Have you seen it?"

He shook his head. "Nope."

"Great kids' piece based on Noah and the ark. Terrific humor elements and challenging musical pieces. But not too challenging."

He looked at her admiringly. "Sounds perfect. Can you track down a copy of the libretto?"

"Of course."

"Eugene needs an answer by the weekend so he can put his stamp of approval on it. I hardly slept at all last night trying to come up with something," Colin confided.

"You should have called me," she said with a yawn. "I was up."

"At two o'clock in the morning?"

Jessica nodded. "I had a hard time sleeping, too. But I wasn't thinking about opera. For a change."

"Wedding plans?"

"Not really." She shrugged. "I'm not sure what was bothering me. I just couldn't seem to rest. I guess I'm just too excited about the kids. They're so great. Still, I know that they have to go home to less-than-desirable circumstances. That really bothers me. I want to do so much more for them." She began to talk in earnest about the children, and her eyes glistened with a renewed shimmer.

"You're a godsend, Jessica," he said when she finished. "I don't know if I've ever really told you that, but you are definitely an answer to prayer. And I can tell you love the kids—really love them. That's so important."

Her smile broadened. "I do." She gazed at Colin with admiration. "You've led by example. And, in case I haven't said it enough, thank you so much for everything you've done for me. I don't know when anyone's ever taken such a risk with a newcomer like you have. Especially after all I put you through back in Houston. But I'm honored you chose me. I don't know if I've expressed that adequately."

"You don't understand, Jessica," Colin said from his heart, driven by the conviction that her arrival in Dallas had little, if anything, to do with himself. "I didn't choose you."

"You didn't?" She gave him an adorable little pout that, for some bizarre reason, nearly sent his heart through the roof.

Colin looked intently into her eyes as he spoke in earnest. "The fact of the matter is—God chose you."

Chapter 12

The following Sunday evening Colin handed out copies of Christmas music to the elderly choir members at church. Though the holidays were still weeks away, he knew how long it would take to pull this mishmash group of vocalists into shape.

As he handed Ida a copy of "O Holy Night," she looked at him suspiciously. "You're not going to make me sing the solo in this one again, are you?" she asked.

"I was counting on it, Ida," he said. "The Christmas program wouldn't be the same if you didn't."

"I told you last year I wouldn't do it again. Haven't changed my mind." She pressed the music back into his hand.

Colin groaned. The woman's stubbornness could be endearing at times, but this was not one of them. With opera rehearsals heating up, the children's production plowing forward, and so many Christmas carols to be learned, he had far too much on his plate to bicker over technicalities.

"I was thinking of someone younger taking over for me." The older woman placed her stocky hands on her hips and peered at him over the rim of her narrow spectacles.

"Younger?" He looked around the room at the white-haired group. "Did you have someone particular in mind?"

"We were thinking," Walter piped up, "that—"

"Whoa, whoa! What's with this 'we' business? Have you all been conspiring against me?" Colin looked at them in surprise as they began to murmur among themselves. "Well?"

"It's like this, Colin," Ida explained. "We're not getting any younger here. It's about time we had an infusion of youth. We were thinking that one of your lady friends up at the opera might like to take over my solo this year."

"Lady friends?"

"Sure. What about that gal—the one who came up from Houston?"

"Jessica?"

"Jessica." Ida looked mighty pleased with herself as she continued. "I've heard you say she has a lovely voice. Well, why not get her in here to help us out? And bring along a few others, as well."

Colin scratched his head as he pondered her request. "Folks," he said finally, "you don't understand. The Dallas Metropolitan Opera is a professional organization with a paid staff. I couldn't expect vocalists of that caliber to perform for free."

"So much for the Christmas spirit," Walter mumbled.

"Besides," Colin said, choosing to ignore the comment, "the Met is in a production of its own right now. We're up to our earlobes in rehearsals. On top of that, in case I forgot to mention it, I'm helping with a children's Christmas production. This is a very busy season."

"Humph." Ida pursed her lips then spoke her mind, as always. "I know you'll miss hearing me sing. A part of me will miss doing it. I've sung that same carol for twenty years now. But I'm looking forward to passing the opportunity on to someone else. It's as simple as that. I'm not saying I *won't* sing. I'm just saying I don't *want* to sing the solo." She sat with a thud and crossed her arms in marked victory.

Colin shook his head in disbelief.

"Well?" Walter asked.

"I'm thinking." How could he ask Jessica to give more of her time when she had already stretched herself so thin? On the other hand, with so many anxious eyes peering at him now, how could he not?

Jessica sat at the computer late Sunday evening, doing her best to communicate with her fiancé online. "What do you think of the ivory dishes with the dark green trim?" She typed the words into the tiny box on her computer screen and clicked the Send icon.

"They're okay," Nathan responded. "Not really my cup of tea, no pun intended."

She chuckled. All evening, the couple had bantered back and forth across the Internet, trying to decide which china and crystal patterns to choose. He felt strongly about solid white; she tended to gravitate toward rich colors.

"Come on, Nathan," she typed. "I've been looking at this stuff for days." Not that she really minded. In fact, shopping for the wedding always brought a familiar comfort. And she felt great about the fact that she had narrowed her fine china list to three or four possibilities. Katie and Kellie had even climbed aboard the wedding registration bandwagon, and together, they had chosen beautiful patterns. But Nathan didn't seem to like any of them.

"Do we really have to have china?" he asked. "What's the point?"

"It's expected." It might not make much sense to ask people to purchase something so seemingly frivolous to a young couple, but she could envision setting the table—a heavy, dark table—with beautiful dishes and crystal goblets. Even if it meant only getting a few pieces now and adding more at a later date, when they could justify it.

"When would we ever use this stuff? Can't we just buy paper plates?"

She smiled at his illogical attempt at humor. "We'll use it, I promise," she typed. Jessica could think of all sorts of occasions for beautiful dishes. Now that she had connected with so many new people, she could see inviting them to dinner, hosting parties, even catering special events for the parents of the children she had grown to love. *Stop thinking like that. You're not going to live in Dallas.*

"I guess."

"And we still need to decide on flatware." She began to open a new Web site, anxious to move on. "Let's not forget that."

"What's flatware?"

Jessica groaned. She had already sent him links to three sites so that he could be choosing. "Knives and forks. The everyday stuff."

"Oh." For a moment neither of them typed a thing. Finally, a message came through from his end. "Can we change the subject for a minute?"

"Sure." She leaned back in her chair and rubbed at her eyes. After an evening of looking through Web pages, they ached.

"I want to talk to you about something serious."

Jessica braced herself. Already, two times this week, he had broached the topic of their long-distance relationship, and never from a positive standpoint.

"What's up?" she asked.

"My fingers are tired, for one thing," he responded. "And I'm not getting much sleep now that our only form of communication is over the Internet. I can't type as fast as I can talk, and this is wearing me out. My fingers will be thin before this is over."

Jessica sighed loudly. "I know," she typed. "But I can't use my cell phone until the end of the month. I'm already over my minutes."

"This is just such a bummer," he wrote. "Is it worth it, Jess? Are you really happy up there?"

She leaned back in the chair, deep in thought. *I wish he hadn't picked this weekend to ask that question.* The last few days had been rough. Despite Mr. Snyder's assurances, she felt oddly out of place amidst so many competitive vocalists in the adult company. "I'm happy." She took her time typing the words. "It's not everything I hoped it would be, but I still love it."

"I'm just lonely without you."

Jessica's eyes watered immediately. "Me, too." Her heart suddenly felt as if it would burst, and tears started to flow. *Lord, have I made a mistake? I miss him so much, and this is harder than I thought it would be. A lot harder.*

"I'm busy, and that's a good distraction," he wrote. "But something about all of this just seems wrong. Off. Haven't you noticed?"

Not until tonight. "I don't know, Nathan."

"I'm probably just tired. I haven't slept much this week. My workload at school is crazy, and I'm drowning at the office, too."

"Well, we should wrap this up so you can get some sleep then," she typed. "We really need to register online tonight, if we can."

He didn't respond, and Jessica wondered for a moment if he had dozed off.

"So, which pattern would you like?" She typed the words carefully.

"I don't really care, to be honest," he responded. "Why don't you just pick something?"

"Are you sure?" *That would be so much easier.*

"Yeah. I really need to sign off. My dad needs to check his e-mail. But I'll talk to you tomorrow night."

"Same time, same station?" she asked.

"Right."

"I love you," she typed.

"Back at ya."

He disappeared, and she closed out the message screen. With determined zeal, Jessica turned her attention to the department store Web site, where she quickly selected china, crystal, and flatware. The whole process took about ten minutes. When she finished, she clicked the computer off with a satisfied smile and turned her attention, once again, to her music.

Chapter 13

"Okay, kids. Let's settle down and get to work." Colin wiped a bit of perspiration from his brow as he faced the room full of boisterous children. "Miss Chapman has an announcement to make this afternoon."

His coworker approached the center of the room, all smiles. "I'm happy to report," she said, "that every member of the youth chorus will be given four free tickets to see the Metropolitan's performance of *Madame Butterfly* in two weeks."

The kids reacted with cheers, and Colin smiled at their enthusiasm.

"Are you really playing the lead, Mr. Phillips?" one of the boys asked.

He nodded, suddenly feeling a crater in the pit of his stomach. Just two weeks to pull it all together. To be honest, the Met's upcoming production had already taxed him beyond belief, and with such a short time until opening night, he was certainly feeling the heat. *Why did I agree to carry such a heavy load when my heart is here with these kids?* And yet he knew the answer. His heart was also set on the stage, where he could share the gift God had given him with full abandon.

How could he possibly complain, at any rate? The Lord had given Colin the opportunity of a lifetime this year—carrying his first real lead in a professional company and directing the children—all at the same time.

It was the "all at the same time" that seemed to be giving him fits right now. *I think I'm just tired. If Jessica hadn't come, I don't know what I would have done.* He glanced across the room at his enthusiastic counterpart. The autumn sunlight streamed through the window and picked up the color in her hair, dancing it across the room. For a brief moment, it held him captive. Then, a youngster's giddy voice interrupted his reverie.

"You're the best singer I've ever heard," twelve-year-old Melissa Grover said with a dreamy-eyed giggle.

Colin tried to squelch the preteen's enthusiasm, though he noticed Jessica nodding her agreement from across the room. "I appreciate the compliment," he said, "but I still have a lot to learn, just like all of you. Trust me."

"Don't let Mr. Phillips fool you, kids." Jessica stepped to the center of the room. "He might still be on a learning curve, but he's the best baritone I've ever heard, and I've heard a lot of them."

Colin's cheeks immediately warmed, and he winked his appreciation.

"Thank you, Miss Chapman." He bowed with great dramatic flair.

"You're more than welcome." She saluted in his direction, and the kids laughed.

Jessica's voice rang out above their very vocal response. "Okay now. It's time to settle down. I have another announcement to make."

Colin watched with amazement as she managed to quiet them down with her playful, singsong voice. "The youth chorus has been asked to do three extra performances of our Christmas production."

The kids erupted in lively conversation, and Colin tried once again to bring the noise level down to a dull roar.

Jessica filled the children in on the details. "We'll be performing at the Old City Park in the historical district. And we'll also be adding two performances at a large church on the south end of town. Then, of course, we'll have our regular performances on the dates we've already discussed. I've got all of the information right here." She waved a stack of papers. "You'll need to get this information into your parents' hands as soon as possible."

The children swarmed around her like bees to honey, and Colin immediately dove into action. "Careful, careful!" He made his way through the crowd and took the papers from Jessica's outstretched hand. As their fingers brushed, she seemed to blush slightly, and the freckles on her cheeks became even more pronounced. *They always do that when she's happy.*

Her eyes glistened with excitement as she spoke. "I have more to tell you," Jessica continued. "But only if you're all sitting down quietly." With a little more encouragement, the children took their papers from Colin, then sat in their seats with looks of curiosity on their faces. "Mr. Phillips has some exciting news for those of you who want to learn a little more about the process of singing."

She gave a grand bow to usher him to the center of the room. The children stirred in their seats. Colin couldn't help smiling as he spoke. "I'm happy to announce that the Dallas Metropolitan Opera has agreed to offer free individual vocal lessons to those of you in the youth program, beginning next Thursday afternoon."

The room grew quite loud once again, and he raised his hands to quiet them. "Now that Miss Chapman's here, we have the best vocal instructor in the world on our team." He gestured toward her, and the kids cheered.

Jessica's cheeks immediately reddened. "You flatter me too much, Mr. Phillips." She turned to face the children, and her enthusiasm seemed to grow. "But I am excited to be able to have this opportunity, and I can't wait to schedule your lessons. So, as soon as we finish up today, come and see me to arrange a time."

The voices of the students rose again, and Colin moved forward into the rehearsal, handing the reins off to Jessica, who took charge with her usual grace and flair. She managed to lead the children through more of the material than he had planned, which certainly eased his mind. *Maybe all of those extra performances won't be such a challenge after all.*

When the session with the children ended, Jessica remained behind to clean up the room. She seemed to be in a particularly chatty mood this afternoon. In fact, she talked nonstop as she pushed folding chairs back into tidy rows.

"I had a great time today. These kids are amazing," he said.

"Yes, they are." Then her smile faded somewhat. "Oh, by the way, I just wanted to remind you that I'll be out of town this weekend."

"That's what I figured. How are your wedding plans coming along?"

She looked at him with an alarmed expression. "We're behind schedule, to be honest. We still haven't ordered invitations. I was supposed to be taking care of that the last time I went home."

"Really? Would you like the name of the guy who prints all of our programs for the Met?" he asked. "He's really good. And he's a graphic artist, so he can pretty much do anything you need."

"Is he reasonable?"

"I'm sure he'll give you a break since you work for us."

Jessica's lips turned up in a smile. "I'll be so relieved to get some of this done, but I have to admit, the children have been a distraction. A good distraction, don't get me wrong. But I've got to stay focused on everything at once."

"Oh, speaking of staying focused. . ." Colin finally worked up the courage to ask the question that had been weighing on his mind all afternoon. "I don't suppose you'd be up to singing a solo at my church a couple of weeks before Christmas."

"What?" Jessica looked stunned, and he immediately regretted asking. "I'm so sorry."

"No, I'm just surprised, that's all," she said. "I do need to get involved in a church while I'm here. If I hadn't spent every other weekend driving back and forth, I would have done so already. But two weeks before Christmas? Do you think we'll be done with the children's performances by then?"

"Yes. Unless we're asked to add more to their schedule."

"Well. . ." She paused, pursing her lips.

"Listen." Colin waved his hand to dismiss the whole idea. "Please forget I said anything."

"Not so fast, not so fast." She grinned. "What's the song?"

" 'O Holy Night.' "

Jessica's eyes lit up in amazement. "That's my grandmother's favorite. I used to sing it every Christmas back home. Interesting."

"I dare say your church choir back home was probably a little different from the one I'm talking about." He dove into a quick explanation, and Jessica grinned.

"They sound awesome, and I'd be happy to do it, Colin."

"Thanks so much. You'll never know what this means to my little choir."

"My pleasure."

"And back to our original conversation," Colin continued, "I'll be praying that the Lord shows you how to keep everything in balance. In the meantime. . ." He swallowed hard. "Say a couple of prayers for me, too."

"What's up?"

Colin didn't respond for a moment as he struggled to come up with the right words.

"Are you worried about *Madame Butterfly*?" she finally asked.

"Not really worried." He exhaled deeply. "I just hope I didn't bite off more than I can chew. Whatever made me think I could handle two productions less than a month apart?" *The kids' performance would have been enough, but with the adult opera season in full swing. . .*

"You'll do great," she said.

He shrugged. "I'm a little behind on memorizing my music for the second act. And, to be honest, this will be the first time I've ever carried a lead role. Don't know if I mentioned that before. Between you and me, I'm a little—"

"Nervous?"

"Maybe a little. I don't want to disappoint anyone. Snyder. The company. My family."

"I don't see that as a possibility." She smiled. "I don't know if I've mentioned this before, but you don't sound like a rookie. And if there's anything I can do to ease your burden on this end—with the kids, I mean—just let me know."

"You've been great, Jess." He reached out and gave her hand a squeeze. "I don't know what I would have done without you."

For a moment his hand lingered on hers. He withdrew it as he suddenly remembered his other prayer request. "Oh, and one more thing." His voice grew shaky. "I, uh—"

"Yes?"

"I'm thinking of asking someone out." *There, I said it. I've finally spoken the words.*

"Katie?" Jessica broke into a broad grin as he nodded. "I think that's great! She's so much fun, and she's so talented, too, Colin. Whenever I hear the two of you singing together, I can't help thinking about what a cute couple you would make."

Cute? "I don't really know for sure about that, but I guess I'll never know if I don't ask her out."

"Oh, I have a wonderful idea!" Jessica's eyes lit up. "Nathan will be here in a couple of weeks to see *Madame Butterfly*. We should all get together and double-date. It would be a great way to ease him into my world here. And," she said as her eyes grew large with excitement, "to make it even more fun, I should ask my brother and Kellie to come along, too. That way everyone would have a partner. What do you think?"

Colin wasn't sure what to think. Somehow, the idea of going out with Katie seemed a little less appealing now that he had voiced it aloud.

"You'll never know unless you ask her!" Jessica gave him a playful punch in the arm.

He rubbed the spot and gave a thoughtful response. "I guess you're right. I'll never know unless I ask her."

On Saturday morning, Jessica made the familiar drive to Houston. The crisp November day provided an array of colorful distractions as she headed south on Interstate 45. The pine trees on either side of the freeway were usually green and full. Today, they seemed browner, less dense. On some level, they served to remind her that this season of her life would pass far too quickly. All too soon, her time in Dallas would be over.

"I need to stop feeling sorry for myself," she said aloud to the empty car. "I need to be grateful for the time I do have." Jessica chided herself for feeling blue and reaffirmed her commitment to approach everything in her life with both joy and balance.

About the time she passed the midway point in her journey, Jessica's cell phone rang, and she fumbled around inside her purse with one hand to retrieve it. Looking down at the screen, she had to smile. She answered the phone with great enthusiasm. "Grandma, is that you?"

"It's me. Just wondering if you're going to be on time. I'm anxious to get rolling."

Jessica glanced at the clock on her car stereo. "I should be pulling into the Houston area a little after noon. Want to meet me for some pizza before we go shopping?"

"You know pizza's my favorite. And your grandpa Buck never lets me eat it. He thinks it's for kids."

"Kids like me." Jessica laughed.

"And me, too. So, what's on the agenda for today?" her grandmother asked. "Still looking at wedding dresses?"

"Uh-huh. And flowers. Today I just want to get some ideas. Maybe I'll place an order next time. Right now, I don't even know what I'm looking for."

"Good thing I know my flowers, right?"

"Right." Jessica couldn't help smiling. "I know Mom wanted to go with me, but she and Andrew are at some sort of seminar."

"It's that 'Song of Solomon' romance thing up at the church," her grandmother said with a giggle. "I wanted to go myself, but Buck wouldn't hear of it. He figured people would think we had a troubled marriage."

Jessica laughed. "Anyone who knows you would know better. I envy your romance with Buck."

"Thanks, honey," her grandmother said, "but still—I think it would have been fun, and you know, it wouldn't hurt you and Nathan to sign up for something like that before you tie the knot, either."

"I know." Jessica calculated her response. She and Nathan could certainly use some help in the romance department. Bickering seemed to be their primary form of communication these days. "But right now I guess I'd better focus on the big day."

"No point in having a big day without a big life to follow it. And a big life needs a little rehearsal, just like one of your shows."

"I know, I know." Jessica groaned.

"Speaking of your shows, how are rehearsals coming?"

"Great. I can hardly wait for next weekend." Jessica dove into a lengthy discussion about *Madame Butterfly*, thankful for the reprieve from the focus on her love life.

When she finished giving her grandmother the colorful details of all that been happening in Dallas, the elderly woman responded, "Sounds like you're having the time of your life."

"I am. I don't think I've ever been happier."

"That's my girl."

"So. . ." Jessica looked at the clock and realized with some surprise that she had been talking nearly half an hour. "Where would you like to meet for lunch again?"

"Pizza. That all-you-can-eat place in The Woodlands suits me just fine. Just don't tell my hips, okay?"

"I promise."

"Or your grandpa Buck."

Jessica laughed. "No problem." She hung up the phone with a grin on her face. More than an ally and close friend, her grandmother had proven to be a source of comfort over the past few weeks, sending countless e-mails and offering encouragement with words of humor and wisdom. *Thank You, Lord, for blessing me with such a wonderful grandmother.*

As she continued the drive, Jessica thought about all she must accomplish in the next thirty-six hours. *I've got to find a dress, visit with my family, see Nathan. . .* She struggled with the emotions that followed the thought of her fiancé. *Something just feels wrong. Off.* Were those his words or her own? Why did nothing these days seem to feel like it should? *Probably just prewedding jitters. I'm nervous about getting married. That's pretty common.*

As was so often the case, Jessica's thoughts shifted to the goings-on in Dallas. She enjoyed her new life more than she had dared dream. And, at the center of it all stood a friend who towered above her, not just vocally but spiritually, as well. Colin Phillips. A strange mixture of emotions flooded Jessica when she thought about him. She would never have thought to feel guilty about her budding friendship with Colin if Nathan hadn't brought him up time and time again. "He likes more than your voice."

Lord, I'm sure that's not true, she prayed. *But if this friendship is outside Your will, please show me. Then help me figure out a way to avoid any unnecessary contact with Colin. I don't want anything—or anyone—to stop me from Your plan for my life.*

Still, she didn't feel at peace about staying away from the tall, dark-haired songster, either. Colin, perhaps more than anyone else, seemed to understand where she was coming from—not just musically, but emotionally and spiritually, as well.

One day Nathan will understand me like that. In time. When we're married. . .

Jessica couldn't seem to complete her thought. Something about all of this just felt very, very wrong.

Chapter 14

Colin glanced across the stage at Katie. His palms, damp with sweat, trembled as he approached her. *Easy, man. You're making this harder than it is.* As he drew near, he smelled the intoxicating aroma of her perfume. "Katie." *Why do I sound so insecure?*

She turned to face him and immediately broke into a broad smile. "Colin. What's up?"

"I, uh, I just wanted to talk to you."

"Really? What about?"

"I, um. . ."

"Colin, are you ready?" Eugene Snyder called out to him from the front row of the auditorium. "We're already running late."

Colin glanced at his watch. *Seven forty.*

"What is it?" Katie whispered. Her beautiful blue eyes sparkled with excitement.

"Can you stay after a few minutes?" he whispered back. "I need to talk to you."

She nodded with an impish grin, and Colin's heart began to beat double time. *What is wrong with me? I feel like I'm in high school again.*

He took his place in the center of the stage and tried to prepare himself for the rehearsal. Things started well, but over the course of the next hour and a half, calamity struck several times. He seemed to be off tonight. Way off. His voice cracked and wavered, and his pitch stayed more than a little low.

Eugene Snyder brought the orchestra to a screeching halt. "Colin!"

"Yes?"

"You're flat," the frustrated director called out from across the auditorium.

"I know." Colin groaned. "I'm working on it."

"Well, work harder. We're down to the wire here. In less than a week you'll be standing in front of thousands of patrons who have spent their hard-earned money to hear you sing."

"I know. I know." Colin vowed to do a better job but, for some reason, couldn't seem to get control of his breathing tonight. The orchestra started once again, but things only seemed to get worse. He tried to focus—tried to stay on top of things—but his mind seemed to be playing tricks on him tonight. At one point, just as he reached a high note, he tripped across a loose cable and nearly lost his balance. If Katie hadn't grabbed his arm, he would surely have hit the floor. Out of the corner of his eye, Colin caught a glimpse of Jessica. Her face, etched with concern, held him captive.

All the while, Colin argued with himself. *What are you doing? What is your problem? Are you really hung up on Katie, or are you just kidding yourself?* As the rehearsal drew to a close, he found himself losing his initial courage. *Don't ask her. Don't do it. If she says yes, you'll get caught up in something you're not ready for.*

On the other hand. . .

On the other hand, could this fear be the very thing to keep him from the relationship God had planned for him all along?

There's no way to know if I don't work up the courage to ask her.

After the rehearsal, Katie approached him. "I'm sorry you had such a hard time tonight, Colin." Her lips curved downward in an exaggerated pout. "Old man Snyder can be downright cruel sometimes."

"No, he was right on target. I'm the one who was off."

"You sounded great." Katie shrugged. "I don't know what his problem is. He has no patience."

"Trust me, he was more than patient tonight," Colin said.

"Anyway. . ." She grabbed his arm. "You said you wanted to talk to me. What's up?"

From across the stage, Colin sought out Jessica's face. *Why do I care if she's watching? What difference should that make?* She gave him an encouraging wink and a thumbs-up. He immediately felt every ounce of courage drain out of him. *I can't do this.* He turned to face Katie.

"Yes?"

"I was wondering if you had an extra copy of the opening number from Act Two. I've lost mine." *That's true, anyway.*

Katie's smile immediately faded. "You need a copy of my music?"

"Yeah. If you don't mind." *You're such a coward, Colin.*

"I think I have one." Her face lit up once again. "It's at my place. Would you like to follow me back there? We could fix some coffee and run through the music if you like."

Now what are you going to say? "I, um. . . I'm too tired, to be honest. Could you just bring it tomorrow night instead?"

"Sure. I guess." Her eyes seemed to lose a little of their sparkle.

"Thanks for being such a great friend." He reached out and gripped her hand, and she squeezed his in response.

"See you tomorrow night, music in hand." Katie gave him a girlish wave as she left the stage.

Colin's shoulders sagged in defeat.

"So?" He turned at the sound of Jessica's cheery voice. "Did you ask her?"

"I didn't." His gaze traveled to the floor, where he carefully examined the tops of his shoes.

"Why not?" Jessica crossed her arms, a clear sign of her disappointment.

"I don't know." Colin groaned. "I just couldn't seem to do it. Maybe it was just something about tonight. Everything about me seems to be a little. . ."

"Off?" She chuckled.

"You noticed?"

"Yeah, but don't let it get you down. We all have off nights, trust me. In fact, that's been my word of the week."

⌒

"I'm exhausted." Jessica spoke through a yawn as she drove Katie home from the rehearsal. "What about you?"

"I'm too excited to be tired," her friend said. "I think Colin's starting to soften up. I hope so, anyway."

"He's such a great guy, Katie. You two would make a perfect couple."

"I agree. But I don't know if I can wait forever. Is he ever going to make his move?"

Jessica pulled onto the interstate as the conversation continued. "I think he's just a little shy. Around women, anyway. But you should see him with the kids. He's very outgoing with them."

"And with you."

Jessica thought she detected a bit of animosity in Katie's voice. "What do you mean?" she asked.

"He's obviously very comfortable around you," Katie said with a shrug. "You two are always laughing and talking together."

Is she jealous? "You know how guys are." Jessica spoke in her most reassuring voice. "They always feel comfortable talking with women they're not attracted to. That's why he's less nervous around me. I'm more like a buddy. A pal. When he's with you. . ." Silence permeated the vehicle for a moment as Jessica fought to complete the sentence. "When he's with you, he's probably a nervous wreck trying to figure out what to say, how to say it. You know."

"I hope."

"I hope, too."

Jessica gripped the steering wheel with both hands and tried to conquer the doubt that suddenly gripped her. For some inexplicable reason, she felt a little uncomfortable around Katie tonight. *All this time I've been thinking about how good Colin would be for her, but I've never once thought about whether she would be good for him.* Jessica fought to push the nagging doubts from her mind as she focused on the road ahead.

Chapter 15

When the curtain pulled back on the night of the first *Madame Butterfly* performance, Jessica could hardly contain her emotions. Even from her current position far upstage right, she could hear the whisper of voices and the creaking of chairs as patrons stirred in their seats. *They're anxious. So am I.* She couldn't make out any faces from here, especially not with the blinding lights in her eyes, but somewhere out there sat her family. And Nathan. *He'll be so proud.*

She attempted to press down the lump in her throat, but it wouldn't budge. When it came time to sing, Jessica tried to distract herself. Her hands trembled and, for a moment, she felt as if she might be sick. Finally her nerves steadied themselves, and she released herself to enjoy the experience. *Lord, this is so amazing. Thank You so much.* From the stage, looking out, the whole thing felt more like a dream than reality.

Jessica sang with full release—from the depths of her soul. When she exited the stage for her first costume change, she paused long enough at the backstage entrance to listen to Colin as he completed his first solo. *He's really on tonight. I'm so glad.* The crowd erupted with applause as he hit the final note of the song, and she found herself applauding along with them.

Then Katie's solo began. Jessica stood in awe. The young woman lit the stage with her incredible vocal presence. Jessica looked back and forth between Colin and Katie with a feeling of satisfaction. All of her doubts from the other night seemed to vanish. *They're going to make quite a couple. In every conceivable way.*

"Move, please." A stage tech tapped her on the shoulder, and she suddenly remembered where she was—and where she was supposed to be. Jessica quickly scurried back to the changing room and slipped into costume number two.

By the time intermission came, she felt like a pro. Jessica chatted backstage with others in the chorus as she awaited her next entrance. Somehow, the wait felt like an eternity.

As she entered the stage once again, the lights and the swell of the orchestra pulled her into their spell. *Father, I've waited for this moment all my life. This is my passion. This is what You created me to do.* She opened her mouth and began to sing with the others. The joy that enraptured her seemed to take root in her soul, and Jessica knew she would never be the same again.

At one point during the second act, she caught Colin's attention to give him

208

an encouraging nod. He winked at her, and an immeasurable joy gripped her heart. *He's the reason I'm here. He knew. He knew I had to come.* Somehow the realization overwhelmed her. To think, the Lord had gone to such trouble to bring her to Dallas. What if she hadn't listened? What if she had missed all of this?

Jessica never found time to contemplate the matter. The performance came to an end all too quickly. She pressed back tears of relief and excitement as she took her bow alongside others in the cast. When Colin approached center stage, the audience roared. Most of them stood. Jessica didn't blame them and, in fact, clapped until her hands ached.

When the curtain closed, she exited the stage in the stampede of excited vocalists. For a moment, she almost forgot about meeting her family in the foyer—almost forgot the hastily planned dinner at a nearby restaurant.

For now, all she could think about—all that mattered—was the music. Katie approached from her right, and Jessica embraced her tightly. "You were absolutely—without a doubt—the most amazing thing I've ever heard."

"Quite a compliment coming from one of the best voices in the company."

"I mean it, Katie. You were awesome tonight."

"And didn't you think Colin just brought the house down?" Katie squeezed her hands impulsively.

"He was great. I'm totally impressed."

"I just wish he was as brave off the stage as he is on." Katie sighed and pulled off a piece of her costume jewelry.

"He hasn't asked you out yet?"

"Nope. Still waiting." Katie turned to visit with her parents, who had just arrived backstage. The elderly couple offered their congratulations boisterously, clearly proud of their daughter.

Jessica leaned against the back wall, suddenly drained of all strength.

"Jess?" She turned as she heard Colin's resonant voice. "Was it everything you hoped it would be?"

"Oh, Colin. It was. . . It was. . ."

Tears flowed, but she didn't even try to stop them. Jessica reached up to embrace him, then pulled away, embarrassed.

"It's okay," he whispered, his own eyes moist, as well. "I'm feeling it, too."

"You were just wonderful." Jess took his hand. "I've never heard anything like it."

"You flatter me, Miss Chapman." He ran his thumb along her fingers. "But you haven't told me if you liked it. Was the experience everything you hoped it would be?"

"Everything and more!" Jessica could scarcely catch her breath. "I could feel the orchestra, Colin! Not just hear them but feel them. The whole stage seemed to be electric. And when we all sang together, the entire auditorium felt full of music.

We weren't just a chorus of strangers singing together. We were a multitude—a heavenly choir. It was the most unbelievable experience of my life." Tears coursed down her cheeks, and she used her fingertips to brush them away.

"I'm so glad. I knew it." He took her hand again. "I knew you would love it."

Yes, he knew. "Thank you for bringing me here," Jessica whispered. Her arms seemed to instinctively reach for his shoulders once again. "I can never thank you enough."

"You're welcome. If anyone deserves this opportunity, you do." He returned her hug with a warm squeeze. "I predict this is just the first of many performances for you."

"Thank you." In his arms, with the crowd pressing in around her, Jessica could barely breathe.

"Jess?" She looked up as she heard another familiar voice. Nathan stood to her left, a puzzled expression on his face.

She pulled away from Colin's embrace with an embarrassed warmth flooding her cheeks. "Nathan! I'm so glad you're here."

"I can see that."

Lord, please don't let him misunderstand. I don't want anything to ruin this wonderful evening.

"Good to see you again, Nathan." Colin extended his hand and, thankfully, Nathan shook it warmly. Colin excused himself and returned to the throng of well-wishers.

Once they were alone, Jessica gazed into her fiancé's eyes for a look of assurance.

"I hope you don't mind that I came backstage." His words seemed a little stilted.

"Of course not. It's wonderful." She slipped her arm around his waist. For some reason, he didn't respond by pulling her close, as usual. Instead, Nathan pressed a bouquet of flowers into her hand.

"These are for you."

"Thank you." Her lips brushed his in thanks.

"Your mom and Andrew are waiting in the foyer," he added.

"Did my grandmother make it? I know she wasn't feeling well a couple of days ago."

"She and Buck are both here. And Kent."

"Looking for Kellie, no doubt."

"He found her." Nathan shook his head. "In fact, she sat with us tonight."

"Really?" Interesting, since the double date idea hadn't panned out. *Maybe God has a few matchmaking plans of His own.*

"How long will it take you to get ready?" Nathan looked at his watch.

"Not long. I'll meet you out front in a couple of minutes." She gave him a peck on the cheek before heading back to the costume room. *He didn't even say if he liked the show or not. I'll have to remember to ask him later.*

Jessica met up with her family in the foyer after the crowd thinned out. They stood in a cluster, with Kent at the center of their conversation. He fought to hold Kellie's attention, though she looked a little distracted at the moment. Nathan interrupted Kent's antics to tell a joke, and everyone laughed. Except Kent.

"I'm here!" Jessica waved her hand triumphantly. Everyone swarmed her at once.

Her mother whispered in her ear, "We're so proud of you. The whole thing was wonderful. Just wonderful."

"I'll bet you had the time of your life up there," Andrew added.

"Oh, I did. It was heaven. Probably one of the highlights of my life."

"That's my girl." Her grandmother slipped her arm around Jess and pulled her into a gentle embrace. "So, was it everything you hoped it would be?" she whispered.

"And more," Jess whispered back. *She knows me so well.*

The family chatted nonstop as they walked the two city blocks to the Italian restaurant Jessica had chosen. She clutched Nathan's hand tightly in hers and silently thanked the Lord for this, the most eye-opening night of her life.

Colin left the theater alone. *Might as well grab a bite to eat on the way home. But where?* Many of the cast members had decided to have a late-night supper at a nearby coffee shop. Somehow that just didn't sound appealing tonight. He looked up as Katie approached. She smiled warmly, and his loneliness vanished almost immediately.

He gave her a warm smile. "Hey, you."

"Hey, you." She reached up and embraced him. "You were awesome tonight, Colin."

"Thanks. You were pretty awesome yourself."

"We make a good team." She gave him a shy look.

Unusual. She seems a little nervous tonight. "Yes." He paused to look into her blue eyes. "We do."

Katie took hold of his hand and squeezed it tightly. "Are you hungry? Would you like to get something to eat?"

"I'm starved," he admitted. *But I would never have the courage to ask you out.*

"There's a great new Italian place a couple of blocks away. It'll probably be pretty quiet. I think everyone else went to the coffee shop."

"Right."

"So. . ."

"I'll tell you what. . ." He took her arm and placed it firmly in his own. "Tonight it's just you, me, and a plate of spaghetti."

She gave him a satisfied grin, and the two walked, arm in arm, to the door. As they made their way to Traviatta's, Colin found himself relaxing. *She's such a great girl. I can't believe I've waited this long to ask her out. Not that I really did the asking, exactly.*

She shivered against the cool evening breeze, and Colin pulled his jacket off. "Here. You take this." He wrapped it around her shoulders, and she looked up with a broad smile.

"You're so thoughtful."

Colin shrugged.

"I'm so glad we're finally going to get this chance to get to know each other," Katie said. "Without the whole group looking on, I mean."

"Me, too." Colin pulled the door of the restaurant open and immediately found himself in a whirlwind of activity. *Great. This place is packed.* From across the room, he heard the sound of laughter.

"Hey, that's my sister!" Katie squealed. "Go figure. And there's that guy she keeps talking about."

"Guy? What guy?" Colin's gaze followed her pointing finger to the table where Jessica's entire family sat, engaged in joyous conversation. "Oh, Jessica's brother?"

"No," Katie whispered in his ear. "Actually, that's not the one she's interested in." She gave a light giggle.

"Excuse me?" Colin peered at the group a little closer. "Who else is there?"

Katie jabbed him in the ribs and nodded her head in a direction that left him without any doubt.

Nathan. Kellie is falling for Jessica's fiancé.

Chapter 16

For days, Jessica floated around on a cloud of pure adrenaline. She walked herself through the performance time and time again. Each thrilling note had held her in its grasp. Her role in the chorus of *Madame Butterfly* had served not only to boost her confidence; it opened a whole new world of possibilities.

Every now and again she would wonder why a bit of guilt would seep in and catch her unawares. *Why should I feel bad about doing something I love so much?* Perhaps, she reasoned, it was because of Nathan's lack of enthusiasm. The morning following the performance, he had brushed a kiss across her cheek and scurried off to the airport.

Her grandmother, on the other hand, had offered enough support for a dozen people. "You were born for this," she had whispered in Jess's ear after the show. "And your father would have been so proud of you."

As the days rolled by, Jessica found strength in those words. She moved forward with plans for the children's production, though staying focused wasn't an easy task.

An unexpected call came late one Thursday afternoon, just as she pulled her car out of the parking garage at the opera house. At first, she could barely make out her mother's frantic words. Finally, however, she managed to pull a few key phrases from the conversation, enough to send her thoughts and heart reeling.

Grandmother. Stroke. Probably won't pull through.

Through a haze of tears, Jessica now fought her way beyond the crowd of people at the Dallas airport. Colin moved alongside her, his shadow towering over Jessica and offering an odd sense of comfort. When they reached the security gate, her arms went to his neck immediately. They stood in silence for a moment, and she could feel his heartbeat.

"I can't thank you enough," she said. "I never would have made it here in my car."

"No problem." He held her in a warm, brotherly embrace. She trembled in his arms and whispered a frantic prayer for her grandmother as she rested her head against his broad chest. When she pulled away, the tears ran in rivulets down her cheeks, an uncorked bottle of grief.

"I'll be praying." Colin spoke in a reassuring voice as he squeezed her hands. "God's still on the throne, Jess."

"I know." She forced a weak smile. Jessica then stumbled through the security process in a numb fog and boarded the plane for Houston. As she took her seat on the 747, she released herself to the emotion, allowing gut-wrenching sobs to emanate. Never mind the guy in the seat next to her. Never mind the flight attendant with her niceties. *Lord, my grandmother! Don't take her from me, Father. Please!*

The flight seemed to last for hours, though her watch ticked by the forty-five-minute flight with uncanny accuracy. By the time she arrived at Houston's hectic Bush Intercontinental Airport, Jessica felt a heaviness she could not explain. Somehow, she knew. She just knew. *Grandma is gone.*

Her brother met her at the baggage claim area, his face ashen. Though he never spoke a word, Jessica read the truth in his somber expression.

"I'm too late." She whispered the words, and his eyes swiftly brimmed over.

Kent nodded then reached to hug her. "Jess." As he pressed his arms around her, she shook with sobs. By the time she stopped, Jessica felt completely drained. Her eyes stung unmercifully, and her chest ached. All of the tears in the world couldn't make her feel any better.

"Where do we go from here?" she asked.

"Everyone left the hospital about fifteen minutes ago," Kent explained. "Mom and Andrew have gone home to rest. They were up all night. I doubt they'll get much sleep, though. Mom was pretty shook-up."

"Bad?"

He nodded. "The whole thing was just such a shock. Came from out of nowhere."

"What about Buck?" A lump rose in Jessica's throat as she thought of her grandfather and the pain he must be feeling right now.

"He's at our place." Kent reached out and took her bag. "For now, anyway. Mom insisted. He'll have to go home later on to track down some life insurance papers and other stuff, but for now, he's with us."

Jessica nodded then followed her brother out to the parking garage in silence. *She's gone. The one person who understood me best in the world is gone.* She suddenly felt guilty for thinking such a thing. *How can I be so self-centered?*

As they climbed into Kent's car, Jessica reached for her cell phone. She quickly dialed Nathan's number. *I've got to talk to him. He needs to know.* The phone rang several times. Finally the recorded message kicked in. "This is Nathan. Leave a message at the beep, and I'll get back to you."

I can't do it. I can't tell him in a recorded message. She snapped the phone shut and leaned her head against the seat in quiet desperation.

About twenty-four hours after Jessica left for Houston, a chill settled over the Dallas area. Unseasonably cold weather locked the city in its grip. Colin fought to continue his work as if nothing had happened. He struggled with his feelings as he waited to hear something, anything, from Jessica. *Should I call? Send an e-mail?* Anything at this point seemed like a better option than waiting, not knowing. For some reason, every time he thought about her, a pain gripped his heart.

Colin shivered against the cold as he crossed the parking lot after Friday's rehearsal with the children. In spite of Jess's absence, they had excitedly tried on their costumes and rehearsed their more difficult numbers. With a show in less than two weeks, Colin had his work cut out for him. Especially if Jessica found herself unable to return.

Ironically, just as he reached his car, Colin's cell phone rang. He breathed a sigh of relief as Jessica's number appeared on the tiny screen.

"Hello?"

"Colin?" Her voice broke immediately, and he braced himself for the worst. "My grandmother. . ."

He listened to the rest with an aching heart. *Lord, help her. Give her strength.* The more she spoke, the more he found himself wanting to hold her—to tell her everything would be all right. After giving him funeral details, she paused for a breath.

Colin finally felt free to share his heart. "Jess, I want you to take your time. Stay with your family as long as they need you."

"But we have a show in eleven days." Her voice broke again.

"That's not important. The most important thing now is to be there for your mom. She needs you. I can handle the kids."

She began to cry in earnest now. "I—I miss. . .my kids. But don't tell them what's happened. Please. I don't want to make them sad."

How does she do it? She's thinking of the children when she should be thinking of herself. "Jessica, don't worry about the kids. They're doing great."

"They are? Do they miss me?"

"Yes, of course, but our rehearsal today went well."

"What about the costumes?" She sniffled, and Colin tried to picture the look on her face.

"All done. The costume department came through, as promised. Jeffrey Weaver had a small problem with his robe. Too short. Other than that, everything looks great."

Jessica sighed. "I wish I could have seen them. I'm sure they were adorable."

"You'll see them when you get back," he said. "In the meantime, get as much rest as you can and spend some time with your folks. Just keep me posted. I've been worried about you."

"You—you have?"

"Well, not really worried. Just concerned. I. . ." Suddenly Colin knew what he wanted to say, though the words rocked him to the core. He wanted to say, "Don't you know how much I care about you, Jessica? I want to be there, to walk you through this. I want you to rest your head on my chest again and let me tell you everything's going to be okay." *Where did that come from?*

"Colin? Are you still there?"

"I, uh—I'm here. I miss you, Jess. And I'm praying for you. But I want you to feel free to take your time." *Oh, but please don't take too much time. I miss you so much already.*

"Okay. Once the funeral is over," she said and sniffled again, "I'll spend some time with my mom. I'll probably come back next Sunday night."

"If you're ready."

"If I'm ready." Her voice seemed to change a little. "I'm so sorry, Colin, but I'm going to have to skip the performance at your church. I hate to let you down, but there's so much going on right now, I just don't think I could handle one more thing. Can you find someone else?"

"I'm sure I'll find someone," he said. "Please don't think a thing about it."

Jessica sighed. "Thanks for understanding. Oh, and, Colin. . ."

"Yes?"

"I just want you to know how much I appreciate you. You've been such a great friend to me. I didn't realize how much I've come to depend on your friendship. I don't know what I would have done without it. I really don't."

"It's easy to be your friend." His heart suddenly swelled with emotion.

"That's so sweet. I appreciate that more than you'll ever know. And I'm so grateful for everything you've done—everything you are doing."

"I love you, Jess." Where the words came from, he had no idea. "And I'll keep praying. For you, your mom, and everyone down there."

A long silence greeted him, followed by a hushed, "You're awesome."

"Good-bye, Jess."

"Good-bye."

As soon as the line went dead, Colin suddenly felt as if he would be sick.

~

I love you, Jess.

All afternoon long Jessica pondered Colin's words. His statement, though hurried and clearly impulsive, had truly left her speechless. Surely, he meant he loved her as a friend. However, the more she thought about it, the less sure she felt. *Lord, have I said something, done something to lead him on or give him the wrong idea? I love Nathan.*

For some reason, Jessica's thoughts immediately shifted to an earlier conversation with her grandmother, the day she had first tried on wedding dresses. "You can force something to fit," the precious older woman had said, "but that doesn't make it right. Living with something that's uncomfortable or 'not quite right' is never a good thing."

Sorrow overtook Jessica, and she crumpled to her knees in a haze of tears.

Chapter 17

Is it always this cold in December?" Jessica asked her mother on the Wednesday afternoon following her grandmother's funeral.

"I don't ever remember a December this chilly." Laura Dougherty pulled her sweater a little tighter and continued to pace the room, as she had done for days now. The week had been a whirlwind of activity, and none of the pieces of the puzzle seemed to be coming together for any of them quite yet. The continual throng of people had brought some sense of comfort, but it felt good—really good—to finally have some time alone to grieve.

"Mom, you've got to stop," Jessica said. "You're going to wear yourself out."

Her mother shook her head. "I'm just thinking."

"About?"

"Something your grandma said to me a few days before she passed away." Laura's voice broke, and she paused for a moment. "She—she told me to follow my dreams, not to let anything stop me."

"She said the same thing to me a few months back," Jessica replied. "That's odd."

"That is odd." Laura paused. "Funny thing is," she continued, "my dream—the one I've put on hold for so many years now—is to open a bookstore. One of my own. I had almost forgotten."

"Right." For as long as Jessica could remember, her mother had longed to have her own shop. For years, she had worked in a large bookstore, but all along she had held on to the dream of one day becoming a proprietor herself.

"The oddest thing has happened. I don't know if it's just a coincidence or if God is at the center of it."

"What, Mom?"

"Madeline is selling the shop. She's moving off to Abilene to be near her parents."

"Really?" Jessica had known and loved Madeline from the time she was a preteen. If she left the store, everything would change. Of course, everything was already changing—and so quickly, too.

"I'm just wondering if your grandmother's words of advice were in some way—I don't know. . . ."

"Prophetic?"

"Not to overspiritualize, but yes."

"It is a little strange, Mom," Jessica confided. "Like I said, Grandma had a similar conversation with me awhile back—about following my dreams. That's why I decided to go to Dallas when I did."

"You're kidding. Your grandmother had something to do with your decision to move?"

"She had everything to do with it." Jessica wrung her hands together and formulated her words. "And it was the right choice. I haven't regretted it for one minute. It's not that I don't miss you guys. I do. And I miss the children at church, too. Of course, from everything I've heard, they've been too busy to miss me much."

"That Mrs. Witherspoon," her mother said with a smile. "She's a pistol."

"I know. I heard all about her from Grandma the last time I was in town. She's having a ball with those kids."

"Their Christmas show is this weekend." Laura's face lit up. "Will you be staying?"

"Yes. I'll be here till Sunday night," Jessica explained. *Colin, I'm so sorry I won't be able to sing at your church like I promised.*

"That's great, honey. It's been so good having you here." Her mother's eyes watered once again, and Jessica embraced her.

"I hate to leave at all, Mom, but I really need to get back so I can get to work. We've got a show of our own next week, and my kids are missing me. I've already talked to Colin three times this week. He says they're going through withdrawal." She stopped to reflect, then drew a deep breath. "I miss my students, Mom. I miss Dallas. I miss the opera."

"Is that all?"

"What do you mean?" Her heart lurched.

"I'm just wondering if you have the same sense of loss for Nathan when you're up there. He's the only person you haven't mentioned." Her mother's face reflected more than just a passing curiosity.

"Haven't I?" Jess paused as she thought back over the conversation. "Of course I miss him. I love Nathan."

"I know you do, Jess," her mother said, "and I'm happy you've had some time together over the past few days. But you two don't seem to be struggling through this separation as much as I anticipated, that's all. I'm not trying to pass judgment. Just wondering. Are things—I mean, is everything okay between you two?"

"We're fine. We're just so busy. Not that I regret the busyness." *If you only knew, Mom. I love it. In fact, I don't know when I've ever been happier.*

"I'm thrilled for you. I really am."

For a moment, the two women sat in silence. Jessica picked up a photo of her grandmother and examined it closely. "Everyone tells me I resemble her," she whispered.

"Not just physically." Her mother gave an assuring smile.

Jess held the photo a little closer. "What do you mean?"

"Your grandmother has—I mean, had—a lot of spunk. Not rebellion, just tenacity. It got her in trouble when she was younger. I've heard lots of stories about her antics. But mostly I've heard about the efforts she went to, to make sure everyone got a fair shake, especially the underdog."

"Wow. I am like her then."

"Be proud of that, honey."

Andrew entered the room and shifted her mother's attention in a different direction, but Jessica couldn't seem to stop thinking of what she had just been told. *If I'm like my grandmother, there must be some reason. I need the same tenacity in my work and in my relationship with Nathan.* In her heart, Jessica vowed to rekindle the romance with her precious fiancé. He was worth it.

They were worth it.

Later that evening Nathan stopped by for a much-anticipated visit. After a quiet dinner with the family, he and Jessica took a walk to the neighborhood park, as they had done so many times over the years. Bundled in heavy coats and locked arm in arm, they talked. About everything. Missing each other. School. Work. Insecurities. Jealousies. And so much more.

With words of hope whispered in each other's ears, the excited couple reestablished feelings and committed to work harder on their relationship. The joy of planning their wedding took root again, and Jessica made herself a promise to do anything and everything to make this thing work.

———

I love you, Jess. Colin still felt a little queasy as he contemplated the words he had spoken less than a week ago. Where had they come from? Why couldn't he seem to control them as they poured forth from his mouth?

"Jessica." Even as he whispered her name, joy flooded Colin's heart. *Lord, take care of her in Houston. Bring her back safely this weekend. Give her wisdom about the music. If she's supposed to stay in Dallas long term. . .*

Colin stopped his prayer immediately. *She's like a sister to me,* he reasoned. *I brought her to Dallas, and I feel a need to take care of her. That's all.*

Is that all?

Of course that's all. She's engaged. She'll be another man's wife soon. I need to focus on my own love life. Even as the thought drifted through his mind, an idea occurred to him, one he could not ignore. He picked up the telephone and nervously dialed Katie's number. *Keep your cool.*

When she answered with a cheery "hello" he almost hung up but somehow forged ahead with the words fresh on his mind. "Katie?"

"Yes?"

"I have a huge favor to ask. Feel free to say no." He went on to explain the predicament he now faced at church: Jessica had agreed to sing "O Holy Night" this coming Sunday morning but couldn't make it due to her grandmother's death. Would Katie be interested in singing it, instead?

"Oh, Colin! I'd love to. I'd be honored." Her excited response both relieved and impressed him. And why not? Katie professed a genuine love for the Lord. Besides, she had an amazing voice. She would blow the choir away. And Ida would be thrilled to learn that he had actually located another vocalist worthy of the coveted solo.

All the way to church, Colin thought about Katie. Truth be told, he had grown quite comfortable around her, perhaps even more so than he had been willing to admit to himself. Their evening together at the Italian restaurant had been truly enjoyable. In spite of the crowd, they had managed to find a table apart from the others, where they had visited at length. Her sense of humor amazed Colin. *Why didn't I ever notice it before? She's been such a blessing and she's been so patient with me. All this time, she's waited to see if I would show an interest in her.*

Am I interested in her?

Colin paused at a red light and gave himself over to the what-ifs in his love life. *Father, if Katie is the one You have in mind for me, please open my eyes—and my heart—to the possibility. Otherwise, Lord, please shut the door.*

Firmly.

The choir settled in for their final rehearsal a short while later, and Colin grinned with pleasure as he introduced a blushing Katie to thirty curious onlookers. When she opened her mouth and began to sing the beautiful carol, Walter very nearly dropped his teeth. The others sat in stunned silence. When she finished the song, the entire group rose to their feet and shook the room with their applause.

All but Ida. The elderly woman sat, arms crossed, in her chair with a skeptical look on her face. Clearly, she had issues with Katie. Jealousy, perhaps? As he moved forward with the rehearsal, Colin couldn't help wondering what thoughts his fiercest advocate held captive in her silence.

He didn't have to wonder long. As soon as everyone left for the night, Ida approached him in the church foyer. "Wrong girl."

"Excuse me?"

"That's not the one I've been praying for."

"I'm not sure I understand, Ida. Not the right one to sing your song?"

"Not the right one for you to marry," she explained.

"Who—who said anything about marriage?"

"Don't waste your time on the wrong girl," she huffed.

"Ida."

She left the foyer, muttering all the way. "Don't know why I bother to give my opinion. No one ever listens to me anyhow."

Colin shook his head in disbelief and turned toward the door. He drove home in dazed silence, trying to sort out his jumbled thoughts. *Lord, is this Your answer? Is Ida Your mouthpiece?* He could not seem to quiet his aching heart. For some reason, every time Colin tried to focus on Katie—her voice, her charm, her beauty—he could only hear Ida's firm voice, laced with irritation. *That's not the one I've been praying for. Don't waste your time on the wrong girl.*

Chapter 18

When Jessica arrived in Dallas the following Monday morning, she scarcely had time to collect her thoughts before finding herself in a musical whirlwind. The children met her with nervous anticipation. Colin greeted her with news of an additional performance opportunity. He assured her it would only take place if she felt up to it. She convinced him she could handle it. No problem.

However, with the deadline for the first show looming, Jessica had to wonder if she had taken on more than she could handle, both emotionally and physically. She found herself irritable and exhausted much of the time, and the children seemed to bear the brunt of her frustration. *I've got to try harder.*

With just a few days left before their performance, Jessica fought to give them her undivided attention. Try as she may, however, she couldn't seem to see past the fog of grief. Many times she found herself picking up the cell phone to call Nathan. He talked her through each moment in his usual practical way, and Jessica realized she missed him more than ever before. For the first time since arriving in Dallas, she truly felt torn between both worlds.

And yet she had little time for such confusion. The children's first performance of *Amahl and the Night Visitors* was upon her before she knew it. The excited youngsters sang their hearts out at several community functions in the two weeks prior to Christmas. Their final show would be held in two days on the big stage at the Met. They could hardly contain themselves as the big day approached. Jessica felt a little unnerved, as well. There was much at stake, after all. Several dignitaries from the city would be in attendance, as well as opera patrons and sponsors. This would be an awesome way to show off the new children's chorus and place the program in good standing for the upcoming spring season.

But Jessica couldn't stop to think about the spring right now. She just had to make it through this cold, hard winter—one day at a time. Though the weather had warmed a little, her heart remained in a frozen state, unable to thaw. Grief held her in its tight grip.

Many times Jessica stopped mid-sentence as something would remind her of her precious grandmother. A word. A smile. A warm embrace. Someone would mention something silly—like pizza—and she would burst into tears. Jessica found herself unable to let go of this woman who had meant so much to her. *Lord, I'll never let go.*

And yet, she must shift her attention to the children. They needed her, especially now. In the same way her grandmother had always been there to offer courage and support, Jessica now found herself having to give pats on the back and whisper words of comfort and advice. The children looked up to her with admiring smiles, and their hopeful faces lifted her spirits when she needed it most.

On the night of the big show, Jessica dressed in a new gown—a burgundy, ankle-length chiffon. When she arrived at the theater, she found the children in a state of nervous panic. Many seemed irritated or even physically ill. She recognized the signs of stage fright all too well. She asked Colin if he felt comfortable starting off the evening's festivities with prayer, and he never hesitated. The kids, dressed in biblical attire, formed a circle and allowed him to pray a rich, heartfelt prayer for the evening ahead.

Then the curtain went up. Jessica watched from the wings as the children she had grown to love sang joyfully. *Was it really just a month ago I stood on this very stage myself? How amazing to think these children will have the same opportunity. Lord, don't ever let them forget how special this is. And thank You, Lord, for letting me be a part of this. I can never thank You enough.*

Every now and again her gaze would drift to the auditorium, and she would strain to locate Nathan. He should be sitting in the third row—somewhere near the middle of the theater. *Ah. There he is.* The young woman to his left looked strangely familiar, and Jessica realized, with an odd sense of betrayal, that Kellie was seated next to her fiancé. Why should that bother her? She was a good friend, after all. It was only natural they would sit together. In the meantime, she must stay focused on the children.

When the curtain came down after the final song, Jessica cried like a baby. All of her pent-up emotions of the past two weeks came tumbling out. In order to avoid the children's curious stares, she pressed her way beyond the crowd to the props area. Here, she could be alone to think, to pray. Her thoughts were a jumbled mess. Between snatches of memories about her grandmother, she found herself facing inevitable questions about her relationship with Nathan. In spite of their recent conversation, she still felt something was amiss, though she couldn't quite put her finger on the problem.

"Jessica?" She looked up as she heard Colin's voice. "Are you okay?"

She nodded. She quickly dried her eyes, determined not to let him see into her heart. *I don't need to be sharing my emotions with anyone except Nathan. It would be wrong.* She quickly dismissed herself to the foyer, where she congratulated the children and visited with their excited parents. One by one, they thanked Jessica for her work. Many shared, through tears, the difference this program had made in the lives of their family. *Coming to Dallas was not a mistake. I would have missed all of this.*

As she made the rounds from child to child, parent to parent, Jessica couldn't stop wondering about Nathan. *Why isn't he here? Did he forget we were supposed to meet after the show?* She finally excused herself from the joyous crowd and made her way to the theater. There, in the third row, Nathan and Kellie stood, completely engaged in a lively conversation. Jessica approached cautiously, trying to squelch the feeling of betrayal that now gripped her.

"Nathan?"

He turned to her, a wide smile on his face. It seemed to diminish a little when their eyes met. "Jess. Are you ready to go?"

"Yes. I've been waiting in the foyer," she explained. "Did you forget?"

"I'm afraid that's my fault," Kellie said with little giggle. "I had a financial question for him. I've been thinking about getting into day trading and thought he might have some advice."

"I see." Jessica rolled her engagement ring around her finger and eyed her fiancé for some sign of response. When he said nothing, she asked, "Did he?"

"Did he what?" Kellie's lips curled up in a cute grin, and Jessica noticed for the first time how truly adorable her neighbor was.

"Did he have any advice for you?" she asked.

"Oh yes!" With an admiring smile, Kellie dove into a detailed explanation of Nathan's words of wisdom.

Jessica couldn't seem to focus on Kellie, however. Her gaze remained fixed on her fiancé, who hadn't seemed to notice she was still in the room.

From the stage, Colin looked out across the near-empty auditorium with curiosity. Jessica, Kellie, and Nathan stood just a few yards away. For some reason, he couldn't help thinking of Katie's whispered confession over dinner that night at the restaurant. *Kellie is crazy about Nathan.*

But what about Jessica? Where did that leave her? Colin had to wonder if she knew about Kellie's feelings. She didn't need to be hurt, especially not now. It wouldn't take her long to figure things out.

Colin felt a little sick as Jessica watched Kellie toss her blond hair. Her giggle bounced across the room. *Jessica looks upset. Should I say something, do something?* He looked at Kellie once again, wishing above all that she didn't resemble Katie so much. That only served to complicate his already confused feelings.

Right now, Colin had to confess, he only felt an overwhelming need to protect Jessica, to keep her from being hurt. *She's been through too much in the past few weeks.* He left the stage and slowly walked toward their row, approaching from an angle that gave him clear access to Jessica's expression. By the time he came up behind the group, there was little doubt in his mind about where things stood. Her beautiful green eyes overflowed with the pain of betrayal, though she continued to paint on a quiet smile. *I know what you're thinking, Jessica Chapman. Go on and admit it. He's hurting you. Right now.*

And Colin wanted to hurt him right back. *Stop it. This isn't your battle. And you don't know for sure that Nathan is to blame for this.*

He managed to catch Jessica's gaze and silently whispered, "Are you okay?" She nodded, but a lone tear slipped out of her right eye. Then he spoke. "Hey, everyone."

"Oh, hi, Colin!" Kellie turned with a gasp. "You snuck up on us. I didn't even see you there."

"Sorry. Didn't mean to scare you." He tried to gauge Nathan's expression. "What did you guys think of the children's performance tonight? Didn't Jessica do an amazing job with those kids?"

"Amazing," Kellie echoed.

"She's great." Nathan reached out and gave Jessica's hand a squeeze, then dropped it almost immediately. This did not go unnoticed.

"So, what's the plan now?"

"Oh," Jessica said, "Nathan and I have a quiet dinner planned. We're going to that new Greek restaurant on Stanton."

"Great place. One of my favorites." Colin nodded.

Jessica reached for Nathan's arm. "Well, I guess we'd better be going now. It's been a long night, and I'm tired."

Nathan extended his hand in Kellie's direction. "It was good to talk to you again. I'm sure we'll be seeing each other."

"Oh, of course." Her eyes, lit with excitement, spoke of her hope for future visits.

Colin didn't miss a thing. *How is Jessica taking this? She looks frustrated. No, she just looks exhausted.* He raised his hand to wave good-bye as the couple turned to leave. "Good night, you two."

Jessica muttered a quick good night. Nathan, however, simply nodded in his direction and kept walking.

Chapter 19

Christmas came and went, and before Jessica knew it, the New Year crept in. She spent the first day of January back in Houston with her family. A cloud of grief still hung over the group, and the usual cheerful exchanges did not take place. No countdowns. No parties. No celebrations. Instead, the day passed uneventfully. Even Nathan seemed oddly distracted. His quietness concerned her, and she tried to use her most cheerful tone when they talked, but something just felt. . .

Off.

That's the only word Jessica could use to describe how things were going. In spite of their earlier conversations, in spite of her attempts to make everything better. She tried to put her feelings of anxiety to rest, but they would not be quieted. In her heart, Jessica knew that something had changed, though she could not bring herself to voice the words. Instead, she tried to reason with herself. *I can make this work. I just have to stay focused.*

But staying focused wasn't easy, especially in this somber crowd. Jessica tried to serve as the cheerful one, often attempting to shift the conversation in lighter directions, but they would not be moved. Her mother melted into a pool of tears on several occasions, and Buck sat silently in the recliner, watching a muted television screen. Andrew made himself at home in the kitchen, fixing snacks and offering food to anyone who ventured near. Kent stayed away. A lot.

Jessica couldn't force herself to leave; though in her heart, she already longed to be back in Dallas—where a new season of music would soon kick off. Both the children's chorus and the adult company would dive right into auditions for spring productions, and the anticipation was almost overwhelming. Every time she thought about her life apart from her family, she felt guilty. Every time she thought about leaving Dallas in three months and giving up her dreams, she felt even worse. How could she pretend nothing had changed when everything had shifted into neutral?

For days, she swung between lethargy and bouts of nervous energy. Some mornings, she could hardly pull herself out of bed. Other days, she spent countless hours in a cleaning frenzy, doing everything she could to help her mother. She washed draperies, swept corners, and ironed shirt collars. And yet nothing seemed to bring a sense of relief. In her heart, Jessica truly longed to be home. With her children.

Nathan didn't seem to notice much change in her behavior. He spent a portion of the holidays with his family, and in the days prior to her leaving, seemed consumed with signing up for more classes at the college. In all, they barely had more than a day or two together. No time for wedding planning whatsoever, though the list continued to grow.

Jessica drove back to Dallas on a Sunday evening, the second weekend in January. As she pulled out of the Houston area, her spirits lifted immediately. Her excitement grew by the mile as she contemplated all that awaited her back home. Just three short months were left before her internship would come to an end. Jessica knew she must take advantage of the time. *God, thank You so much for giving me this opportunity. It's been the most awesome experience of my life.* Tears flowed down her face, and joy consumed her.

Joy, mixed with sorrow. *What will I do when it's over?*

Of course, she knew what she would do. She would become Mrs. Nathan Fisher, and he would make her the happiest woman on the planet.

Happy. When she contemplated the word, Jessica felt an emptiness she had never known. *If this is happiness, why don't I feel. . .happy?*

Jessica sighed then allowed herself to think about her musical plans once again. The adult company would be performing a Gershwin review for Valentine's Day, and their springtime production of *The Bartered Bride* was sure to be amazing. And the children's chorus was growing—by five. She and Colin had been given permission to audition some new voices for the group, and she could hardly wait to look over the résumés.

Colin.

For some reason, Jessica couldn't stop thinking about him, and always with a smile on her face. *He's one of the greatest men I've ever known. And he's so awesome with the kids.* Guilt immediately consumed her, though she wasn't sure why. He seemed to know her better than almost anyone—except her grandmother, of course. He knew what kind of music she loved. He knew her favorite colors. He understood her passion for music and even shared her love for the children.

In short, everything about him brought a smile to her face, though that smile was always followed by an overwhelming sense of guilt. Jessica attempted to push all thoughts of Colin from her mind, knowing they were a distraction from the wedding plans. *I should be thinking about the wedding cake we're going to order next weekend. And I need to make a final decision about my bridal bouquet.*

And so she continually forced her attention to the wedding. With only four months left until the big day, Jessica knew she must hurry.

I don't want to hurry. I want everything to slow down.

Then the tears started once again.

———

Colin pushed the fork around in the piece of chocolate turtle cheesecake, leaving an artistic imprint. He pulled the utensil back to examine his work. *Not bad.*

"Are you okay?" He looked up as Katie spoke. From across the table, he could see the concern in her eyes.

"I, uh—I'm fine." He dropped the fork onto the table with a *clink.*

"It's a brand-new year," she said. "A time for starting new things. A time for happiness."

"I'm happy."

"Right." She took a little nibble of chocolate before continuing. "You just seem a little quiet tonight. Something on your mind?"

Yes. I can't stop thinking about Jessica—can't stop worrying about her, wondering how things are going in Houston without me. Can't deny that I think she's wasting her time on that fiancé of hers. . . . Can't help wondering why you don't wipe that smudge of chocolate off your right cheek. . . .

"Colin?"

"I'm sorry, Katie. I really am." He shook his head in defeat. "I'm afraid I'm not very good company."

"You're unusually quiet." She wiped at her cheek with a heavy cloth napkin. "But I don't really mind. Just wanted to make sure you were okay."

"To be honest. . ." *How much should I tell her?* "I have a lot on my mind."

"About us?" Her hopeful eyes locked in on his.

"*Us?*" *How can she call us, us? We've only been on a couple of dates—both initiated by her. And I've certainly never done anything to—Stop it, Colin. Of course she thinks we're a couple. I've never had the courage to tell her what I really think: that this is a waste of time. That Ida was right. That I shouldn't—*

"Colin?"

"I'm okay. I promise. I'm just a little distracted tonight. I think maybe I'm coming down with something. To be honest, I haven't felt well for days now."

"You do look a little pale." Katie reached up and felt his forehead. "Nope. Not hot."

"I don't have a clue what's wrong with me." He sighed and pushed his chair back from the table. "Something just feels off tonight."

"Maybe I should go."

He looked up from his plate with a shrug. "I don't want to hurt your feelings." *You're such a coward, Colin.* "Do you need a ride home?"

"No. I've got my car, remember?" She jangled her keys in his face, and he fought the impulse to be irritated at the little clinking noise they made.

"Right."

"Well. . ." She stood and reached for her purse. "I can tell you're not exactly yourself tonight. I'll just give you a call tomorrow."

"Okay. Sorry, Katie."

She left the restaurant with a dazed expression on her face, and Colin sat to finish his cup of coffee in silence. He tried to think about the upcoming auditions, tried to force his thoughts to the children. But all he could think about—all he wanted to focus on—was Jessica.

Guilt consumed him every time he remembered. *She's not mine. She's going to be another man's wife.* Then, just as quickly, the guilt was overshadowed by a tremendous sense of loss. Sorrow. She would be leaving in three short months. *Why do I feel so empty every time I think about losing her?*

For the children's sake, of course. They would miss her. They adored everything about Jessica. And why not? She had been sent from heaven to head up this program. For a season, anyway.

Colin took a sip of the coffee. Now lukewarm, it hardly brought him any satisfaction. He reflected on the fact that the children weren't the only ones who had gained an ally in Jessica Chapman. In his heart, he had grown attached, as well. *I've lost something that was never even mine in the first place. If I could only keep my mind on the music and just forget about her. . . .*

Suddenly Colin remembered something his mother had said many months ago. How had she put it, again? Ah yes. "It's time you settled down. Found yourself a wife. Had a few kids. I mean, the opera is a good thing, but there's certainly more to life than music. It's one thing to follow your dreams; it's another to give up your personal life."

Colin shoved the fork into the cheesecake and stood to leave.

Chapter 20

On the night of February 14, the Dallas Metropolitan Opera hosted a special evening of love songs—a tribute to George Gershwin. Just before the show, Jessica fought against her own emotions as she dressed. Nothing seemed to be going right tonight, though she couldn't put her finger on why. As she struggled with the red bow tie, she argued with herself. *Get it together, Jessica. What's wrong with you?*

In her heart, however, she knew. Something in the Gershwin tunes had struck a chord. Love—the kind she had been singing about—didn't exist. At least, not between herself and Nathan.

"But love isn't really just about feelings," she whispered as she twisted the bow tie into a knot. Still, she wished for a few feelings right now, especially since she had received the news that Nathan wouldn't be able to join her tonight. *Valentine's Day without my valentine.*

Somehow, it didn't hurt as much as she thought it would—and that worried her. They should be missing each other more. Shouldn't they? And why didn't the words of the love songs make her think of him?

Jessica stepped back to have a look in the mirror. Her black dress pants, white tuxedo shirt, and shiny bow tie made her feel more like a penguin than a vocalist. However, when Katie appeared at the door of the costume room dressed in the same attire, Jessica felt a little more comfortable.

"Are you ready? Snyder's a little snippy tonight." Katie's flushed face shone with excitement.

"I'll be right there." Jessica dabbed on a bit of lipstick and examined herself in the mirror. "I guess this will have to do." She scurried across the backstage area and into the rehearsal room, where fellow vocalists sat, preparing for a final run-through of tonight's songs. As she entered the room, she noticed Colin's eyes. They sparkled as he turned to face her.

"You look great," he whispered.

She chuckled. "We all look just alike."

"No. Not you. You always stand out above the others."

"Maybe it's the red hair," she acknowledged with a smile.

"Nope. Not that. Although you do have beautiful hair. I think it's something else—something that comes from way down deep inside you. You're beautiful from the inside out."

Jessica marveled at the joy in his eyes. The depth. The caring. "You flatter me, Mr. Phillips."

"You make it easy, Miss Chapman."

She felt her cheeks flush and quickly moved to take a seat in the front row, amidst the other sopranos. Colin took his place in the third row. For some reason, Jessica's heart fluttered as he moved away. Something undeniable seemed to be stirring. *I don't get these same feelings around Nathan. Maybe I never did. Lord, what's wrong with me?*

As she took her seat and began the warm-ups, Jessica tried to focus on her wedding vows, which still needed to be written. Somehow, every time she rehearsed them in her mind, they came out sounding like Gershwin tunes. *I can't even think straight anymore.*

The music began, and Jessica's heart began to twist inside out. *I'm just lonely because Nathan's not here. I'm missing him.* But in her heart, she knew this wasn't true. Jessica finally began to acknowledge what she had probably known for some time now. She glanced across the room at Colin. The speed of her heartbeat nearly doubled, and she had to voice the inevitable. "I care about Colin," she whispered. "As more than just a friend."

The words nearly knocked her out of her chair.

All through the rehearsal, Colin fought a rapid heartbeat. He felt physically ill, though he couldn't quite figure out why. Probably just nerves. But he never got nervous—not like this, anyway. Why tonight? He joined the others as they traveled from the rehearsal room to the stage entrance. From here, he could hear the people in the auditorium and could almost envision their faces.

Almost. Funny. The only face he could see with any clarity was Jessica's. Her smile. Her whimsical pout. Her freckles. Her rich, auburn hair.

Colin traipsed behind the others to enter the stage. He took his place on the third row of the risers and waited for the curtain to rise. He had looked forward to tonight's performance above almost any other. The Gershwin music seemed to speak to him, perhaps even more so than the traditional classical music he had always loved. In his heart, he knew why. These songs voiced the very thing he had been afraid to speak.

Love.

What a wonderful, terrifying word. Love for a woman. Colin gasped as the revelation hit him like a freight train coming around the bend. The one thing he had been trying to avoid for months now seemed inevitable, and it very nearly knocked the breath right out of him. He had fallen in love with Jessica Chapman, and he must tell her.

He would die if he didn't.

From upstage right, Colin struggled to get Jessica's attention. "I've got to talk to her, or I'm going to explode," he whispered as the music swelled. *Father, if what I'm feeling, if what I know in my heart to be true is wrong, then stop me. Please. Settle these emotions, Lord.*

As they sang the familiar love songs, Colin watched the most beautiful woman in the world out of the corner of his eye. She stood out above the others, and he had voiced it well a little earlier. *It's not just her outer beauty, though she is prettier than the other women here. There really is something about Jessica—something that goes all the way to the core.*

Colin recognized her spiritual depth, that which gave her true beauty. She was by far the most amazing woman he had ever met. Probably the most amazing he would ever meet. *I don't deserve her.*

Oh, but I want her. And I want her to want me. He struggled with his feelings as the love songs continued. When his solo, "Love Walked In," began, Colin fought to swallow the lump that had grown in his throat. Love had walked into his life, and he could deny it no longer. He would deny it no longer. The words spoke more truth than he had ever been willing to face. He felt the depth of the words as they tumbled out of his mouth: "Love walked right in and drove the shadows away; love walked right in and brought my sunniest day. One magic moment and my heart seemed to know that love said, 'Hello,' though not a word was spoken."

I did know. I knew the minute I laid eyes on her. I knew that day back in Houston when she walked on that stage. Love walked into my life and changed everything. How could I have been so blind not to see what was in front of me all the time? Didn't I want to see? Guilt immediately seized him, and Colin begged the Lord to forgive him for these feelings.

And yet he didn't want them to end.

Colin looked her way as his song ended and her beautiful solo began. Clearly, Jessica favored her song above all others. "Someone to Watch Over Me," seemed to suit her—not just vocally, but in all other ways, too. Snyder had chosen Jessica to sing the beautiful female solo, and she did it justice like no one else could have. When she began the melancholy piece, the audience responded with cheers and whistles.

"There's a saying old, says that love is blind." She sang with her eyes closed. "Still we're often told, 'Seek and ye shall find.' So I'm going to seek a certain lad I've had in mind." Colin silently willed her to open her eyes, to see the desperation in his own.

I'm that lad, Jessica. I'm the one you've been looking for.

As she continued on, he suddenly felt nauseous. Running from the stage seemed to be his best option. Instead, he drew in deep, calculated breaths and tried to focus. *How can I focus on anything but her?* Her gaze finally locked on his as she reached the chorus of the song. *Is it just a coincidence? She's supposed to be facing stage left, not stage right.*

Tears shimmered in her eyes as she sang—not to anyone else in the auditorium. Only to him. "There's a somebody I'm longing to see. I hope that he turns out to be someone who'll watch over me." Colin's heart leapt into his throat.

His gaze spoke a thousand words from across the stage. *I'm that somebody, Jessica. I want to be the one to watch over you. You'll never have to be alone.* But, then again, she wasn't alone. Nathan, her fiancé, provided an ever-present reminder. *If he's so in love with her, why isn't he here on Valentine's Day? Oh, but I'm so glad he's not here. If he had come. . .*

None of this would be happening.

Jessica continued to sing, and Colin found himself caught up in watching her—so much so that he almost forgot to join in on the chorus. *This is reaching a crazy point. I've got to do something, say something. I can't wait any longer. My heart can't take much more of this.*

When the song ended, he managed to get her attention and mouthed the words, "I need to talk to you." She nodded with a mixture of terror and curiosity etched on her beautiful face.

The final song of the evening drew to a conclusion with the whole group in choreographed formation, which, blessing upon blessing, placed Colin and Jessica side by side. As the curtain came down, he took advantage of the opportunity by grabbing her hand and whispering in her ear. "Jessica. I need to talk to you. It can't wait."

She looked up at him with a panicked expression and nodded silently.

"If I don't tell you this, I'm going to die." He pressed her hands into his own as he spoke above the excited voices onstage. "Remember that day on the phone when I told you I loved you?" She nodded, and her hands began to shake as he continued. "I didn't mean to say those words. I wasn't even sure where they came from, to be honest. But the truth is—I do love you." His words, rushed and passionate, astounded him.

She began to cry, and Colin gripped her hands even tighter. "I love you, Jessica. I've tried not to. I've prayed about it, worried about it—tried to forget about it. But I can't. I know that God brought you here—not just because of the music—but because we're supposed to be together. I prayed for a helper, and He sent me the best one on the planet."

"Oh, Colin." Her eyes filled with tears, and she squeezed his hands. Then, just as swiftly, she backed away and placed her hands over her mouth. "What are we doing?" she whispered. "This can't be happening." Thunderous applause continued from the other side of the closed curtain.

"It is." He pulled her to himself. "And it's too late to change anything. I love you, Jessica." And then, without planning a thing, their lips came together in the most orchestrated moment of Colin's life. The world seemed to disappear in a joyous haze as he held this gift, this amazing woman in his arms. The roar of love nearly deafened him.

Only when an elbow jabbed him in the ribs did he realize the roar came from the audience. When had the curtain gone back up?

For a second, Jessica looked as if she might faint. Her cheeks blazed with color. From stage right, Katie stared with her mouth hanging open. Several people in the audience began to cheer, and Colin realized, all too late, that he and Jessica had just exposed their feelings not only to each other—but also to the entire city of Dallas, Texas.

Jessica tossed and turned in her bed, fighting the mixture of emotions that held her in their grip. *He loves me. Colin loves me.* The revelation brought wonder.

And terror.

I love Nathan. Don't I?

She wrestled with the truth, and it nearly strangled her in its grasp. *I don't love Nathan. Not like I should, anyway. But what do I do about that? Do I marry him anyway?* She twisted around in the sheets for nearly an hour before finally falling asleep. When she dozed off, familiar dreams swept her away to a place she recognized all too well.

Jessica saw herself on a stage, singing her heart out. She wore an exquisite, flowing dress in shades of cream and burgundy. To her left, a beautiful set filled the stage—an antiquated Italian city with houses, fountains, and cobbled streets. From inside the window of one of the houses, a man sang to her in a rich baritone voice, which resonated across the theater.

She responded to his words in Italian. Her soprano voice matched his as they joined together in harmony to complete the song. He disappeared momentarily, only to reappear in the doorway of the house. The tall stranger with dark hair moved toward her, never taking his gaze off of hers.

Only now did she recognize him.

Colin. I've been dreaming about you all along!

With great joy, he swept her into his arms and sang lovingly to her as he danced her across the stage. She found herself captivated by the moment and completely lost in his gaze. They seemed to mirror each other perfectly. From there, the dream faded to a dismal, gray haze.

Jessica awoke in a pool of sweat. She shook uncontrollably as truth overwhelmed her. Somehow, lying here in the bed with no one but the Lord to confide in, Jessica had to admit the truth.

I'm in love with Colin Phillips.

Chapter 21

The week after Valentine's Day gave Jessica the time she needed to seek God's will concerning her love life. After much turmoil, she had to conclude that she could not carry through with her plans to marry Nathan. This revelation caused pain at first, but it had been followed by an overwhelming sense of relief.

Now she must tell her fiancé that she couldn't possibly marry him. Many times she ran through the conversation in her mind, trying to decide the best way to word things. And opportunities seemed to abound. She could have told him of her decision over the phone on several occasions. She could have shared the news as they chatted online. She could have told him any number of times in any number of ways.

But fear always stopped her. *He's going to be so hurt. He'll never understand.*

Besides, he always seemed to be more than a little distracted and even moody when they were together. Often, he didn't have time to talk at length anyway. His school schedule was tight, and his work commitments seemed to be growing daily.

Not that she had much time, either. The children's spring production was in full rehearsal, and the children offered hours of distraction from her woes. They were a chaotic delight, as usual. On top of their antics, Jessica had another amazing distraction. She had been offered the opportunity of a lifetime—a solo role in the adult spring performance of *The Bartered Bride*. With so much going on simultaneously, she had little time to contemplate the very real consequences of bartering her own romantic feelings.

In order to maintain a sense of openness before the Lord, Jessica made a commitment to cease any personal conversation with Colin. This proved to be quite difficult, in light of the hours they spent together daily, but she managed to avoid any private conversations and kept her thoughts and emotions to herself. Until she settled the issue with Nathan, she had no other choice. Everything was just too confusing right now. Instead, she made the whole matter an issue of prayer and committed her heart—and her future—to the Lord. Even if it meant spending the rest of her life alone.

By the time she drove to Houston the final weekend in February, Jessica felt more at peace about the whole situation. She knew the Lord would show her what to do. He could be trusted with her future. Hadn't He already directed her this far? Hadn't He given her the courage to come to Dallas to audition for the opera? He knew her heart, and He remained in full control.

In the meantime, Jessica knew she must confide in her mother at once. To wait any longer would be too difficult. Besides, she needed the assurance and the love of one who had already lived and loved so well. What better person than her own mother, who had always shared her heart so openly?

When she arrived home, Jessica took advantage of the first available opportunity to pour her heart out to both her mother and Andrew. She spoke carefully, thoughtfully, and didn't leave out a thing. She told them of her most recent revelation—that her feelings for Nathan were not what she had always thought. Though somewhat shaken, her parents seemed to take the news a little better than she had hoped.

"To be honest," her mother responded at last, "I'm not that surprised. In fact, I think I've known for a while. That's probably why I asked so many pointed questions when you were here last."

"It doesn't change your opinion of me?" Jessica wiped tears from her eyes as she spoke.

"Never." Her mother's eyes misted, as well. "I felt a little bad for putting you on the spot before, but now I know that God was obviously on the move. I can see that now."

"I'm so relieved. Thank you both so much for understanding." She looked at them with great appreciation.

"We trust your judgment," Andrew added. "And you know in your heart whether Nathan is the right man for you."

"It would be far worse to marry a man you were never intended to marry," her mother added. "I've known far too many people who did, and they struggled for years to try to make the marriage work. I don't want that for you, Jess. I want you to be able to have it all—the romance, the music—everything."

Then I have to tell them the part about Colin, too.

Tears flowed now, and Jessica freely shared all that had happened on Valentine's Day. At first, as always, guilt consumed her. But when she reached the point where Colin confessed his love for her, she couldn't help smiling. Her heart came alive, and her hands began to tremble. Even her lips quivered as she spoke the words, "I feel so bad about feeling so good."

For a moment, her mother didn't say a word. Then, when she did speak, her words startled Jessica. "I never thought I could fall in love twice in one lifetime." She took hold of her daughter's hands. "When your father passed away, I just accepted the fact that I'd be by myself for the rest of my life. I was so surprised when the Lord brought Andrew into my life."

"In a good way, I hope." He slipped his arm around her shoulders.

"A very good way." She patted him on the knee, and they hugged at length.

"You two are so romantic," Jessica said with a sigh. "I want a relationship like that. I really do. I didn't realize how much I wanted and needed that."

"Romance is very important," her mother said. "But love—real love—far exceeds any feeling or emotion. I know I don't have to tell you that."

"I always thought I knew what love was like." Jessica shrugged. "But now I'm not sure I know anything anymore. I feel like a little girl, all over again."

"That's not such a bad thing," Andrew said. "Just put your trust in God. He's still there."

"Just remember," her mother said, "God's methods don't always fall in line with what we expect. And He has an amazing sense of humor. Sometimes we forget that."

"I had almost forgotten. These past few months have had very few light-hearted moments. Between Nathan and myself, I mean. Up in Dallas, I've had lots of fun. I don't know when I've ever felt so fulfilled or so needed."

"I'm thrilled for you, honey." Her mother stood to give her a warm embrace. "Just promise me you won't make any rash decisions where your love life is concerned. These things take time, trust me."

Jessica wrapped her arms around her mother's waist. "I won't, Mom. Other than work-related things, I haven't even spoken two words to Colin since Valentine's Day."

"I'm not so sure that's good, either."

"I just haven't known what to say, so I haven't said anything. I think it's more important at this point to talk to Nathan and resolve our relationship in a way that honors God—and him. But I'm so scared I'm going to hurt him, Mom. I'm so scared." She dissolved into tears, and her mother held her in a warm embrace.

"You can't let that stop you from doing the right thing."

"I know." Jessica reached for a tissue and dried her eyes.

"One day at a time, honey. And one battle at a time."

As they wrapped up their conversation, Jessica finally felt free to breathe again. Now she could move forward with her life. Just as soon as she talked to Nathan.

She found her first opportunity to speak with him later that same evening. He arrived around six to pick her up for dinner. All the way to the restaurant, she sat in silence, planning her words. Just as they pulled into the parking lot, she turned to face him. "Nathan, I need to talk to you about something. Important."

"What's up, Jess?" He turned to face her as he pulled into a parking space.

"I need to tell you—"

At that moment, his cell phone rang, and he reached to grab it. "This will just take a minute. I'll get rid of them." He answered the phone, and Jessica tried, once again, to collect her thoughts. Unfortunately, his call lasted quite some time and seemed to be complicated. Something about one of his classes. Obviously something important. He remained on the phone nearly twenty minutes. When he finally hung up, she opened her mouth to begin again, but he managed to get the first word in.

"I can't believe that guy!" Nathan dove into a lengthy explanation of all that had transpired over the phone. On and on he went, sharing every detail. Something hurtful had happened at school. He had been victimized. Someone else was to blame. He had tried to make things right, but nothing seemed to work in his favor.

Jessica listened intently, but at some point in the story, she felt all of her courage drain away. As she and Nathan entered the restaurant together, she decided this would surely not be the night the Lord had in mind to break her fiancé's heart.

I've lost her. The words ran through Colin's mind over and over again as he prepared the room for the children's arrival. *Why did I tell her? Why did I—how could I have kissed another man's fiancée? What's wrong with me? Why didn't I just wait and. . .*

And what? Live in misery without letting her know? Let her think he felt comfortable just being her friend when, in reality, he wanted to sweep her into his arms and hold her?

Forever.

But clearly, that would never happen now. She had gone back to Houston and, with the spring productions just a few weeks away, he knew she would only return for a brief time.

Then she'll be gone. What will I do without her? His heart twisted as if in a stranglehold, and he felt a lump rise in his throat. *Lord, help me resist these feelings. Don't let me give in. Help me do the right thing, Father.*

Colin pushed the lump back down and forced himself to focus on the children—on the upcoming rehearsal. With so much to do, who had time to worry about being in love anyway?

Chapter 22

Weeks went by, and Jessica never found the right opportunity to share her heart with Nathan. She tried valiantly, but every time—every single time—something would happen to interrupt their conversation. Many times she found herself questioning both her motives and her feelings. Would it be better to hurt Nathan by telling him the truth or to marry him, knowing he wasn't the right man for her? If she married someone outside of God's plan, the consequences could be devastating for both of them.

And what about Colin? Jessica pressed all thoughts of him from her mind time and time again. But he would not go away. At night, in her dreams, he would reappear. In her thoughts, he would speak words of kindness to her. Jessica couldn't seem to shake his image, no matter which direction she turned. And working with him every day didn't help matters much. Continually, she was reminded of his warm smile, his love for the children, his passion for the music they both loved.

And his comments to her on Valentine's night.

Though the two never mentioned all that had taken place after that infamous performance, she could not stop thinking about his words, could not help remembering what it felt like to be wrapped up in his arms. It had felt so good, so right. But how could it be? *God, forgive me if what I'm feeling is wrong. I don't want to be out of Your will.*

But how could marrying Nathan be right, either? What good was a marriage that would only end in misery? She wouldn't be giving Nathan her whole self, even if she vowed to try with all her heart.

No, Jessica finally concluded, she could not marry Nathan. Even if God chose to close the door on a potential relationship with Colin, she could not—would not—carry through with the marriage to her fiancé. To do so would be to deny her heart and would be unfair to him.

But how could she tell him?

On the final weekend in March, she finally found the right opportunity to speak with Nathan and give him the dreaded news. He had agreed to drive her back to Dallas so they could have some time together. Alone. At first, she was thrilled at the opportunity. However, as the car pulled away from the curb, Jessica began to wonder if she could go through with this. *Lord, I need Your help. I don't want to hurt him. Help me, Father.*

Just as she opened her mouth to begin, Nathan spoke. "Jess, I need to talk to you."

"Okay. I need to talk to you, too."

"This is really important." He pulled the car off the road and gazed at her intently. "I, uh. . ."

Obviously very important. "Go ahead, Nathan."

"I need to tell you something, but I don't want to upset you. Really," he continued, "I guess there's no way to tell you this without upsetting you."

"What is it, Nathan?" Now her curiosity kicked in.

"I, um, I've had a lot of time to myself over the last few months."

"I know. I'm really sorry about that."

"Don't be," he said. "The time alone has given me a lot of opportunity to think—about who I am, where I'm going, all that stuff. I might have seemed stressed about being by myself, but God was using it to prepare me for something."

What is he going to say?

"I've had a lot of time to ask Him about the direction my life should be headed. And He's answered me. Pretty specifically, actually. In fact, I've been pretty amazed at all He's had to say."

"That's awesome, Nathan."

"Yes and no." He paused and shut off the engine. "What God has been sharing with me affects us both."

"Really?"

"I know I've been distant lately." His gaze shifted out the window. "I'm pretty sure that's been a subconscious thing. But I've had some issues to work out on my own—things that I couldn't tell you about."

"Like what?"

He turned back to face her. "Part of it has to do with school stuff—and my future. I've put out a lot of résumés over the past few months."

"Really? Any leads?"

"Yes, actually. I received a job offer last week. A really great one."

"Nathan, that's awesome. Where at?"

"Ironically," he said slowly, "in Dallas. It's with an oil and gas accounting firm. With my background in the industry, they felt like I'd be a good fit."

In Dallas? He's moving to Dallas? Lord, what are You doing here?

"That's what makes this next part so difficult." Nathan drew in a deep breath and shifted his gaze to the seat.

"Say it, Nathan."

"I don't want to hurt you."

"Just say it." A peace suddenly overwhelmed Jessica, and a sense of God's presence filled the car.

"I, uh, I've been thinking a lot about us, too," he whispered.

"And?"

"And I think—no, I know that we're—we're. . ."

"Go ahead." She reached out and gripped his hand.

"We're not supposed to get married." Now his words seemed rushed, and his gaze locked on hers as he forged ahead with a passion. "It's not that I don't love you, Jessica. I do. I've always loved you. But I don't think it's the same kind of love that a husband would have for a wife. I didn't want to hurt you, and I've been trying, for a while now actually, to make myself feel something I didn't really feel."

Jessica's heart soared. How could she possibly be happy with such terrible news? And yet, it wasn't terrible. "Nathan, you don't have to say another word."

"I don't?" He looked at her intently.

"No. I totally understand. And. . ." She swallowed hard. "I have to agree. In fact, I've been trying to tell you for weeks that I've felt the same way. I just couldn't bring myself to do it."

A look of sheer relief passed across his face. "Really?"

"Yeah." She grinned.

He rubbed at his brow. "It's been torture, hasn't it?"

"Yes," Jessica agreed. "And no. I wouldn't trade our friendship for anything. And God has taught me so much as we tried to force this thing to fit when it really didn't. And I know that there is a love between us—one we've shared since we were kids. Maybe we just misunderstood and thought it was the 'happily ever after' kind when it really wasn't."

"I never meant to hurt you," he whispered.

"I didn't mean to hurt you, either."

"I suppose it would have hurt a lot more if we had discovered this after we got married, don't you think?" He released her hand, and his eyebrows elevated slightly.

"Yeah."

"Jess, you're great. And I know God has big plans for your life. I'm sorry I haven't been more supportive. I'm not really into the opera thing as you know."

She shrugged. "No harm done. And I know the Lord obviously has some big things planned for you, too. But what do we do now? Do you still want to come to Dallas with me for the performance, or should we turn around and take you home?"

"Actually," he said and smiled, "I have an appointment with the new company tomorrow afternoon. I plan to stay for your performance and then I'll fly back on the red-eye."

"I see." She leaned back against the seat and closed her eyes, rethinking all that had just taken place.

Nathan started the engine, put the transmission back into gear, and pulled out onto the highway. For the next two hours, he and Jessica had one of the best conversations they'd had in months—sharing their hearts, laughing, and marveling about God's goodness in their lives.

Colin moped around his apartment in sheer misery. Weeks had gone by, and he couldn't bring himself to say a word to Jessica about his feelings. Right now, his heart felt like a lump of lead in his chest. *Lord, if this is love, I'm not sure I can take it.* A prayer arose out of his spirit and poured forth like water tumbling over river rocks. *What good is an occupation without a personal life? What if I worked all of my life and had no one to share it with, no one to come home to in the evenings?*

Colin could think of nothing worse than coming home to an empty house.

Except, perhaps, coming home to the wrong person in that house. Visions of Katie with those sparkling blue eyes tore at him, and Colin knew, beyond a shadow of a doubt, that Ida had been right all along. Katie wasn't the one he had been praying for, either. She was awesome. Amazing. Very nearly perfect, in fact.

Just not for him.

"How many people do that, Lord?" he whispered. "How many get defeated and settle for something—someone—less than the person You've selected for them?" The idea sent a shiver down his spine. "I'd rather be single forever than settle for the wrong woman. Help me, Father. Help me."

Chapter 23

On the night of the opening for *The Bartered Bride*, Colin's trembling fingers fidgeted with his costume. *Just two more weeks and she'll be gone forever. Just two more weeks.*

He couldn't seem to stop the thought from rolling through his mind. Jessica would leave him—and the children—and would return to Houston to be married. She would become Mrs. Nathan Fisher in just a few short weeks.

And there was nothing he could do to prevent it.

Every time he considered the possibility of losing her, Colin felt weak in the knees. Children's program aside. Opera aside. He needed her. In so many ways, she fulfilled him. And yet, she did not belong to him. She belonged to another, and he would simply have to get used to that idea, whether it killed him or not.

Just one more time. If I told her just one more time how I feel, she might. . .

No. To say it again would only complicate an already chaotic matter. She clearly wasn't interested. She had hardly spoken a word to him in weeks, after all—and there had been plenty of opportunity.

Colin glanced at himself in the mirror once more before leaving the room. A light tap at the door interrupted his thoughts.

A stagehand spoke. "Curtain call in five minutes, Mr. Phillips."

"Thanks." He returned to fidgeting with the buttons on his shirt. Another light tap resounded on the door. For some reason, it irritated him, and he yanked the door open, ready to do battle—until his gaze fell on the beautiful angel on the other side. "Jessica?"

"Colin, do you have a minute?" Her eyes seemed to carry a new glow, an anxious glimmer.

"Just a few, actually. They've already called us for curtain." *This is it. This is the moment I've been dreading.*

"I have to talk to you," she whispered. Her eyes filled with tears immediately. "I wish we had more time."

"So do I." Now his eyes filled, as well. "But we're almost out of time, aren't we, Jess?" He reached for her hands and squeezed them.

"Yes."

"But I want you to know," he spoke with fervor, "that these last few months have been the best of my life. I don't know what I would have done without you. I really don't. You've been such a blessing to me. The children have fallen in love

243

with you, and so have. . ." *No. Don't say it.*

"Colin, I have something to tell you."

"Curtain in two minutes, Mr. Phillips." The stagehand appeared again, this time looking quite anxious.

"Let's talk as we walk to the stage." Colin took Jessica's hand and led her to the backstage entrance. Somehow, with her hand in his, everything in the world felt right again. He could breathe again. He could sing again.

He could live again.

"I just wanted to make sure you knew—before you leave, I mean—how much it means to me that you came to Dallas in the first place." Colin looked at her intently. "I may never get the chance to say this again, but you've been a godsend. You've been a direct answer to prayer."

"Places, please!" the stage manager whispered with a firm hand on Colin's shoulder.

For a moment, Jessica looked as if she would faint. "I need to talk to you when this is all over," she whispered. Then, as she crossed the stage to take her place, her green eyes spilled over with tears.

She's going to miss the children. She's going to miss singing on this stage. She's going to miss. . .

The curtain lifted, and an audience full of spectators began to applaud wildly. Colin tried to focus on the show, tried to remember his first lines, but his heart, now torn in two, wouldn't allow it.

By the time the show ended, Jessica found herself in a befuddled state of despair. Many times throughout the performance, she had tried to catch Colin's eye. Either he simply wasn't interested anymore, or he was trying to avoid her. At any rate, she must speak to him. Her heart couldn't wait any longer.

As the curtain came down that opening night, Jessica fought her way through the crowd to get to him. There, in the corner, he stood, surrounded by lovely prima donnas. They would have to wait. She had something to tell him. Something urgent. Eagerly, she pressed her way through the group and to Colin's side. She took his hand and squeezed it to get his attention. "Colin?"

"Jess?" He peered down at her with a look of eager curiosity.

"I need you."

"Excuse me?" His eyes began to twinkle with a bit of mischief, and the young women surrounding him took the cue. One by one, they began to scatter.

"I, uh, I need to talk to you. I have something to tell you."

"Right now?"

"Right now. It can't wait. Even a minute." Jessica couldn't seem to stop the grin from spreading across her face as she led Colin by the hand to the backstage door. With a triumphant swing, she thrust the door open, and they stepped out into the moonlight together. A night of wonder swept her into its trance. "Wow. It's beautiful out here." She turned in circles and gazed up at the sky, forgetting for a moment what had led her to this place.

"Sure is," Colin agreed. "But I'm a little distracted by something more beautiful right now."

"More beautiful?" She looked at him with heart racing. "You mean—"

"I mean," he said as he moved a step closer, "I can't see anything but you, Jess. I haven't been able to for months. I feel like a blind man staggering around in the dark, and yet I don't think I've ever seen more clearly. Does that make any sense?" He took her by the hand, and she immediately felt as if she might never be able to speak again.

When she didn't respond right away, his words poured out in a torrent. "Of course it doesn't make any sense." Colin raked his fingers through his thick, dark curls. "Nothing makes sense anymore, does it? I mean, on one hand, the world looks completely sane and normal. On the other hand, nothing seems logical anymore. I can't think straight. I can't sleep at night. And it's your fault. No, that's not right. It's not your fault. You haven't done anything. It's me. It's all me. I've fallen in love with you, and I don't know what to do about it."

Her heart leaped into her throat, and Jessica felt tears welling up in her eyes. "Oh, Colin." She could hardly contain her emotions and wanted to tell him— quickly—that she shared his feelings.

He took a giant step backward. "But it's wrong," he whispered. A lone tear tipped over the edge of his lashes, and he brushed it away with a vengeance. "You're not mine. And I can't feel this way. I'm breaking God's heart." He leaned against the brick wall in defeat. "I'm breaking my own heart."

"No." Jessica reached up and ran her fingers over his damp cheeks. "No broken hearts necessary. Not God's or yours. Certainly not mine." Now the smile spread from ear to ear. She could no longer hide her feelings. *I love this man. I have to tell him, or I'll die.*

"What do you mean?" His large hands suddenly felt as if they would crush hers.

"I have something to tell you. I've been trying to tell you all night, in fact."

"What, Jess?"

"It's just that. . .Nathan and I aren't—well, we aren't 'Nathan and I' anymore."

"Are you serious?" He let go of her hands and stared at her as though in wonder and disbelief.

"I'm serious. We decided, both of us, that we couldn't go through with the wedding. We realized that our relationship just wasn't part of God's plan for our lives."

"It wasn't?"

"No." Jessica swallowed hard. "After all," she whispered, "you can't marry one person when you're. . ."

245

"You're. . . ?"

"You're in love with someone else." Her gaze sought out his dark eyes in the moonlight.

"Do you mean that?" His voice soared with joy.

She nodded. Colin pulled her close, and as she laid her head on his chest, his heart raced in sync with hers. She knew, without a shadow of a doubt, that God had answered every prayer in one heartbeat.

"You are the most amazing thing that has ever happened to me." He planted tiny kisses on her forehead then lightly traced her cheekbone with his fingertip.

"I love you, Colin. And I'm so blessed. I don't know what I ever did to deserve you." Jessica choked back the tears that now threatened to overwhelm her. "But do you think there's any hope for us? Is it too late to start over again?"

With the moonlight guiding his way, Colin's lips found hers, giving his final answer on the matter.

Epilogue

The costume director for the Dallas Metropolitan Opera appeared at the door with a gorgeous gown in her hands. "All of the alterations are complete, Miss Chapman." Her breathless words were rushed. "I'm really sorry it took so long. I just wanted this one to be perfect."

Jessica looked up from the mirror, where she had carefully applied an adequate amount of stage makeup. "Thanks so much, Amanda. I can't wait to wear it tonight." She examined the dress carefully, amazed at the intricate stitching and marvelous colors. "You did an awesome job. I can't believe how pretty it is."

"Thanks." Amanda grinned her appreciation. "You're going to look beautiful in it. Speaking of which, would you like some help dressing? All of those buttons might present a challenge."

"No thanks. I'm expecting help to arrive any moment." As the door to the room closed, Jessica turned to look in the mirror once again. Then, with her hands shaking, she stood and reached for the dress. Tonight's performance would be the opportunity of a lifetime—a chance to put to rest all prior fears and concerns. It would end all speculation and open doors to a beautiful and hopeful future. As she took the stage tonight, Jessica would realize the fulfillment of a dream that had begun years ago—a dream given by the Lord Himself.

A rap on the door interrupted her thoughts. She pulled her dressing gown tightly around her. "Come in."

Her mother peeked inside. "How's everything coming? Need my help?"

"Sure. I'd love that, Mom."

Her mother entered and smiled broadly as she faced the beautiful gown. "Oh, it's gorgeous, Jess! You're going to look amazing."

Jessica's anxious fingers tripped over the tiny buttons. "I don't know what's wrong with me tonight. For some reason, I'm a nervous wreck." She pulled the dress off of the hanger and slipped it over her head, nearly getting tangled up in the long, flowing sleeves. "I usually don't get preshow jitters," she said from inside the layers of chiffon, "but this is so different."

"What's that expression you theater people use? Break a leg?" her mother asked as she helped Jessica adjust the gown.

For the first time, Jessica noticed tears in her mother's eyes. "Right."

"Well, all I can say is, there's no way you could possibly sneak in an extra rehearsal for tonight's show. You have to count on God's ability to direct this one."

She began the arduous task of buttoning the twenty-five pearl buttons that ran up the back of Jessica's dress.

"Mom, I can't tell you how happy I am." Jessica felt tears arise and immediately began to fan her eyes, hoping not to ruin her makeup. "When I think of how far I've come in the past year or two, I'm amazed. God has answered every prayer. Not exactly the way I thought he would, but He has definitely given me the desires of my heart."

"He's full of surprises, isn't He? But I'm not surprised the Lord has chosen to use you in so many ways, honey. And I know His blessing is on you. Tonight is just the beginning of many opportunities yet to come. I only wish. . ." Her mother choked back tears. "I only wish your father could have been here to witness this. And I can't help thinking of all the witty things your grandmother would have said."

"It's not the same without them." Jessica sighed as she held her mother in a tight embrace.

"No, it's not." The older woman stood back with a determined look. "But enough tears for us. You have to be on the stage in just a few minutes."

"How's the audience?" Jessica asked as she turned back to examine herself in the mirror one last time.

"Quite a crowd for an opening night performance. They're here because they love you, Jessica. And I love you, too. I don't know if I've said it enough, but I do. And I'm so proud of you. You've been such a godly example to all of the children here, and you've certainly taught me a thing or two."

A knock on the door interrupted their conversation. "Miss Chapman?"

"Yes?" She peeked outside to respond to the stage manager.

"Curtain in five minutes. You sure don't want to be late for this one. They can't start without you tonight."

Jessica smiled. "You're right." She turned to face her mother. "You'd better take your seat, Mom. I don't want you to miss anything."

"Okay." Her mother held her tightly for a moment. "Oh, by the way—Andrew's waiting at the back of the theater. Do you remember where to meet him?"

"I remember." Jessica grinned and reached for the exquisite bouquet of red roses to her left. "And I can't wait."

From upstage left, Colin waited. Tonight's performance would seal his future and write in stone every God-given dream upon his heart. Tonight—in just moments, in fact—Jessica Chapman would enter the stage and take his hand.

For the rest of his life.

From behind the Mediterranean backdrop, Colin waited for the music to begin. He sneaked a peek through the window, and his gaze fell on Nathan and Kellie, who sat, hands tightly clutched, in the third row. Their wedding, just weeks ago, had been a lavish, upscale affair. He and Jessica had attended with great joy.

Just in front of the newly married couple he located another old friend. Ida Sullivan sat in the second row with a look of pure satisfaction on her wrinkled face. Walter Malone was seated next to her, dressed in a suit that must, surely, be older than Colin himself. The elderly man leaned in to whisper something in Ida's ear, and she responded by smiling broadly. Colin took a second look. *Is he holding her hand?*

He barely had time to contemplate the matter. The stringed quartet began the introduction, and he swallowed hard as the familiar strain of music gave him his cue. His heart pounded in anticipation as he stepped through the doorway at the designated moment and began to sing. The love song he and Jessica had chosen was in Italian. Of course. Nothing else would have done.

He had rehearsed at length, though his nerves now kicked in, and Colin found himself barely able to get the first few words out. And yet he must continue. He would sing beyond the tears that now formed in his eyes. He would sing over the lump in his throat. He would sing the song of angels, and she would join him in a heavenly chorus, one that would require no interpretation.

As the words began to soar like ribbons on the wind, Jessica made her entrance from the back of the theater, stepfather Andrew at her side. The audience stood to their feet, and Colin could hardly contain the emotion that held him in its twisted embrace. *My bride!* By the time he reached the chorus, Andrew had released Jessica's hand, and she crossed the beautifully decorated bridge across the orchestra pit to join him onstage. By the time the second verse began, Colin's solo had become a duet.

Jessica fought back tears as she crossed the stage. Roman columns, draped with tulle and twinkling lights, framed a beautiful Italian village, hand painted by the best set designers Dallas had to offer. She hardly noticed it, however. She couldn't seem to take her gaze from the man she loved, the one the Lord had dropped into her life when she least expected it.

Her grandmother's words of encouragement flitted through her mind rather unexpectedly. When had she spoken them? Ah yes—that day she had tried on wedding gowns. *You're going to be a beautiful bride, honey, and that radiance is going to shine through like a light that can't wait to escape the darkness, because it will spring up from your innermost being.* For the first time, Jessica understood. From the very core of her being, she understood. *I love this man. Honestly and truly love him.* And the light in her eyes must surely radiate the love she now felt.

His eyes seemed to dance with excitement, as well. The handsome baritone, tall and striking in his romantic Italian apparel, sang to her in a voice she had only dreamed of. She eagerly took Colin's hand and joined him in song. Their voices rose and fell, and emotion carried them through to the end of the piece. Then, as the dramatic piece ended, the minister made his entrance.

Together, he led the two through the rest of the ceremony. With all her heart, Jessica vowed to love this man. To cherish him. *You make it so easy, Colin.* She wiped tears of joy from her eyes as he shared his heart openly and clearly for all to see and hear. His handwritten vows seemed to ignite her heart and set it ablaze. *Have I ever loved before? No. I've never known love until now.*

Now, at this very moment, all of her dreams ran crazily, merrily into truth. Into reality. Tonight, she would cling to the hand of this man God had given her and commit to raise her voice alongside his for all of time.

Never again a chorus of one.

Banking on Love

Dedication

To all of my married daughters and their spouses:
Randi and Zach, Courtney and Brandon, Megan and Kevin.
The weddings are behind you, but the fun is just beginning!
I'm praying for Happily Ever Afters!

Chapter 1

Kellie Fisher pulled the keys from her purse and sprinted across the parking garage in search of her new sports car. "I was on level 2." She looked around, confused. "Right? Or was that yesterday?" Her days, filled from morning to night with work, seemed to run together into a dizzying haze. She could hardly remember her own name, let alone where she had parked the car.

She glanced at her watch and groaned. 6:47 p.m. In exactly thirteen minutes, in an exquisite downtown hotel ballroom, her husband would be honored for his work at Siefert and Collins, one of the busiest oil and gas accounting firms in the state of Texas. He would deliver a speech she had helped him craft. And she would miss it if even the slightest thing went wrong. Finding the car was critical to her survival.

She took the elevator to the next level and located the vehicle at once. The stunning silver sports car gleamed—a gem among the oceans of cars in the parking garage. Still, it was little consolation for her tardiness. "Please, Lord," she prayed aloud as she climbed inside, "please don't let there be any traffic. Just this once."

The new car started with ease, and Kellie made her way through the traffic in the parking garage, hands gripping the steering wheel. As she pulled out onto Westheimer, one of Houston's busiest streets, a mob of cars greeted her. Horns honked. Drivers shouted. An officer, face etched with frustration, directed traffic at the corner.

Kellie slapped herself in the head. "Not tonight. I can't be late. I just can't." If she missed even a minute of tonight's event, she would have a hard time forgiving herself. *I can't let Nathan down. I just can't.*

Then again, maybe she could use this time wisely. Kellie glanced in the rearview mirror. Her short blond hair needed a good brushing, and her cheeks, usually tanned and healthy, looked as if they hadn't seen the light of day in months. *I'll have to get to the tanning salon. Soon.* In the meantime, a little blush would have to do.

She stuck her hand in her purse and fished around for the small hairbrush. Once found, she pulled it out and ran it through her hair. She opened a tiny silver compact and swept soft rosy blush along each cheekbone. "There. Much better."

A whistle blew several times, and Kellie realized she'd been holding up traffic. She shot forward a few short feet, waving her apology at the police officer.

"It's not as if we're really making progress," she grumbled. "And it's not as if I'm going to get there by seven either."

In the three years since she and Nathan had been married, Kellie rarely made it to an event on time. Her reputation for being fashionably late irritated Nathan, but what could she do about it? After taking on the job at Walsh and Weston, Houston's largest full-service brokerage firm, she'd scarcely had time to breathe, let alone eat or spend quality time with her husband. Her emotions ran up and down with the stock market, the highs and lows nearly taking her captive at times.

"We'll have more time together once things settle down." She spoke the words aloud to reassure herself, as always. In the meantime, she and Nathan would continue to build bank accounts, develop portfolios, and elevate their status on the job.

"Everything in its time." And time was critical, especially now.

She took a quick left onto a backstreet and wound her way through an up-scale neighborhood, shooting for the short street that would empty into the west end of downtown. Kellie looked at the homes in awe as she sailed past them. Someday she and Nathan would own a house like one of these. They would sell their condominium and move up. When the children came.

"Everything in its time." She repeated the words again and glanced at the clock. 6:57. Three minutes. She focused on the road and forged ahead. She was grateful traffic seemed to be of little issue now.

Kellie allowed her thoughts to ramble a bit. She offered up a scattered prayer for Nathan, knowing his nerves were probably a jumbled mess as he prepared to face the crowd to speak. He always seemed to struggle with recognition and no-toriety. As they had worked together on his speech late into the night, she could sense his edginess and slight embarrassment.

"You'd better get used to it," she had encouraged. "By the time all is said and done, you're going to be CEO. You'll be giving lots of speeches."

He responded with a shy smile and a slight shrug. "You'd better be praying a lot then."

"I am."

And she did pray for him. Every day, in fact. As she traveled back and forth to work, Kellie offered up words of thanks for the awesome man the Lord had dropped in her lap more than three years earlier while living in the Dallas area. At the time they'd met, Nathan had been engaged to someone else.

But God. . .

The Lord clearly had other plans. After the most lavish wedding anyone in the state of Texas had ever witnessed, the Lord had shifted Kellie and Nathan into a joyous honeymoon season. The years since had been spent in pure marital bliss. He'd opened doors for them to move back to Houston, prepared the way for her job at Walsh and Weston, and ultimately swung wide the doors for Nathan to move up quickly at Siefert and Collins.

Kellie was extremely proud of her husband's accomplishments, especially his ever-growing desire to help the underdogs he encountered along the way. She saw his commitment to the firm—and to her—and thanked God they had found one another.

With a prayer of thanks on her lips, Kellie pulled up to the hotel's valet parking area at 7:09. She checked her appearance in the rearview mirror one last time. She applied a dab of soft pink gloss and climbed from the car. She tossed the keys to the attendant with a quick thank-you.

"You're welcome." He tipped his cap in her direction, then gave a whistle as his gaze fell on the car. "Wow. She's a beauty."

"Thanks." Kellie pressed her way through the crowd at the front door of the hotel and entered the grand foyer. Opulent light fixtures hung from the lofty ceiling, and expensive artwork framed the walls. For a moment she nearly let herself get lost in the splendor of it all. Until she remembered her purpose in being there.

Where is the ballroom again? Ah yes. Up the escalator and to the left. Or is it right?

She made it to the escalator in record time but managed to step aboard after an elderly couple, who stood their ground on the step above her. She glanced at her watch again—7:11. Surely the banquet would start late. These things rarely began on time.

At the top of the escalator Kellie glanced to her left. Through the open doors to the ballroom, she could see her husband seated onstage next to his boss. His lopsided sandy blond curls appeared a little more controlled than usual, but his long, gangly legs jutted out in front of the chair. No hiding that tall, thin physique. Kellie smiled in his direction. Nathan's stunning gray-blue eyes met hers as she entered the room.

"Sorry I'm late." She mouthed the words as she took her seat at the table nearest the stage.

Nathan shrugged and flashed a grin.

"At least he's not mad." Had she really spoken those words aloud?

"Kellie, it's nice to see you."

Kellie started as she heard her mother-in-law's words. For the first time, she realized she was not alone at the table. "Well, hello to you, too." She reached to give the older woman a soft kiss on the cheek.

"Glad you could make it." Nathan's mother smiled and turned her attention back to the stage. Kellie tried not to read too much into her words. *Did she think I wouldn't come, or is she scolding me for arriving late?*

Kellie's father-in-law reached to squeeze her hand and gave her a wink. She responded by gripping his hand tighter. Then, with nerves a bit frazzled, she leaned back in her chair and focused on her husband.

Nathan sat at his appointed place on the stage, twisting his cloth napkin in nervous anticipation as his boss made the necessary introductions. Truth be told, he didn't like it when people bragged about his accomplishments. It was hard to hear and even harder to talk about.

And yet, that's exactly what he must do. Tonight Nathan must stand before a roomful of his peers and discuss his achievements in the world of oil and gas accounting. That's what they expected. Why else would the firm have chosen to honor him as their Man of the Year? Why else would the bigwigs from Dallas have come down to Houston to share in his moment of glory?

Nathan looked out to the front table, where Kellie sat with his parents. *Lord, she's beautiful—inside and out. I don't know what I ever did to deserve her.* On the other hand, he didn't know what he would do without her. They were truly one flesh, sharing common interests, common goals, and common likes and dislikes. Not every couple could say that, and he didn't take it for granted. He hoped he never would.

I'm not sure when I've ever seen two people more jointly fit. That's what the pastor had spoken over them on their wedding day. And time proved him right. Kellie was Nathan's equal in every way. In some ways her head for knowledge and ability to play the role of chameleon when necessary gave her an added edge over him. She seemed to be moving up at the brokerage house almost as quickly as he stepped up the ladder at the firm.

Nathan snapped back to attention as his boss, Marvin Abernathy, turned to face him and loudly proclaimed, "Please welcome Nathan Fisher—a man with a head for numbers and a heart for the people. He's one of the hardest workers I've ever met, and he's our Man of the Year at Siefert and Collins."

Beads of sweat popped out on Nathan's brow. He wiped at them with the back of his hand, willing the lights overhead to dim.

As he stood and took the first step toward the podium, Kellie erupted in applause. Nathan threw a "Please don't do that—you're embarrassing me" look, but it did no good. She stood to her feet and clapped with great gusto. Others in the crowd followed her lead, and by the time he reached the podium, the whole place was on its feet.

"Congratulations, Nathan." Mr. Abernathy extended his hand. Nathan shook it warmly and then reached into his pocket for the speech he and Kellie had written together.

His hands shook, and he tried to still them as he spoke. "Thank you all." He looked over the crowd as they took their seats once again. "I can't thank you enough for being here tonight. It's an honor and a privilege to work for a company like Siefert and Collins, and an even greater honor to stand before you—my friends and peers—tonight."

His hands continued to vibrate as he reached to unfold his notes. *Lord, please help me through this. You know how nervous I get.*

His gaze fell on Kellie, who smiled broadly and gave him a thumbs-up sign. Her encouragement and support, as always, motivated him. With Kellie on his side, he could do anything.

He muddled forward into his speech, spending a few moments talking about his transition from Dallas to Houston, then diving into the many changes he had brought to the firm. None of the things he mentioned was fabricated or at all exaggerated. He had accomplished a lot over the past several months. With the Lord's help, of course. But listening to everything laid out in such a succinct, practical way now floored him, perhaps more than anyone else. It did seem a bit overwhelming that the Lord had blessed him so much.

By the time he finished his speech, Nathan's armpits were a soggy mess. Droplets of water slid down the sides of his face, and his throat felt constricted by his collar. As he moved across the stage to take his seat, he fought the feeling that he might be sick. Still, in spite of the obvious struggles, he felt a small sense of satisfaction.

He looked out at Kellie, who dabbed at her eyes with a cloth napkin. She blew him a kiss, and he winked in her direction. In a few moments, when this nonsense came to an end, he would take her in his arms and kiss away those tears—even if they were tears of joy.

Chapter 2

Nathan mulled over the pastor's words as he and Kellie left the sanctuary of the large metropolitan church. *Relationships are like gardens. They need tending. Leave them to themselves, and they'll be overgrown with weeds in no time.* Nathan contemplated the words as he made his way through the crowd.

He looked over at his gorgeous wife. *Lord, I know I've been busy. I can't seem to avoid it. But I also know things are changing in my relationship with Kellie. Even when we're together, we're not really—together.*

They reached the spacious foyer hand in hand and stopped for a breather as the crowd thinned. "Where do you want to go for lunch?" Kellie tucked a loose blond hair behind her ear and looked up at him with those crystal clear blue eyes of hers.

"I heard some people in Sunday school mention that new Italian place on the interstate. We could go with them. That might be fun."

"I don't know." With a Sunday school class of one hundred plus, there could be a potential mob scene if they all showed up at the same place. Besides, he had been looking forward to some alone time with Kellie. And it wasn't as if they'd had much time to develop friendships with others in the class. They were too busy. In other words, they wouldn't be missed.

"What were you thinking? I'm totally open."

"Hmm." An idea struck. "I was thinking that new deli. They're close, they have good food, and we can be in and out in less than an hour."

"Good point." She gave him a suspicious look. "Do you have to work this afternoon?"

Nathan drew in a deep breath, knowing how many things needed to be taken care of today. "We'll see. I'm hoping for some downtime."

"Me, too." She nuzzled against his arm. "Sounds good."

"Just a quick lunch then." He smiled. "And maybe the afternoon will be kind to us." *Maybe there will be enough hours to accomplish everything and still spend some quality time together.*

They chatted all the way across the parking lot as they searched for the car among the other vehicles. One of these days, they'd arrive at just the right time and get a good spot. Today wasn't that day.

Kellie's eyes lit up as she spoke. "Since we're alone, I guess I should tell you something."

"Really? What's that?"

"I've wanted to talk to you about our financial portfolio," she explained. "I have quite a few ideas for diversification."

"I'm always open to new ideas," he agreed. "As long as the payoff is good."

"Not good." Her eyebrows elevated playfully. "Great."

"Speaking of great, I have some great news about one of my newer accounts. It's doing really well." He dove off into a lengthy explanation but stopped himself midsentence when he realized what he'd done. *I'm talking about work. Again.*

They both grew silent at the same time.

Kellie broke the silence with a soft chuckle. "We're a mess, aren't we? We don't know how to talk about anything but work." She climbed into the driver's seat of her sports car, and Nathan took the passenger seat.

"Sure we do," he argued. "We talk about all sorts of things." All related to the future, of course. In his heart, he had to admit the truth. They rarely talked about what they were thinking, feeling, hoping in the here and now. More often than not, he and Kellie talked about 401(k)s and stock options. They discussed the possibility of one day selling their newly renovated condo in favor of a brick home. They talked about the what-ifs of one day having a child, where that child would attend school, and what sort of day care options might be most viable during the formative preschool years.

What they did not talk about, however, was today. But right here, right now, he would change that. "I'm starved." He grinned in her direction. "I'm going to order the biggest sandwich they have."

"I love their salad bar."

They plunged into a lengthy discussion about the benefits of adding fiber to their diets, which led to a discussion about staying fit, which in turn led to an intense discussion about the recent stock surge among fitness centers on the West Coast.

At some point along the way, Nathan stopped for a belly laugh. They couldn't seem to win for losing.

"Catch!" Kellie tossed the keys in Nathan's direction with a smile.

He caught them and gave her a curious look. "Is this your way of saying you want me to drive your new car?"

"If you don't mind." She pulled her cell phone from her purse. "I need to call my mom. She left three messages this week, and I haven't had time to get back with her." Something about her mother's messages left an uneasy feeling, one she couldn't explain. At any rate, she would feel better after talking to her. Her mind would be eased and her conscience relieved of the guilt she now carried—guilt over being too busy to stay in touch with the people she loved the most.

"No problem." Nathan clicked the doors open and climbed inside.

"Whatever happened to the days when you opened the door for me?" She scooted into the passenger seat, punching numbers into her phone.

"Huh?"

"You used to—" *Ah, never mind.* She wasn't one of those girlie girls who needed a man to open doors for her anyway. And Nathan was far too busy—and too distracted—to remember a little thing like opening the door for her.

She finished entering the number, and the phone rang once, twice, three times—and finally shifted to the answering machine.

"Great," she mumbled. "It's the machine."

"You've reached the Conways." She recognized her father's cheery, south Texas drawl. "We're not here right now. Probably out back tending to the animals or up at the church singing in the choir. Leave us a message, and we'll get back with you."

"Daddy." She spoke with conviction. "Daddy, this is Kellie. I'm calling Mom back. She actually called me a couple of times this week, but I've been swamped with work. Tell her I'm free this afternoon if she wants to give me a call. I love you both."

Kellie clicked the phone closed and leaned back against the seat.

"Not home?" Nathan put the car into gear and pulled out of the parking lot.

"Guess not." She shrugged. "I'm a little worried. According to my mom's latest message, my dad hasn't been himself lately. Lots of headaches, that sort of thing." She closed her eyes and realized she had a headache coming on, too.

"Probably the change in weather." Nathan shifted gears and headed toward home. "Allergies always get to me, too. Springtime is the worst."

"Still. . ." Kellie drew in a deep breath and rubbed at her aching neck. "It isn't like her not to be home on a Sunday afternoon. They're pretty settled into their routines."

"Just like us." Nathan reached over to squeeze her hand.

Kellie shot him a hopeful smile. "I hope you're not saying you've decided to spend this afternoon working after all."

"Well. . ."

"Nathan. It's Sunday. Even the Lord took one day off."

"I know, Kellie." He focused on the road. "It won't take long, but I have some figures to go over. If I want to make partner this year. . ."

"I know, I know." She bit her lip and fought to keep from saying more. "It's fine."

She could probably get some work done, as well. But that's not how she wanted to spend the day. She wanted to spend it cuddling with her husband. Watching a movie. Eating ice cream.

"Everything okay?" He looked her way as he shifted gears once more.

"Uh-huh. Just lost in my thoughts."

"I know things are crazy right now, Kellie." He squeezed her hand again. "But we're going to have so many chances to make up for it. Someday. We'll take that trip to Europe. Just the two of us. We'll find the perfect spot to renew our wedding vows. Just name the place and I'm there."

"Austria." The word slipped out before she had time to analyze his proposition. She paused, thinking. "No. Germany?"

"Any place you like." He nodded in her direction as he headed onto the interstate. "This will be your trip—the vacation of a lifetime. Whatever you want to do, we'll do."

"A boat ride down the Rhine? Touring ancient castles?" She smiled, remembering the television travel show that had triggered such lofty dreams.

"We'll do it all," he spoke with assurance. "And we'll stay in the best hotels, too."

Kellie shrugged. "I don't care about that. It might be as much fun to find some quaint bed-and-breakfasts along the way. I don't always need the best of everything, honey."

He shrugged. "Agreed. But I want to give you the best. Anything wrong with that?" His cell phone rang, and he took the call.

"No. Nothing wrong with that." Kellie muttered the words, then slipped off into her thoughts for the rest of the trip. By the time they arrived at the condominium, she felt as if she could fall asleep the moment her head hit the pillow. They took the elevator up to the seventh floor, while she yawned the whole way.

Nathan opened the door to their condominium, and she stepped inside. No matter how sleepy, the sheer magnificence and beauty of this place captivated her. Granite countertops, recently installed, gleamed. Brand-new stainless steel appliances looked right at home sitting alongside them. Wood floors, special ordered, beckoned.

But Kellie had only one thing on her mind. She wanted—no, she needed—to spend time with her husband. Nothing else mattered right now.

"I know you have to work, but"—she put her arms around him and rested her head against his chest—"I thought maybe we could—"

His cell phone went off again before she could finish her sentence. He answered it, and she marched into the bedroom to change.

Once there, she slipped into a worn nightshirt she had owned since high school and climbed into bed. She turned on the television, hoping for an old movie, something romantic. She settled on an old episode of *The Andy Griffith Show*. At least it was in black-and-white.

Kellie had dozed off when the bedside phone rang out, startling her. She answered it with the most "awake" voice she could muster. "Hello?"

"Is that my Kellie?"

"Mama?" She sat up immediately, plumping the pillows to her satisfaction.

"How are you, baby?"

She leaned back against the pillows and yawned. "Sleepy right now. But good. How are you? How's Dad?"

"I'm doing pretty well," her mother responded. "But Daddy's still not feeling very well. The headaches are getting worse."

"You should take him to see Dr. Baker." Kellie tried to sound firm. "There must be some reason for them."

"We have an appointment for tomorrow morning, honey, so don't worry. I'm sure everything will be fine." She paused a moment, and Kellie noticed a change in her voice. "Now tell me, how are you and Nathan?"

"We're fine." Kellie sighed as she looked across the bed.

"You sound tired."

"We're both so busy—" Kellie changed gears, opting to keep her private life private. No need worrying her mother unnecessarily, especially not on a day like today, when her father wasn't feeling well.

"Do you think you'll have time to slip away for a visit anytime soon? I'd love to see you, and you know how hard it is for Daddy and me to make that drive now. He's not much for getting out on the freeways anymore. I'm not either, to be honest. And the whole city of Houston is looking more like one big freeway every day."

Kellie could sense the seriousness in her mother's voice and responded as best she could. "You're right about that. And the construction is quite a challenge, too." She tried to sound encouraging. "We'll come soon. I promise."

"Thatta girl." She could hear the smile in her mother's voice. "Greenvine's not that far away. Just an hour and a half. Lots of people drive that far to get to work in the city."

"I can't imagine it." Kellie shook her head. "I'm glad I live so close to the office. I don't know how people commute."

"I don't either, but folks seem to do it." She paused. "I keep forgetting to tell you that several of your friends from high school have been asking about you. Did I tell you Julia is pregnant?"

"Again?" Kellie flinched upon hearing her former best friend's name. "Wow. How old is her little girl? Just a little more than a year, right?"

"Yes."

"Pretty close together, I'd say."

"Some people do it that way."

Kellie calculated her words before speaking. "And some choose to wait until they can afford to give their children a good life."

Her mother laughed. "Some folks would be waiting forever then. I'm glad your daddy and I didn't wait till the money came rolling in. You and Katie probably wouldn't have been born at all."

Kellie looked up as Nathan entered the bedroom. He pulled off his tie and slipped out of his shoes. He glanced in the mirror above the dresser, then raked his fingers through his sandy, lopsided curls. Then he turned to face Kellie with a wink and a pout.

"I need to let you go, Mom." Kellie smiled back at him, understanding his wink. "But call me tomorrow after you get back from the doctor's office, okay?"

"I will, baby. But don't worry. God's in control."

"Yes, He is. But call me anyway."

They ended their call, and Kellie looked up in time to see Nathan ease into the spot next to her. She nuzzled into his arm and planted tiny kisses on his cheek. "I thought you had to work," she whispered.

He smiled gently and traced her cheek with his finger. "Everyone needs a day off."

She was glad they could enjoy the rest of it together.

Chapter 3

When the phone rang in the middle of the night, Kellie's heart raced. She shot a glance at the clock. 2:53 a.m.

"Who is it?" Nathan's voice, groggy and confused, spoke out of the darkness.

"I can't see the caller ID. Hang on." She rubbed at her eyes and snatched the portable phone from its base as she recognized her mother's cell phone number.

"Hello?"

"Kellie?" Her mother's frightened voice greeted her. "It's Mom."

"Mom." She sat up in the bed and turned on the lamp. "What's happened?"

"Your daddy"—her mother's voice broke—"he's—"

Kellie's heart twisted.

"We–we're at the hospital. They've taken him for a CT scan. Or maybe they said an MRI. I—I can't remember."

"I don't understand." Kellie tried to order her thoughts. Still half asleep, she struggled to comprehend her mother's breathless words. "Is it because of the headaches?"

"Yes. He felt much worse this evening, so he took some ibuprofen and went to bed around eight thirty. I was working on a craft project for the children's program at church. I should have checked on him sooner." Her mother began to sob in earnest now. "I feel so—so b–bad."

"What happened, Mom?" Kellie's heart pounded against her chest wall. *Dear Lord, please. . .please. . .*

"I crawled into bed around eleven thirty and tried to wake him. I wanted to see if he felt better. But he wouldn't respond." Her mother's words were rushed, emotional. "I couldn't wake him up. He wouldn't budge."

"Oh, Mom." Kellie leaped from the bed, phone still clutched in her hand. She reached into a dresser drawer and pulled out a pair of jeans. She pressed the phone between her shoulder and her ear and began to shimmy into them.

"At first I thought he was just sleeping. You know what a sound sleeper he is."

"Yes." Her father had always had the uncanny ability to fall asleep anywhere and everywhere—and to sleep through anything, including thunderstorms.

Her mother's voice choked again. "B–but he wasn't just asleep. At some point I knew we were dealing with something much more than that. That's when I called 911."

"What are the doctors saying?"

"They're not sure. Maybe a stroke. Or an aneurysm."

"Oh no." Kellie fastened her jeans.

"What are you doing?" Nathan crawled out from under the covers and gave her an odd look. "What's happened?"

"It's my dad." She mouthed the words so her mother wouldn't hear. "He's in the hospital."

Nathan flew into action.

"Mom," Kellie said with as much determination as she could muster, "Nathan and I are coming."

"Oh, honey. I'd be so—so grateful." Her mother's sobs intensified.

Kellie made her way into the bathroom and reached for her toothbrush. "Where are you?" She smeared toothpaste over the bristles.

"At the hospital in Brenham."

"Brenham?" She nearly dropped the toothbrush. "Why is he there? He needs to be here—in Houston at the medical center. We've got the best doctors, the best technology."

"Honey, we were in too much of a hurry. The paramedics wanted to get him to the closest facility, and Brenham was the logical choice."

"But—" Kellie stopped herself before entering into an unnecessary argument. They could always arrange to have him transferred later—with her mother's co-operation. "We'll be leaving here in just a few minutes. We can probably be there by"—she glanced at the clock again and saw that it was three—"by 4:45, I'd say."

"Just come in through the emergency room."

"I will. And I love you, Mom. Give Dad a kiss from me. Nathan and I will get there as quick as we can."

"Promise me you'll drive carefully. And pray, honey."

"I am already." As she hung up the phone, Kellie burst into tears.

Nathan wrapped her in his arms. "It's going to be okay," he whispered as he stroked her hair.

"I don't know. . . ." She stood frozen for a moment, then stepped away and brushed her teeth with fervor. When she finished, she turned to Nathan. "We have to hurry. I want to get there as fast as I can."

"Well, you can't go in that." Nathan pointed to her outfit, and she suddenly realized she still wore her nightshirt over her jeans.

"Oh. Good point." She slipped on a blouse and pulled another one from the closet to take with her. *Just in case.*

"I hate to bring this up, but didn't you say you had a meeting at work this morning?"

Kellie stopped dead in her tracks and tried to focus. "Oh. Yes, I do. It's with a new investor. Great opportunity. Could be a lot of money involved—for him and the firm. And ultimately for you and me."

"What will you do?"

Kellie sighed. "I'll pass him off to Bernie." She hated to lose the opportunity, but this was significantly more important. "It's not as if he's alone anyway. We have a couple of trainees on our floor. They'll do whatever he asks."

"That's good."

"What about you? Anything critical happening at the office today?"

He pursed his lips. "I think I can manage, as long as I call by seven and let them know. I can always take my laptop, and I'll keep my cell phone handy."

"Me, too." Kellie felt guilty talking about such things when her father lay in a hospital bed in an uncertain condition, but what could they do?

Within minutes, she and Nathan were on the road, headed west on Highway 290. With her nerves a shaky mess, she felt better that he had automatically taken the wheel. He seemed to be calmer, cooler. She looked at him as they traveled along, new thoughts ripping at her emotions. Her feelings for her father were strong, but a guilty conscience tore at her as other thoughts emerged.

Lord, what would I do if something like this happened to Nathan? I love him so much. I couldn't make it without him.

She pushed desperate thoughts from her mind and turned to him for comfort. "Nathan?"

"What, baby?"

"Could we pray together?"

"Of course." He began to pray aloud, and her nerves calmed almost immediately. When he finished, she picked up where he left off, offering an impassioned plea for her father's health and safety. They finished the prayer, and Nathan reached to snap on some music.

"I'm thinking praise and worship music would be good right about now." He adjusted the stereo to play a new CD.

As he fumbled with the knobs, the words from one of Kellie's favorite scripture verses came to mind. " '*I have told you these things, so that in me you may have peace. In this world you will have trouble. But take heart! I have overcome the world.*' " That verse from the Gospel of John had carried her through more than one tragedy. With God's help this mountain could be tossed into the sea, as well.

A familiar worship song kicked in, and she leaned back against the seat in an attempt to relax. Somewhere between the words of the scripture, the lyrics of the song, and her husband's hand squeezed tightly in her own, hope took root.

Nathan paced the halls of the small hospital, praying silently. In the hours since arriving, he and Kellie had taken turns consoling her mother and speaking with the doctors. From what he could gather, his father-in-law's prognosis was grim at best. He frowned as he relived the doctor's words: *Ruptured aneurysm in the brain.*

Immediate surgery to reduce bleeding and swelling. Medically induced coma. Chances of survival—less than fifty percent. Recovery time undetermined. Possibly weeks or months.

Without a miracle he might not make it.

Nathan continued to pace, his thoughts churning. He was plagued with unanswered questions. If Kenton survived, would he ever be the same again? Would he have to relearn how to speak, how to walk? Would he be able to return to work? *Lord, I don't understand. How do these things happen? Kenton loves his work. And the people of Greenvine love him.* They also needed him. Kenton's work as city comptroller had garnered him the respect and appreciation of friends and neighbors. How would they manage without him?

"Nathan?"

He started at his wife's beckoning. "What, baby?" He looked up into Kellie's tearstained eyes, then opened his arms to her.

She leaned her head on his shoulder. "What will happen if he doesn't get better?" she whispered. "What will my mama do? What will I do?"

Nathan couldn't muster up the words to respond. And Kellie's question raised other troubling thoughts. *Lord, what would I do if anything ever happened to Kellie?* He didn't have answers, at least not yet. But one thing was for sure: He had to devote more time to her and less time to work. He had to let her know she took precedence over his job. And he must start now.

"This is the first time I've ever had to face the possibility that I could lose someone I love." Kellie continued to speak in hushed tones. "It's scary." She paused for a moment. "I mean, I know God's in control, and I know for sure where my father would be, but still. . ." Tears filled her eyes. "I would miss him so much."

"Let's don't think like that." Nathan sat up straight in his chair, determined to put a more positive spin on the situation. "We're going to keep praying and speaking words of faith over him when we go in there. I've heard that people in comas can still respond to our words."

"I've heard that, too." Kellie's eyes reflected hope. She bit her lip, then looked at him squarely. "I have an idea."

"What's that?"

"I have my portable CD player in the car. And I have tons of worship CDs. Maybe they'd let me play some music when we go in to see him. I know Daddy loves worship music. And hymns. I've got that great new collection of classic hymns my sister recorded. He loves that one." Her eyes lit up for the first time since they'd arrived.

"Great idea." Nathan squeezed her hand. "And we'll pray every time we go in. Out loud. He'll hear us—I know he will. And even if his body doesn't respond, his spirit will."

Nathan drew Kellie to him and kissed her on the head.

"I'm so proud of you," she said.

"Why?" He looked down at her in vague curiosity.

"You're such a man of faith. Sometimes I feel so. . . .inadequate. When the rubber meets the road, my faith flies right out the window."

If only she knew how weak I feel. "No, it doesn't." He kissed her on the forehead. "You have more faith than almost anyone I know. You just need time to adjust to all of this."

Her cell phone rang out, startling them both.

Nathan looked at his watch. 7:53 a.m. "Who's calling this early?"

"It's Caroline from the office," Kellie explained, looking at the caller ID. "I'm sure she only wants to check up on things."

Kellie took the call, and Nathan's thoughts wandered as her conversation shifted. He could tell she wrestled with the need to be in two places at once. He understood that dilemma. Work beckoned, but how could they leave? Kellie would never forgive herself, and he wasn't sure he'd be able to either.

Nathan glanced at his watch one more time. 7:56 a.m. He toyed with the idea of calling his office while he had the chance. So many things remained undone. The pressures were greater than ever. And yet he must stay here, at his wife's side. She needed him. And, in so many ways, Kellie's mother needed her. Norah Conway was one of the strongest women he had ever met, but she clearly longed to have her daughter nearby at a time like this.

Lord, You're going to have to work out the details. I've got too much on my plate to figure it all out.

Peace eluded him at the moment. With so much going on, he would truly have to hand this situation over to the Lord. Not that Nathan could fix it anyway. But it would surely feel better to relieve himself of the responsibility.

Over the next few minutes, as Kellie continued her phone conversation, Nathan came to a difficult decision. No matter what, he would do all he could to support Kellie and her family during this difficult time. No sacrifice was too great.

He came to another conclusion, as well. He would hold her closer than ever. He would redeem every moment.

Chapter 4

Kellie stared at her reflection in the tiny restroom mirror and grimaced. The bags under her eyes grew larger daily. Each morning she attempted to swipe on a bit of eye shadow and mascara, but it seemed so pointless now. For nearly forty-eight hours, she had barely slept. Instead, she and Nathan shuffled in and out of the neurological ICU alongside her mother.

She occasionally gathered her wits about her long enough to think about what she might be missing at the office. Even then, she couldn't keep her thoughts straight. What did it matter anyway? Her father's life hung in the balance. How could she even justify thinking about fluctuations in the stock market or the potential loss of a client? What if she lost her father?

The news about his condition had fluctuated, as well—sometimes up, sometimes down. Her emotions seemed to follow suit, though she struggled hour by hour to call on God. *Where is my faith? I'm a spiritual wimp.* Still, she managed to garner up enough fortitude to face her mother with her chin up each and every time. She needed to be strong for her.

At least today things appeared more hopeful. With the bleeding under control, the swelling in her father's brain was receding. This was the first good news they'd had all along. And she clung to it with a fierceness that would not relent.

Soon—perhaps in the next few days—the doctors would allow him to rouse ever so gently from the medically induced coma they'd kept him in since his surgery. When the moment came, she would be right there at his side, even if it meant losing her job. Even if it meant going without sleep until they had some news.

Kellie exited the bathroom, gripping the doorknob with a paper towel in her hand. No point in taking chances. Not here, with so many germs floating around. She walked out into the hallway and stretched. Nathan approached her and wrapped her in his arms.

"I'm sure I smell just awful." She looked up into his understanding eyes.

Nathan shook his head and shrugged. "No more so than the rest of us."

She yawned. "Mom says you and I should sneak over to her place and take a shower. Maybe even try to sleep a few hours. What do you think?"

"I, uh. . ." He pulled back and shifted his gaze.

"What?"

Nathan's words were quiet but rushed. "I hate to say this. I really do. But I've got to get back to the office. They're falling apart without me." He paused. "Well, not falling apart literally—but they act as if they are. My whole department is in turmoil."

Kellie didn't respond at first. She fought to push down the growing lump in her throat as she leaned her head against her husband's chest. She didn't want him to leave. She needed him, more than ever. "I wish you wouldn't—" She stopped midsentence. Why inflict guilt unnecessarily?

"I know. But it won't be so bad. I was thinking I could go back for a couple of days and get caught up, then come back to your mom's place. Sound okay?"

Not really. But I understand. "You have to do what you have to do." She pulled away from him and shrugged. "I'll be fine." She felt silly pouting but couldn't seem to help herself. After all, she was missing work, too. Didn't he see that?

"If it would make you feel better, I could drive back and forth," he explained. "That way I could still spend time with you in the evenings."

"That doesn't make any sense," she argued. "You need your sleep if you're going to work. You can't work all day then come up here and stay awake all night. How would you drive back the next morning?"

"You need some rest, too." He reached to brush a stray hair out of her eyes. "I know you've got to be exhausted. At least I've slept a little in the waiting room. You haven't rested for days."

"I know." She sighed. "But every time I think about relaxing, I start to worry. What if I went home for a shower and Dad woke up? What if something happened to him and I was asleep?"

Nathan shook his head. "You can't control any of that. And besides, you put way too much on yourself. You always have."

She argued with herself before responding. When she did speak, the words came out sounding terse. She didn't mean for them to. She couldn't seem to control the emotion behind the explanation.

"You don't understand, Nathan." She crossed her arms at her chest. "I'm all they have. Ever since my sister moved to New York, I've been the logical choice. I have to be the one to pick up the slack."

"I know, but you can't be everything to everyone. You have to take care of yourself, or you won't be any good to your mom. And it's not as if she'd be alone." His face lit up with that slow, crooked grin she loved. "You've seen all her friends from church. At least three or four of them at a time are always here, tending to her every need."

"I know." Kellie sighed because he clearly didn't see her point. "It's just that. . ." It's just that her schedule at work had prevented her from spending enough time with her parents, and the guilt was eating at her like nothing she'd ever known.

"You don't have to be a superhero." He pulled her close once again and ran his fingers through her hair.

"I know." Tears welled up, and she let them travel in little rivers down her cheeks. "But I don't know how to rest. It goes against my nature. You know what a 'Martha' I am."

He smiled. "Yes, I know. But Jesus would have preferred that she sit at His feet like her sister, remember?"

I could tell you the same thing. You work just as hard. Maybe harder.

"I'll follow you and your mom out to her place," he said. "And then I'll head home to get some work done. Just a couple of days, honey. Then I'll come back."

She nodded. "It's fine." As the words were spoken, an unusual peace washed over her. It was fine. God was in control, and He would remain in control whether Nathan stayed or went. *Our love for each other is stronger than any separation. And God's love for both of us is even greater than that.*

Nathan glanced at his watch. "The next visitation time is in ten minutes. I won't leave until I've had a chance to see your dad once more. I want to pray with him before I go."

"Okay." She whispered the word and gave the situation over to the Lord.

She and Nathan went in search of her mother. They found her in the waiting room with three of the ladies from her church. All four women were huddled in a circle, praying and crying. For two days it had been like this. People from the small congregation had been a consistent part of the process for her mother. They wouldn't leave her side. They brought everything from fast food to casseroles, blankets to pillows, and devotion books to printed lists of God's promises. They prayed consistently, loved consistently, and gave consistently.

Kellie remembered this kind of love. As a child she had always known it. *Funny.* She hadn't appreciated it then. But now she missed it with an ache that couldn't be squelched.

Lord, will I ever experience true friendship again? I barely know anyone at my church. Who would take care of us if something like this happened? She pushed the thoughts from her mind. *Don't be selfish. Be glad they're here for Mom. That's the important thing.*

She and Nathan slipped across the hallway to the doors of the ICU. They used the hand sanitizer pump on the wall as they waited for the doors to swing open. When they did, Kellie was the first one inside. She had to get to her daddy, had to let him know she was still here, still praying. She had to see his face, to reassure herself he would be okay.

Nathan gripped her hand as they made their way across the crowded room to the bed where her father lay, still and silent. The bed was surrounded with monitors and IV poles. The light clicking sound continued on the monitor as his heart beat, steady and strong. She checked the numbers on the monitor to see if the pressure in his brain had subsided.

Funny how much she had learned in such a short time.

Sadly his numbers remained unchanged. She pressed back the lump in her throat and reached to take her father's hand. "Daddy, we're here. We love you." Salty tears slipped down her cheek and dribbled across her lip, but she swept them away. *No sadness here. Only hope.*

Nathan wrapped his arm around her waist and pulled her to him. She drew in a deep breath and continued. "You have a lot of friends here, Daddy. Half the church has come by to be with Mom and to let you know how much they love you. People are praying in the hallways, praying in the waiting room—"

"And praying right here." Nathan took a step closer to the bed and reached out his hand to touch her father's arm. In a voice quiet and genuine, he began to pray aloud. Kellie couldn't remember when she had ever heard him speak with such faith, such assurance, and even boldness.

And yet here he stood, taking a position of authority at the very moment when she needed him most. He finished the prayer, and she added her "amen" to his. She noticed another, quieter voice behind them and turned.

"Mom." She took her mother's hand and drew her closer to the bed. "I'm sorry. We thought you were still in the waiting room with your friends. I hope you don't mind that I rushed in ahead of everyone. I couldn't wait."

"Of course not." Her mother smiled. "I'm so glad you did."

Kellie noticed how tired her mother looked—and older than she could ever remember. She saw the pain in her mom's weary eyes and wanted to do something about it—but what could she do?

"You're doing what I've called you to do."

She started as she heard the words resound in her spirit. *Yes, Lord.*

The three of them stayed for a few minutes until a nurse with a brusque voice reminded them they were limited to two visitors at a time.

"I have to go anyway." Nathan planted a kiss on Kellie's head, then reached to grab her mother's hand. "I hope you don't mind, Mom, but I have to get to the office for a few days. I'll come back on the weekend."

"Of course I don't mind. You've been more than wonderful to come and stay as long as you have. It's far more than I would have expected, and I'm so grateful."

"I wouldn't have been anywhere else," Nathan said. He gave her a hug, then turned to Kellie.

Kellie's mom gave her a serious once-over. "You should take this girl with you. I'm sure she could use some rest."

"Mom, I'm not going home. I'll be fine." Kellie wasn't trying to be stubborn. She couldn't imagine leaving.

Nathan shook his head. "You're not fine—at least you won't be if you don't get some rest." He turned to face her mother. "I'm sending her to your place for a few hours to get some sleep. And a shower."

Kellie rolled her eyes. "He thinks I smell."

"I'm sure we all do." Her mother chuckled. "Speaking of which, if you're going to my place, I could use a change of clothes." She gave Kellie a list of items to fetch, and good-byes were said.

Kellie and Nathan left the hospital arm in arm. As she climbed into her mother's older-model sedan, she glanced in the rearview mirror. Nathan gave her a smile and a wave from the driver's seat of her sports car.

With tears in her eyes, Kellie turned the key in the ignition and put her mother's car in gear. For once she would have traded it all—the job, the condo, the car, everything—for a few more minutes with the man she loved.

Nathan shifted his wife's car into gear and headed out onto the highway toward Houston. He tried to still his thoughts, but they would not be silenced. Guilt ate at him like a cancer. How could he leave her there? Would she think his job took precedence over her? It wasn't true, but how could he prove it? Did he need to try?

Is my job too important? Have I focused too much on what's going on at the office and not enough on what's happening at home? He shook his head and concentrated on the road. A man had to work. And he had done a pretty good job of balancing his work life and home life.

Nathan prayed aloud as he clutched the steering wheel. "Lord, I know You've called me to provide for my family. Kellie is my family. I won't be able to provide for her if I lose my job." He drew in a deep breath. "Please give me wisdom. And please show me how to spend more time with her. I want to be with her."

I need to be with her.

He swallowed the lump in his throat and kept driving. His thoughts shifted to the office. With this current quarter drawing to a close, the workload was unbelievable. And for some reason tempers flared—even over the phone. The atmosphere of the whole place seemed to be changing right before his eyes. "It's the pressure of the season we're in. This is going to pass."

He hoped.

In the meantime, work waited. Balancing the phone in one hand and the steering wheel in the other, he punched in the number to his office.

Chapter 5

Kellie hung up the phone and turned to her mother with a sigh.

"Everything okay at work?" Her mom's forehead wrinkled in concern.

"I guess." Kellie took a seat at the breakfast table and nibbled at a piece of toast. Things weren't going as well as she'd hoped, but she certainly didn't want to concern her mother with unnecessary details. Her boss called every hour on the hour. Not to worry her, he insisted, but to keep her abreast of all she was missing.

Missing. . .

She fought to swallow the lump in her throat. She missed her husband with an ache that wouldn't subside. Though she had tried valiantly to sleep, she'd spent much of the last few nights tossing and turning. How could she sleep without Nathan by her side? Three years of marriage and they'd spent only four or five nights apart. And now this.

Her mother lifted a fried egg out of the skillet on the stove and slipped it onto her plate. "I'm sure I'll be fine, Kellie. You should go back home—at least for a few days."

"I can't do that, Mama. What if—" She stopped herself. In the four days since Nathan had returned home, she'd watched her father lie quiet and still in a hospital bed. She had prayed more prayers, cried more tears, and paced more hallways than ever before in her life.

And the prayers appeared to be working. His numbers had dropped substantially—enough for the doctors to pull him out of the medically induced coma. Anytime now, they predicted, her father should begin to awaken. What would happen after that was far more questionable. Regardless, she must be here—at her mother's side.

And yet. . .

Kellie's heart ached, and she brushed away the tears that clung to her lashes. She couldn't let her mother see her crying. The tears would have to be left to late-night hours, tumbling out onto crisp white pillowcases on the bed in her parents' guest room. They could never fall openly. If her mother knew how much Kellie's heart ached to be with Nathan, she would insist upon a rapid trip back to Houston.

Better to stay focused on the task at hand. "What time should we leave?" Kellie flashed a brave smile.

Her mother sat down across from her and took a bite of bacon. "Hmm." She glanced at the wall clock. "Probably about twenty minutes or so. Can you be ready that quick?"

"I'm the queen of quick." Kellie couldn't help but chuckle. "You have no idea how fast I can move, Mom."

"Oh, I can imagine. You've always been an overachiever, trust me. But you get that from your dad, not me. I'm a little simpler than that, as you know. Greenvine is the perfect place for a gal like me. We're pretty laid back around here. Just how I like it."

Kellie reflected on her words before responding. "I don't miss the fast-paced life as much as I thought I would, to be honest. It's weird—not having to set my alarm clock to be up before daylight. And I can't remember when I've had a real breakfast." She took another bite of toast and leaned back against the chair, happy for a few minutes of rest and relaxation.

"I've never known anything but this life." Her mother took a sip of her coffee, then continued, "Guess that's what happens when you've settled on a small-town environment. Life is slow. Simple. There's plenty of time to enjoy people—and things. Time to intercede for those who need it. And time to visit folks who need visiting."

Kellie shrugged. "Life is a lot slower here," she acknowledged. "I had almost forgotten."

"You didn't seem to mind when you were growing up," her mother said with a smile. "But I think your father and I always knew you'd end up in the big city."

"Really? What made you think that?"

"You seemed"—her mother gestured with her hands—"bigger than this place. You and your sister both. She was destined to sing in the opera, and you—"

"What?" Kellie couldn't help but wonder what she'd say next.

"You were so good with numbers. A real math whiz. And talk about saving money. Do you remember that piggy bank you had when you were little?"

"Yes." Kellie leaned her head down against the table. "Don't remind me." She couldn't help but smile as she thought about the bright pink ceramic pig with hand-painted eyelashes she'd received on her sixth birthday. She'd saved every penny that came her way, pressing each coin, each bill, through the narrow slot on his back.

"All of your birthday money, any cash you earned doing chores—you socked it all away in that little piggy bank."

Kellie shrugged. "Yes, but if memory serves me correctly, the payoff wasn't very good."

"That's right." Her mother's eyes narrowed to a slit. "You lost it."

"Not exactly *lost*. Misplaced would be the right word." Truth be told, she had hidden the ceramic pig away in a safe place once his belly had been stuffed full of money. She didn't want to run the risk of someone walking off with him. In the end she'd done the goofiest thing an eight-year-old kid could do—forgotten where she put it.

"We searched for that piggy bank for years, didn't we?"

"Yeah." Kellie sighed as she picked up the piece of toast again. "Lost forever."

"You learned a hard lesson from that, to be sure." Her mother smiled. "But a good one. Made you a lot less selfish with your money." She clamped her hand over her mouth, obviously embarrassed. "I'm sorry. Selfish might've been a strong word."

"No, that's about right." Kellie frowned as she contemplated her mother's words. She had been selfish as a child, perhaps more than she'd realized. And as an adult. . .

Am I still selfish? Is that why I work so hard—to put as much money into my "piggy bank" as I can?

She shrugged. "I'd like to think I've outgrown a lot of that, but I'm not sure. I do enjoy working, but it seems as if I spend a lot of time at the office."

"You're a hard worker, that's for sure." Her mother reached to squeeze her hand. "You always have been. That's nothing to be ashamed of. And I'm happy that you're happy." Her eyes misted over. "Both of my girls are doing what they love."

Am I? Kellie bit her lip. In her heart she wasn't sure. All the work earned a great lifestyle, but what good was a great lifestyle when you were too worn out to enjoy it?

"What, honey?"

"It's not that I don't love my work. I do. I really do."

"It's important to have an occupation you enjoy." Her mother gave her hand another gentle squeeze. "But I think I know what's bothering you."

"You do?"

Her mother nodded. "Remember to take time for yourself and Nathan. Don't let the work dictate who you are."

"I hadn't thought about it like that before." *I've always been Kellie the stockbroker. Not Kellie the woman or Kellie the wife or Kellie the child of God. Just Kellie. . . the stockbroker. The overachiever. The one who has to prove something to everyone.* The revelation nearly took her breath away.

They finished their breakfast in quiet contemplation, then left for Brenham. With her mother behind the wheel of the small sedan, Kellie took the opportunity to call Nathan.

He sounded thrilled to hear her voice. "Is that really you?"

Kellie felt the corners of her lips curl up. "Do you miss me?"

"Like crazy. I've been really. . ." He hesitated, then spoke in hushed tones, almost sounding embarrassed. "Lonely."

Kellie felt the familiar lump in her throat and fought to push it down so he wouldn't notice the pain behind her words. "Me, too."

His voice softened more but carried a hint of mischief. "I miss sleeping in the same bed with you."

"Me, too," she whispered.

"I miss you curling up next to me on my side of the bed—crowding me out."

Me, too.

"But most of all," he said a bit louder now, "I miss your snoring. I haven't slept a wink for days—it's been so quiet."

She groaned. "Hey, what's up with that?" She shook her head in disbelief. "I don't snore."

"Sure you don't." Nathan chuckled. "But the nights have been the hardest."

Kellie sighed. "I agree."

"We'll make up for it tonight. I'll be there by seven thirty at the latest."

"Why so late?"

"I have a lunch appointment and two afternoon meetings. I should be able to get out of here by five, but then I have to swing by our place and load up the car."

"Ah. Speaking of which, did you get that list of things I need from the condo?" Kellie thought back over the e-mail she'd sent the night before. Had she left anything out?

"I almost ran out of ink printing up the list. And I'll have to rent a moving truck to get it all to you."

She sniggered. "Very funny. It's only a few things."

His voice changed a little, and a seriousness took hold of the conversation. "How is your dad? Any changes?"

"Nothing"—she glanced at her mother and chose her next words carefully—"nothing significant."

"I don't know when I've ever prayed more in my life."

"Same here," she confessed. In truth, she had devoted hours each night to prayer.

Nathan sighed. "I was hopeful he'd be awake by now."

"I know." She checked on her mother out of the corner of her eye. "Me, too."

"Well, I'm certainly bringing enough stuff for you to stay at least a week or two." He paused. "Did you talk to Mr. Weston about getting some work done from up there?"

"I did." Not that she wanted to talk—or think—about work.

"What did he say?"

"He told me to take a couple more days to see how my dad's doing. Then, if it looks like I'll have to stay longer, he'll give me the go-ahead. I think he's more worried about me than the business, to be honest. At least he sounded like it. And he knows Bernie can take care of my people while I'm gone. If you don't mind the fact that I'm not picking up any new clients, I'm certainly content to stay for now." She had barely missed her life at the brokerage. If only she and Nathan could be together, she would almost be at peace here awhile longer.

"Of course I don't mind. And I'm glad Weston wants you to take a little more personal time. You need it."

"I know."

"Things are a little more complicated here." Nathan's voice seemed to tighten as he talked about his job. "Tempers are rising, and problems are escalating. Nothing I'm in the center of—I'm thankful for that—but all the same, it's been pretty tense around the office ever since I got back. I sure don't think I could get away with being gone too long."

Kellie tried to focus on the good. "I understand. But you can stay all weekend. That's all that matters."

"Yes." He paused, then rushed through the next few words. "That's my other line. I'll call you when I get on the road, okay? I love you, baby."

"I love you more." She whispered the words, then snapped the phone shut. With tears she could no longer disguise, Kellie leaned her head back against the seat and turned her face to the window. She began the arduous task of counting the minutes until she would see her husband again.

Just as she began to lose herself in the emotion, Kellie's phone rang out. Her hands trembled the moment she recognized the number on the caller ID. With a fresh sense of fear gripping her heart, she glanced across the front seat at her mother, then spoke the necessary words. "Mom, it's the hospital."

Nathan drove toward Brenham in a frenzy. Kellie's rushed call from the hospital had been enough to cause him to cancel both afternoon meetings and come right away. He had quickly put together a bag of clothing items from her list but felt sure he'd left something out.

Not that it mattered. All that mattered now was getting to Brenham. He pulled off the highway at a quarter till four. Five minutes later, he drove into the crowded parking lot of the hospital. By four o'clock straight up, he was standing at the door of the ICU, preparing to go inside. Kellie stood alongside him, hand tightly gripped in his own.

"When did they call you?" he asked.

Her fingers twisted nervously inside his palm. "It was after I hung up from talking to you this morning."

"And what did they say again? Tell me every word."

"They—" She started to explain as the doors to the ICU opened and a nurse ushered them inside. Nathan followed along behind Kellie and her mother to his father-in-law's bedside. From outward appearances, nothing seemed to have changed.

And yet everything had changed.

"Daddy?" Kellie spoke softly at first, then a bit louder. "Daddy, you have visitors."

Nathan watched in stunned silence as his father-in-law's eyelids fluttered open then shut—open then shut again.

"Can you hear me, Kenton?" Norah implored. "If you can hear me, squeeze my hand twice."

They all looked on in shocked amazement as he slowly squeezed her hand two separate times. Tears rushed down Kellie's cheeks, and Nathan felt as if his heart would leap from his chest. *It's true. He's awake.*

For nearly twenty minutes, with tears in every eye, they celebrated the quiet victory. Nathan watched in awe. Though his father-in-law couldn't seem to formulate words, the older man's mind was clearly at work. Moisture brimmed his lashes as each person communicated their love and well wishes.

By the time they left the ICU, Nathan had little doubt his father-in-law would recover. The only question now was how long it would take. Regardless, he would do all he could to lend support, knowing that was exactly what any one of them would have done for him.

They drove back to his in-laws' house to spend the night. Along the way, Nathan couldn't drop the nagging feeling that he'd left something at home—something important. It wasn't until they arrived at the house and Kellie asked about her laptop that he realized what it was.

Chapter 6

Kellie opened the front door to her condo and tentatively stepped inside. For some reason, she expected it to look different—more inviting maybe. Instead, it felt oddly cold. *I've been away too long.*

Ten days, to be exact. Ten long, exhausting days—days filled with prayers and fear, conversation and hope. Days filled with more time to think clearly than she could remember in a long time.

She dropped the stack of mail on the kitchen countertop and stepped back to look over her home. Sooner or later she would feel right about being here again. In the meantime, something felt off, odd.

"What's that smell?" She looked around, nose wrinkled. *Ah.* They must have exterminated while she'd been away.

No doubt many things had happened while she was in Greenvine. The first thing to tackle would be the monstrous stack of mail on the kitchen counter. She gave it a quick glance. *Bills. Ads. Junk, mostly.* One caught her eye, however. She ripped open an envelope and glanced at her bank statement inside. Her heart lifted as she took in the total. "Not bad, not bad."

"Everything okay?" Nathan appeared at the door, her luggage in hand.

She set the envelope back down. "Yep. Thought I'd lost you."

"After I dropped you off up front, I headed to the parking garage. But I had a whopper of a time finding a spot. If you can believe it, I had to park on the top floor."

"Again? Who took our spot?"

"The guy in 712. Want me to report him?"

Kellie sighed. "It won't do any good."

"You're right." He smiled. "I see you got the mail." Nathan gestured toward the countertop. "Should we sort through it tonight?"

"I already did. Nothing that can't wait till morning. I'm too tired to mess with bills tonight, to be honest."

"I hear ya." Nathan carried her luggage into the bedroom and lifted the larger suitcase onto the bed.

Kellie followed behind him and opened it right away. "I'm sure my clothes are a wrinkled mess." She groaned as she pulled out the soft green designer blouse on top. *Ninety dollars—and look at it.*

"I need to make a run to the dry cleaners anyway," Nathan said. "I'll be glad to drop off your things, too."

"You're awesome." She gave him a kiss on the cheek, and he drew her close.

"You know, you could do this in the morning." He gestured toward the suitcase. "I can think of a lot of things I'd rather do than unpack laundry."

Kellie tried to avoid his gray blue eyes. "I know. Me, too."

He whispered in her ear, "I've missed you, Kellie. It just hasn't been the same without you."

"I know." She planted tender kisses on his cheek. "It's been awful."

"I don't know how people manage," he said. "I could never be one of those husbands who had to travel all the time. It would drive me crazy to be away from you."

She sighed. "It couldn't be helped. I needed to be there. And I'm going to have to go back—at least on the weekends. As long as Daddy's in rehab, my mom's going to need me. It could be weeks. Even longer maybe." Her heart twisted with the words. Even now she longed to get in the car and head back to where they'd come from.

"I know. And I'll be there with you as much as I can," he said. "But your mom had a long talk with me. She's concerned that you're missing so much work. I think she feels a little guilty about it."

"I hope I didn't make her feel that way." Kellie pulled back a step, deep in thought. "It probably didn't help that Mr. Weston called so much. He was an ever-present reminder, I'm afraid."

She sat on the edge of the bed and contemplated this revelation. *But she's right. I do need to go back to work.* To stay away much longer could potentially put at risk all the well-laid financial plans she and Nathan had settled on. If they didn't meet their financial goals, they would have to put off their dreams of buying a house—and having a child—even longer.

Nathan continued, clearly oblivious to her ponderings. "Your mom wants the best for everyone," he said. "For your dad, for you. . ." He paused and looked into her eyes with some concern. "She's so used to taking care of everyone. I'm sure it must feel odd that everyone is now sweeping in to take care of her."

"She needs it. I'm so glad Katie was able to fly down for a few days. Otherwise I don't think I could have left." Kellie reached to pull a gray skirt from the suitcase. *Great. This one has to go to the dry cleaners, too.*

"True. And you've been there for her every step of the way. But doesn't it feel great to be home again?"

She looked around the familiar bedroom and nodded. There was a certain comfort to this place—a familiarity. In spite of the smell. In spite of the pull to be elsewhere. This was still home.

"Now"—he zipped the suitcase closed and lifted it down onto the floor—"what do you say we forget about dirty clothes and parking spaces for a while and focus on us?"

"I think"—she gave him a teasing look—"that sounds perfect."

In the days that followed Kellie's return to Houston, Nathan watched over her closer than ever before. He couldn't help it. Something in her demeanor had changed. Sure, she had settled in at the condominium. She had even returned to work with a vengeance. But something was—off. He could feel it.

Daily she called her mother for an update. The news remained unchanged for the most part. Though her father had been transferred to a rehab facility, his recovery would be slow, tedious. Kenton could put together a few words but would have to relearn how to function in most every area of life.

"I can't even imagine." Nathan voiced his thoughts aloud as he eased his car through traffic on Houston's busy 610 loop. To lose your ability to function, to work. . .

How could a person reenter the job force after something like that? Would Kenton ever return to his job? Would his God-given skills regenerate, or was he destined to live a half-life? Nathan shrugged that idea aside. Of course his father-in-law would make a full recovery. They wouldn't give up on praying for that very thing.

As he reached the Post Oak exit, Nathan wound his way through the cars and counted the minutes until he arrived at the restaurant where Kellie probably already waited. He had planned tonight's outing with much anticipation. After so much time apart, he now chose to take advantage of each moment.

He pulled up to the valet parking at Le Jardin, one of Houston's classiest restaurants, known for its tempting French cuisine. After handing over the keys, he sprinted toward the door. He reached in his pocket to feel for the familiar jewelry box. In a few moments he would draw it from its hiding place and set it on the table in front of the most wonderful woman in the world.

The host led Nathan to a small table in the back of the restaurant where Kellie waited. She sat with her laptop open, typing with a vengeance.

"Hey, baby." He kissed her on the forehead.

She started, then looked up into his eyes with a smile. "Hey. Just catching up on some work. Can you believe they have wireless Internet access in a place like this?"

"I believe it." He shook his head. "It's scary, but I believe it." He smiled at his beautiful bride. "So, how are things at the office? Getting settled back in?"

She groaned. "This probably wouldn't be the day to ask."

"Ah. Well, things are finally slowing down for me. I was able to sneak away to the health club for an hour this afternoon."

"Good for you. I'm going to try to do that tomorrow. I haven't worked out in weeks. And with all the food my mom's friends brought in, I've probably added at least three inches to these hips of mine." She flashed him an impish grin. "I don't think I've ever seen so much fried chicken in my life. Or cakes. Have you ever seen that many cakes in one place?"

Nathan's heart twisted. *Lord, how long has it been since I've seen her smile like that?* "The food was great, but you haven't changed a bit. You look terrific."

"Thanks, baby." Kellie snapped her laptop shut and picked up a menu. "But all this talk about my ever-widening hips has reminded me—I'm starving! What sounds good to you?"

"I don't know. Let's have a look." They settled on lobster bisque and steak with béarnaise sauce.

Once their waiter—a stocky fellow with a contrived French accent—disappeared, they sat in silence a moment. *The clinking of silverware and soothing instrumental music provides the perfect backdrop,* Nathan reasoned. He and Kellie would enjoy an intimate meal together and fill the empty spaces with conversation that excluded work-related things.

"I haven't been here in ages." Kellie looked around the room in quiet contemplation.

"Me either. It seems like we're always eating on the run." Nathan garnered up the courage to continue. "In fact, that's one of the reasons I wanted tonight to be so special. I wanted to let you know I think we should have a regular date night."

She smiled. "That's a nice idea. I'll take a look at my calendar and pencil you in." She was teasing, but something about her words bothered him.

"No." He felt his lips curl down. "We have to stop fitting each other in. We have to make sure we put our relationship above our jobs."

"Wow." She took hold of his hand and squeezed it. "That sounds like something I had planned to say to you tonight. I don't know how much longer I can go on with things the way they've been. I mean, what's the point of having great jobs, a great place to live, and all that if we hardly have time to see each other?"

"Amen." He flashed a broad, heartfelt smile. "Sounds like we've prepared the same speech." He paused and gazed into her eyes. "So what do you think we should do about that?"

She shrugged. "I like the date-night idea. It might be a little harder, now that we're driving back and forth to Greenvine every weekend. But I have Tuesday evenings free, for sure. What about you?"

"Tuesdays are good for me. At least for now." He pulled out his handheld PC to double-check. "Yep. That'll work."

"And we can take advantage of our drive time to my mom's place," she suggested.

"What do you mean?" Nathan's curiosity got the better of him.

"I mean"—she grinned mischievously—"we could spend that time talking. Really talking—about our hopes, our dreams, our innermost thoughts."

"Our innermost thoughts?" Nathan smiled. Kellie had such a definitive way with words.

"You know." Her gaze shifted to the table. "We need to talk about things like. . .children. When we're going to have them."

"Aha. *Those* innermost thoughts." Nathan nodded. "I agree." He reached into his pocket and grasped the tiny box. "But in the meantime, I have a few innermost thoughts of my own I'd like to share with you."

Her face flushed. "Right here?"

"I can't think of a better place." He stared into her eyes and shared his heart. "I love you, Kellie. I want you to know that. You're more important to me than anything else."

Her eyes filled with tears. "I love you, too, babe."

"I have something for you." He pulled the box up to the table and set it in front of her.

Kellie's eyes grew large. "What's this?"

"Open it and see." He could hardly wait to see the look on her face.

Kellie tentatively lifted the lid to the box and gasped as she gazed at the diamond bracelet inside. It matched the necklace he'd given her on their wedding day. "Nathan!"

He stood and approached her side of the table. Reaching into the box, he pulled out the delicate bracelet and fastened it around her wrist. "You deserved something special. You've been through so much lately."

She looked a bit dazed. "But this is too much. . . ."

"Nothing is too much for you." He gripped her hand and spoke passionately. "I mean that, honey. You're the most valuable thing in the world to me. And there's nothing I could ever give you—nothing I could do—to show you how much you mean to me. This bracelet is a small attempt on my part to share something huge that's on my heart."

Tears ran in tiny rivers down her cheeks. "I love you," she whispered.

"I love you more." He winked in her direction. They turned their attentions to the meal and to one another. Nathan relaxed as they chatted back and forth. For the first time in weeks, he felt some sense of direction.

Chapter 7

Kellie stepped out of her father's private room at the rehab facility and leaned against the wall. She didn't like this place—the smells, the people in varying stages of brain damage, the nurses scurrying to and fro, caring for patients who often cried out in pain or shouted foul insults. They couldn't be blamed, of course, but it was too much to take in.

With her eyes brimming over, she stared at the door leading to her father's room. On the other side of that door, a man she barely recognized lay in a bed, fighting to relearn everything.

"Lord, I don't understand." How could he ever become the strong, intelligent man she had always known? And why was everything moving so slowly? She fought with her feelings, one moment up, the next down. Would this roller-coaster ride ever come to a satisfactory end, or were they destined to spend the rest of their lives loving a man who barely remembered his own name, let alone how to function in the world?

"Kellie?"

She looked up as her mother stepped out into the hall, and guilt overwhelmed her at once. She couldn't let anyone know her fears, her doubts. She must remain positive, upbeat—at all costs. Kellie brushed away the tears, ashamed to let her mother find her in a moment of weakness, and then offered up a smile. "What's up, Mom?"

"I'm concerned about you. Are you okay?"

Mom, you're always comforting me. It's supposed to be the other way around. I'm supposed to be helping you through this. "Everything is moving so slowly." Kellie sighed. "I wish we had some kind of button we could push to speed him through this."

"I know." Her mother smiled. "You're the queen of quick. I remember."

Kellie groaned. "I can't believe I said that."

"I guess some things can't be rushed." Her mother shrugged. "But while your dad's relearning, I suppose we'll have to learn a few things, too."

"I guess." Kellie paused. "It's just so hard to. . .to. . ." She choked back tears. "To see him like this."

"I know." Her mother drew her into a tight embrace and whispered, "It's hard on all of us—but it has to be harder on him than anyone. I can't even imagine."

"I can't either. He's always been so strong. And his mind. . ." She pulled back and gazed into her mother's weary face. "He has the brightest mind of anyone I've ever known."

"That's what I'm counting on." Mom smiled. "I know he's still in there, honey. And he's fighting with all of his strength. I can see it in his eyes."

"I can, too." Kellie brushed away loose tears. "And I'm so proud of him. It's just so hard to watch. I don't know if I have it in me to make it through the emotional ups and downs. Sometimes I wonder. . .if things will ever be the same again." She paused as she examined her mother's face for a response. "Are you ashamed to hear me say that?"

"Ashamed?" Her mother's eyes watered. "Oh, honey, of course not. If anyone understands what you're thinking and feeling, I do. Trust me." Her mother took a seat. "I'm up here every day, watching. And praying. But that doesn't mean I don't get discouraged."

Up here every day. Kellie cringed. How she wished she could be here every day. How she longed to drop everything and race to her father's side as he walked through this valley. How guilty she felt for going about her daily work as if nothing had changed—when everything had changed.

"I'm relieved to hear you say that," Kellie confessed. "You're so full of faith. It helps to know you have your down moments, too."

"I don't think we'd be human if we didn't. It's not my faith I question. I have faith. I think we grow weary sometimes. But those are the times the Lord has to carry us—when we admit our weakness. We're completely dependent on Him."

"I know you're right. I hadn't thought it through like that." Kellie's spirits lifted at her mother's words. "And I know Daddy's getting better every day. He's taking baby steps, but every one is a step in the right direction."

"Yes," her mother agreed. "And he knows we're here, even when he can't voice his feelings. It means the world to him. I can see it in his eyes."

Kellie sat next to her mother, quiet for some time. "I wish I could be here more," she said finally. "It doesn't seem like enough to come on weekends." *It isn't enough.*

"Don't be so hard on yourself." Her mother patted her hand. "You have a husband and a job. Daddy understands that, even if he can't say it. We all do."

For some reason Kellie couldn't let the idea rest. In her heart she yearned to do more. In her heart she saw herself here—every day—alongside her mother. She wanted to play an important role in her father's healing. He needed her. "I could take some time off from work," she said, suddenly determined.

"But you've already done that." Kellie's mother gave her a quizzical look. "You've lost over a week's work already."

"No. I mean, I could take an extended leave of absence." Kellie paused, deep in thought. "Or better yet"—she felt her excitement rising—"I could work from here. I could focus on day-trading. As long as I have Internet access, I could make it work. I know I could."

"Day-trading?"

"Yes. I could work a few hours in the morning and then come up here for the rest of the day. I know I could handle the workload." My income might drop a little, but what difference would that make, in the grand scheme of things? And it's not as if I can't make up for it later. I can. I know I can."

"But what about Nathan?" Her mother's eyes registered concern. "Think about what you're saying, Kellie. You might be able to make it work for you, but it would be terrible for the two of you to be apart. I watched you try. It's not fair to him—or to you."

Kellie felt as if the wind had suddenly been knocked out of her sails. "I know." She sighed deeply. "If only we could find some way to—"

"To have your cake and eat it, too?"

Kellie looked up as she heard Nathan's quiet interjection. "Nathan. H–how long have you been standing there?"

"Awhile." He sat next to her and leaned his head back against the wall.

"I'm sorry," she whispered as she leaned her head against his shoulder. "I know I'm not making much sense."

"I understand, baby." He kissed her on the forehead. "This is hard."

She sighed. "Have you ever wished you could be in two places at once?"

Nathan pursed his lips. "Only when you were here and I was at home alone. I wished it every day."

She dropped the subject. "I'm sorry. I know it's impossible. Just wishful thinking on my part."

"No harm in that." He slipped an arm around her shoulders. "I wish I had the answer for you. I really do. But we'll keep praying. God will give us direction. I know He will. And in the meantime, we'll keep coming every weekend. We'll be here as often as we can."

Kellie nodded. *Lord, I wish I had his faith.* She looked up as Dr. Koenig, her father's neurologist, joined them in the hallway. He spoke in hushed tones, as if somehow that would shield her father from whatever he had to say. In truth, Kellie had to admit, her father probably wouldn't make much sense of their conversation, regardless of the volume.

Dr. Koenig gave them a sympathetic smile. "I know you're anxious to see him progress."

Everyone nodded in agreement. Kellie gripped Nathan's hand in her own.

"The truth is, he is progressing, even if it's not apparent to the naked eye," the doctor continued. "We can't discount how far he's already come. The fact that he's awake and able to move is very hopeful. And his ability to speak, albeit only a few words, is also a good sign."

Kellie fought to push thoughts of frustration from her mind. The few slurred words coming from her father sounded little like the man she knew and loved. "How long?" She voiced the question everyone surely wondered. "How long will he be in here? How long before he's back to. . .to normal?"

Dr. Koenig drew in a breath and looked her squarely in the eye. "I wish I could answer that. I do." He paused and shook his head. "Some of my neurological patients enter the rehab in dire straits, then end up staying only a few weeks. They leave as if nothing had ever happened. And then. . ."

Kellie glanced up as he gestured to the recreation hall, where patients with varying degrees of neurological problems visited together. Some watched television. Others struggled to stand, to walk. Some swore at nurses and shouted insults to those walking by. Still others sat in silence in their wheelchairs, staring out of windows.

"Some of my patients have been here quite some time," the doctor explained. "There's truly no way to predict. It's too soon to tell how quickly Kenton will progress. But I'm very hopeful. And he needs you to be, also."

"We are." Kellie's mother reached out and placed her hand on the doctor's arm. "We're not going to give up, and neither is he. I know that man of mine. He's a fighter. He wants to get through this."

Kellie felt the familiar lump rise into her throat. She tried to push it down as she spoke. "We're going to be here for him."

"That's the key thing." Dr. Koenig smiled warmly. "He will respond to the familiar. The more time you can spend with him, the better. I can't express how important that is. Having your support will be better than any medication I can give him."

Kellie noticed Nathan's palm grew sweaty in her own.

As the doctor turned to leave, she turned, as well. Kellie looked her husband in the eye and prepared herself to ask him for the impossible.

Nathan listened intently as he drove to his mother-in-law's house. Kellie's heartfelt words left little to the imagination. They brought to light feelings she had not fully voiced in the days prior, feelings he now struggled to reconcile with his own. With tears flowing, she poured out her heart, expressing her desire to stay in Greenvine so she could be closer to her father.

With a lump in his throat, Nathan fought to respond. But what could he say? How could he reciprocate her feelings when he wasn't even sure he understood them? In truth, he couldn't make much sense out of Kellie's emotional request. Could she be serious? How could they settle in a town like Greenvine, even for a short period of time? And, if so, how could he go along with such a thing? How would they continue to work? What would happen to their condominium, their jobs, and their lifestyle?

He drove in silence, conscious of her breathing as the tears continued to fall. *Lord, help me. I don't want to blow this. Give me Your words to say.*

"I didn't know I would feel this strongly," Kellie explained with great passion. "I've never been through anything like this before. I don't have anything to compare it to."

"We're both on a learning curve," he acknowledged.

"I guess this whole experience has made me reconsider some things." She looked over at him with those sad eyes, and Nathan forced himself to stay focused on the road. He bit his lip and continued to drive.

"What kinds of things?"

"Things like fancy cars, expensive condominiums, and high-paying jobs," she said. "These days I spend more time thinking about the things that are really important—family, relationships, and quality time with the people I love—that sort of thing."

"I hear you." Nathan chose his words carefully. "And I agree that those things are more important. I don't see an answer to this problem, though, at least not one that would satisfy both of us. I know you want to be with your dad—"

"And with you," she said adamantly. "That's why the only way it would work is if we were in agreement. Together both physically and psychologically. But that means we'd both have to be willing to make some changes."

"I don't do change well," he said. "And, to be honest, I can't even imagine staying here. Your mom already has her hands full, and I don't think I'd want to give up my privacy by staying in her house. It just wouldn't feel like—"

"Like home?" she asked.

"Right. Home."

"I think I have a solution." Kellie smiled, and Nathan realized she had already come up with a plan, had already worked this out in her head. Without him.

"What's that?" He turned onto her mother's street and listened carefully as she explained.

Her eyes sparkled with excitement as she spoke. "What would you think about renting a house?"

"What?" He hit the brakes and pulled the car off to the side of the road so he could make sure he'd heard correctly. "Renting a house here? In Greenvine?"

Her energy level rose with each word. "Yes. I've given this a lot of thought, baby. There's a house for rent two blocks from here. At least I hope it's still available. I saw the sign out front last time we were here. It's so inexpensive that you're going to laugh when you hear how much they're asking."

"I doubt it." He pursed his lips.

"I know what you're thinking." She grabbed his hand and gazed at him with a look of desperation in her eyes. "You're thinking we won't be able to balance everything out. But I think we can do this, Nathan. I—I know we can." She raced ahead, nearly breathless. "I can work over the Internet. I can spend time with my mom and still have plenty of time with you in the evenings and on weekends. And it's not really that far for you to drive, is it?"

"Kellie, I don't know."

Her eyes widened more with each impassioned word. "I mean, an hour and a half each way. . .people do it every day. We could keep our condominium. Or rent it out. Whatever you think. I mean, we're only talking about a few months after all—not a lifetime."

He shook his head in disbelief. "I'm floored. I don't know what to say. It sounds as if you've got everything worked out, right down to the house. But you've completely left me out of the equation." He fought to keep his temper in check. How could she see this as an answer?

"I–I'm sorry." She lowered her head, and droplets of tears fell onto her blouse as she spoke in hushed tones. "You're right. I just don't know what else to do."

They sat in silence for some time before Nathan put the car in gear again. Try as he might, he couldn't think of anything to say. With a heavy heart, he turned the car in the direction of his mother-in-law's home.

Chapter 8

Kellie crossed the parking lot of the small community church with her husband's hand tightly clutched in her own. She smiled as she spied the new education building off to the left. Children raced across the sidewalk, scurrying from place to place. Not so many years ago, she had been one of them. "This place has grown," she said.

"It has?" Nathan looked around, clearly surprised.

Kellie had to laugh. "I know it doesn't look like much, but it's about twice the size it was when I was a kid. And my mom tells me they've renovated the sanctuary. I can hardly wait to see it." In truth, she could hardly wait to see the people inside the sanctuary. How many would remember her? How many would she still connect with?

They entered the building, and Kellie braced herself for the inevitable. Sure enough, as they crossed into the foyer, a host of people greeted them.

"Why, if it isn't little Kellie Conway!" An elderly woman grabbed her hand and squealed in glee.

"It's Kellie Fisher now, Mrs. Dennison." She smiled broadly as Nathan extended his hand. Her heart swelled with pride as she introduced him. "This is my husband, Nathan."

"Nathan." The older woman released her hold on Kellie and grasped Nathan's hand. She looked him in the eye. "Yes, I heard all about your wedding. Heard you did it up right. Folks 'round these parts aren't accustomed to such fancy to-dos, but we can't fault you for pulling out all the stops." Here she paused and gazed tenderly at Kellie. "She's worth it, after all. You have an amazing girl here. She was quite a little pistol as a child. I should know. I was her Sunday school teacher."

Kellie felt her cheeks flush. "Mrs. Dennison taught my Sunday school class for several years," she explained. "She took us all the way through the Old and New Testaments. We studied over a hundred Bible characters."

"Probably more," the older woman said. "And I could have taught much longer, but I had to retire after my hip surgery." She finally let go of Nathan's hand and smiled admiringly at the couple. "But I'll never forget this girl. She was our class treasurer her freshman year in high school. Took great care of the offerings."

Nathan smiled. "That doesn't surprise me."

"She was always a whiz with numbers," Mrs. Dennison continued. "Never quite figured out how she kept up with it all, but she devised some sort of system for keeping track of funds even before they came in."

Nathan chuckled. "That's my girl."

"I'm still working with numbers," Kellie explained. "I'm a stockbroker at a firm in the Houston area."

"I believe your mother told me that. We're so proud of you, honey." Mrs. Dennison beamed with joy. "Now me, I can barely balance my checkbook." She chuckled, but eventually a serious look returned to her face. "But speaking of your mother, is she here?"

"I believe she'll be here any moment now," Kellie explained. "She stopped off to see Dad on her way."

"I saw him myself this morning." Mrs. Dennison smiled. "I try to go by on Sunday mornings before church to pray with him. And, of course, Wednesday is my day to work crossword puzzles with him. He's always loved those crossword puzzles."

Wow. "I remember," Kellie said. "Thanks for spending so much time with him. I know it has to bless my mother to have all her friends close by."

"Well, that's what friends do, honey." Mrs. Dennison chuckled. "I wouldn't be able to look myself in the mirror each day if I didn't follow the leading of the Lord in times like these."

A man with white hair and a rounded belly interrupted their conversation. "How's your father, Kellie?"

She looked up into the eyes of Hal O'Keefe, her father's best friend.

"A little better, I think." Kellie grinned at the older man's familiar crooked smile. "We went to see him yesterday. Stayed a few hours. He's able to eat now, with help, of course. We're headed back over there today after the service."

"Well, I'll see you up there this afternoon then," he explained. "I always take communion to the shut-ins on Sundays."

"That's wonderful." *These people are amazing.*

"Hal and his wife have done more than their share. Everyone has." Kellie's mother interrupted their conversation with her thoughts on the matter, and Kellie smiled in her direction.

"Hi, Mom. How's Dad doing this morning?"

"Oh, about the same." Her mother shrugged. "But he wanted to make sure I passed along a message to his friends at the church. He's so grateful to you all." She spoke to the whole room now, and they responded with comforting smiles and nods in her direction. "You've brought so much food—I could never eat it all. You've gone above and beyond the call."

"Well, we love you and Kenton," Hal said. "When you love folks, you can never do too much for them."

Kellie marveled at their easy exchange, so intimate, and yet it sounded so foreign to her. The conversation swung in several different directions at once as people came in droves to inquire after her father's health and hug her. Kellie listened in stunned silence as her mother took the time to connect with each person personally. *Lord, she really knows how to love people.*

From inside the sanctuary the opening song began to play. Kellie turned to Nathan, who looked a little uncomfortable. "We'd better go get a seat."

He nodded, and they made their way inside.

The pianist began to play the first song, a triumphant melody Kellie recognized right away. The worship leader stood and encouraged the congregation to join him. All across the room, people stood, many reaching to hug a neighbor or family member as the first words were sung.

As the song continued, Kellie looked around the room. Many of the people had aged, no doubt, but many remained seemingly unchanged. She caught the eye of Julia, her best friend from high school, and gave a little wave. The pretty redhead held a sleeping child in her arms—a little girl with cherub cheeks and hair every bit as red as her mother's. Julia's husband, Frankie, sat to her right. For some reason Kellie's heart lurched as she watched the three of them together. She couldn't explain the feeling and tried to cast it off, choosing instead to concentrate on choir members, who sang jubilantly.

A feeling of comfort enveloped her, and she settled into the familiar routine. The service flew by. Kellie couldn't remember when she'd enjoyed church so much or when a message had impacted her more. She glanced at her watch as the final song was sung. *Noon.* Enough time to grab a bite to eat with her mom and then visit with her father for a couple of hours. She and Nathan would have to be back on the road by four in order to make it home in time to prepare for work tomorrow.

"Are you okay?" Nathan got her attention as the pew emptied out.

"Oh yes." She nodded. "Just thinking."

"About?"

"Oh, about all we have to do today."

"That's what I was thinking about, too." They stood and made their way through the crowd down the center aisle of the church. "I'd like to take care of something before we leave."

"Oh?" She wondered what he meant.

At that very moment, Julia approached with the baby in her arms. "Kellie. It's so great to see you again."

"You, too." She embraced her old friend. "And who's this little angel?"

Julia beamed with pride. "This is Madison. She's a year and a half now."

"Well, she's a beauty." Kellie ran her fingers through the child's soft curls. "And my mother tells me you have more news."

"Yes." Julia flashed an embarrassed smile and brushed her hand across her belly. "I found out eight weeks ago. The babies will be a little more than two years apart." She shook her head and giggled. "But I'm not complaining. I love being a mom. I think I was born for this."

Kellie felt the usual tug on her heart. "Well, if the next one is half as pretty as Madison, she'll be a doll."

"Thank you. But we're hoping for a boy."

Nathan squeezed Kellie's hand, and she took the hint. "I hate to leave so soon, but we're headed up to the rehab to see my dad."

"Give him my love, will you?" Julia said. "I'll be back up there on Tuesday. Your mom told me how much he loves reading the paper, so I try to spend a little time reading to him. And he loves seeing Madison. I'm pretty sure he remembers her; his face lights up every time I bring her in the room."

"Wow. That's great."

Julia shrugged. "It's the least I can do. Your parents have always been so wonderful to me." She paused as she gazed intently at Kellie. "Will I see you there?"

"No. I, uh. . ." Kellie's heart twisted once again. "I'll be back in Houston. I have to work."

"Oh, I'm sorry to hear that. But it was great to see you." Julia gave her a warm hug and turned to visit with others nearby.

Nathan and Kellie forced their way through the crowd in the foyer and then managed to make it out into the parking lot together.

"I never would have believed they could fit that many people into such a small space." Nathan gave the building an admiring glance. "I'm impressed."

"This place has been bursting at the seams for as long as I can remember." Kellie pulled her keys from her purse. "But even with the renovations, they're still pretty full. I wouldn't be surprised if they have to go to two services soon."

"Sounds logical."

They continued to chat as they crossed the parking lot. As they approached the car, Kellie extended her hand with the keys. "Would you like to drive? My mom wants us to meet her at the Country Buffet out on the highway."

"I don't mind." He took the keys. "But I was hoping to change your plans a little."

"What do you mean?" Surely he didn't want to leave for Houston right away.

"I mean," he said as he unlocked the car, "that I've given a lot of thought to what we were talking about yesterday."

"You—you have?" She bit her lip and waited for his next words.

Nathan opened her door and nodded. "I have." He paused, and his brow wrinkled a bit with his next words. "I don't have a permanent solution, but I'm willing to consider the idea of driving back and forth—at least for a while."

Kellie caught her breath. "You are?" She could hardly contain her excitement but didn't want to alarm him by responding with too much zeal. "Oh, Nathan. I know we can make it work. I know we can."

"One thing," he said firmly. "I don't want to rent out the condo. I'm sure we won't need to stay here that long. But I've been thinking about that house you told me about. I thought maybe we could swing by after lunch and take a look. Maybe, just maybe. . ."

Maybe. Kellie's heart sang. Maybe she *could* have her cake and eat it, too.

After lunch, Nathan pulled the car into the driveway of the rickety white house with the FOR RENT sign out front. It didn't look like much, but looks could be deceiving. He hoped.

With Kellie's fingers laced through his, they crossed the overgrown front yard and knocked on the door. Nathan tried to push aside the heaviness in his heart as they waited for someone to answer. He had wrestled with the Lord all night over this decision, but the Lord had eventually won out. Kellie was right. She needed to be here with her mother. And he needed to do whatever it took to make that possible. In spite of the daily drive. In spite of the concerns over the cost.

"Well, hey there." A large man, nearly as scruffy looking as the yard, answered the door with a suspicious grin. "What've we got here?" He rubbed at his whiskery jowl and took them in with a lingering gaze.

The whole thing made Nathan more than a little uncomfortable. "We've come to take a look at the house." He tried to sound self-assured as he spoke.

"Have you now?" The man's face lit up like an evergreen on Christmas morning, and suddenly there wasn't a frightening thing about him. "Well then, come on in. The name's Chuck Henderson, by the way." He extended his broad hand, and Nathan shook it warmly.

They entered the house, and Nathan knew right away why Chuck had opted to charge so little rent. The place was a disaster. The paneled walls appeared to be coming loose in places. The sofa, an old plaid number from the seventies, was threadbare. A large dog of the Heinz 57 variety lay stretched out across a broken recliner in a sound sleep.

"That's Killer." Chuck gestured toward the mutt. "He's my watchdog."

The monstrous creature rolled over and yawned, then dozed off again.

"Uh-huh." Nathan would have said more, if every word he'd ever known hadn't escaped him.

"He takes good care of this place."

"Right." It looked as if someone needed to take care of the place.

"What do you think?" Chuck spoke with his hands as he showed off the room. "It's really something, ain't it?"

Nathan nodded politely. "At the very least."

Kellie looked around, clearly stunned. "It's not exactly what I was expecting."

"Lots of folks say that." Chuck smiled. "It's big, ain't it?"

In comparison to a cracker box? Nathan tried to be open-minded, but logic prevented it.

"It don't look like much from the outside, but these rooms are bigger'n people expect," Chuck explained. "And look at that carpet."

I'm looking. Nathan stared in shocked silence at the dingy gold rug.

"You don't find shag carpet like that these days. Folks is laying down those noisy ceramic tiles or fake hardwoods." He took off his shoe and raked his toes through the carpet. "Nothing fake about this. And there ain't nothing like the feel of real shag between your toes." He flashed a contented smile and slipped his shoe back on.

Nathan couldn't seem to think of a response. Instead he and Kellie followed the fellow into the next room—the kitchen. The countertops, crafted of butcher block, were clearly worn down by the years. The appliances probably all dated back to the late sixties or early seventies. The cabinet doors hung from broken hinges, and the sink was filled with dirty dishes. In short, it was nearly the worst kitchen he'd ever laid eyes on. Or smelled, for that matter.

Nathan tried to read Kellie's mind. *She's used to granite countertops, top-of-the-line appliances, hardwood floors. Surely she'll see this would never work.*

His beautiful wife looked the place over in complete silence. He couldn't seem to read her thoughts.

"We got three bedrooms here." Chuck led the way down a narrow hallway to a door on the left. "The first one is kinda small. My daughter tells me it'd make a great office. I've been using it for storage." He pushed the door open, and Nathan gasped.

Storage? The room was filled, top to bottom, with junk. Nathan could hardly believe his eyes.

"Wow." Kellie mouthed the word, her eyes widening.

"If you liked that, you'll love the next room." Chuck led them down the hall to a second small bedroom, equally as messy. "This one's bigger. You two could put a baby in here."

Never in a million years would I put a child in that room.

"Well, we don't have any children," Kellie explained. Her cheeks flushed bright red.

"I can't wait for you to see this." Chuck grinned as he pushed open the door to the master bedroom, and for the first time, Nathan noticed a tooth missing on the upper right. "The master suite—fit for a king and queen."

Together they entered a room that was surprisingly big—and not terribly hard on the eyes. It needed a fresh coat of paint, but this was the only place in the entire house Nathan could see himself in. For a few moments, anyway.

"What about the bathrooms?" Kellie asked the question quietly, and Nathan tried to imagine what she must be thinking about all of this.

Chuck led them through the bedroom to the master bath. It was dated and in much need of cleaning. The discolored tiles appeared to be coming loose from around the tub, and the grout had fallen in clumps.

"Wow." Nathan made use of his one-word vocabulary again.

"Yep. She's a beauty." Chuck turned on the light and gestured to the shower. "Now that showerhead is new. I bought it at the hardware store and installed it myself. It's a fancy one."

Nathan nodded silently.

"So what do you think?" Chuck looked him squarely in the eye. " 'Cause I've got another couple interested."

Sure you do. "Well—" Nathan looked at Kellie to gauge her thoughts.

She stared at the room with interest. "Would you let us paint and paper?" she asked.

Nathan put a clamp on the gasp that wanted to escape.

"No skin off my teeth," Chuck said, "as long as you don't choose any of those bright colors. Don't want to bring down the value of the house." He gave them a knowing look.

Kellie smiled, and Nathan could tell she was fighting not to speak her mind. "And you're sold on this carpet then?" she asked.

"Well, yeah." Chuck shrugged. "I like it. But there's real hardwoods underneath 'em, if you prefer that kinda thing. Not as comfy on the feet, but I guess they're in pretty good shape."

"I see." Kellie looked around again. "When will the home be available?"

Nathan could hardly believe his ears. She must see something in this place that he didn't.

"I'll be moving midweek," Chuck said. "My daughter and her husband bought one of those fancy houses up in Brenham. They want me to be close. I, uh. . ." He stumbled over his words. "The doc says I've only got about three or four months." His gaze shifted to the ground.

The older man's words almost knocked the wind out of Nathan. "I–I'm so sorry," he stammered. No wonder he'd let the house go. And no wonder he needed to move so quickly.

"Oh, Mr. Henderson." Kellie's eyes filled with tears.

Chuck broke into a broad smile. "Three or four months of chemo, I mean. My daughter wants me to be close to town so I don't have to drive back and forth. I figure I'll be ready to move back to Greenvine in about six months. Didn't want the house to sit empty all that time."

"It won't be empty." Nathan extended his hand. "We'll take it."

"We will?" Kellie looked up at him with tears still glistening against her lashes. "Are you sure?"

"I'm sure." And with a shake of their hands, they sealed the deal.

Chapter 9

Kellie looked around her new home with mixed emotions. The wood-framed house, far cleaner than the day she first saw it, was now filled with brand-new furnishings—at Nathan's request. He'd insisted on pulling up the gold shag carpeting before the furniture went in. She hadn't minded, though the floors underneath needed refinishing.

She glanced at the kitchen. Gone were the old appliances. In their place, Nathan had installed a practical black stove and refrigerator, contemporary in design. He'd insisted these changes were necessary—that this was the only way she would ever feel comfortable—but Kellie wasn't so sure. In fact, she thought the new items looked a bit odd up against the dilapidated structure. She would never hurt Nathan's feelings by sharing this thought, though, not after the trouble he had gone to in order to make things nice for her.

Kellie glanced at her watch. 10:35 a.m. She didn't have time to worry about the house now. It presented far less grief than her current problem—signing onto the Internet. Kellie hadn't counted on the inability to soar across the World Wide Web at the usual rapid pace. Here, away from the city, she had to resort to dial-up. *Dial-up.* She shook her head in disbelief as she sat down in front of the computer.

The disbelief continued as Kellie fought with an uncooperative phone line for an hour and a half. Just about the time she signed on, she would get knocked off again. And today of all days! She'd been advised by a client to purchase a specific number of shares of stock at a current reduced rate. Unfortunately the ups and downs of the market made that transaction impossible, at least without reliable Internet access.

Kellie gave up as the clock struck twelve. She'd lost the opportunity to make the purchase, and nothing could be done about it. With the phone in one hand and laptop in the other, she placed the call to the client and prayed the loss wouldn't be held against her.

After an aggravating conversation that involved groveling and a plea for another chance, she hung up and plopped on the couch. Kellie rubbed her forehead and leaned back to relax. But she couldn't still her mind. Her thoughts bounced back and forth from stock prices to gas prices—Nathan's latest complaint as he traveled back and forth to Houston—to the cost of the rehab where her father now resided.

Kellie sprang from the couch, her mind suddenly made up. Only one thing could make her feel better about this. She needed to get out of the house for a while. She needed to go to town.

She turned the computer off, grabbed her keys and cell phone, and headed out to the car. As Kellie threw the vehicle into reverse, she began to relax. In less than twenty minutes, she would walk through the door of the Bluebonnet Rehab in Brenham. Her father would be waiting. They would share some smiles, and she would fill him in on the things that happened over the past twenty-four hours, as she had yesterday and the day before.

Kellie reached for the cell phone and pressed Nathan's number. He answered on the very first ring, as she pulled her car out onto the highway.

"Kellie?"

Kellie's heart raced as she heard his voice. "Hi, baby."

"On your way to see your dad?"

"Yep. How'd you know?"

He chuckled. "I think I have your daily schedule down to a science. Every day at 12:10 p.m., you call me. I was actually sitting here, waiting."

"Really?" She felt her lips curl up a bit as she imagined what he must look like, sitting there waiting.

"Really."

"We've gotten pretty good at this," she said. "Can you believe it's only been a week?"

"Seems like years." His voice suddenly sounded tired.

She fought to change the direction of the conversation. "I'm shocked at how much we've gotten done in such a short time. It's pretty amazing when you think about it."

"Maybe that's why I'm so worn out."

"Well, as soon as you get home tonight, I'm going to pamper you." She smiled as she thought through her plan. "I'm cooking chicken cacciatore."

"My favorite."

"I know." She continued to formulate a plan, one she knew he would appreciate. "And I'm going to pick up a cheesecake while I'm in town."

"In town?" He chuckled. "Brenham is 'in town' now?"

"Yes." She laughed. "Funny how things change. Brenham is now the largest town in my little world. But it seems to have everything we need, so I'm not complaining."

"Well, Houston is looking bigger every day," he said, "and emptier than ever, now that you're not here. I went by the condominium this morning on my way in to pick up some more clothes, and it felt. . .odd. It's not the same without you in it."

"Aw." Kellie's lips curled down in a pout. "I miss you, too, but you know what?"

"What?"

"We're going to have a great evening together. Very relaxed. And after dinner, I'm going to rub those aching shoulders of yours," she said.

"Sounds incredible." Nathan paused a moment to take another call. He returned with an abrupt "Can I call you later? They need me down on the third floor."

"Sure." She kept a steady eye on the road. "I'm almost there anyway. I'll see you tonight, baby."

"Later, gator."

Kellie smiled as she finished the drive. *Lord, You've been so awesome to me. You made a way where there was no way.* In her heart she felt a peace, in spite of the current situation. Something about being here, in the place where she grew up, felt right. She would relish every moment—even if it were for a short time.

She pulled into the rehab facility at twelve thirty and climbed from the car, anxiety mounting. As she entered the lobby of her dad's now-familiar home away from home, she waved at the head nurse. "How are you today, Sharen?"

"Fine, girl. How about you?" The jovial woman with the ever-present jumbo loop earrings greeted her with a hug.

"I'm good." *I really am good.*

Sharen smiled. "Well, I'm glad you're here. Your father's been asking for you all morning."

"He has?"

"His speech is getting better every day," Sharen said. "And that man does love to talk."

Kellie responded with a grin. "My father is a very social man."

"I'd say." Sharen nodded, and her earrings bobbed up and down.

They walked together toward his room. Sharen paused for a moment outside his door. She looked at Kellie intently. "Before you go in, I should tell you one thing."

"What?" Kellie prepared herself, in case the news was bad.

"I caught him crying this morning."

Kellie felt tears well up in her eyes. "Are you sure?"

"Yes." The nurse nodded in sympathy. "I think he was overwhelmed. We were trying to get him dressed for the day, and things weren't going well. We asked him to lift his right arm, and he lifted his left—that sort of thing. I think he was embarrassed and maybe a little confused."

Kellie fought to keep her tears in check. "Is he okay now?"

"Yes. The choir director from your church came by a few minutes later and had him singing a song of some sort."

"He has his singing voice back?" Kellie's hopes rose instantly. Her father had always sung—for as long as she could remember. Maybe the Lord would use that singing to bring him out of this awful situation.

"Well. . ." Sharen shrugged. "It was an attempt. At any rate, they were loud. Woke up Mr. Scoggins in the next room, and he had quite a whining session about it."

They giggled together. Kellie then thanked the nurse for the information and braced herself for the usual rush of emotions as she opened the door to her father's room.

"I'm here, Daddy."

He lit up immediately. "K–Kellie."

"How are you today?" She walked to the bed and gave him a hug. His eyes, though full of love, still had a look she couldn't place. *Vacant.* That's what it was. He wasn't quite himself. Not yet anyway.

"F–fine." He sat up, and she plumped his pillows.

Kellie took a seat in the chair next to him and struck up a conversation. Of course she did most of the talking, but her father responded with as many words as he could muster. His eyes spoke the rest. She told him about her morning, about her Internet woes, and her business. She shared what it was like to be back at the church of her childhood and how she felt when she saw Julia and Madison. In short, she talked his ear off.

At one point her father interrupted with one shaky word. "N–Nath–an?"

"Nathan's in Houston, Daddy." Her heart ached, even as she spoke the words. "He's at work today. But he'll be home tonight."

"H–home?"

She reminded him of the rental house in Greenvine and tried to put his mind at ease. Clearly he didn't understand how Nathan could be in one place and she in another. She rushed past the explanation in the hope that a little would suffice.

"W–where is your m–mother?"

"Ah." *I should have told him right away.* "Mom's at a luncheon at the church today. She'll be here in about an hour."

Her father nodded and smiled. "L–love her."

"I know you love her, Dad." Kellie winked at him. "And she loves you, too."

His eyes filled with tears, and he brushed at them with an undeniable look of anger crossing his face.

Kellie's mind reeled as she contemplated his reaction to her words. Why would that upset him? Of course her mother loved him. After a moment she figured out his thoughts. *He's worried that he's unlovable in this condition. That's what it is.*

She stood and embraced him. "Daddy, you're still the love of her life. That will never change, no matter what."

He nodded, his eyes still moist. "I know." He squeezed her hand and looked directly into her eyes. "L–love you, K–Kell."

"I love you, too, Daddy." She gave him a kiss on the cheek, then sat to chatter awhile longer.

⁓

Nathan pulled in the driveway—if one could call it that—and turned off the car. He sat for a moment, staring at his new home in the dusk. It had an eerie look, one that still made him a little uncomfortable. In some ways the whole experience reminded him of a movie.

"And people think living in the city is scary." He spoke to no one but himself. Of course he had been doing a lot of that lately.

Nathan took the keys out of the ignition and reached for his briefcase. As he climbed from the car, he caught a glimpse of Kellie through the front window. She scurried around the kitchen with her short blond hair in a disheveled mess. He stared in silence as his bride shifted from the stove to the table. She looked— what was the word?—relaxed. She looked relaxed and happy. *Funny*. He'd almost forgotten what that looked like.

Nathan opened the back door of the car and pulled out an overnight bag. With the bag in one hand and briefcase in the other, he crossed the overgrown lawn. Sooner or later he would get to it. Probably later rather than sooner. Nathan entered the house with a rehearsed smile on his face. He didn't want Kellie to see the exhaustion or any hint of frustration. She had been through enough.

She greeted him with a warm hug and a brush of light kisses along his cheek. "How was the drive?"

Nathan fought the temptation to say *long*. He opted, instead, to go another route. After all, the Lord had given him plenty of time to make calls while on the road. And his prayer time had increased, to be sure. Besides, it was a pretty drive, especially in the springtime with the bluebonnets to keep him occupied.

Nathan smiled as he said, "Not bad. I've been listening to tapes from that conference in Austin. I actually made it through the first two."

"Great." She took the briefcase from his hand and set it aside. Her lips turned down in a bit of a pout as she continued. "I had a little trouble signing onto the Internet today, but I called the phone company. They're going to send someone out tomorrow to look at our line."

He had worried about this. In her line of work, an instant connection was critical. "Any consequences?" He almost dreaded her answer.

"Yes." Her gaze shifted downward. "But nothing a little pleading couldn't take care of." She sighed.

He shook his head. "I'm sorry, honey."

"C'est la vie." She gave a wave of her hand, as if to dismiss the whole thing.

Nathan wasn't ready to let go of his troubling thoughts. "What are they saying at the office? Are they okay with this change in plans?"

"So far, so good," she said. "I'm thankful for that."

Nathan breathed a sigh of relief. "Well then, I'll pray the phone company gets the kinks worked out. Looks as if the Lord's already taken care of the rest."

"Yep." She ushered him toward the table. "Hungry, I hope?"

"Starving." He'd barely had time for lunch. Somewhere between the two drives and the workload, he hadn't found time for food today.

She pointed at the dish of chicken cacciatore and the salad and beamed. "I've been working hard."

"I can see that. It looks great." Nathan sat at the unfamiliar table in an unfamiliar chair and ate off an unfamiliar plate. All the while, Kellie chattered merrily. She never picked up on his discomfort, and he never gave her any reason to. He took big bites and listened as she told him about her day. Had she always been this talkative? For some reason he couldn't remember this much gabbing after work. Then again, in the city she had people to talk to all day. Here...

Well, here things were different. *Clearly.*

"I went to see my dad." Joy laced her words. "I think he's doing a little better." She paused, and her lashes dampened with tears. "You should see him, Nathan. His face lights up every time I come in the room. The doctor says he'll be up to walking outside by next week. I can't wait. I hope the weather cooperates. I checked the weather report today, and we're supposed to have a lot of rain in the next ten days."

"You checked the weather report?" He didn't recall her ever doing that before.

"Well," she explained, "I read the paper up at the rehab. I've been doing a lot of reading lately."

"Wow." Nathan smiled at her enthusiasm. *I haven't seen this side of her in a long, long time.* Somehow, seeing her so relaxed helped relax him, too.

He decided then and there that he could handle the drives, the loss in income, and the bills from the new house and furnishings—as long as he could look at her peaceful face every night.

Chapter 10

Kellie stopped at the grocery store in Greenvine on the way home from visiting her father. She entered the store with the list of needed items in one hand and the cell phone pressed to her ear. She continued an ongoing conversation with Nathan, one that had started twenty minutes prior, as she pulled out of Brenham.

"How late will you be?" Kellie spoke into the phone as she grabbed a shopping cart and headed it toward the produce aisle. One of the wheels didn't seem to be working properly so she switched out one cart for another. Unfortunately, the next one appeared to have the same problem. *Oh well.*

"From what I've been told, this meeting could go on until seven or eight," Nathan explained. "Looks like I'm not going to make it home till ten or after."

She paused long enough to pout. "No way."

"Way."

"Man." Kellie tossed a head of lettuce into her shopping cart and sighed. "I had planned a great dinner. King Ranch Chicken and a brand-new taco-salad recipe I found in a magazine up at the rehab." Her father seemed to spend more time dozing than awake, so she'd had ample time to browse the facility's worn selection of women's magazines. She'd discovered recipes, developed a desire to redecorate, and even come under conviction to intensify her romantic life. Amazing what a few words of encouragement could do.

"I'll still eat when I get in," he said. "But don't wait on me, okay? Go ahead and do your own thing."

Do my own thing? "Are you sure?"

"Yeah. And don't stress so much over the cooking. You're going to make me fat." He chuckled, but Kellie didn't join in the fun. She had grown to love preparing a homemade meal each night, and as thin as Nathan was, she could scarcely imagine him growing plump. In spite of her new recipes.

Nathan let out a groan. "Great. That's my other line. I have to run."

"I miss you, Nathan."

"I miss you, too. See you tonight."

He was gone, and Kellie turned her attention to shopping. Even if he came home late, she wouldn't let that stop her from making a meal he would enjoy. She would continue to do everything she could to let him know how much she appreciated him.

She pushed the cart along, broken wheel bouncing with a *clack, clack, clack*. She glanced to her right and left, still adjusting to the outdated grocery store. It in no way compared to the contemporary, well-stocked markets back home in Houston. To start, it was a fraction of the size. And it offered little variety. In particular this tiny store carried very few of the natural, organic fruits and vegetables she had grown to love.

Well, no bother. *The next time I'm in Houston, I'll go to the whole foods market.* In the meantime, this would have to do. She sorted through the bell peppers, finally choosing two she could tolerate. Next she headed to the tomatoes. She picked her way through the limited selection, bagging three small ones and placing them in the front of her basket next to the peppers.

Kellie rounded the corner onto the bread aisle. She reached for a loaf of bread and placed it in the basket. As she did, a familiar voice caught her attention.

"I have a great recipe for homemade bread."

Kellie looked up into her friend's eyes. "Julia!" she squealed. "I can't believe it."

"Why not?" Julia smiled. "In a town this size, we run into each other all the time. Better get used to it."

"I guess so." Kellie paused as she thought about it. "It's kind of nice. Doesn't happen much in the big city."

Julia quieted Madison, who'd started to squirm in the front of her basket. "This little girl's sleepy. She missed her nap today. We had a tea party for preschool girls up at the civic center. That's why she's so dressed up."

"Well, she looks adorable," Kellie acknowledged. In fact, Madison looked like the cutest thing she had ever seen with her ruffled dress and patent leather shoes. "And it sounds like a lot of fun."

"I'm the activities director for the center," Julia explained. "We do everything from inviting in speakers to taking road trips together. It's a blast."

"Wow." Kellie pondered her friend's excitement. *How can anyone muster that kind of enthusiasm for a children's tea party?*

Julia continued to tend to Madison, who clearly wanted out of the basket. "So, are you getting settled in?" she asked, as she reached to scoop the rambunctious little girl into her arms.

Kellie nodded. "Getting there. The house still needs a lot of work." She and Nathan had spent a great deal of time on the place already, but it would take months to transform the little house into a comfortable living space. Not that they had months.

"Frankie and I bought a little fixer-upper a couple of years ago," Julia said. "It's been a challenge, but we've learned a lot about ourselves along the way. We've done a ton of work on the house—everything from remodeling the kitchen to laying down a wood floor. And I've developed an addiction to home improvement TV in the process." She flashed Kellie a broad smile. "You name it; I watch it. Design shows, landscaping shows, even those funny surprise makeover shows. I love them all."

It looked as if Julia's enthusiasm wasn't limited to her daughter's social life. Kellie couldn't help but wonder about her friend's lifestyle. Did Julia spend her days as full-time mom and activities director and part-time home decorator? Whatever she did with her time, it certainly brought her joy.

"I'd love to come by and see the house sometime," Kellie said. "And you, too, of course. When are you free?"

"I'm pretty open in the afternoons," Julia said. "I'm still teaching art classes at the junior high in the morning. They were great to work around my schedule."

"Oh!" Kellie nearly squealed again. "You're an art teacher. I'd almost forgotten. I sure could use your help choosing paint colors for the house."

"I'd love that." Julia bounced Madison up and down on her hip. "When do you want to get started?"

"The sooner the better."

The two plunged into a lengthy discussion about paint chips and name brands. They contemplated color choices and textures. They debated faux finishes and wallpaper. In short, they had a grand time talking about the what-ifs of home decorating.

After a while, Kellie changed the direction of their conversation. She had been wondering about Julia's husband for some time now and couldn't wait to ask about him.

"What's Frankie like?"

"Oh, he's awesome." Julia's face lit up. "He's got the most amazing sense of humor. He keeps me laughing all the time."

"What sort of work does he do?"

"He's a mechanic. He works at Clayton's Automotive up on 290. You've probably been by it a hundred times."

"Oh, I think I've seen that place."

"I met him when my alternator went out." Julia chuckled. "We've always said the Lord brought us together. Only problem with that theory is it cost me about three hundred dollars to have the crazy thing fixed."

Kellie smiled.

Julia continued with great enthusiasm. "But you should see him with Madison. They're the perfect father-daughter team. And he treats me like such a queen. He does most of the cooking—not because he doesn't like mine, but because he enjoys doing it. He might not be the most handsome man"—she paused for a moment and seemed to disappear into her thoughts—"and we'll probably never live in a really nice home or anything like that. But he's the man of my dreams, no doubt. God knew what He was doing."

Kellie looked at her friend with newfound admiration. "Well, he sounds great. And I can't wait to get to know him better." A thought suddenly came to her, one she could not let go of. "You know, I think Nathan could use some friends from the area. He's private, but I can tell he gets a little lonely sometimes. Maybe you and Frankie could come over sometime for dinner. Maybe we could watch a movie or something after."

"Sounds like fun." Julia's brow wrinkled as she continued. "But I'd have to bring the baby. Would that be okay?"

Kellie reached to play with Madison's curls once again. "I wouldn't have it any other way."

Madison began to fuss a bit, and Julia placed her back in the front of the basket. "I guess I'd better get this little girl home," she said with a sigh. "Her daddy's going to be arriving any minute now."

Daddy. As soon as the word flitted through her mind, Kellie's eyes watered. *Lord, please heal my dad. And, Lord—give Nathan the desire to be a dad.*

Where the words came from, she had no idea.

⁓

Nathan awoke early Saturday morning. He glanced at the clock. 5:55. *Why can't I ever sleep past six?*

He knew the answer. His body had grown accustomed to the early morning hours. But on Saturday? Surely on the weekend, he could catch a few more winks.

The first hint of sunlight peeked in through the window. Nathan closed his eyes to shut it out. Unfortunately nothing could drown out the noise of birds chirping in the tree outside their bedroom window. He would never grow used to it, not if he lived here a hundred years. He yearned for the noises of the city—the sound of cars racing by, horns honking, tires squealing, people hollering back and forth. He strained to hear those wonderful, familiar sounds.

Nothing. Only the irritating hum of crickets and the wind blowing through the trees. How did people live like this? Nathan rolled back over and punched the pillow. *I'm going to sleep if it kills me.* He lay in silence for a few minutes, willing himself into a slumber. Kellie's gentle breathing almost made him envious. *Am I jealous of my wife?*

He drew in a deep breath as he pondered the thought. He had been more than a little envious of her over the past couple of weeks, though he hadn't admitted it to anyone. Even himself. But how could he not feel some small degree of resentment? It must be nice to be able to sleep in every day, then wake up to a quiet home. No people shouting orders, racing up and down hallways, pressing into elevators. No looming deadlines or irritable coworkers.

He punched the pillow again. *Be fair, man. She's working from home. It's not as if she doesn't have a job. And even if she didn't—*

The concept hit him like a meteor plunging from the sky. What if she didn't?

What if Kellie turned out to be one of those women who simply wanted to stay home and raise babies? Would that be so awful? He swallowed hard, thinking about it. Sure, it interrupted their well-conceived plan, but what if God had a different plan in mind all along?

Nathan lay silently as he pondered the thought. *We'll have children one of these days, and they'll have everything we can afford to give them. They'll go to the best schools. They'll get the best possible care from a private nanny, if need be. At any rate, they'll be well taken care of.*

Well taken care of. He looked over at Kellie once more. Her back rose and fell with each breath. Nathan noticed how she'd changed over the past few weeks. He saw a peace in her that he hadn't sensed before. She'd lost the frenzied, worried look that so often etched her eyes. In its place, a bright-eyed, well-rested woman greeted him each night as he entered the house. With a tasty meal on the table, to boot.

"She's well taken care of now." He whispered the words, then sat up in the bed to look at her more pensively. Here, in this place, she appeared to be thriving. The only thing missing from her life was—well, to be honest—him.

But there's nothing I can do about that. It's not my fault. He wrestled with the Lord a few moments over the issue. How could he handle so much at once—a mortgage, rent, bills, the commute—and still give her the things she needed? Surely he had shown Kellie in a dozen different ways how much he loved her, even if he couldn't give her the time she needed.

Nathan thought back over the gifts he'd given Kellie over the past three years. Gifts to make up for not being there as much as he should. Gifts to bring a smile to her face. Gifts to replace the one thing she wanted.

Time. All she needed was time with him. That's all she'd ever needed or wanted. *She's about quality time. That's how she wants me to show her love. But how, Lord? How do I do that when I have no time?*

Then again, he had time right now. Nathan reached over and ran his finger across Kellie's cheek.

She awoke with a start. "Nathan, is everything okay?"

"I'm sorry." He pulled his hand back, repentant. "I didn't mean to wake you." He drew closer to her and kissed her on the cheek. "Unless you want to be awake, that is."

"What time is it?" She looked at the clock and groaned. "Whoa."

"We can sleep awhile longer." He leaned back against the pillow and yawned.

"Okay." She rolled over and leaned her head against his chest. About the time he thought she'd fallen asleep again, she reached to plant a tiny kiss on his shoulder. Nathan responded by wrapping her in his arms.

Chapter 11

Kellie nudged Nathan with her elbow more than once during Pastor Jamison's sermon the following Sunday. She didn't see how anyone could doze through such a life-changing message. How long had it been since she'd heard the gospel preached with such clarity? And how long had it been since she'd found herself in such a peaceful setting to take it in?

She glanced around the room, still listening. The same organ sat to the left of the stage, the grand piano to the right. She'd played that piano as a child with her sister Katie singing along.

And that pulpit. How many sermons had she heard from behind that hand-carved wooden pulpit? How many times had Pastor Jamison given a call for people to come forward for prayer? And how many times had she found herself at the altar, weeping? Those memories faded into one clear reality. This room held a host of memories—all wonderful. In this place, she had given her heart to the Lord. In this place she had come to understand His call on her life. And now in this place, she sat with her husband at her side, content.

Kellie continued to look around the room as she listened to the pastor's words. The stained glass windows caught her eye. Each was unique to itself, perhaps not as brilliant as those in the city churches but with every bit as much meaning. Perhaps more. Her gaze came to rest on one in particular—Jesus making His way up the hill toward Calvary. Sunlight from the outside brought the colors to light. Each red and blue seemed more brilliant than she'd remembered.

Though Kellie couldn't read the inscription from where she sat, she knew from memory what it said: IN LOVING MEMORY OF KENTON CONWAY SR.—her grandfather—one of the founding members of this church. She remembered his laugh and the way his breath always smelled of mint. She remembered his silver hair, sculpted in place with slick hair gel. But more than anything, she remembered that eventful Sunday during her seventh-grade year—a few short months after he'd passed away. Pastor Jamison had dedicated the colorful window with tears in his eyes. In fact, everyone in the place had damp eyes.

Just as she did now. But the window stirred other feelings now—feelings she couldn't seem to control. Staring at the window made her think of her father and brought a sense of sadness. She pushed it aside and focused on Pastor Jamison.

Of course it was a little difficult, with Nathan dozing off to her left. Every five or six minutes, his breathing changed, grew heavier. Then, about the time she found herself captivated by the message, he would let out the tiniest bit of a snore. The little girl in the pew in front of them seemed to find it amusing. The darling youngster turned around on several occasions and made funny faces. Kellie tried to stay focused but found it difficult. She was thankful her mother was off in children's church. She was the sort to find this funny, too. Kellie found the whole thing more difficult.

On the other hand, she reasoned as she jabbed her elbow into his side for the umpteenth time, *it's not as if he's getting enough sleep. He's wearing himself out driving back and forth so I can be here. He's making all the sacrifices, and I—*

She pursed her lips as she contemplated what Nathan must think of her. *Does he think I'm lazy? Does he think I don't care about his workload? I do care.* But had he misinterpreted her motives? Had she in some small way let her love for her father seem more important than her love for her husband?

Kellie gave a little shiver as the thought sank in. She tried to stay focused as the pastor wrapped up the message but couldn't seem to let go of the thought that Nathan must be harboring some internal frustrations he wasn't voicing. Perhaps they would have a good, long conversation about it. *This afternoon.*

As the service drew to a close, Nathan seemed to be more himself. He sang reverently, with his eyes shut, during the invitation and stood in silent prayer for those who responded. He clutched her hand and eased her along through the crowd toward the back of the sanctuary as the service was dismissed. They encountered more than one interruption along the way.

"Kellie, where is your mother this morning?" Mrs. Dennison asked. "I didn't see her."

"Oh, this is her week to teach children's church," Kellie explained. "She wouldn't miss that for the world."

"I should've known." The older woman opened her arms for a warm embrace. "She's such a worker bee."

"Yes, she is."

Kellie willingly allowed herself to be hugged, then turned back toward Nathan, worried he had grown bored and wanted to escape. Instead, she found him involved in an easy conversation with Hal O'Keefe. She caught the tail end of Hal's story— something about a fishing trip he planned to take the following week. Was he—no, surely he couldn't be inviting Nathan. Nathan had never fished a day in his life.

When the words, "I'd love to, sir," slipped from her husband's lips, Kellie thought perhaps the time had come to get her ears checked.

Hal slapped him on the back before heading off into a conversation with one of the deacons.

"You didn't have to do that," she whispered into Nathan's ear as they made their way into the lobby. "I'm sure his feelings wouldn't have been hurt."

Nathan's lips turned down into a frown, and his wrinkled forehead spoke volumes. "But I want to go fishing. I never get a chance to do stuff like that."

"You do?" She stared up at him with a broad smile as relief swept through her. "I thought you were afraid you'd hurt his feelings, that you were scared to say no to him."

"Do you think I have trouble saying no to people?" His question was almost accusing.

Only to me. She shook her head, frustrated. "No, Nathan, I don't. And I'm excited you want to go fishing with Hal. I just didn't want you to feel obligated."

He shrugged. "Sounds like fun, actually. And it's not as if I won't be up at five thirty next Saturday anyway. You know me."

Yes. She knew him, and that's what worried her. He hadn't rested in weeks. But perhaps next Saturday's trip to the river with Hal would give him a chance not only to connect with a wonderful man of God but also to get some well-deserved rest. With a pole in his hand.

Kellie squeezed his fingers as a sign of approval, and they took a few steps into the crowded lobby. She quickly found herself engaged in a conversation with Julia, who'd appeared with Madison in tow. Frankie, ever his wife's social equal, gabbed at length with one of his friends off to her left.

"A bunch of us are going up to the cafeteria on the highway for lunch," Julia explained. "I thought you two might like to join us. And your mom, too, of course." She bounced Madison up and down on her hip as she spoke.

"Oh, it sounds. . ." Kellie hesitated before responding. How would Nathan feel about eating in a cafeteria with a mob of church friends? She looked up into his eyes for her answer.

"Sounds great to me," he said. "If you think we've got time."

Kellie glanced at her watch. 12:15. "Dad's not expecting us till two. Surely we'll be done by then. And maybe"—she smiled at the thought—"maybe we can take him a plate of food—offer him something different for a change." She nodded in Julia's direction. "We'd love to meet you."

"So you're coming with us?" Frankie turned to join them with a broad smile. He scooped Madison into his arms, and she let out a squeal as he lifted her into the air above his head.

"Frankie, don't do that." Julia gave him a firm scolding, but he seemed to take it in stride.

"She's not scared," Frankie insisted.

"I know, but. . ."

Kellie smiled as Madison let out another squeal from above the crowd.

"She's a daddy's girl." Frankie lowered his daughter to his chest and planted a kiss on her forehead.

Julia shook her head, then turned her attention back to Kellie. "Men."

Kellie didn't dare look into Nathan's eyes. She might read too much into his expression. Instead, she took his hand, and they pressed through the crowd into the parking lot.

"Oh, wow." She glanced up at the sky, brilliant blue and as clear as a glass of water. Not a cloud in sight. "It's a gorgeous day. And I can't believe it's this warm."

"It's spring, all right," Nathan said. "I've been watching the bluebonnets up and down 290 as I drive back and forth. I don't remember seeing anything like it before."

"They've always been there," Kellie pondered aloud. "I guess we've never paid that much attention before." Funny how much they hadn't noticed before—like the melodic sound of birds singing outside their bedroom window and the tiny beams of sunlight peeking through the shade first thing in the morning. She loved every bit of it.

"Right." He squeezed her hand, and they walked a few steps in silence.

Several feet from the car, Kellie's mother met up with them. Nathan shared their lunch plans, and she quickly agreed to come along.

"Sounds like fun," she said. "And it's just what Kenton would want me to do."

Kellie found herself smiling all the way to the restaurant. She and Nathan chatted about the service, the people, and the warm reception. He seemed eager to visit with her father today and oddly eager to meet with Hal next Saturday. And something else was different about him, too, though Kellie couldn't put her finger on it.

Nathan seemed. . .relaxed. Yes, that's what it was. In all the years she'd known him, she had rarely seen this side of him.

But what she saw, she liked.

⌒

Nathan sat next to his wife and chatted at length with Frankie about her new car. The fellow, who had first come across as a country bumpkin, seemed knowledge-able about the particular make and model, even commenting on the engine size and gas mileage.

"When you're ready for an oil change, just bring it in to me," Frankie said with an inviting smile.

"Well, we get free oil changes for the first year," Nathan explained with a shrug. "So. . ."

Frankie nodded. "I figured. But you have to take it into the dealership for that, right?"

"Right." *Hadn't thought about that. When could I possibly—*

"Just bring it to me," Frankie said. "I'll take good care of you."

Nathan nodded. "Sounds good. To be honest, it's hard to find a mechanic you can trust—" He started to say "in the city" but held his tongue and let it rest there.

The conversation shifted to the house and the work still undone. Nathan chuckled as Kellie described, with some sense of drama, their first visit to the place. Her eyes grew large as she told everyone at the table about poor Mr. Henderson and his dilapidated home. But those same eyes brimmed over with tears when she reached the part about his cancer treatments. The whole table grew eerily silent.

"We'll add him to our prayer list," Julia said. "We have a great prayer chain up at the church."

"Prayer chain?" Nathan asked.

His mother-in-law piped in, "When there's a need in the church, they let Mrs. Dennison know, and she makes a call to the next person on the prayer chain. They pray together aloud over the phone, and then that person calls the next one on the list. And on it goes."

"Ah."

Julia nodded. "We've seen so many miracles on our little prayer chain." She reached to squeeze Kellie's hand. "And I just know your dad is going to be one of them."

Kellie gripped his fingers and gave him a smile of contentment. For some time, Nathan sat like that—with her hand firmly clasped in his own—tuning out the conversations around him. He wanted to stay focused, wanted to join in more, but something else drew his attention away at the moment.

Hal O'Keefe. His father-in-law's good buddy and his soon-to-be fishing partner. Nathan had his suspicions about why Hal wanted to spend a little private time with him. The good-natured older fellow had telephoned a few days prior with news that he'd hoped would stay quiet on Nathan's end.

The city of Greenvine was in trouble. Financial trouble. And Kenton, for years the city's dutiful comptroller, remained blissfully unaware in his current condition.

"I thought you might be willing to give us some advice," Hal had said over the phone. "Not trying to get you too involved. But since Kenton's in rehab and can't take care of this personally, the rest of us are clueless. We need someone with your expertise."

For once Nathan was glad his father-in-law wasn't fully aware of the goings-on around him. Knowing Kenton the way he did, he'd want to be back up at the office, fixing things.

But fixing things this time might take some doing.

Nathan pondered the situation a few minutes, trying to decide how involved he should get. *My plate is so full already. I don't have time to think about taking on much more.*

A shock wave of laughter brought him back to the present. Julia's little girl had strings of spaghetti hanging from her hair. Her tiny bulb of a nose was covered in red sauce, and she grinned like a Cheshire cat.

Nathan looked over at Kellie, who laughed so hard her face turned red.

She faced him head-on with a cockeyed grin. "Isn't that the funniest thing you've ever seen?"

He answered with the most serious face he could muster. "Nope."

"It's not?" Her lips turned down a bit.

"This is." Nathan reached to pull a string of spaghetti out of her hair and placed it on the table in front of her for all to see.

Kellie gasped, and her hands shot up to her hair to search for more. Finally convinced she was pasta-free, she turned back to the group with cheeks ablaze. "Why didn't someone say something?"

Everyone began to laugh and talk at once. Nathan pushed aside thoughts of the city's financial woes and turned his attention, instead, to the beautiful woman at his side.

Chapter 12

Kellie sailed through the following week, shocked at the passage of time. With each new day, her father's condition improved, though ever so slightly. With each new day, she also faced work-related challenges and countless phone calls from her office in Houston. Every few minutes, she questioned their decision to be here—in Greenvine. Every few minutes, she wondered how—or if—she would ever be able to leave.

On Thursday afternoon, after visiting her father, Kellie went by the civic center to meet with Julia and the children. All the way there she praised God for the news. Her father had taken giant leaps forward over the past week. Just this afternoon he had eaten on his own. Held the fork in his hand and taken real bites. He was also starting to speak in clear, coherent sentences. Almost clear anyway. And he'd taken several steps with the aid of a walker yesterday and seemed to be responding to the daily dose of physical therapy.

Kellie could hardly wait to tell Julia. She knew her best friend would praise God alongside her.

She walked in on a bustle of activity and shared her news. As expected, Julia let out a loud "Praise the Lord" and lifted her hand in praise toward the sky. Kellie smiled. Clearly her friend was enthusiastic about more than home improvement. Her love of the Lord was evident in all she said and did.

Kellie looked down at the room full of exuberant youngsters. They sat at a table loaded with craft items. Colorful beads, sequins, and feathers filled the center of the table.

"We're making drama masks," Julia explained as she placed a bright red and purple sequined mask in front of her face. The lips curled up in a smile. "This one's comedy." She spoke in a happy voice. She replaced it with a black and gold one with lips turned down. "This one's tragedy." She spoke in a somber voice.

Kellie clasped her hands together, ready to join the fun. "Cool. Sounds like a blast. Can I make one?"

"Of course!" Julia shoved several supplies her way and gestured to a seat.

Kellie sat down and joined the fun. The children laughed at length as the project consumed them. On more than one occasion, Kellie sprang to rescue some little one from near disaster. She soon became absorbed in their stories as she worked alongside them.

"You've worked with kids before," Julia observed.

"Um. . .not really."

Julia's face reflected her surprise. "Well, you're a natural at it."

Kellie pondered her friend's words. She'd never considered herself a natural at anything—except numbers.

Wow. I hope that's not my legacy. Won't look very good on my tombstone. "SHE WAS GREAT WITH NUMBERS."

Kellie pushed aside the nagging thought and tried to stay focused. As the children busied themselves, Julia whispered a few quiet words on a subject that startled her a bit.

"I guess you've heard—"

"About?" Kellie looked over at her friend, puzzled.

Julia looked around to make sure they weren't being overheard. "The trouble."

"Trouble?" Kellie thought of the church, and her heart quickened. "No, I haven't heard anything. What's happened?"

Julia pursed her lips. "We found out a couple of days ago. Frankie's dad is mayor now—did you know?"

Kellie's mouth flew open. "I've been so focused on everything else that I didn't make the connection. I'm sorry."

"Oh, don't be." Julia shrugged. "It's just that we hear a lot of what's going on with the city before some of the others."

"The trouble has to do with Greenvine?" Kellie set her mask down on the table so she could concentrate.

"Yes." Julia drew in a deep breath. "It's something pretty big, too. I don't understand the technical lingo. Something about arbitraged. . ." She bit her lip, clearly trying to remember the rest.

"Arbitraged bonds?" Kellie asked.

Julia shrugged. "I think that's right. Something about a bad investment."

Kellie's heart felt as if it would hit the floor. "Or a bad *investor*," she was quick to add. "Someone scammed the city leaders?"

"Pretty much."

Julia turned her attention to one of the little girls who needed help, and Kellie pondered her friend's words.

"Daddy." She whispered the word, suddenly aware of the truth. Her father had apparently put his trust—and ultimately the city's trust—into the hands of someone who'd proven him wrong. And he didn't even know it.

Kellie put together a plan in her mind. She would find out the *who*s, *what*s, and *when*s and would get to work. But she would need help. She would need—

Nathan.

She would need Nathan. Where her knowledge ended, his began. Together they could work as a team to help Greenvine reclaim what it had lost. Together they could—

She stopped herself in the middle of the thought. *I can't do that to him. He's overwhelmed with work already. He hardly has time enough for—*

Kellie struggled with the next thought. Nathan hadn't had much time for her lately, but she certainly couldn't blame him for that. Not with the house in such a state of disrepair and the drive back and forth to Houston.

And something else seemed to be missing from his life, as well. His passion for God seemed to be—what was the word? *Waning.* She didn't see him reading his Bible much these days, and it had been ages since they'd had one of their famous "let's talk about how we're doing spiritually" conversations. He always initiated those.

But not now. Now he was just too busy. So how could she ask more of him?

Kellie squirmed in her chair, thinking. She ached for Nathan. She missed him, maybe more than she had ever missed him back in Houston. This was a different kind of missing—the kind that created a tight grip around her heart and wouldn't let go.

Lord, I have to give this situation over to You. I don't know what else to do with it.

She and Nathan would get through this season, she felt sure. She loved him with a passion that seemed to exceed any fears or frustrations. Yes, her love had changed over the years. This was a different, more committed kind of love—of the "in it for the long haul" variety.

Her relationship with Nathan was key.

On the other hand, she loved Greenvine and wanted to do what she could to help. She would try, at any rate. She would make her father proud. And when he was on his feet again, he would get back to work, doing what he loved best. Somehow, she would manage to do it all.

"Earth to Kellie."

She looked up into Julia's laughing eyes. "Hey."

"Hey to you, too." Her friend reached to pat her on the back. "Thought we'd lost you there for a minute."

"No, I'm still here." Even as she spoke the words, Kellie understood their depth. She was still here—in Greenvine.

And here she wanted to stay.

⌒

Nathan sat at lunch with his boss in a crowded downtown restaurant. All around him people hollered out conversations to one another above the din of clinking silverware. Busboys loaded their trays, and waiters took orders. The whole place was abuzz with activity, and he loved every bit of it.

Mr. Abernathy looked him in the eye. "Nathan, I've wanted to talk with you awhile now. I'm proud of the work you've accomplished at Siefert and Collins."

"Thank you, sir." Nathan took a sip of tea and tried to relax. Something about these one-on-one meetings with his boss still made him a little nervous.

"There's just one thing." The older man looked at him intently.

"Sir?"

"Well." Mr. Abernathy stared him down as he spoke. "You haven't exactly been yourself lately. You seem distracted, to be honest."

"Ah." Nathan should've been prepared for those words but wasn't. "I, um. . ." No point in arguing about it, especially when it was true.

The older man gave him a sympathetic look. "I know you've been through a lot in recent weeks. And I know you're torn between two places right now."

"Yes, sir. But I've tried hard not to let that interfere with my work."

"It's not your work that's suffering necessarily," Mr. Abernathy explained. "I'm more concerned about your health."

"My health?"

A look of genuine concern filled his boss's eyes. "You seem worn out most of the time, and that concerns me. Are you getting enough sleep?"

Nathan sighed. "I'm trying. It's an adjustment. And the drive. . ." The drive was wearing on him. What had begun as a great opportunity to spend more time in prayer had turned into a daily battle with his own internal thoughts. Many times he had all but pressed God out of the conversation altogether. Without meaning to, of course.

"Have you given any thought to staying at your condominium a few nights during the week?" Mr. Abernathy's words brought Nathan back from his ponderings.

"Yes. In fact, I plan to stay in town tonight. I've got too much on my plate to drive home."

"Home?" The word sounded more like an accusation.

Why did I say home? I didn't mean home. I meant Greenvine.

"Well, Greenvine is more of a home away from home." Nathan braved a smile, hoping to bring assurance. "It's certainly not the kind of home I've planned for my family and myself."

"Of course not." Mr. Abernathy's eyes narrowed. "I know better than that. You fit right in here in the city. Always have."

Nathan thought about those words as they finished their lunch. He'd been born and raised in Houston and had never planned to leave. His parents were here. His job was here.

His home was here.

Chapter 13

The following Sunday morning, Nathan had a hard time waking up. He'd spent the better part of the night tossing and turning. He couldn't seem to still his mind. Problems at work, coupled with his concerns over Hal's revelations during their fishing trip, kept his mind occupied

He glanced at the clock several times during the night. 2:15, 4:36, 5:44. He must have rested somewhere between those times, but he sure didn't feel like it when the alarm went off at seven. And then there was that ever-present aggravation of birds shrieking outside his window. There weren't enough pillows in the world to drown out that nuisance.

Kellie rolled out of bed with her usual ease. She gave him a soft kiss on the cheek and headed to the bathroom to brush her teeth. He would join her in a minute. Right now he had more important things to take care of.

At 7:20, Kellie eased him back away with her gentle words. "Getting up, sleepyhead? I've already had my shower." She leaned down to kiss him on the forehead.

"Uh-huh." His head felt heavy against the pillow. For some reason, he couldn't seem to budge. *Just a few more minutes won't hurt.*

She awoke him again at 7:55, a look of concern on her face. "Are you sick, Nathan?" This time she didn't sound quite as gentle.

He tried to focus on her words but couldn't keep his eyes open long enough. "I–I'm fine."

She stared at him with a degree of concern registering in her eyes. "You never sleep this late. I already have my makeup on, and breakfast is getting cold."

"Okay." He sat up slowly, then leaned back against the headboard. "I don't know what's wrong with me."

She gave him an encouraging nod. "I'm sure you'll be fine after your shower."

Kellie padded off into the kitchen, and Nathan allowed the weight of his eyelids to pull them down, down, down once more.

It seemed like only a second more, and Kellie shouted in his ear. "Nathan, what's going on?" He wiped the drool from the edge of his lip and shot a glance at the clock. 8:37. She stood before him, fully dressed, purse slung over her shoulder, Bible in her hand. Clearly ready to leave. And clearly in a bad frame of mind.

"I–I'm coming." He swung his legs over the side of the bed and stretched. But how could he leave when his head felt heavier than a bucket of lead?

"I don't see the point." She pursed her lips and crossed her arms at her chest. "Are you mad at me?"

"Not mad." Her eyes reflected a strange sadness. "I know you're tired."

"It's not just that," he tried to explain. "I couldn't sleep at all last night. There's too much going on in my head. And speaking of which"—he rubbed his aching head, willing the dull ache to go away—"my head is killing me."

Kellie's expression softened, and she let her arms fall to her sides. "I'm sorry, baby. Do you need something for the pain?"

He nodded, and she went to the medicine cabinet in search of the pills. When she returned to his bedside with a glass of water in one hand and medicine in the other, he offered up a smile. "Thanks for taking care of me."

"Wish I could do more." She glanced at her watch. "But I need to go. It's getting late, and I don't want to miss Sunday school. I'm supposed to be reporting on my dad's condition. He's doing so much better, and I can't wait to tell them."

"I know, Kellie." Nathan stood to give her a kiss. "And I'm sorry I'm going to miss it. I wish I could be there."

"I'll see you afterward," she said. "But it's going to be later than usual. We have that fund-raiser dinner for the missions trip the teens are taking to Nicaragua this summer. I promised I'd help with the slave auction. I'm handling the money part of it."

"Man." Nathan paused to think. "I forgot about that. I told some kid I might buy his time. Maybe get him to come and do some work on our yard." How could he have forgotten when their overgrown yard beckoned?

"That was Jerry Chandler," she reminded him. "But I'll explain you're not feeling well." Kellie walked toward the bedroom door, then turned back to look at him. "I could still arrange for him to come and work on the yard next Saturday, if you like. Might cost a little more than we'd pay otherwise, but it's for a good cause."

Good girl, Kellie. I knew I could count on you to take care of that for me. "That's fine. Whatever you think is best."

"Okay." She paused for one last time. "I should mention that I'll be at rehab from two until about four or so. If you want to join me—"

"I'll be there." He sat back down on the edge of the bed. "I promise."

"Okay. Well. . ." She turned and walked from the room. He heard the front door slam as his head hit the pillow.

Can I help it if I'm worn out? Can I help it if my head is killing me?

Nathan pouted in silence. He didn't want to get up. He didn't want to face a church full of carefree, smiling people. Not today.

No, today he wanted to lie right here, snoring peacefully. The world could go on spinning without him for a while longer. Kellie could—

He punched the pillow and fought to get comfortable. Kellie could surely face her friends and family without him this once. After all, it wasn't as if she'd been the one working 24/7. What more could she expect?

And of course he'd be there to see her father at two. What kind of person did she think he was? An internal argument began, one he couldn't seem to squelch. It wasn't as if she'd spent any time with his family over the past month. Or that she'd spent a lot of time talking to him about his struggles, his thoughts, his concerns.

Nathan rubbed at his aching head and tried to still the frustrations that had erupted from out of nowhere. *Lord, I don't know where this is coming from. I had no clue I was this bugged about things.*

"I'm just tired." He spoke aloud to the empty room then let out an exaggerated yawn. "That's all that's wrong with me."

Nathan thought about his work back in Houston. The company seemed to be going in a thousand different directions at once. He had hoped the meeting with Mr. Abernathy would bring some order to the confusion in his mind, but things had only grown worse. Chaos reigned at Siefert and Collins. And somehow he managed to be stuck in the middle of it. This coming week he'd have to spend at least one or two nights in town to accomplish all that needed to be done. He'd stay at the condo.

The condo. Nathan slapped himself on the head, remembering. He'd received a call on his cell phone on Friday about a problem with the condominium. Something about a leak in the bathroom that had caused flooding for a neighbor downstairs. The maintenance people had stopped the flow of water, but he still needed to hire a plumber to fix the problem.

I'll take care of that first thing tomorrow morning. Right now I need to get some sleep.

He gripped the pillow with both arms and clamped his eyes shut. Sunlight streamed through the cracks in the wood shutters at the window. Outside, a flock of birds continued to chirp in a crazy chorus, nearly driving him out of his mind.

"Why is it so stinkin' noisy in the country?" He rolled over in the other direction and put the pillow over his ear. *And why is Kellie so infatuated with this place?*

He pondered the thought, eyes still squeezed shut. She loved it here. The thought plagued him. At the root of his headache, his frustrations, his pent-up anger lay that one, horrible thought.

Kellie loved it here. And perhaps she always would.

But what could he do about that? How could he counteract it? Something needed to be done—and quickly.

An idea took shape, one that wouldn't leave him alone. She had forgotten what it was like to be in the city. He would take her back to Houston for a couple of days. They'd have a night on the town at that great little French restaurant. They would talk about the condo and their investments. They would start planning that trip to Europe to renew their vows. Everything would be like it was.

Do I want things to be like they were?

He punched the pillow again, sleep a distant dream. Did he want life to return to normal? Wasn't Kellie more peaceful? Didn't he enjoy getting to know the people at church? Wasn't the Lord providing for all their needs?

Nathan groaned, then sat up in the bed. He swung his legs over the side and bowed his head in shame. *Lord, what's wrong with me? What is going on?*

With turmoil still eating at him, Nathan slipped down onto his knees. Enough with all this arguing. What he wanted—what he needed—was time with the Lord.

———

Kellie cried as she drove along the country road toward town. Frustration moved her to tears, not anger. At least not anger at her husband. At the enemy perhaps.

She didn't blame Nathan for not getting out of bed. She understood his need for rest. She could relate to his exhaustion. She'd lived in an exhausted state for the past three years.

She didn't hold any grudges. He had done so much for her. She only wished this season would somehow resolve itself so they could have more time together.

With a heavy heart, Kellie continued her drive to the church.

Chapter 14

H ow does this sign look?" Nathan stretched his arms up as high as he could, lifting the banner above the front door of his in-laws' home.

Kellie clasped her hands over her mouth, then released them triumphantly. "Oh! It looks great."

He scrambled to get the large vinyl banner hung straight. After he was sure he had it up properly, he stepped down from the ladder for a look.

"Welcome home, Kenton." He whispered the words, thrilled at the joy they brought.

"Can you believe it?" Kellie slipped her arm around his waist. "He's coming home." A tear slipped out of the corner of her eye, and she brushed it away with a fingertip. "I'm not sad," she assured him. "Not at all. In fact, I'm so happy I just can't hold the tears back."

"I know, babe." Nathan's heart swelled as he pressed a kiss on her forehead.

Kellie beamed. "And having Katie here makes everything perfect. I've missed her so much."

"I know your sister is glad to be back," Nathan said.

Kellie glanced at her watch. "We only have ten minutes. Mom called when they left the rehab and said six thirty."

The front door swung open, and Mrs. Dennison stepped outside. "I've got everything ready in the kitchen." She beamed with pride. "Do you need my help out here with anything?"

"I think we have it covered." Nathan folded up the stepladder and carried it to the garage as she headed back inside. Even from here, he could hear the bustle of the crowd in the house. The noise level was at a cheerful high. At least ten or twelve of Kenton's nearest and dearest friends awaited his arrival. They would welcome him home in style—with good food, good conversation, and even a few tears. Nathan could see it all now.

It must be nice to have friends like that, he reasoned. *People who stick with you through thick or thin.*

He had friends, of course—men he played racquetball with, coworkers he'd grown to admire and converse with on a personal level. And then there were the guys he'd grown up with, his buddies from high school. Of course they hadn't seen one another for years. They had no—what was the word?—longevity. They had no longevity. He had temporary friends. Well, near-friends really.

This more intimate type of friendship had somehow eluded him. For a moment Nathan wondered who might be waiting in the living room for him, if he were in Kenton's place.

"Everything okay out here?" Kellie appeared at his side.

"Yes." He pressed the ladder against the wall and turned to pull her into his arms. "I was just thinking."

"About what?" Her face filled with concern immediately, and Nathan knew why. He'd done more than his share of grumbling over the past week. The plumber overcharged him for work at the condo; a tire blew out on his car on the trip back from town Wednesday night; and—to top it all off—Kellie hadn't been able to join him for that in-town romantic getaway he'd planned.

Not that he blamed her. With the excitement surrounding her father's upcoming release, she had been needed here, in Greenvine.

He turned to face her. "I was thinking about how blessed your dad is." Nathan ran the back of his index finger along the edge of Kellie's cheek. She responded by leaning into his chest as he continued. "He has some great friends."

"Yes. They're awesome." She paused, then came alive with her next words. "Oh, speaking of friends, Frankie said to tell you those new wheels you ordered are in. He said they look great. You're going to love them."

"I can't wait." He had happily ordered them at Frankie's suggestion, knowing they would dress up his vehicle.

"Speaking of Frankie, he and Julia are inside with the others. They just got here."

"Great." Nathan smiled and took her hand. They walked in the house arm in arm, then separated to greet the crowd. He grinned as he made the rounds from person to person. There was no lack of conversation—or love—in this room.

When his father-in-law arrived at last, the atmosphere changed immediately. Tears of joy sprang up in nearly every eye, and his friends ushered him in like royalty. After he took his place on the sofa, Kenton looked over the room, his own eyes filled.

"It's. . .it's good to be home."

Nathan felt Kellie's hand tighten in his own.

"We're happy to have you home, Daddy." Kellie sat next to him and planted a tender kiss on his cheek. The sight of Kellie with her father warmed Nathan's heart. When her sister, Katie, joined them on the sofa, the chattering began in earnest.

The room became lively again as people made their way over to the couch, one by one. They offered warm words, prayers, encouragement, and even a laugh or two. Nathan watched it all from a careful distance—close enough to let Kellie know he wasn't going anywhere, far enough away to give her the space she needed with her dad.

Hal prayed for the food, and everyone loaded their paper plates, chatted merrily, and ate with abandon. Nathan filled a plate with meatballs, some little sausages, cheese and crackers, and an assortment of fresh veggies with dip. He'd come back for dessert later.

On second thought. He reached to grab two peanut butter cookies and a piece of cheesecake while they were still there to grab. In this kind of crowd, what he wanted might not still be there when he got back.

Balancing the plate in one hand, Nathan popped a piece of cheese into his mouth.

Hal slapped him on the back, nearly sending the piece of cheese down his throat. "Getting enough to eat?"

Nathan nodded, then reached to pick up a paper cup from a stack on the table.

"Here, let me get that for you." Hal took the cup. "What did you want in it?"

"Some of that punch would be good. I'm not in the mood for soda." He took a bite from a meatball and watched as Hal filled his cup. *This guy has a real servant's heart. Then again*—he looked around the room—*they all do.*

Gripping the plate in his left hand, Nathan took hold of the cup of punch with his right. He swallowed down a big drink. "That's good stuff."

"My wife made it," Hal confided, his voice a bit concealed. "I've had that same punch at over twenty parties this year alone." He laughed so loud, his joy reverberated around the room. "I can't stand the stuff, but she loves it." He gave Nathan a knowing wink, and his voice softened again. "These women of ours. They're good at what they do, aren't they? And their hearts are as big as Texas."

Nathan looked across the room at Kellie, who held Madison in her arms. "Uh, yes."

Hal dove off into a conversation about goings-on at the church, and Nathan found himself squarely in the middle of a debate over whether or not the Prime Timers should replace their worn chairs with new ones. He didn't mind. In fact, he rather enjoyed the one-on-one time with Hal. Felt almost. . .natural.

At one point he shot another glance in Kellie's direction. Her face was alight with joy as she bounced Madison up and down on her hip.

That's a side of her I've never seen before. She looks. . .natural. Nearly everything about Kellie felt natural here. She fit in here. She was at home here. And there was a glow about her, something he couldn't quite place. Perhaps it was the pleasure of being in a place where so much love abounded.

His heart twisted with that revelation. Now that her father was doing better, perhaps he and Kellie could talk about going home again. He hoped she would carry some of this joy with her.

⌣

Kellie didn't know when she'd ever had a better night. As she looked around the now-messy room, her heart swelled with joy. In one night everything she had hoped and prayed for this past month had finally come to pass. Her father had returned home. Her sister had joined them. And Nathan was able to be here, relaxed and well rested. He'd visited with everyone in the room, from young to old. And she—

She felt a sense of anticipation, as if some private door to the world had opened up just for her. She couldn't figure out why. In years past she might have attributed this feeling to something going on at work, but this time things felt different. This time her wants and wishes had changed. *Substantially.*

Occasionally she would catch Nathan's gaze from across the room. He seemed more himself tonight—certainly more so than last Sunday morning. Something had happened that day—she suspected exhaustion had driven him to a point of frustration. But his countenance had improved by midday. And now, nearly a week later, he seemed a new man. *Reformed.*

She watched as he popped a cookie into his mouth, then chatted with Frankie at length. They were surely discussing his car—the latest gadgets and gizmos he hoped to add to it for better performance. Or perhaps they had slipped off into a conversation about the city's financial woes. She hoped not. Why ruin a perfectly good night?

On the other hand, she had hoped Nathan would take an interest in the town's plight, hadn't she? With his brilliant mind at work, they might stand a chance at turning things around.

Kellie looked at the men with a more discerning eye. Frankie had a broad smile on his face.

"Having a good time?"

Kellie turned as she heard her mother's voice. "Mm-hmm. I'm so glad Daddy's home. I know you are, too."

Her mother's eyes filled with tears. "I am. I'm a little nervous, though. I hope I can take care of him."

"You'll have a nurse stopping by every day, right?"

Her mother sighed. "Yes. She'll be a big help. But he's taking so much medicine, and he'll have to be driven back and forth to physical therapy every day. It's a lot. I hope I'm up to it."

For the first time, Kellie noticed the extent of the weariness in her mother's eyes. She reached out and touched her arm. "I'll be here with you, Mom. I'm not going anywhere. You won't have to go through this by yourself, I promise."

Her mother nodded, and her short gray curls bobbed up and down. "I appreciate that, honey. I don't know how I could have made it through any of this without you. I've thanked God every day for sending you back. And I know your father has, too."

"I wouldn't have done anything differently." She embraced her mother, then gestured to Nathan. "And it looks as if he's starting to fit in."

"I've spent a lot of time praying about that." Her mother's brow wrinkled. "He's been so patient with all of us. But I'd imagine he'll be happy to get back home before long."

Home. For the first time in a while, Kellie thought about her life in Houston and cringed. *Lord, please don't send us back yet. Give me a few more weeks—a little more time here.*

She looked up as Julia's familiar laughter rang out across the room. Madison made a face as she bit into a large dill pickle. Everyone nearby watched her with broad smiles.

"That little girl is a doll," Kellie said.

"She is," her mother acknowledged. "And Julia is such a great mom."

Kellie grew silent and allowed her thoughts to roam as her mother moved on to talk to a friend. The desire for a child had come on Kellie gradually since arriving in Greenvine. What was it about this place that made her think she could settle down—give up everything she had worked and planned for—and live a simple, uncomplicated life?

She found herself almost envying Julia and Frankie. True, they didn't have much in the way of material things, but they clearly shared a love and faith in their future. In some ways they seemed better prepared to face the days ahead than she and Nathan were, though they had given it their best effort.

Kellie continued to watch Madison from a distance. She felt the familiar pangs of desire but pressed them down. It didn't make any sense to dream about such things. Not yet anyway. Everything in God's time.

Oh, how she wished she knew more about His time frame!

Kellie started as Nathan slipped his arm around her waist.

"You're mighty quiet tonight."

"Am I?" She turned to face him with a smile. "I don't mean to be. Just so happy."

"Me, too." He pressed kisses onto her forehead, and she melted into his embrace with a happy sigh.

"I love you, Nathan."

"I love you, too."

She pushed back the lump in her throat. "I'm so grateful to you. I don't know how I can ever thank you for giving me this season with my dad."

"I'm so happy he's doing better. Maybe things will be back to normal before long."

Back to normal. Kellie gave him a weak smile. "Right now I'm happy to be with all the people I love."

"Me, too." He pressed another soft kiss on her brow. "You, especially."

She blushed a little but allowed him to give her a warm kiss in front of the whole room. Who cared if others knew they loved one another? She wasn't ashamed to show her affection for her husband. Not here, among friends and family.

After a moment alone, Kellie and Nathan made the rounds to say their good nights. Then, as the crowd thinned and her father retreated to the quiet of his bedroom, they made the drive home.

Once there, they enjoyed some quiet time together. Here, in this country place with no distractions, Kellie could think more clearly, give more freely, and even love more deeply.

With the taste of her husband's kisses still sweet on her lips, she eventually drifted off to sleep, content.

Chapter 15

Over the next two weeks, Kellie settled into a happy routine. She awoke each morning, had her quiet time with the Lord, spent a few hours on the Internet and the telephone, then went to her parents' home. Along the way, she enjoyed the flowers that bloomed in every yard and noticed the variety of trees. She waved to now-familiar neighbors and lowered the windows in the car so she could enjoy the fresh air.

Once she arrived at her parents' place, she helped her mother with everything from cleaning the kitchen to driving her father to physical therapy. Their hours were spent telling stories of days gone by, listening to music together, and discussing the prayer needs of friends at church. Occasionally they would go out to lunch at the cafeteria in Brenham and stop off at the outlet mall on the way home.

By the time she got back to the house, Kellie had enough time to decide what to cook for dinner and tidy up a bit. Then, when Nathan arrived home, they talked about their day, ate together, and spent some time watching television or cuddling.

Occasionally they'd have dinner at Frankie and Julia's place. Kellie marveled at her friend's ability to balance everything—her workload at the school, her activities at the civic center, her daughter, and her marriage.

Or was it the other way around? As she watched, it became clear that Julia put her family well above her work. In fact, she spent more time talking about the people in her life than things.

Kellie took careful notes.

And she observed something else. In the past week, her friend's waistline had expanded a bit. Kellie watched in amazement. How wonderful and how frightening all at the same time. Julia's cheeks carried a rosy glow, and she beamed like a ray of sunshine when the ultrasound revealed the baby's sex: a boy. Their little family would be complete, at least for now.

Kellie couldn't imagine what it must feel like—or what she would look like if the same blessing were bestowed on her. She tried not to dwell on the pangs that gripped her heart each time she held a baby in her arms. Instead, she fought to ignore them. But a seed of hope had secretly begun to grow, one she'd have to share with Nathan soon or push to the back once and for all.

On Thursday afternoon, as she arrived back at the little wood-framed house, Kellie looked the place over with an inquisitive eye. In her somewhat overactive imagination, she could see it developing into a fine-looking home. Knock down a wall here; put up a wall there. Install new windows; replace the tub and tile. She could see it. And with the size of the property, they could expand when the time came.

She spent a moment reflecting. Something about this tiny place continued to captivate her. What was it? Perhaps it was the idea that a family had once lived here. Children had played in that yard—chasing one another and throwing balls. A wife and mother had cooked in the tiny dilapidated kitchen. A loving father had cradled his child in that living room.

Kellie thought about Mr. Henderson specifically now. She prayed for his health and his treatments. Soon she would see him again. But in the meantime, she wondered what his life had been like in earlier days as he resided in this very spot. Had he watched his children swing from the tire hanging in the front yard? Had he watched his daughters grow into young women, entering the front door with beaux on their arms? Had he cared for his ailing wife in the bedroom they had once shared? Had he watched the rooms grow empty as, one by one, his life became solitary?

A little shiver ran through Kellie, and she prayed for him again. How sad to live to such an old age and be alone. She thought about her own parents—how rich and full their lives were. What made the difference?

Relationships. Family. Friends. These things they all took for granted. And these were the very things she would sacrifice when she left Greenvine and moved back to Houston.

"Don't think like this," she scolded herself. "It's not going to make things easier. Pretty soon you'll be going back home."

Home.

She could scarcely remember what the condominium looked like. How could she ever feel at home there?

And yet she must prepare herself to return. Tonight, when Nathan arrived home, she would open the door to that conversation. She had put it off long enough. Now that her father's physical therapy sessions were dropping to twice a week, Kellie's list of excuses for staying in Greenvine had dwindled rapidly. She must come to terms with it.

But would the brokerage firm take her back full-time? She'd been assured it wouldn't be a problem, but situations weren't always what they presented themselves to be. Regardless, she must do her best to shift her thoughts in that direction. Already, Kellie had given the matter over to prayer. Now she must remove her hands from it altogether. Surely God was big enough to handle the pain this decision caused. Surely He could deal with her broken heart.

Nathan pulled his car out onto Highway 290 West in the direction of Greenvine.

He'd fought traffic for the past thirty minutes, but things seemed to be thinning out now. It was the first moment all day he could relax and spend a little time thinking and planning. And with so much on his mind, preparing for the future came naturally.

Joy filled Nathan, coupled with a sense of anticipation. The Lord was surely at work in his life. All the pieces to his puzzle seemed to be coming together. Things at work were finally slowing down; he and Kellie would soon be headed back home to Houston. And the best surprise of all—he had booked a trip to Europe for late summer. He could hardly wait to tell her. She would be thrilled.

Nathan let his mind dwell on the details for a moment. They would fly into Frankfurt and take that much-anticipated boat ride up the Rhine. They would tour ancient castles and find the perfect place to renew their wedding vows.

Just as Kellie had suggested months ago.

To cap things off they would drive into Austria and Switzerland to look at the mountains. Nathan practically beamed with excitement. Kellie would be so proud of him for taking matters into his own hands and planning this trip. Sure, it had put a damper on his savings plans for this summer, but who cared? Nathan felt like a man released from prison.

"Thank You, Lord—for freeing me from the idea that I have to store up treasures for myself. Kellie is my treasure. . . . *You* are my treasure."

These lessons had come from the past six weeks in Greenvine, to be sure. The Lord had been teaching, and Nathan had been on a learning curve. His well-laid plans for the future now paled in comparison to what he had in front of him at this very moment.

Kellie. Nathan smiled. The past few nights, in particular, she'd shown her love more than in years past. "Must be something in the water," he reasoned. Whatever it was, he hoped it lasted.

No. No complaints in that area. And he could find little to complain about in other areas either, now that he thought about it. Their life together seemed more simplistic, quieter, and more intimate. Even their conversations were better directed, more heartfelt.

And his sweet Kellie—always the last one to arrive at every function—seemed to be showing up every place on time these days. The frenzied look had left her eye. She was a well-rested version of her earlier self, and he liked what he saw.

Now, if only that bliss would follow them back to Houston, he would truly be a happy man.

Houston. Nathan thought about the city with a smile. Kellie would soon be back in the condominium, fussing over her latest purchase or complaining about the parking situation. She would buzz around the place, preparing for the workday ahead. She would settle back into the routine quickly. *I know her. She loves to work. She loves what she does.*

Moving back to Houston seemed logical. Still something bugged him, something he couldn't put his finger on. He tapped his finger on the steering wheel. *What is it, Lord? Why do I have this nagging thought something remains undone?*

Aha. There was still that one unanswered question about the financial trouble in Greenvine. But it wasn't his problem to solve. He didn't live in Greenvine. *Not really.* Of course it probably wouldn't hurt to make a few calls, check on a couple of things. And maybe, now that Kenton was home from the hospital, he might feel well enough to answer a few questions, offer some clarity.

These things often turned out to be a simple misunderstanding. Perhaps he could take a little time to help the fine people of Greenvine sort things out. After all, they had been mighty good to him.

Nathan reflected on his new friendships for the rest of the trip. He smiled as he thought about Hal pulling that catfish from the river. The loving older man had measured the monstrous fish, bragged about its size, then tossed it back into the water with a cockeyed grin. And that comment about the punch had thrown him for a loop. Who would've thought the fellow didn't care for his wife's prized punch recipe?

And Frankie—Nathan marveled at his new friend. Though worlds apart in so many ways, they shared a kindred spirit, of sorts. Nathan admired Frankie's work ethic—how he'd taken that little garage and turned it into a profitable shop. Still, in spite of his business, Frankie's world seemed fairly simplistic. In fact, he and Julia seemed to live the most carefree life Nathan had ever witnessed. A simple home, a precious little girl, and another child on the way.

Child on the way. There was something else he'd left undone. Nathan knew Kellie longed to talk about the possibility of children. Now that they were headed back home, he felt released to start thinking in that direction. *Perhaps in Europe.* He pondered the thought. What better idea than to conceive a child in some wonderful, foreign place? Yes, that trip would be the start of something new—in many ways.

As he pulled the car into the driveway, Nathan looked at the house. He had to smile, remembering what it had looked like that first day. Kellie had since painted the shutters and replaced the front door. Even the yard looked better, now that Jerry Chandler had invested some time and elbow grease. She had even talked the young man into putting in some new springtime flowers last Saturday.

Nathan rubbed at his chin, deep in thought. Yes, the home had surely made progress.

Then again, so had he.

Chapter 16

Kellie sighed as she looked around the cluttered kitchen. She stretched to grab something from the top cupboard but couldn't quite reach. "Nathan, can you come and help me with this?"

He entered the room, and she laughed at his appearance. His ragged T-shirt and faded jeans looked a little out of place on him. And the tennis shoes, once white, were now covered in splotches of paint. He even had paint in his hair.

"Wow. That's quite a fashion statement." She giggled.

He shrugged. "No point in getting dressed up just to work on the house. I want to get that back bedroom finished before Mr. Henderson gets here."

Kellie drew in a sigh. Yes, Chuck Henderson was due to arrive in a couple of hours. She wondered how he would take the news that they were moving out of the house earlier than planned. Perhaps he missed the place and was ready to return home. That would make things easier.

Then again—she looked around with a smile. This was hardly the same home he'd left behind two months ago. The space had been transformed. *Literally.* Would he feel like a stranger in his own house?

Nathan interrupted her thoughts. "Did you need me for something?"

"Oh." She started to attention. "Yes. I'm trying to get those plastic storage containers." She pointed to the top cupboard. "But I can't reach."

"Not a problem." He pulled the containers down, one by one. "What do you want me to do with them?"

She sighed again. "I guess just leave them on the counter for now. I'm almost out of boxes." She looked around the kitchen at the five large boxes she'd already taped up. "Which reminds me—would you mind carrying these out to the garage?"

"Sure." Nathan reached to pick up one. "But remember—you don't have to get all of this done today. We don't have to be home for another week or so. And we could always come back and get the rest later."

"I know. But my weekdays are already taken up with work and several last-minute things for my parents." She brushed aside the mist of tears that mounted her lashes. "And I want to spend every minute I can with them while we're still here."

"I understand." Nathan gave her a gentle peck on the cheek. "But Rome wasn't built in a day, and you sure don't have to get everything packed up right away."

He looked around the kitchen, lips pursed. "What are we going to do with all this stuff back in Houston anyway?"

"I'll leave a lot of it here," she explained. "I'm sure Mr. Henderson would like to have it. It's certainly newer—nicer—than what he had."

"True." Nathan headed out to the garage, and Kellie threw herself back into her work. After a few minutes, however, she had to take a break. For some reason the day's activities had worn her out.

Nathan finished with the rest of the boxes, then plopped down onto the sofa next to her. "Ready for some lunch? I'm starving."

"Mmm." Her stomach growled, but the idea of food didn't sound terribly appealing. Not yet anyway. "I guess. What did you have in mind?"

"Let's see what we have in here." He stepped into the kitchen, opened the refrigerator, and pulled out all sorts of things. "Turkey. Ham. Lettuce. Mayo. Two kinds of cheese—Monterey Jack and Swiss. And we still have plenty of that homemade oat bread Julia sent over."

"Mmm."

He stood in the doorway. "Want me to make a couple of sandwiches? You look beat."

"I am." She leaned back against the sofa. "I guess you were right. I've been trying to do too much too fast."

"Told you. But rest for now. I'm on it." He returned to the kitchen, and she could hear him slapping sandwiches together.

A few minutes later, he entered the living room with two plates in hand. "Sandwiches, chips, and a soda for my lady." He extended a plate in her direction, and she took it willingly.

"Thanks. I think I am hungry. Starving, actually." She took the plate and set it on the coffee table, smiling as she noticed he'd garnished the sandwich with a pickle.

"It's my cooking," he bragged. "You can't turn it down."

Kellie wasn't sure when she'd ever seen him look so proud. Or so adorable.

"Right, right." She smiled and bit into the sandwich. "Mmm. Not bad."

"Not bad?" His lips curled down. "Come on and admit it. That's the best sandwich you've ever eaten."

She put on her most serious face. "It's okay."

"Okay?"

Kellie chuckled. "It's mahvelous, dahling. Simply mahvelous!"

A look of relief swept across Nathan's face. "That's more like it."

They chatted as they ate. Kellie tried to force a smile as he talked about their plans for the future, especially the part about going to Europe.

Funny, though. Right now even Europe doesn't sound that appealing. Lord, help me get beyond what I'm thinking and feeling. I need to be with my husband—not just physically, but psychologically and emotionally.

They talked of Europe and other things as they finished their lunch. Afterward Kellie returned to her work in the kitchen. She smiled as she looked at the new appliances. Mr. Henderson would be tickled pink at the changes. She only hoped he didn't mind the house sitting empty until he could return. She and Nathan would continue to pay rent until the agreed time anyway.

At two thirty a knock on the door interrupted her work. She pulled the door open to find a much thinner Chuck Henderson standing on the other side. He still maintained the same mischievous eyes. A young woman stood next to him, her arm linked through his.

"Mr. Henderson." Kellie extended her hand. "Welcome home."

"Thank you."

He gave her hand a light shake, and she noticed he was clearly weaker than the last time she'd seen him.

"How have you been?" She asked the question tentatively.

He flashed a cockeyed grin, and a glimpse of his former personality emerged. "Fitter'n a fiddle." He turned his attention to the nice-looking young woman who stood at his side. "This is my daughter, Linda."

Kellie extended her hand toward the young woman, who looked to be not much older than she was. "It's so nice to meet you. Thanks for coming out on such short notice. Please have a seat." She gestured toward the sofa.

Linda nodded. "Look what they've done with the place, Daddy," she said with an admiring smile. "It's beautiful. It hardly looks like the little house I grew up in." She smiled as she looked at Kellie. "Not that that's a bad thing. It looks great."

"Thank you. I'll get my husband, and we'll be right with you." Kellie headed down the hallway to fetch Nathan.

As he entered the living room, Nathan extended his hand. "Good to see you again, Mr. Henderson."

"None of this Mr. Henderson stuff," the older man said with the wave of his hand. "Call me Chuck."

"Chuck." Nathan nodded and sat on the couch next to Kellie. She gestured for Chuck and his daughter to sit across from them.

"Nice to see you, too. I. . ." Chuck hesitated and looked at his daughter, who gave him a reassuring nod. "I've been meaning to get by to talk to the two of you anyway."

Ah. He's wanting to come home sooner than expected. That will make things so much easier.

"You have?" Nathan asked.

Mr. Henderson looked down at his hands. "I have. And now that I'm here, I feel more confident than ever." He gazed around the room. "You have done wonders with the place, just like Linda said."

"Thank you." Kellie and Nathan spoke in unison.

"Not exactly my taste," the older man acknowledged, "but still it's nice."

Kellie felt her cheeks flush. "Well, we can always recarpet if you like."

"No, no." His eyebrows furrowed a bit. "Don't want you to do that. You've gone to a lot of trouble already."

"Well, it's your home. We want you to—"

"It's like this," Mr. Henderson interrupted. "I've decided not to come back."

"What?" Nathan's face paled, and Kellie was afraid for a moment he might overreact.

An embarrassed grin crossed the older man's face. "I never thought I'd live to see the day, but it turns out I like big-city life."

His daughter smiled. "As if anyone could call Brenham a big city." She rested her hand across her father's arm. "But, to be honest, we love having Daddy with us. Our boys adore him, and our house is so big. We have plenty of room."

"They've got cable television." Mr. Henderson grinned. "Two hundred channels." He nodded matter-of-factly, as if that settled the deal.

"So"—Kellie glanced at Nathan for help—"so what were you thinking? You're going to sell the house?"

"That's right." The older man's gaze shifted down to his hands. "Look—I know it's not worth much. It's not big-city living, for sure. But it's very homey, and it sure looks like you two have taken a liking to it." He gestured with his hand. "You've pert near turned it into a palace. And besides"—he looked at his daughter again—"I could sure use the money. Medicare covers most of my treatments, but I don't have any real insurance to speak of."

Kellie felt a lump in her throat. How could they tell him they planned to move out next week? "Oh, Mr. Henderson."

"Daddy tends to worry too much." Linda patted her father's hand. "I don't think there's much to be concerned about financially, but it would ease his mind a great deal if he could sell the house. That would be one less thing for him to think about."

Nathan cleared his throat and looked in Kellie's direction. She wondered how he would handle this, what he would say. His cheeks flushed red, a sure sign thoughts were stirring. But what sort of thoughts?

"Would you excuse us a moment?" Nathan asked.

He took Kellie by the hand, and they made their way down the hall toward the master bedroom. They entered and sat on the bed. Neither of them said a word. Finally Kellie broke the silence.

"Oh, Nathan." She buried her face in her hands. "What are we going to do?" She lifted her face to gaze into his eyes.

He drew in a deep breath, forehead wrinkled. "Well, I have an idea. I don't know how you'll feel about it, but here goes."

As he laid out his plan, Kellie's mind eased at once. It was the only thing that made sense. Yes, it would require great sacrifice on their part, to be sure, but they had grown accustomed to sacrifice over the past several months.

Yes, she reasoned. *This could work.*

With her husband's hand tightly clutched in her own, Kellie traipsed back up the hallway to give Mr. Henderson the news.

Nathan returned to Houston on Monday morning, his head full of ideas. He stopped by the condo on his way into the office to check the mail. He smiled as he looked around the place. *Quite a contrast to our current living conditions.* He and Kellie had nearly grown used to living with middle-of-the-road furnishings and appliances. But not for long.

Their time in Greenvine was rapidly drawing to a close. Boxes were packed and cupboards nearly bare. Soon—in less than a week—they would be here again. Where they belonged. It would require at least one truckload of boxes, but they'd see to that this coming Saturday. Once they got settled in, he and Kellie would travel back and forth to Greenvine on the weekends as they had planned from the beginning.

Not that he'd minded the past few weeks. Truth be told, Nathan had grown to love the people of Greenvine. And the changes he and Kellie had faced over the past seven weeks had made him a better man.

Nathan drew in a satisfied breath and thought about how he'd drawn closer to God during this season. And the Lord responded by speaking, giving direction. Nathan heard His voice clearly these days, with much more clarity than in years past.

His decision regarding the house in Greenvine had been God-inspired, to be sure. They would buy the property from Mr. Henderson and rent it out. With a little TLC, the home would make for a great investment.

Of course he must take care of the technicalities. A Realtor would have to be hired, and the repairs would need to take place right away for the house to pass inspection. But Nathan didn't mind, especially since he wouldn't be the one doing the work. He couldn't—not with so much going on already.

"Nothing like taking a little more on your plate when it's already full." Nathan smiled. "But we're getting pretty good at balancing a lot at once."

He pulled his car into the parking garage at the accounting firm and shut it down. For a moment he leaned his head back against the headrest and prayed. All the pieces to his puzzle seemed to be coming together. *Well, almost all.*

Why couldn't he get Greenvine's financial problems off his mind?

He knew why. After several phone calls last Friday, the truth was clear. The city had been taken for a ride and had lost a small fortune—almost enough to sink them if someone didn't intervene—and quickly.

Nathan's concern for his father-in-law deepened with each revelation. Kenton had been taken advantage of, to be sure. He had acted out of honesty and sincerity and clearly felt awful about the whole thing. No one held him to blame. That's how the people of Greenvine were. They cared far too much about him to point any fingers. And right now his health required that he remain positive, upbeat.

Nathan sighed as he contemplated the most worrisome thing. His father-in-law's ability to reason clearly had not returned—at least not in full. Perhaps in time. But for now he couldn't handle the situation. He could barely handle the small things, like dressing himself and fixing a bowl of cereal each morning. How could he be called upon to save the city from financial ruin?

Lord, I don't understand. It's too much for one man to handle.

"He needs help solving this." Nathan pursed his lips. "But what can I do? It's too late to recoup their money."

The best chance the city of Greenvine stood right now was a concise, practical investment plan for the future. They'd probably need to raise taxes a little to accomplish this and would need someone they could trust to advise them regarding future investments. Someone with a head for financial matters. And someone who genuinely cared about the townspeople—cared about more than their financial interests. Someone who cared about them as people, not as taxpayers.

Nathan's thoughts flashed back to the night he'd been honored as Man of the Year. What was it Mr. Abernathy had said of him? *"Please welcome Nathan Fisher—a man with a head for numbers and a heart for the people. He's one of the hardest workers I've ever meet, and he's our Man of the Year at Siefert and Collins."*

Nathan trembled as the words rolled through his memory. "Oh, Lord, surely You're not asking me to do this thing." *Surely not.*

He reached for his briefcase and sprinted from his car, forcing the ludicrous idea from his mind.

Chapter 17

Kellie paced around the house with a string of nonsensical prayers flowing. *Lord, I don't understand. What are You up to? Oh, Lord, I'm going to need Your help.*

This changes everything.

She stared down at the white plastic stick in her hand for the umpteenth time. *Yep. Positive.* Just like the last million times she'd looked at it.

"Pregnant." She spoke to the empty room. But how? They had been so careful. If truth stared her in the face, then the Lord certainly had a sense of humor.

And interesting timing. Kellie plopped down onto the sofa, deep in thought. How in the world could she accomplish working full-time and raising a baby? And where would she raise it? They had no room in their tiny condo for a child. One bedroom. One medium-sized, not-ready-for-anyone-else bedroom.

And Nathan. What would he think? Would he assume she had planned this to trap him?

"Oh, Lord. You've got to help me. I don't know how to tell him."

Then again she couldn't go without telling him for long. Her body had begun to betray her. What had started out as mere queasiness a week ago had developed into full-blown sessions of toilet-hugging. Every morning for the past three days, she'd spent more time in the bathroom than out. She was thankful Nathan had already left for work before the episodes began.

Clueless. He's clueless.

The phone rang, and Kellie nearly jumped out of her skin. She glanced at the caller ID. *Nathan.*

She tried to sound as normal as possible as she answered. "Hello?"

"Hey, babe," his cheery voice greeted her. "I just got to the office. Thought I'd call and check on you."

"Oh?"

"You were sleeping like a rock when I left." He sniggered. "I haven't heard snoring like that in a while."

She groaned. *I'm snoring for two now.* "I'm fine. I'm about to start packing up the bedroom. And I have a couple of calls to make. Bernie wants me to come in Monday morning. I hope I'm up to it by then. This weekend is going to be crazy." *Maybe crazier than we thought.*

"I know. That's part of the reason I'm calling. I rented a small moving truck.

I'll pick it up in Brenham on Friday night. I don't think we'll need anything more than that. And Frankie said he'll come by Saturday morning to help load up. That means I only have to find someone to help once we get back to the condo."

"Right. Well, I appreciate him, for sure." *I can't do any heavy lifting now.*

Kellie listened as Nathan carried on about how they would transport the two cars back and forth but didn't take much in. Instead, her mind wandered to the obvious. She put her hand on her stomach and waited for something to happen.

Nothing.

"Kellie? You there?"

She jolted back to reality as she heard Nathan's voice. "Oh yeah. I'm sorry. I'm distracted today. Too much on my mind."

"That will end soon." His voice resonated with calm, practical assurance. "Before you know it, we'll be back home and everything will be back to normal."

"Yeah." She glanced down at the white stick. *Still positive.* "Back to normal."

"Well, almost normal anyway." He paused for a moment, and she felt a shift in the conversation. "Things at work are—strange. That's the only way I can describe it. Everything is so hush-hush around here today. I don't know what's up, but I get the feeling something's about to blow."

"Yikes. No clues?"

"No," he said. "But I'm trying not to read too much into it. In fact, I've been a little distracted myself. To be honest, there's something I can't stop thinking about. Something completely unrelated to the firm."

As he paused, Kellie felt the queasiness return. She drew in a deep breath and waited for it to pass. "W–what do you mean?"

"I, uh, I was trying to figure out how to go about offering my help to your dad. I can't get Greenvine's financial issues off my mind."

"Ah. I see." She ignored the tingling in her cheeks as she contemplated his words. Had the Lord convinced him of this? Were they supposed to be getting involved? "I've spent a lot of time praying and thinking about it myself," Kellie acknowledged. "And I think we could help them. But it would take time. Effort."

"Right." He sighed. "That's the hard part. I don't have a lot of time right now. And my efforts seem to be so divided already." He sighed. "And once we get back home. . ." His voice trailed off. "I don't know, Kell. It just seems impossible. But if it's impossible, then why won't the Lord leave me alone? Why does He keep dropping this into my heart, into my spirit?"

Fresh feelings of nausea rose and then settled down almost as quickly. Kellie was better able to focus on the conversation, to take in the full meaning of his words. "I can't answer that, babe," she said. "But if God is speaking, all I can say is, we'd better be listening."

A dead silence permeated the air for a moment. When Nathan finally responded, his words startled her. "I don't think I like what I'm hearing. Is that awful?"

Kellie forced back a smile. If he thought his news complicated things, wait until he heard what she had to say.

Another call interrupted them, and Nathan had to leave abruptly. With the telephone still in her hand, Kellie looked heavenward. "Lord, I'm not sure what You're up to." She glanced at the house full of boxes. "But I hope You'll show me before I pack another thing."

Nathan pulled his car into the condo's parking garage. *Great.* Someone had taken his spot. Again. With frustration mounting, he drove up to the top floor and parked on the roof. He needed time to think anyway.

He shut off the car and grabbed his laptop. With a determined stride, he headed for the elevator. On the way there, his thoughts jumped from one thing to another. *The office.* He contemplated today's revelations. Things at Siefert and Collins were definitely in a state of transition. Today, less than an hour ago, he'd been offered a new position at the firm.

Partner.

Finally Nathan had been offered the coveted position he'd prayed for.

"Why don't I feel right about this? What's wrong with me? I should be calling Kellie. I should be celebrating."

A *ding* brought him back to his senses. He stepped into the elevator and punched the number seven. Surely a good night's sleep would put everything in perspective. He leaned back against the elevator wall and closed his eyes.

By the time the elevator arrived at his floor, Nathan resolved himself to the inevitable. He must pick up the phone and let Kellie know, even if she recognized the discomfort in his voice. He must keep this ball rolling. It was too late to stop it now.

He trudged along the hallway until he reached his condominium. The maintenance man greeted him outside the door.

"Good evening, Mr. Fisher."

Nathan eyed him suspiciously. "Bobby. Is everything okay?"

"Well. . ."

"It's okay. Just tell me, whatever it is."

Bobby tucked a flashlight into his tool bag. "The AC unit froze up this morning. We've had to shut everything down in order to thaw it out. We'll probably have everything up and running by tomorrow."

"Right. Tomorrow."

Nathan pulled at his collar as he braved the heat inside the condo. He checked the thermostat. Eighty-two degrees. "It's not even summer yet. Why is it so ridiculously hot?"

Nathan pulled off his shirt and slacks and slipped into a T-shirt and shorts. Then he scrounged around in the kitchen, looking for something to eat. They would have to do some heavy-duty grocery shopping once they moved back for good. For now he decided on a can of soup and some stale crackers.

He settled onto the sofa with a bowl in hand. As he ate, Nathan reached for the remote control. He listened to the evening news in shocked silence. Were the stories always this negative, or was his hometown just suffering a particularly bad day?

He switched the channel, choosing an old movie. Not five minutes into it, he muted the television and picked up the telephone to call Kellie. He needed to hear her voice and needed to tell her about his promotion. She would cheer him up. She would bring everything into balance.

Kellie answered with an unusually weary sound to her voice. She went on to assure him everything was fine, but the conversation left Nathan feeling uneasy. As he told her about the partnership, he expected to hear rejoicing on the other end of the phone. For some reason her voice seemed to choke up.

She's just happy for me.

She ended the call rather abruptly—something about needing to turn off the bathwater. Nathan tried to take it in stride but felt in his spirit something was wrong.

He dropped into bed a little before nine, exhausted and frustrated. His thoughts shifted for hours between the job, the sale of the house, and Greenvine's financial problems. Sleeping was out of the question, especially with the heat presenting such an issue.

At two fifteen he arose from the bed and walked out onto the balcony. He stood in silence for a moment as he rubbed at his aching brow. The hum of traffic from the street below provided the perfect backdrop. Nathan sank into the deck chair and leaned back with his eyes closed. He couldn't possibly make it through this night without focusing.

Not on himself or his problems, but on the Lord.

Chapter 18

Nathan picked up a small moving van in Brenham on Friday night. With Kellie following along behind him in her car, he traveled the now-familiar road toward Greenvine. On the way there, his thoughts tumbled round in his head. He contemplated not the move but the meeting he'd just called at the civic center.

He glanced at his watch. 6:48. In twelve minutes city leaders, his father-in-law included, would converge upon the tiny civic center for an informative gathering Nathan had initiated after a near-sleepless night. Once there, he would lay out the financial plan that hadn't given him a moment's rest.

A plan to save the city of Greenvine.

Nathan turned off onto the country road that led to the center of town. The moving van jolted up and down with each pothole. His nerves, once jumbled and on edge, settled down, in spite of the bumpy road. Now that a plan had formed, his body seemed more relaxed.

He glanced in the side mirror to catch a glimpse of Kellie's vehicle. Her sports car seemed tiny in comparison to this monstrous van. But still she looked regal, sitting behind the wheel.

He loved to see her like that, in a seat of honor. She deserved it. No one worked harder than Kellie or had loftier plans. She was truly a queen—and not just the queen of quick, as she called herself. She sat like royalty upon his heart.

He squinted against the setting sun to see her face more clearly. Immediately concern registered. Were those tears? He rolled down the window and twisted the mirror a bit, trying to get a better look. Why would she be crying?

His heart twisted as the truth prevailed. She was sad about leaving Greenvine. He knew that. He'd always known this transition back to Houston would be tough on her, but—*tears?* Kellie wasn't a crier, by any stretch.

He looked in the mirror again—and nearly drove the vehicle off the road in the process. "Stay focused, man." He gripped the steering wheel, unable to remember where he was headed. Kellie's emotions now consumed his thoughts.

She was clearly keeping her tears hidden from him. She was going along with his plans and not saying a word. *But why?* Was she scared to tell him how she felt?

Nathan drew in a deep breath as he turned down the road toward the civic center. As he bounced up and down in the cab of the moving van, reality hit. He'd made so many decisions, but had he somehow pressed the voice of the Lord to the background and shifted onto a road of his own? Had he left Kellie out? His thoughts drifted back to that day when he'd accused her of the same thing. She'd left him out of the equation initially, but who was to blame now?

He looked in the mirror again and caught a glimpse of Kellie drying her eyes with rushed fingertips. *She doesn't want me to know she's unhappy.*

His words with the Almighty now flowed from a place of truth—of open honesty.

"Lord, show me Your will. I've made so many plans. Have I asked You to come on board after the fact? If Your plans are different from mine—"

His heart quickened. If the Lord's plans were different, could he live with that? Common sense kicked in. Of course the Lord wanted them in the city. He'd given them a clear-cut plan for their future.

Future.

The word hit hard as he glanced in the mirror once again. The future was—tomorrow. It wasn't the here and now. And what good was a happy tomorrow if you had a miserable today?

The revelation slammed against his seared conscience. He'd been living for the future and spending far too much time worrying about the outcome of life's situations.

The Lord, it turned out, was apparently more interested in the journey.

Kellie took a seat near the front of the room. She reached over to grip her daddy's hand and gave it a tight squeeze. "How are you feeling?" she whispered.

"Better." He gave her a wink, and her heart almost sang.

Almost. Another thought immediately put a damper on things. *We're leaving. Tomorrow. This is my last night with my family, for a while anyway.*

Kellie sat with her father's hand in her own as Nathan stood before the people. The crowd grew quiet as he began to speak. She listened with great joy as he outlined a detailed plan to get the city back on its feet. She wondered, though, how the citizens of Greenvine would take the news that they must begin again.

Begin again.

Hmm. She tried to still her trembling hands by placing them across her belly. Inside, life was beginning. A piece of her. A piece of Nathan. She would tell him soon. This news couldn't wait much longer.

As Nathan wrapped up his speech, the place came alive. One by one, the good folks of Greenvine poured out their questions, sought his counsel. He responded to each one thoughtfully and clearly with their best interests in mind. Kellie's heart swelled with pride as he took the time to think through his answers and voice them in love.

"That's quite a guy you've got there." Her father whispered the words into her ear, and she nodded with a lump in her throat.

"I know."

As the meeting drew to a close, Kellie joined the other women in the kitchen, preparing snacks for the crowd. They set out platters of fresh-cut vegetables and tempting fruit, and she entered into conversation with several of the ladies as they worked alongside one another.

"Nathan is so great," Julia observed. "I mean"—she looked at him admiringly—"I've always known he was a great accountant. I guess I didn't realize he was so good at the people part. He's a good communicator, and he seems to care about us."

"He does." Kellie nodded. "I know because he's lost a lot of sleep over this." She didn't add that he'd called her three times in the night to ask her opinion on his ideas, particularly those related to investments. He cared about her expertise, as well, and had wanted to get her take on his plan. And she was happy to link arms with him on this project. In fact, she didn't know when she'd ever felt so good about anything.

Julia shrugged. "I guess it's pretty rare to find someone with a head for numbers and—"

Kellie finished for her with words that seemed to leap from her throat. "A heart for the people."

Why does that sound so familiar? Ah yes. They were Mr. Abernathy's words as he'd introduced Nathan a few short months ago.

She looked across the room at Nathan, who spoke with his hands to a group of men. They hung on his every word, nodding and patting him on the back. Nathan was brilliant, to be sure. But his love for people far exceeded any academic gifting. Now, with the people behind him, he seemed to spring from his shell, energized by their enthusiasm.

Kellie turned back to her mother and Julia to wrap up her thoughts on the matter. "He wants to do what he can to make things better for you guys."

Her mother leaned over to give her a peck on the cheek. "He let you spend these last few weeks with us," she whispered. "That's definitely made things better for all of us. I don't know what I would've done without you."

Kellie reached up to give her mother a warm hug. "I'm going to miss you. But I need to be with Nathan, and he wants to be"—her voice broke—"back in Houston." She brushed at damp eyelashes.

"We wouldn't have it any other way, hon. You need to be together."

Kellie looked to the front of the room, where Nathan and her father stood in concentrated dialogue. The spark in her husband's eye intrigued her. She hadn't seen this kind of enthusiasm in him for a long time. In fact, she wasn't sure she'd ever seen him this excited, hopeful. She liked the new Nathan—and hoped it translated over into their new life in Houston.

New life.

How could she possibly begin a new life when she still harbored old feelings? *Lord, if You're wanting to renew my heart, to clean out the fear and anxiety, then do it. Have Your way, Father. I want to be in the center of Your will—no place else. And if that means Houston—then I'm fine with that.*

Kellie settled the issue once and for all in her heart. She would, as the scripture so aptly said, learn to be content in whatever state she found herself—genuinely, peacefully content.

She crossed the room to where Nathan now stood alone. She slipped her arm in his and gave him an adoring gaze.

He glanced down with a look of concern. "Are you okay?"

"Sure." She smiled up at him. "Why?"

"Oh, nothing." He brushed a stray hair out of her eye. "I just want you to be happy."

Kellie's heart twisted. "I—I am happy, honey."

"Really?" His brow furrowed, and she wondered if he'd been listening to her earlier thoughts.

Kellie's gaze shifted to the ground, and she fought back the tears. "I–I've loved every minute of being here," she said finally. "But I know we have to be where God wants us to be. And wherever that is, I'm okay."

He nodded but said nothing.

"I figure," Kellie continued with enthusiasm mounting, "that as long as we're in the center of God's will, we're in the safest place on earth, regardless of where we live. Right?"

He nodded again but said nothing.

"Where we are physically isn't half as important as where we are with Him." Kellie beamed now. "So wherever He calls us to go—I'm going. As long as you're going, too."

Nathan drew in a deep breath and pulled her close. He planted kisses in her hair and then whispered, "You're the smartest woman I know."

Kellie giggled. "Then you don't know many women—that's all I've got to say."

Chapter 19

Nathan awoke early on Saturday morning. He lay silent in the bed for a while, listening to Kellie breathe. For some time, he drank in the stillness of the moment.

Nothing could have prepared him for her sudden bolt from the bed. He watched in amazement as she sprinted toward the bathroom, hand over her mouth.

"What's wrong?" He followed her to the bathroom door, but she closed it in his face.

Kellie never answered, but he could hear the noise from the other side.

"You're sick?"

Still no answer. When she finally emerged from the room, her face was pale and drawn.

"Kellie?" He followed her to the bathroom sink, where she reached for a toothbrush.

She checked her appearance in the mirror. "Ugh. I look as bad as I feel." She slathered toothpaste on the brush and stuck it in her mouth.

"I'm sorry you're sick." Nathan reached to pull her hair out of her eyes as she brushed her teeth. "Do you think it's something you ate?"

She shook her head but never looked up.

"Some kind of stomach bug?"

She didn't answer. Instead, she continued to brush her teeth in silence. When she finished, she finally looked him in the eye. "I feel a lot better now. I'm sure I'll be fine."

"Still." He ran his hand along her cheek. "I want you to take it easy today. We've got lots of people coming to help. No need in you doing too much."

"I'll take it easy," she assured him. "But don't worry. I'm sure I'll be fine."

He nodded, then headed off to the shower. As the hot water beat down on his neck, Nathan planned for the day ahead. Frankie would arrive at nine. With his help they would load up the boxes and clothes. After that he and Kellie would hit the road for home. They would return to Greenvine next weekend to tie up loose ends and prepare the house for inspection.

Nathan exited the shower, his mind in a whirl. He tried not to let his thoughts slow down much. If they did. . .

No, he wouldn't stop to think. He must plow forward with the task at hand.

He would have plenty of time to think later.

Once dressed, Nathan entered the bedroom. Surprise filled him as he looked at the bed where Kellie lay curled up, still in her nightgown.

"Not feeling any better?" he asked.

She sat up with a start. "Oh." She gave him a quizzical look. "I'm just—"

"It's okay, honey." He walked over and kissed her lightly. "I told you to take it easy."

He sat on the edge of the bed and ran his fingers through her hair. She pushed his hand away and rolled over.

"Are you mad at me?" Nathan asked.

She shook her head.

He wasn't convinced. "Do you want to talk about it?"

No response.

Nathan stood up and walked to his chest of drawers to pull out jeans and a T-shirt. How could he go about reading her mind? On the other hand, maybe she didn't want him to. Maybe she needed space.

He dressed quickly and headed to the kitchen to make some coffee. Moments later he sat at the table with a cup in his hand. A knock on the door roused him from his quiet thoughts. Nathan glanced at his watch. *8:42. Frankie's early.*

He trudged to the door and opened it, startled to find his in-laws on the other side.

"Well, good morning." He greeted them with a hug.

"Can we come in?" Kenton asked.

"Of course." Nathan ushered them into the kitchen and offered them a cup of coffee.

They sat together at the table, and he quickly explained Kellie's absence.

"Should I go and check on her?" Norah asked.

He nodded, and his mother-in-law slipped off into the other room.

Kenton sat in silence for a moment, then finally looked Nathan in the eye. "Norah was doing me a favor by leaving," he explained with a twinkle in his eye. "She knows I came to speak with you. Guess she thought I needed some privacy."

"Privacy? What's up?" Nathan took a sip of coffee, then leaned back in his chair.

Kenton looked at him intently. "Nathan, I've got a problem."

Nathan laid a hand on his father-in-law's arm. "What do you mean?"

"I mean"—Kenton's gaze shifted down—"I'm not getting any younger. And even though I'm getting around better, I'm still—still—" He paused, and his eyes filled with tears. "This is what I'm trying to say, Nathan. I don't believe I can return to my job. I've overstayed my welcome as it is."

"Sir?"

"The fine people of Greenvine have entrusted me with the position of city comptroller for years." Kenton spoke slowly, carefully. "But I'd be looking at retirement in another year or two anyway." He looked up, his eyes brimming over.

Nathan tried to swallow the growing lump in his throat. "What are you saying, Kenton?"

"I'm saying"—the older man stared directly into his eyes—"that I'm beyond the point where I can do this city any good. But you're not."

"Excuse me?"

"Nathan, you're a wonderful young man. You've been the answer to my daughter's prayers—and, in so many ways, an answer to our prayers. We never had the privilege of having a son, but the Lord has sent a fine one our way."

"Th–thank you, sir."

"God has blessed us in so many ways of late; I don't have any business asking for more." Kenton sighed. "But I feel it would be wrong of me not to mention what's been on my heart for the past several days, especially after the people took so well to your plan last night." He looked up, determination in his eyes. "I'll cut to the chase and save you any questions. Elections are just around the corner, and I think you'd make a fine city comptroller for the people of Greenvine."

Nathan set down the coffee cup with a thud. Surely the older man jested. City comptroller? To stay would require putting an end to everything he and Kellie had hoped and prayed for.

"I–I'm not sure what to say." He didn't dare look his father-in-law in the eye, not when his eyes would give away his feelings.

Kenton patted him on the back. "No need to say anything—at least not yet. Just promise me you'll pray about it."

Nathan nodded in numbed silence. *Pray about it?* A knock on the door brought him back to his senses. He glanced at his watch. 9:02. "That's Frankie."

"I'll get myself another cup of coffee." Kenton stood and headed toward the coffeemaker while Nathan plodded to the front door.

"Mornin', neighbor!" Frankie greeted him with a broad smile.

Nathan extended his hand. "Good morning to you, too. Thanks for coming to help."

"No problem." Frankie looked back toward the car. "I've enlisted the troops. Hope it's okay that we brought Madison along." He gestured toward Julia, who lifted Madison from the car seat.

"Of course." Nathan watched with a grin as the little girl squirmed in her mother's arms. Within seconds they joined him at the door.

"Where's Kellie?" Julia asked.

"In the bedroom with her mom." Nathan shrugged. "She's sick."

"No way." Julia trudged off in the direction of the bedroom, and Frankie and Nathan joined Kenton in the kitchen for a cup of coffee. They chatted about the weather, the construction on Highway 290—everything but the move. Finally, when he could sit still no longer, Nathan stood. The time had come.

They'd better get packing.

⌒

Kellie spent a few minutes chatting with her mother and Julia before they stepped into the kitchen for a cup of coffee. She slipped out of her nightgown and robe and into some clothes before heading out to join them. She still battled queasiness but did her best to force it aside. No point in raising suspicions. Not yet anyway. She padded into the kitchen, which was filled with boxes.

"Where are the guys?" She tried to act casual as she reached for a coffee cup from the windowsill.

Her mother gestured out the front window. "They've already started loading up."

"Ah." She looked out of the window in time to see Nathan hoisting a box into the back of the moving truck. Her heart twisted a bit, but she pushed the feelings down.

"I should finish packing up these last few dishes." She opened a cupboard and pointed to a handful of things she'd deliberately held back till now.

"Let me help." Her mother stood right away. "I'm so sorry you're not feeling well this morning."

Kellie shrugged, hoping to still her mother's fears. "I'll be fine." She smiled warmly and changed the subject by turning to face Julia. "So when are you and Frankie coming to town to see us?"

"When do you want us?"

"As soon as you can get there." Kellie reached to grab her friend's hand and fought to keep the tears from rising.

"I'm not much of a city girl," Julia said with a shrug. "But for you, I'll give it a try."

They dove back into their work, chatting like schoolgirls. An hour or so later, a handful of people from the church showed up with food in their hands. They set up card tables on the lawn, then stayed to join in the fun. Shortly thereafter, others arrived with everything from sodas to homemade cookies. They added their food to the existing bounty, and the tiny tables overflowed.

By the time the guys had the truck loaded, lunchtime had arrived. Kellie joined the others on the lawn as they shared sandwiches, conversation, and laughter. It seemed no time at all had passed when Kellie looked at her watch and gasped. 1:25. They had planned to leave before noon.

She left the roar of the crowd for a moment to take one final look at the house. She didn't realize Nathan had joined her until she felt his arms slip around her waist from behind.

"We'll be back next weekend to finish up." He spoke quietly, but she detected an edge to his voice, something she couldn't define.

She nodded and turned to face him. "I know." She leaned her head against his shoulder and tried to relax.

"Kellie?"

She looked into his eyes. For some reason they were etched with concern.

"What, babe?"

He sighed deeply. "There's something I need to tell you before we go."

"Really?" She drew in a sigh of her own. "Because there's something I need to tell you, too."

Chapter 20

All morning long, Nathan had argued with himself, but the truth now raised its head, and he could not press it down any longer. What would be the point, when the voice of the Lord roared so loudly in his ears? Nathan plunged into the conversation with Kellie, spilling everything at once.

He told her about the proposition to run for city comptroller. He shared his feelings of ambivalence toward the partnership he'd been offered back in Houston. He spoke honestly about his confusion over everything.

Kellie said nothing as the words tumbled out of his mouth. He couldn't help but notice the tears in her eyes. At one point he grabbed her hand.

"I feel terrible about the fact that I haven't asked you what you wanted till now." He spoke passionately. "But I've assumed all along I knew what the Lord wanted."

"You've never been the type to assume," she assured him. "I think you've always acted out of practicality, common sense."

"I know, but—" He glanced at the moving truck. Frankie and Julia stood beside it, deeply engaged in conversation with Kenton and Norah. "Look at them." He gestured. "Some people would say they don't have it as good as we do."

Kellie's brow wrinkled as she responded. "Financially, you mean?"

Nathan shook his head. "Not just that. We have our education. We also have amazing jobs with plenty of advancement opportunities. We have a wonderful home in a great city and plenty of money in the bank so we don't have to live paycheck to paycheck."

"What are you saying, Nathan?" Kellie's eyes remained moist.

"I'm saying that maybe, just maybe, I've placed my security in the wrong things. Maybe the Lord wants to free us up—to give us reason to live in faith." His thoughts flowed from the tip of his tongue without constraint. "Maybe He wants us to let go of some of our material possessions and live a simpler life. That's what I'm saying."

Even as the words were spoken, Nathan felt as if a huge weight had been lifted from his shoulders. All of his adult life he'd had to prove himself. Jockeying for a better position at the firm, investing in a better place to live, setting aside money into bigger, better types of accounts.

And for what?

He bit his lip and waited for Kellie's response. He knew she had grown accustomed to nice things—a modern home and frequent gifts. He also knew she'd grown to appreciate and understand their fast-paced lifestyle with its perks. And yet she seemed to thrive here, in Greenvine.

Which would she choose, if given the opportunity?

Kellie choked back tears and fought for words. For days she had prayed Nathan would come to this decision, but now that the Lord had answered her prayers, she could hardly believe the words coming from her husband's lips or the passion that seemed to drive them.

She wrapped her arms around his neck and leaned into his chest. "N–Nathan."

"I can't tell if you're happy or sad." He pulled back to look into her eyes.

She shook her head. "I'm happy, baby. You don't know how happy."

A look of relief flooded his face. "Why didn't you say something before now?" he asked. "You let me go on and on, setting my sights on life in the city. I must've sounded like an idiot."

"No," she whispered, "I told you last night—I'd follow you to the ends of the earth. If you'd said we needed to move to Alaska, I would have gone." She gave him a shy smile. "At least I'd like to *think* I would have. But the truth of the matter is, my heart is here." She gestured to the worn-down little house. "I love this place. I know it doesn't make much sense, but I do. And I can see us here, years from now, with children of our own."

"Really?" He looked at her with some degree of curiosity. "You wouldn't miss living in a nicer place?"

"Nathan, look around you." She gestured to the property, their friends, her parents. "This *is* a nicer place. And I don't need a fast-paced life or lots of money to enjoy myself. I've had the time of my life these last few months. Less is more, you know?"

He nodded as his gaze traveled from person to person. "Yes." He sighed. "I'm just relieved to hear you say it out loud. I've been trying not to let myself get caught up in the lifestyle these people enjoy, but I want to. I want what they have."

She put her hand to her stomach and prepared to speak the words she'd been holding back for days. "Since you've said that, there's something I need to tell you." She took a deep breath and plowed ahead. "Nathan, you're going to have to build on an extra room." She swallowed hard before adding, "A nursery."

"W–what? W–when?"

"In about seven and a half months." Kellie couldn't hold back the grin as his eyes widened. "I've known for a while now."

"You're kidding." He shook his head and stared at her as if they were strangers. Suddenly light dawned in his eyes. "That's why you were so sick this morning."

Kellie nodded but said nothing.

"Why didn't you tell me? I can't believe you didn't say anything."

She shrugged. "I knew your decision to stay or to go would be swayed by knowing. I needed you to make a decision based on your heart, not on our circumstances."

He continued to shake his head, clearly unable to formulate words. "I don't believe it." The edges of his lips curled up. "I'm going to be a dad." Fear registered. "Not that I have any clue how to do that."

"You'll learn." Kellie gestured in Frankie's direction. "And he'll help you, I'm sure. He's an awesome father."

"He is." Nathan looked at her with eyes filled with love. "And you're going to be the best mother in the world."

Kellie smiled. "If I'm half as good as Julia, I'll be doing well. It's going to be quite a change from what I'm used to, but I can't wait." Her heart swelled with joy, and she and Nathan crossed the yard, hand in hand.

Nathan shook his head, overcome by Kellie's revelation. No wonder she'd acted so emotional these past few days. No wonder she didn't want to settle back into her old life at the condo. Her perceptions had changed because her situation had changed.

Kellie interrupted his thoughts with her next question. "Speaking of not waiting—what should we do with the condo?"

He shrugged. "Sell it? Rent it out? Doesn't matter. It's not as if we'll be needing it anymore."

She nodded. "If we sold it, we could use the money to fix up this house." They turned to face the little wood-framed home together, hand in hand.

"Good point." He nodded in agreement.

"We've spent a lot of time talking about the future," Kellie continued. "But the future is here. Now. This is what we've talked and prayed about. It's happening right in front of us."

Nathan wrapped her in his arms and gave way to the lump in his throat. The tears that followed came from a place he'd not visited in quite some time.

The future is now.

And no time like the present to enjoy it.

Epilogue

Fall blew into Greenvine, and with it came a host of changes. None was more wonderful than those in Nathan and Kellie's lovely renovated home tucked away beneath the pine trees. Inside that place love had grown, doubts had dissipated, and a new little bundle of joy now brought a sense of wonder and awe. By the time fall shifted into early winter, a new season of hope had truly begun.

Nathan contemplated these things as he made his way down the hallway toward the baby's room.

"Honey, are you ready?" He popped his head in the door of the nursery to find Kellie changing their son's diaper.

"Almost." She finished the process, then swept baby Logan into her arms. As she cradled him against her shoulder, Nathan thought his heart would leap from his chest.

"That's the most amazing picture I've ever seen."

"What?" Kellie looked at him curiously.

"You and Logan. Together. Like that." He felt the sting of tears. "It's perfect." An idea struck him. "Don't move. I'll be right back."

He raced into the master bedroom and pulled out his new camera. Entering the nursery again, he began snapping photos from every angle. Kellie shook her head as always.

"We have hundreds of pictures of him already."

"So?"

"You're so cute." She walked over to him and placed Logan into his arms. "Would you mind holding him for a few minutes while I put on some powder and lipstick?"

"Of course not." The baby squirmed, and Nathan responded by rocking him back and forth.

"Oh," Kellie added, "and would you go ahead and put his jacket on? It's a little cool out today."

"Sure." Nathan reached into Logan's closet and pulled out the light blue jacket with a bumblebee on the front. They'd purchased it at a local supercenter. Nothing was too good for his son. He slipped the jacket on and held the baby up in the air until he squealed with delight.

"Nathan," Kellie scolded from down the hall. How did she always know?

Nathan made his way out into the living room with Logan in his arms. Once there, he settled down onto the sofa and focused on the baby's face. Soft blond wisps of hair and bright blue eyes seemed only natural on his handsome son. And talk about smart! Not yet two months old and already holding his head up and smiling. It wouldn't be long before he'd be scooting all over the place.

Kellie came back out into the living room. She paused for a glimpse in the hall mirror and fussed with her hair. "I look awful," she said.

"You're gorgeous," he said and meant it. Sure, she'd changed a little over the past year, but those changes had transitioned her into the woman of loveliness who stood before him now. He wouldn't change a thing—about her or the wonderful life they now shared.

As they stood to leave, Nathan took a good, long look around his house. No longer the run-down home it had once been, the place now testified to the wonders of transformation.

Then again, so did he.

"Ready?" Kellie lifted the baby from his arms. "We have a big evening ahead of us. And I know my mother could use my help setting up."

"I'm ready." He helped her gather up the baby's things, and they walked to the car together. No longer a sports car but a practical SUV sat in the driveway. Logan's car seat had its place of honor in the backseat.

They pulled the car out onto the highway, chatting all the way. Kellie told Nathan about her new part-time job at the brokerage house in nearby Brenham. She shared her joy at how well Logan seemed to have adapted to a few hours a day at Julia's house.

Nathan shared his excitement over his work for the people of Greenvine. Then they talked about tonight's big plans at her parents' home.

In short, they talked about today.

"You want to know something funny?" Nathan asked as they pulled into the center of town.

"What's that?"

He smiled as he reflected on what he would say. "Might sound a little cheesy, but I always thought money could buy love."

"What?" She giggled. "Really?"

He nodded. "Well, in a manner of speaking. I thought that if we had the right combination of things—great jobs, a high-end home, expensive trips—happiness would follow." He glanced back at the sleeping child in the backseat. "But I was wrong."

"Funny how different we are from the people we were just a year and a half ago," Kellie said. "But I wouldn't change a thing. Would you?"

"Nope." He reached to give her hand a squeeze. "I wouldn't change a thing."

⌣

Kellie's heart leaped for joy as they pulled into her parents' driveway. Her father stood on the front porch, fussing with the screen door. He waved, then joined them at the car.

"Daddy, you shouldn't be outside. It's chilly out here," Kellie scolded.

He shrugged. "That screen door is getting rusty. Just cleaning the hinges." He gave her a wink. "It's one of the perks of retirement. I can fuss around the house all day. Drive your mother crazy."

Kellie laughed.

Her father's eyes sparkled as he looked into the backseat. "How's that grandson of mine?"

"As feisty as ever." Kellie lifted Logan from his car seat and placed him into his grandfather's outstretched arms. "And very anxious to see his grandpa."

"He's a handsome fellow." Her father ran his fingers through the baby's curls.

"Yes, he is," Kellie agreed. Logan was a dead ringer for Nathan. How could she think otherwise?

They entered the house with hearts full. Kellie headed straight to the kitchen to help her mother. They still had a couple of hours before guests would arrive for tonight's festivities but decided to go ahead and set the table. They shifted back and forth from kitchen to dining room, carrying food, paper plates, and silverware. Kellie set up the punch bowl and checked the refrigerator to make sure she had the necessary ingredients for later.

They finished up as quickly as they could, but when all was said and done, her mother stood back and surveyed the dining room with a look of concern on her face.

"What's wrong, Mom?"

Her mother shook her head. "I feel as if I'm forgetting something. Wish I could remember what it was." She disappeared back into the kitchen. Moments later, Kellie heard a gasp and ran to her mother's side.

"What is it?"

"I just remembered!" Her mother's face lit up. "Mrs. Dennison is bringing the wedding cake, and I wanted to use that lovely old tray my grandmother passed down to me. I thought it would be perfect for your big night!"

Kellie smiled at her mother's thoughtfulness. "Sounds great! Where is it?"

Her mother bit her lip and stood in silence a moment before answering. "Oh, I remember now. I packed it away in a box with some old family heirlooms years ago. It's at the top of the closet in your old room." She looked at Kellie with renewed excitement. "I haven't had a chance to use it for years. It seems kind of silly to have it sitting in a closet when I could be using it. Would you mind getting it for me, honey?"

"Of course not. I'd be happy to."

Kellie passed through the living room, where she would soon renew her vows, gave all three of her men kisses on their foreheads and kept going until she arrived in her old bedroom. Once inside, the usual warm memories surfaced. Her mother had changed little in this room throughout the years, and she loved coming in here to reminisce.

The same twin bed with ruffled floral bedspread sat underneath the window. A worn teddy bear leaned against the pillows. The chest of drawers that had once held her personal belongings stood in its place on the far left wall. Her little study desk and chair sat to her right. A colorful paint-by-numbers rendition of a horse still clung to the wall over the desk. It was every bit as charming as it had ever been, and she drank in the joy it brought.

"Whatcha doin' in here?"

Kellie turned as she heard her husband's voice. "Oh! You scared me."

"Sorry about that." He walked over to her and wrapped his arms around her. "That's the last thing I wanted to do." He looked at her intently. "What are you doing? Thinking of backing out? Leaving me at the altar?"

She giggled. "I came in here to get something for my mother and got lost in my usual little-girl memories."

"I understand. That's the same feeling I get when we're together in our little house with Logan tucked away in bed. I think they call that *contentment*."

"Yes." Kellie leaned her head against his shoulder, overcome by feelings of joy and peace. "I don't know when I've ever been this content. What about you?"

"I"—his voice broke—"I sometimes wonder what we ever did to deserve all the Lord has done for us. He's been awfully good to us."

"And you've been so good to me." Kellie looked up, her eyes filling with tears. "You've sacrificed so much over the past year. You didn't have to, but you did. And I love you so much for it. You'll never know how much."

Nathan pressed tiny kisses into her hair. "It doesn't feel like sacrifice now. Just feels good. Right. Like this room."

Kellie looked around, her heart full. "I feel as if I'm all grown up now. I'm not a little girl anymore. And yet having the baby makes me feel. . .reminiscent."

"Nothing wrong with that."

They stood in silence for a moment. Logan let out a cry from the living room, and Kellie looked up with a shrug. "I'd better go see about him."

"I'll take care of it," Nathan said. "You go back to what you were doing for your mom."

"Sure?"

He gave her a warm kiss, then headed out into the hallway.

Kellie walked toward the closet. It still had that funny smell she remembered so well from childhood. She turned on the light and looked around, trying to figure out where the box might be. "Aha." There. Just above her to the left.

She pulled the chair into the closet and climbed up on it to have a closer look.

The box proved to be heavier than she'd remembered. She struggled with it but finally freed it from its place.

She set the box on the bed and opened it with great care, knowing the value of the things it contained. How many times had she and her mother looked through this box during her childhood? How many times had she and her sister snuck into the closet for another peek at the goodies inside?

One by one, Kellie lifted out the items: an oval photograph of her great-grandmother, a carefully wrapped gravy bowl, and several chipped and worn figurines.

After Kellie lifted out the large tray, her hand hit upon another item wrapped in newspaper. Funny, but this one didn't ring a bell. She examined the newspaper for clues. The stories appeared to be from another era, but not her grandmother's time. More like—

More like my time.

Her heart filled with joy as revelation hit. "Oh, Lord. Is this what I think it is?"

Gingerly she pulled back the layers of paper. Kellie gasped as the small pink piggy bank revealed itself. She clutched it to her chest, and a lump rose in her throat. The memories came back at once. She'd taken the piggy bank, stuffed full of coins, and hidden it away so she wouldn't be tempted to spend the money. She'd tucked it away in a safe place, knowing she might need it in the future.

This is the future.

With the tray in one hand and the piggy bank in the other, she practically sprinted back into the kitchen. She approached her mother with tears in her eyes.

"Thanks so much, honey." Her mother reached to take the tray, then gave her an odd look. "W–what's happened? Is everything okay?"

"Yes." Kellie held out the piggy bank and bounced up and down with excitement.

Her mother clamped her hand over her mouth and shook her head, clearly not believing her eyes. "Kellie, I don't believe it."

"I'm not sure I do either." Kellie clutched the familiar little pig in her hands and smiled. "But there's got to be some reason why the Lord dropped it in my lap, don't you think?"

"I suppose you'll have to ask Him."

At that moment, Nathan walked into the kitchen, mouth stuffed full of cheese and crackers. "Ask who? What?"

Kellie smiled and held up the piggy bank.

"What's that?" He popped another cracker in his mouth.

"My old piggy bank," she responded. "At least it used to be mine. Years ago." She beamed with delight. "I put a lot of time and effort into saving for the future with this little guy."

"Really?" Nathan's eyes lit up. "So you're saying there's quite a nest egg in there? Enough for a second honeymoon?"

She nodded. "Well, quite a little nest egg for an eight-year-old. That's how old I was when I lost him."

Nathan's eyes grew large. "And you just found it now?"

"I did." She grinned. "Just now."

"Wow." He drew near and looked at her intently. "So what are you going to do with all that money?"

"That's a good question." Kellie stared at the little bank with renewed interest. "I worked for years to fill him up."

She had invested all her excess change—had even done without some of the luxuries her sister had enjoyed, all for the future.

This is the future.

The words rang out in her spirit once again, and Kellie knew immediately what she must do. She reached into a nearby drawer and pulled out a hammer. With one fell swoop, she split the little piggy in two. Coins scattered across the kitchen counter, and a few even rolled off onto the floor. She scooped every last one up into her hands and let out an animated holler.

The noise drew her father and Logan in from the next room. Her entire family stood in shocked silence, watching her every move.

"Kellie?" Nathan stared at her in amazement. "What are you doing?"

She looked up into her husband's concerned eyes and laughed. "I'm going to invest in something we can all use—here and now."

"And what would that be?" He took her in his arms and planted happy kisses on her forehead.

She looked up with the most serious face she could muster. "I figure there's a good twenty dollars here."

"Right. So—?"

"So," she looked up at him, joy spilling over. "Twenty dollars might not take us to Europe. I'm not sure it would even put enough gas in our tank to get to Houston. But it's probably about the right amount to take us all out for banana splits."

"What?" Her mother looked stunned. "You don't mean now, do you? We have people coming over in a couple of hours to watch you renew your vows."

Kellie looked at her watch. "In that amount of time we could swallow down enough ice cream to give us all stomachaches." She scraped the coins into her purse with the rest of her family looking on.

"But—it's chilly outside. Who eats ice cream when it's chilly out?" Her mother tried to argue, but Kellie put up a hand and stopped her midstream.

"I do."

They continued to stare, and Kellie erupted in laughter. No doubt they thought she'd lost her mind. But she didn't care. She'd been set free, liberated.

"I won't take no for an answer," she said. "And don't you worry about getting back on time. I'm the queen of quick, remember? I won't be late for my own ceremony!"

Her mother nodded, her forehead etched with wrinkles. "I—I remember."

"Well, then, what's keeping us? Let's shake this place!"

The room came alive with activity as everyone darted this way and that to collect their belongings. Her father took the baby, and her mother scurried off into the master bedroom to retrieve a warm sweater. Nathan wrapped her in his arms and pressed one last kiss in her hair. "It's not exactly Europe," he whispered.

A girlish giggle rose up as Kellie gave her response. "Aw, who cares? I hear Europe is *highly* overrated, anyway." She grabbed her purse, now heavy with coins, and looked up into her husband's sparkling eyes. He nodded his approval, and together they sprinted toward the car.